Acclaim for
The Novel Life Of Coral Ambrose

" . . . THIS HIGH-QUALITY NOVEL IS INSIGHTFUL, ENTERTAINING, POIGNANT, AND OUTRIGHT HILARIOUS . . . It's an ode to a lifelong love of books and will surely be appreciated by true book lovers and those who love authors playing with genres."
- Portland Book Review

"Ballou's skills particularly shine when Coral is using the magic bag and the narrative jumps between Coral's time inside and outside the fictional worlds. EACH GENRE SHE ENTERS IS AS RECOGNIZABLE AS A CELEBRITY CAMEO and it's a kick to see Coral puzzling out the boundaries of each . . . (T)he heart of this book is in its playful dealings with the nature of story. A clever genre-hopper that espouses the healing power of books."
- Kirkus Reviews

"The fantastically original plot is the perfect excuse for the author to indulge us with many genres, great locations and fantastic characters without it seeming like an overload. THE WRITING QUALITY IS EXCELLENT AND I LOVE BALLOU'S WRY SENSE OF HUMOUR. MANY BOOKS ARE DESCRIBED AS PAGE TURNERS BUT THIS ONE TRULY IS, because you simply must read on to see what is coming next. When you start reading, you can expect to have very heavy bags under your eyes the following day!"
- E-Book Planet

"I really enjoyed how well the author managed to present multiple genres in one novel. SHE IS SO TALENTED she plays them all off very well . . . I TRULY HOPE THERE WILL BE MORE BOOKS TO FOLLOW BY THIS AUTHOR. This is also the perfect selection for a reader's group. The author even provides a list of thought provoking questions at the end of the novel that will stimulate interesting discussions."
- ReaderViews

"… she cleverly uses the framework to different types of stories to add excitement, originality, and laugh out loud moments to Coral's story. HER BIGGEST STRENGTH IS HER ABILITY TO INFUSE HUMOR WHILE AT THE SAME TIME SHOWING HER APPRECIATION FOR THE GENRES. Yes, she pokes fun, but she never disparages certain genres. It's clear that BALLOU IS THE BEST TYPE OF WRITER since she has such a passion for reading."

- Self Publishing Review

"A WITTY HEROINE, THRILLING MYSTERY, and the multiple interpretations of various genres within one story highlight THE NOVEL LIFE OF CORAL AMBROSE . . . Ballou manages to weave in several incredibly vibrant worlds as Coral finds herself in genres including horror, western, mystery, sci-fi, and even bodice-ripper. . . Ballou does a marvelous job of balancing the new worlds that Coral enters, along with her real world, with the stakes high in both parallel universes. . . a DELICIOUS PAGE-TURNER that spotlights not only imagination, but the solace of storytelling."

- Indie Reader

-

the novel life of Coral Ambrose

BONNIE BALLOU

Names, characters, places, and incidents are based on the author's imagination. This is a work of fiction. Any resemblance to actual events, locales, or persons, living or dead, is coincidental.

GAGE

DEDICATION

In loving gratitude to all the authors who inspired and entertained me,
taught me what it means to be someone other than myself, made me laugh
and cry, comforted and distracted me when I was down, and filled my life
with friends I never met. And for my husband, a keeper of books, who
agrees that reading is on the short list of life's necessities.

CONTENTS

ACKNOWLEDGMENTS

I wish to thank Dr. Steven Gorshe, Alex Gorshe, Ian Gorshe, Charles Phillips and Shirley Berg for their encouragement, Gayle Brown, Karen Sjoblom, and Kathy Hartrum for their eagle eyes, Dr. Michael B. Harrington for his knowledge of the ways of The Pentagon, Terry Knighten and Kelly Adamson because if I didn't thank them I'd have to ask where my manners were, and editors Thomas Kivney and Carolyn Oliver who were invaluable.

1 A VOICE FROM NOWHERE

Something terrible is coming.
It was that voice again, resonant with dark masculinity.
Coral Ambrose's fingers glowed green in the dashboard lights
as she pushed buttons on the radio while trying to find a station playing
lively music. It didn't matter what kind.
Something terrible is coming.
Anything to drown out the voice in her head, that rumbling
menace.

*" ... where experienced salespeople want you to get the best deal possible on
a ... "*

*" ... That was, I would say, around 1981. We were mostly playing, you
know, dive bars (laughter) and ... "*

*" ... house fire on Rocky Ridge. Authorities are investigating the cause. In
other news, a truckload of ... "*

Something terrible is coming.
She was tired. That's all it was. Nothing was warning her about
anything. Medford was probably an hour away, maybe a bit more. She
could hang on. She would listen to the radio and focus on the beauty
of the mountains of southern Oregon: the stately firs and mist-
dampened grasses freshening even the air inside the car with a resinous,
mossy scent. She'd be pulling in to Medford right around midnight if
all went well.
Something terrible is coming.
With no streetlights on this snaking highway, the dashboard
lights blazed in Coral's eyes. There was probably a way to turn them
down. Maybe one of the cryptic buttons near the climate controls. She
hadn't paid much attention to them when she'd picked up the rental
car at PDX since the late summer weather was mild.

A movement in her peripheral vision caught her attention. There was a brief flash of something pale—round eyes, a face. It looked like a kid. She hit the brake pedal and jerked the steering wheel too hard. The car lost traction and fishtailed.

She hadn't felt a collision. And it couldn't have been a kid out on the road at this time of night.

Pulling over with a death grip on the steering wheel, Coral peered out the window, looking for what she hoped would be a healthy deer on the side of the road, but saw only indistinct shadows between the ancient trees.

Suddenly a fist pounded on the window next to her ear. Her foot hit the gas by reflex and the car lurched forward.

In the rearview mirror, glowing in the blood-red hue of her brake lights she saw a one-eyed football player with a knife stuck through his head.

She braked when she saw it was the Oakland Raiders mascot on a T-shirt worn by a little boy. The mascot was silver on a black background, reflecting her taillights. It *was* a child she had seen, and he appeared unhurt by the car, but terrified.

Coral took a deep breath and let it out slowly, then rolled down the window and called, "Where did you come from? Are you okay? I bet someone's really worried about you."

He didn't answer. Instead, he dashed to the other side of the car and tried to open the locked passenger door. Coral hesitated briefly about letting a stranger in to her car when she was alone and vulnerable, but this was a child. She pushed the doors-unlock button.

"Get in."

"Go! Go! Go!" His voice was small and tight. He said it like a prayer. She couldn't see him well in the dashboard glow. Dark hair, open mouth.

"Okay, okay. I have a cellphone in my purse. We should probably call your family and let them know you're okay." He seemed very small cowering in the seat, maybe 7 or 8 years old. She tried to remain the responsible adult before his panic infected her, and rooted around in her handbag until she found her cell, then turned it on and handed it to him.

"Go ahead and dial the number."

"We don't have time. You need to drive."

"What's your name?"

"Isaac. Just *drive*. Just *go*." He pressed the dashboard with his hands as though he thought he could push the car forward.

"Why do you keep saying that? Are you running away from someone? Was somebody hurting you?" She was going to have to get this boy to a police station.

"It's coming! It's terrible! It's coming!"

Something *was* coming?

"What's coming?"

"Just go. Back that way. Please!"

Coral headed back the way she had come, but when the Ford rounded a corner, she had to hit the brakes to avoid smashing into a massive fir tree lying across the road, blocking both lanes of traffic.

With the car stopped Coral released the steering wheel in amazement. "I was just here! The wind must have just taken it down." The tops of nearby fir trees were only bending gently in the breeze.

Coral tried dialing 9-1-1, but couldn't get a signal this far out. Isaac had curled into a little ball in the passenger seat. There was nothing to do but turn around and continue down the road in the same direction she'd been going in the first place.

That is, until they rounded a bend just past where she'd picked up Isaac and were stopped short by another downed fir, bigger than the first. "What are the odds, huh?" She still saw no evidence of extreme wind. "What *did* that?"

She started to open her door to investigate, but Isaac pulled at her and the door slammed shut. "No, no! Don't go out there! Don't go!"

"What's making the trees come down? Do you know?"

"It's a dragon," he whispered. Tears were rolling down his cheeks. He pressed his fingers to his clenched eyes, trembling.

"There's no such thing as dragons." Was it some weird guy with a chainsaw? That wasn't much more comforting than a dragon.

Isaac shook his head. "I saw it. It's a dragon."

She tried the cellphone again, with no luck. Completely frustrated, Coral looked at the girth of the tree in the cold light of her headlights. Moving the tree herself, even pushing it with the car, was out of the question. It was going to require a wrecker truck with huge chains to move that tree, and that was after someone cut it into pieces.

Should they try to hike out? She'd feel better about that if she knew which direction to go. The boy must have come from someplace—maybe he could find his way home. Or perhaps they should stay right where they were and wait for help. Someone would come along eventually.

But what if another one of these trees fell and crushed the car? Wanting desperately to understand, she rolled down the window to listen for any hint of what was happening in the dark woods.

The rich scent of wood smoke filled the car. It reminded her of campouts with her family, and of the cabin at the lake. It was a homey, comforting smell. *There must be a house nearby*, she thought, until she saw what she at first took for fog and then realized was smoke crawling along the ground like a translucent, malevolent snake.

This was why, when the fir tree in front of them caught fire, she wasn't entirely surprised. But the way it went up in flames, exploding into an orange fireball, made Isaac scream. "Go!" he wailed.

He didn't need to tell her. She was already driving the Ford in reverse as fast as it would go, stopping only when she realized she would soon back into the other downed tree.

"It's the dragon," Isaac moaned. As though to confirm his words, there was a tremendous roar behind them. Both their faces lit up orange when they snapped around to see the source of the sound. A second fir tree, on the hill beside them, had just exploded in flames.

Underbrush was now burning on both sides of the road. Coral didn't know whether to be more afraid of being hunted by some napalm-bomb-throwing, chainsaw-wielding psycho, getting hit by falling trees, or burning up in a forest fire. But then the voice came back.

The terrible, wanting thing had been waiting for centuries for a moment such as this. It was all there for its pleasure: blood and bone helpless in its grasp. The wailing and screeching of its victims when bathed in its fiery spew were poetry. Moments ago it had made its first kills. Before the night was over, many more would fall prey to its roasting breath, gleaming talons, and rending teeth. It was free again. And it hungered.

Then Coral knew. It was a dragon, and it intended to eat them. But how did she know its plans? One moment she was living out a nightmare, and the next she was being given a tour of this creature's desires. It was almost as if she were in a book written in third-person omniscient. A lot like it, actually. Exactly like it.

And then it came back to her: Phil Reddington, the messenger bag, and the horror novel she had placed inside.

She was living in a book. She shook her head.

"This isn't real."

Isaac turned his face to her in confusion.

"Just hold on a second. I need to think this through." *How had this happened? And why?*

It had all begun the day she ran out of room on her bookshelves ...

2 TOO MANY BOOKS

Coral Ambrose's life began to change when she came to the end of the book she was reading. It was, oddly, the necessity of a shelf that set everything in motion. Finishing a book was always something that left her feeling disoriented. That by itself was nothing new. When the problem was resolved and the hero had won, or not, the people she had come to know and the world they inhabited needed to be put on a shelf.

She took a moment to gaze at the cover art one more time, then sought out the books stacked under her bedroom window that were waiting to be read. With her finished book still in hand, she skimmed the contenders' spines, listening for which one screamed loudest to be read. She wanted to read them all, and she would, eventually. But only one of them could be *next*.

After narrowing it down to a few finalists, she took a moment to ask herself which genre she was really in the mood for. Unless books were part of a series, she rarely picked her next book in the same genre as the last. It didn't seem fair, somehow, to invite the inevitable comparisons. The just-completed book she held was a Civil War-era historical novel called *Dixie Forge*. It was time to read something entirely new and let the previous book stand on its own merits. She decided she was in the mood to be shaken up a bit, and not knowing that her real life would shake her up more than enough, she selected a Robert Ludlum spy novel.

Giving its cover one last look of appreciation, she began to hunt for a place on her many bookshelves to put away *Dixie Forge*. Her bedroom walls were covered, floor to ceiling, with bookshelves, except where her bed and dresser were, and the filing cabinet she had no room for anywhere else. She kept her to-be-read stack in the gap below the window that was too short for a bookcase.

6

Unfortunately, she realized, every shelf in her bedroom was full. She headed down the hall, which was also lined on one side with bookshelves that made the pathway so narrow she needed to rotate a bit sideways to pass through. She was looking for a space about an inch and a half wide, just a little place to tuck in this one book. But the hall bookshelves were also full.

Continuing to the living room, where again each wall that could hold a bookshelf did, she gazed around with an uncomfortable feeling. There were no visible gaps on any of the shelves. Four entire shelves were taken up with notebooks—journals and records of various things from elementary school and later. She was a big note-taker and there was very little she didn't write down in a journal. Nothing else would be forgotten if she could help it.

Her apartment, though adequate for one, was not particularly big. Furniture huddled in the center of the room like high school freshmen at their first dance: a sofa, a coffee table, two easy chairs, and a couple of floor lamps. Every person who had ever visited had said, without fail, "It looks like a library." That was perfectly fine with Coral. She liked libraries. It was irritating, though, when her sister Pearl, who thought of herself as artistic, followed the statement up with specific criticisms, such as how the bookshelves seemed to make the walls close in on you, and how there was nothing restful to the eye, like a landscape painting or even a patch of bare wall.

The bathroom had a tiny bookshelf, but it was full. There was no room in the kitchen for bookshelves. Hard as it was to believe, there was no bookshelf space anywhere in her entire apartment to store the book she held in her hand. Hunger gnawed at her and added urgency to the situation. She wanted to eat something and she couldn't eat unless she was reading a book, but how could she start the new book until she found a place to put away the book she had already read?

Maybe she could put it on the bottom of the to-be-read-stack, or store it in her filing cabinet under "Y" for "Yikes." Coral dumped the book on the coffee table for the time being, but clearly needed to come up with a real solution because soon she would be done with her next pick, and the next, and the next, and all the books in her stack would need someplace to go. Wondering why she hadn't noticed before how out-of-control her book storage problem had become, she tucked her straight brown hair into a ponytail, made herself a bagel and cream cheese, sliced an apple, and settled down to eat.

Her cellphone buzzed.

Coral chewed quickly and looked at the Caller ID before picking up. Of course it was Pearl. Hardly anybody else called her.

"Hello, sis," said Coral. "What's up?"

"James is going on a business trip to Belgium. Thought I'd come by soon."

Pearl sounded resigned to the inevitable. Her husband traveled a lot, and rather than give into boredom, she kept herself busy with her own job and friends, including her sister.

"Oh yeah? What's he doing there?"

"Usual stuff. Meeting with investors."

"Oooh, tell him to bring me back some chocolate." Coral's sharp chin and narrow nose made her look almost elfin as she smiled in anticipation.

"I'm telling him to stuff his whole suitcase with chocolate. It's the least he can do for going to Europe without me." Pearl paused in a way that somehow seemed ominous to Coral. "He also dropped a bombshell on me last night but I'll tell you later. Anything new with you?"

"A bombshell?"

"I said I'll tell you later. So what's new?"

"Hmph. Nothing much. I may need to move."

"What? How come?"

Too late, Coral realized she had set herself up for a lecture. "I don't really *need* to move, but I was thinking a bigger place might be good."

"What do you need a bigger place for? It's just you. Aren't you getting a great deal on rent?"

"Yeah. I was just thinking it would be nice." Coral pushed back her chair, took off her glasses, and waited for the lecture.

"You're right by your job. You'd be stupid to give that place up. What brought this on?"

Coral paused to come up with a plausible answer, and apparently the pause told Pearl everything.

"You want more room to store books, don't you? Why don't you just get rid of some of the ones you have?"

"I like to keep them in case I want to read them again later. What if I break my leg and I'm stuck in my apartment for months?"

Even as the words were coming out of her mouth, Coral knew they sounded ridiculous.

"You have every book you ever read. It would take years to read all those books over again." Pearl began to use the voice that had annoyed Coral ever since they were little girls, when Pearl, five years older, had acted like a mother and bossed her around with tragically exaggerated patience. "Nobody is suggesting you get rid of all of them. Just the ones you aren't going to read again. That's what other people do, you know. After all, it's not like you're responsible for keeping them all." Next step: blatant impatience. "You're not the Library of Congress. If you get rid of them they'll still exist somewhere else."

"It's not that. They're a part of my life. I like to remember that I read them. It's hard to explain. But I'm going to think about it."

Coral knew she had built a wall of books around herself, but it was a wall of her own choosing and made of wonderful stories she'd gotten lost in. She put on her brightest, most energetic, topic-changing voice. "So anyway, tell James to have a great time on his trip and to be safe. Call before you come over in case I'm at work. My schedule is all over the place."

"Okay, I will!" There was a muffled conversation on Pearl's end. "Oh, and James just told me to tell you that if you move he's not carrying all those books. He'll help with the furniture though. But I say: don't move."

"Right. Don't move. Got it. Talk to you later."

After Pearl hung up, Coral finished her bagel without resuming the spy novel. The problem of the bookshelves weighed heavily on her mind. She had to do something, and much as she hated to admit it, her sister was right about the apartment. There was no way she would be able to find an apartment as nice or as large in the vicinity of her job for anything close to what she was currently paying. Her landlord had always treated her well. None of the neighbors with whom she shared walls made excessive noise, or if they did, she couldn't hear it through the sound-muffling books. The parking was decent and she could see trees out of both windows. It really was a pretty sweet place to live.

But all those books. Sure, she had more than she needed. What constitutes "need" exactly, when it comes to books? That was what she had to think through. She needed to set up decision criteria and follow the rules: this goes, this stays. If she set her mind to it, she could probably clear a few out.

One book in particular sprang to mind. She had grabbed it at an airport concession once when she had finished a book sooner than she'd planned on a plane trip, leaving her with nothing to read on the final leg of a flight. She hadn't known anything about the book, but had snatched it quickly because the cover reminded her a bit of a book she'd liked once. After quickly paying the clerk, she'd sprinted to the gate for the final boarding call. But the plane hadn't even finished taxiing to the runway before she'd realized it was a very, very bad book.

The dialogue was ridiculous and none of the people were likable enough to root for. The plot was something cobbled together from a couple of popular television shows. Nothing much seemed to happen in it, but emotions were always running very high. At one point there was a car on fire, and then apparently it simply wasn't on fire anymore because in the next chapter people were driving around in it. The book ended when the situation changed without any of the characters in the book doing anything to resolve the problem, or growing or learning in any way. She wondered how it had gotten published in the first place. In theory, that book could go, but it probably shouldn't go into the hands of some other poor sucker; it should probably be put straight in the trash, if she could bear to do it, or, better yet, used in a writing class as an example of how not to write.

Her bagel finished, Coral tucked the plate in the dishwasher and went in search of the terrible book. It was hiding in disgrace on a shelf behind the sofa, where she had probably tried to ditch it a long time ago. It would be going out—somewhere—tomorrow, which left a convenient little gap for the book she had just finished.

She needed to be at work at a quarter to six the next morning to open, so it was definitely time to wash her face and brush her teeth, get into pajamas, and slip between the covers, bringing her new book into bed with her.

When the alarm went off the next morning, there wasn't much to do to get ready. A nice perk of working at a gym was being able to show up in workout clothes without makeup. This was especially handy on the days she needed to open. She would eat and even shower at Strong Body Cooperative, where she kept a locker, so all she needed to gather was a change of clothes, a small handbag with wallet and keys, and of course her book for slow times. Everything fit into a backpack. She headed out the door and down to the street for the brisk run to work.

Unless the weather was horrible, Coral usually ran. The asphalt gray sedan bought for college was parked on a side street near the apartment building, and seemed to acquire new scratches and dents every week. There was something about that car, maybe the color. No doubt the manufacturers had marketed the dark gray as being sophisticated, with perhaps a tailored businessman in the ad, but in real life the color was so exactly like the color of asphalt that people didn't appear to see it. Drivers were always backing into it, cutting corners too wide and sideswiping it, or failing to stop quickly enough when she slowed down. Coral had developed an aversion to driving the thing and hoped someone would hit it hard enough that the insurance company would declare it totaled and give her money to buy something different, possibly something bright red.

There it was, though, in case she needed it to move, for example, or in an emergency. Not that she was anticipating any emergencies, but nobody really anticipates even the common sorts of disasters. In the meantime, the asphalt-colored crashmobile did give her good motivation to keep up with her running.

If she'd had an office job much further away, no doubt the level of fitness she'd gained by running track at school would be eroding instead of improving. Strong Body Cooperative was only seven blocks away, which could barely be considered a workout, but she would use the weight machines or the elliptical during her first break.

The weather had cooled a bit, but it was a nice morning and looked like it would be a pleasant September day. She was heading down her usual route when she turned a corner and came face to face with an older woman walking a young Labrador Retriever. Evidently he wasn't used to being on a leash yet and was straining, trying to get away, pulling the woman nearly off her feet. The dog had a wild, almost frantic look on his face. Even though the owner was calmly giving commands and jerking his leash to get him to listen to her, he was twisting around to bite at the leash and then lunging left and right.

Coral's heart leapt into her throat and she cringed.

Trying to put on a normal-person expression, she nodded to the woman, then turned and darted in the other direction to pick up a street parallel to where she usually ran, chastising herself the whole way for the odd phobia she had about dogs straining at the leash. The owner had seemed nice; it wasn't like she was hurting the dog. He needed to learn to walk on a leash like all the other dogs, and then he'd be fine. But there was something about the collar and the leash and the dog trying to get away that gave Coral a horrible, bleak feeling, like there was nothing inside her. She didn't know why. She had been like this as long as she could remember, and not just about dogs straining at their leashes. She didn't like anything around her own neck, not even a scarf or a necklace, but she understood why she felt that way. There was family history there. She didn't understand why her phobia about dogs was worse.

There had been construction going on along this parallel street when she'd first plotted out her running commute route, but the construction was done and probably had been for some time. A couple of new stores had gone in on the ground floors of the old buildings lining the street. Or perhaps they had always been there, but she had never noticed them before. A dry cleaner, which could be handy if the one she used ever closed. Another espresso bar. Good luck to them, since there were already three within a few blocks. A New Age shop.

The store across the street brought her run to a stop. Art Deco lettering proclaimed it to be Red's Reads: Used Books. This definitely had not been there before. It was dark inside due to the early hour, but there were books in the window. It was open for business. She would come back soon, since it was so close to where she worked. She could imagine spending a lot of time in there. With a smile, she picked up her run again.

It wasn't until she got to her locker that it dawned on her: used bookstores usually buy books in addition to selling them. If she were smart she would sell some of her books, right? Normal people would do that. People who were able to part with books. She knew where she'd be going after work.

3 PHIL REDDINGTON

The old door seemed stuck, its wood groaning as Coral leaned against it. It wasn't locked, but it wasn't opening either. She pushed a little harder and it suddenly gave, unbalancing her and sending her lurching into Red's Reads. A little bell at the top of the door chimed unnecessarily to announce her entrance. Hey everyone! Look at the clumsy customer!

After attempting to regain her dignity, Coral looked around the dim shop for the source of the voice that was saying, "Uh, yeah, I need to fix that. Sorry."

"I'm okay. How long has this store been here? I just noticed it for the first time."

A small man with graying brown hair approached. "We opened, let's see, three weeks ago? Three-and-a-half? So, yeah, new here."

"Welcome to the neighborhood." The ceilings were very high and topped with an ornate tin veneer. The store was scented with eau d'old building mixed with that smell peculiar to all libraries. Shelves ran from the floor to the very top of the walls, each covered in books both hardbound and paperback. She would need to spend many, many hours in here.

Tearing her eyes away from this cornucopia, she said, "I'm looking for Red."

"What do you need Red for?" The man, who was wearing a dark green sweater, paused in his inspection of the contents of a box of books and looked her over.

"I have a book he may want to buy. Is it 'he'? Or is Red a she?"

"A he, I'm absolutely sure of it."

"You're not Red, are you? I was expecting someone with red hair."

"I am, and no." He grinned.

"What does that mean?"

"It's my shop."

"But no red hair. Was it red when you were little? Have people always called you Red?"

"People never called me Red. It's just the name of the shop. They call me Phil."

"Well, hello Phil, glad to meet you. I'm Coral."

Phil extended his hand. "Phil Reddington."

"Ohhhhhh."

"Nice to meet you, Coral. I thought Red's Reads sounded like a good name for a bookstore. What can I do for you?"

"It *is* a good name for a shop." After a last minute perusal of her shelves she had only been able to decide on that one bad book as something she was willing to lose, telling herself she was just testing the water.

Phil looked a bit like the way she imagined her father would have looked if he had lived: the same rather pointy nose and thin lips, and his eyes were warm and kind, almost like he knew and cared about her. The resemblance to her father led to an attack of honesty. "I have a book to sell, but you may not want to buy it because it's a terrible book."

Phil looked amused. "Terrible how? Let's see it."

Coral pulled it out of her backpack and gave it to him. He took it between thumb and forefinger the way one might handle someone else's dirty underwear. "It's not toxic or anything. It's just a really poorly written book. You want it? I should pay you to take it."

"It's not erotica?"

"No. Just idiotic."

"I don't sell erotica here. Almost everything else. Unless it's a cursed book. Was it cursed by evil fairies?"

"If this book is cursed, it's cursed with stupidity. I'm sure you don't want it." She gave him a brief book report, including the bad dialogue, unoriginal plot, and car that may or may not have exploded in fire.

"You're not much of a saleswoman, Coral. Do me a favor: If business picks up and I need to hire help here, don't apply." Phil scrutinized the cover of the book and turned over the first few pages. "This publishing company was only in business a little while. I guess we know why. Would we be doing the world a favor if we just threw it away?"

Coral cringed. "Is that possible? Is it possible to throw a book away? Aren't there laws? Don't the library police come after you?"

"No they don't. People throw books away all the time, usually because they deserve it. Not everything published is Holy Writ."

She felt like a little girl afraid to get in trouble for misbehaving in school. "The school librarian told us all in kindergarten that we must always take good care of books, and I think I may have taken that a little too much to heart."

"I can tell you've never seen what happens to paperbacks the stores don't sell. They strip off the covers, return them to the publishers, and send the pages off to be pulped. The books don't scream or anything. What did you do with textbooks in college? Did you take notes in them?"

"Never!"

"Neither did I!" They were both true respecters of books.

"Is that why you went into the used book business? To rescue books?"

"No."

Coral waited for him to continue, but he didn't. The fact that he didn't made her curious. She sensed there was a story behind that one word. Why did he have this store? To make money? How much money could there be in running a small used bookstore?

Phil walked the bad book over to a large trashcan by the cash register. He held her eyes as he slowly dangled the book over it. "You can stop me. It's your book."

With a sick face, she said, "I don't want it to be my book. I don't want it to be anybody's book."

"After I drop this in, you can forget all about it and move on with your life."

"I don't like forgetting things. Don't say that, it makes me feel sorry for it. Someone ought to remember that even that horrible book once existed."

"So you have to own it to remember it? Doesn't it bother you that it's taking up room in your life?"

"Yes. Fine. You're right. I know. Trash it."

Phil released the book and it fell into the trashcan with a satisfying thunk. "Regrets?"

"Oddly, no. So that's one down and several hundred to go."

"You have several hundred terrible books? You seriously need advice before you buy." He made a sweeping gesture encompassing all the books in his store. "I'd be happy to set you up with some wonderful reading material."

"It's not that. I have wonderful books already—too many. I don't have room for all my wonderful books. Let's just say it's come to my attention that I really ought to part with some of them."

"I'd be happy to take a look at them, make an offer. Why don't you put them in a box and bring them over?"

"You don't understand. There are a *lot* of books."

"Multiple boxes then." His face was kind, like he honestly cared. He nodded encouragingly.

"No. No boxes." To her mortification, Coral's eyes prickled with tears. Darn his kind face. "I don't know how to part with them, or if I want to. I mean, I *don't* want to. But I need to if I'm ever going to be able to have room for new books." *How ridiculous I'm being,* she thought. *There are people who don't have enough to eat and I'm crying because I have too many books. And why am I getting all emotional with this old guy I don't know?*

Phil had seen the trouble she'd had even parting with the bad book, and didn't seem surprised. "I understand. I really do. Can you imagine how impossible it would be to be a bookseller if I felt like that?"

Coral took a swipe at her eyes. "Are you going to recommend a psychologist?"

"Me? Nah. Tell you what. If you'll allow me to see your collection, maybe I can advise you better. As one bookaholic to another." When Coral looked concerned he added, "I understand if you don't want me to intrude. Oh, I'm being intrusive! Terrible idea!"

Coral's first instinct had been not to allow a strange man into her apartment. But her landlord had been good about being present when she'd needed to have workmen in for one reason or another and this was not really different. Perhaps Dan would be willing to be there for this visit too.

"Actually, I appreciate the offer. No guarantee that I'll be willing to sell many of them. I need to coordinate the time with someone else, so maybe we could arrange this by email."

They exchanged email addresses and Coral returned home nervously—but not nervous that he would turn out to be a serial killer. He seemed okay. She was nervous that he was going to persuade her to get rid of a lot of her books. He would use some sort of voodoo that would make her hand over her reading history. The books would no longer be on her shelves ready to access at any time, like little portals she could step through into familiar worlds, and she would forget what she'd read.

Then she would lose part of herself.

4 PEARL

"I come with food."

Pearl looked like Coral would if she were five years older, 30 pounds heavier, and spent a lot more money at salons and department stores. Her hair was lighter than Coral's, chin-length and sleek. She waggled a white paper bag in Coral's face, and then flourished a pink bakery box. "Healthy salad from Cornish's, followed by Napoleons."

"I love those! But I made you lasagna. I already put it in the oven." Food would be a good distraction from James' bombshell announcement that Coral didn't think she wanted to hear.

"So we have lots of food. I can stay for days." Pearl placed the white bag on the counter and opening the refrigerator, hunted around among the fruit and iced tea trying to make room for the Napoleons. "It's pretty crowded in here. We may need to eat these right away."

"What a shame." Coral set out plates. "Those will tide us over until the lasagna is done. Because we can't eat the salad first. That would be boring."

"Works for me. Ooh, wine. Yes, please." Pearl helped herself to the white wine that was chilling.

"Would you care for some wine, Pearl?" Coral said belatedly.

"Don't mind if I do."

"How's work?" Pearl had taken up real estate sales a few years ago and had done well enough. If she was planning on having children one day, she never mentioned it. Coral wondered if raising her had satisfied Pearl's mothering instinct, but never brought it up. "Sell any houses lately?"

"I'm working on a couple of sales right now. Nothing finalized, but they're going to go through."

"Yay!"

"Yeah, yay! What have you been up to? Anything besides reading?" They carried their plates and glasses into the living room and curled up at opposite ends of the sofa like two cats.

"Eating. Sleeping. Working."

"That sounds boring. I keep telling you to go out there and— oh my gosh." The Napoleons' pastry layers were crispy and filled with real thickened custard, not some bizarre whipped substance, with a thick coating of glossy, almost black chocolate alternating with white glaze on top.

Coral took small bites of hers, savoring each one, trying to make it last. She laughed. Crisis averted by food. "I think I could live on nothing but these for the rest of my life. We can run it off later."

"I don't run. You run." Pearl was holding the plate close to her mouth to catch any crumbs before they fell on her silk blouse.

"You should start. You're not getting any younger." Coral made no mention of the extra weight Pearl was carrying around.

"Running doesn't actually make you stop aging, not unless you get hit by a car while you're running and you die. Then you'll stop getting older. None of that working out you do actually makes you any younger."

"Well, yeah, but I'm going to be a "Fabulously Fit Fifty." We have a poster at Strong Body with a woman with spiky gray hair flexing in yoga pants that says that."

Pearl rescued the bottle of wine from the kitchen counter, poured herself a second glass, and topped off her sister's. "You still like working there?"

"It's okay. Not mentally stimulating, but the people are great and I get to work out for free whenever I want."

"Any hot guys?"

"The place is loaded with hot guys." One in particular came to mind, a new guy with dark hair she had seen around but had never spoken to. Not that she'd bring that up to Pearl.

"Any of them ask you out?" Pearl knew her sister was unlikely to make the first move.

"Some of them do," Coral admitted.

"Go, sis!" Pearl nodded in approval. "Anybody special?"

"I don't actually take them up on it."

"What? Why not? Didn't I just say 'go, sis?' Guess I have to change that to '*go*, sis!'"

"You didn't change anything."

"Yes I did, I changed the emphasis."

"Fine, fine. I don't go out with them because they aren't really my type."

"None of the hot guys are your type? You have something against hot guys?"

"Definitely not." Coral sipped her wine and sighed. "I have something against ... I don't want to feel entangled. I don't want to lead a guy on when I know he's not my type."

"What is your type?"

Coral gazed at the trees outside her window and tried to formulate words to describe her type. The problem was that her type had nothing to do with looks or bearing or any of the ways people normally describe types, but she had to answer the question somehow. To be her type, a man would have to somehow fit into this highly controlled life she'd made for herself.

She had come from a horrible background—she and Pearl both had—and she was proud of the life she'd made for herself. She was comfortable, even though her life wasn't very exciting. She didn't want anybody to mess it up. The guys she'd met had come from normal families and had normal problems. She couldn't expect any of them to understand what it would be like to be raised the way she was. She had no reason to believe that anybody would ever take care of her, so she had learned at an early age to take care of herself. If she found a guy who understood that, he would be a real hero. How could she word that?

"He would have to be very caring."

Pearl seized on that adjective and went straight into problem-solving mode. "So maybe someone who volunteers at a pet shelter, or a social worker, or a nurse?"

"Maybe. I don't know. Someone like a hero."

"So a superhero. You're holding out for a superhero. Good luck with that." Pearl had met her own husband, James, her freshman year in college, where they'd clicked over dorm cafeteria tacos, discussing how each of them had been forced to grow up too soon. Since her own love life had been settled very young, Coral's love life, or lack thereof, was a recreational diversion for Pearl.

"He doesn't have to have superpowers. Just someone who cares."

"About you?"

"Well sure, that's obvious. Someone who wants to take care of things. Hard to explain."

"How do you know none of the guys at the gym are superheroes without powers? Maybe they are. Maybe you haven't gotten to know them well enough."

"That is a very good point and if I ever notice someone like that, I'll do something about it. So far none of them have leapt out at me."

"Lucky for them. If anybody ever leaped out at my baby sister she'd use her Aikido moves on them and they'd be very sorry. Nobody messes with you."

Coral grinned her elfin grin. "Just so we're clear."

The setting sun spilled into the apartment and cast a warm glow on the sisters lounging on the sofa with their wine. Coral felt proud of her little home, the way the nubby sofa looked nice with the glass-topped coffee table and boldly patterned rug. She was hoping Pearl wouldn't bring up the matter of the bookshelves. The whole dating thing had been a potential minefield, but they'd had fun chatting about it after all.

Yet now Pearl brought up something guaranteed to suck the joy out of the room.

"I was thinking about Jet the other day." Pearl kept her eyes on the wine in her glass as she said it.

Coral felt the familiar sense of being broken that had haunted her as long as she could remember. Jet was about hiding and silence and chaos, and their father trying very hard to make everything all right when it never could be, and nobody knowing why a little boy was dead.

"Way to bring us down, Negative Nancy."

"I was thinking about his elbows, that they were really sharp and he used to jab me with them in the car and act innocent when I told on him."

"I don't remember that."

"And that one time he gave you all of his plastic dinosaurs. Decided they were for babies."

"I don't remember that."

"You were little. Maybe three or something. What *do* you remember about him?"

Coral rattled off her memories by rote. "There's one where I'm in a little wading pool and he's putting big scary sea monsters in and I'm laughing. There's one where the three of us are lined up in Halloween costumes, all holding plastic buckets. You're a princess, Jet was Spiderman, and I'm a cat, which was really just a black leotard with ears on a headband and whiskers drawn on with eyeliner."

"Those aren't memories. You're describing pictures in the photo album."

"I know."

"So you still don't remember anything about him at all? No actual memories?"

"No memories of him, no memories of myself when I was little, or Dad and you, or Mom, nothing until after he died."

"That's so weird. Not your birthday parties?"

"No, nothing."

"You're like a person in a soap opera with amnesia."

"Yeah, well, lots of people don't remember much that happened when they were really young, I just don't remember anything at all. But you're right, it does sound banal."

"Banal? You're saying it wrong. It's not buh-*nal*, it's *bay*-nul."

"Nuh uh, they're both okay."

"Bet you." Two cellphones were whipped out, fingers typed, and Pearl conceded gracefully that either was correct. "Who says 'banal' anyway? That's the kind of word you only read. Leave it to you to actually use it in a sentence."

"What about you? What do you remember?"

There was a lengthy silence. "I remember everything. What our family was like before. When Mom still lived with us even. All the stuff with the police investigation. How Dad was after it all happened, how he couldn't get over the fact that they never found the killer. He talked about it all the time, that he was going to find out who killed Jet."

"I remember *that.*"

"What got me started was thinking about you and your books."

Coral peered at her sister through her glasses with a guarded expression.

"You started reading right after he died. You and I would hide in our room for hours and I taught you how to read. You picked it up really fast. Once you learned you didn't stop."

"I also remember that."

"Everything was crazy-bad at our house and you would just curl up with a book and you'd be gone. It was like you weren't there."

"Yeah. You went over to friends' houses a lot."

Pearl poured herself a third glass of wine. "I think I'll just stay over if you don't mind."

"My sofa is yours."

Pearl took a big sip and said, "So here's what I've been thinking. Keeping all these books around you, it's like you made fortress walls. Just like when we were kids and you hid inside books."

Coral made a face. "Oh, come on. Don't get all amateur psychologist on me." Pearl was treading on that dangerous line siblings are so good at finding. She wasn't exactly wrong, but she wasn't completely right either, because Coral didn't tell her sister every little thing about how she was feeling. There was no doubt Jet's death had shaped who she was. Everyone was shaped by something. In her case it happened to be the murder of a big brother that took away her trust at an age when most children were being told not to be afraid of the monster in the closet because their moms and dads would always keep them safe.

Coral had learned early what it felt like not to be safe and she hated it—hated it enough to keep her body fit with self-defense classes as soon as she was old enough. Hated it enough to win a scholarship with her running in high school. So what if she was better at running away and also a little slower to let people into her life than some? She could get away. That mattered. She was cautious, not a recluse.

"You were hiding from a sad family when you were a kid, but what are you hiding from now?"

"Nothing! I'm not hiding from anything! I'm not the only person who really likes to read, you know. I just like to keep my books. Jeez. I have a job where I'm meeting the public all day. I'm not hiding." It really made her mad when Pearl got on one of these jags. She knew her life was a little limited, but what was she supposed to do? She was doing the best she could. Pearl had her quirks too, but no good would come of bringing them up. "I'm going to check on the lasagna."

"You're my baby sister and I like to help you."

"I'm not a baby, and no more wine for you. I'm cutting you off." She made a slicing gesture across her throat and headed into the kitchen. "You'll be happy to know I'm talking to a guy tomorrow about getting rid of some of the books."

Pearl followed her into the kitchen. "You're kidding." She faked a faint. Definitely enough wine for her. "A guy, huh? What kind of guy? Like a guy-guy?"

"Well, he's not a giraffe-guy."

"So are you seeing this guy is what I meant. Is he a superhero? A caring guy? Does he work in an animal shelter?"

"Oh, no. An old guy. He has a used bookstore. I can sell some of them to him."

"Excellent!"

The lasagna was starting to brown and smelled delicious. Coral pulled it out of the oven to rest on the counter for a few minutes before cutting. She'd postponed asking Pearl what her news was long enough. Time to bite the bullet. "But enough about me. Didn't you say on the phone James had dropped a bombshell on you? What was that about?"

Pearl furrowed her brows. It was an expression Coral had come to loathe. When Pearl, the strong one who had always protected her, was worried so was Coral. "I don't even want to tell you."

"What?"

"They want him to move to Europe indefinitely. Keep an office in Brussels and be accessible to the entire European market there."

Coral felt a black hollowness in her stomach. "He can't do that. Your job is here." And I'm here, she thought.

"Nothing is settled."

"I can't... tell him you can't go."

"I know."

Coral had lost her mother, then her brother, her memory, and then her father. She couldn't lose Pearl. Just no.

5 THE MESSENGER BAG

Dan the landlord was in the bathroom tweaking the float in the toilet so that Coral wouldn't have to jiggle the handle every time. He was a nice guy, and she hadn't wanted to disturb him about such a small matter, but since he was hanging around being her bodyguard anyway, she brought it up. It gave him something to do while Phil was there.

On the coffee table sat a plate of oatmeal cookies and a small pile of books. Coral had spent three days going over her shelves. There had mostly been a lot of moving of books from one place to another. She was pleased with the reorganization and with her refreshed memory about what she had. The original plan, however, had ended with her giving a big stack of books to Phil so that he wouldn't feel like he wasted his time in coming over. Then she could be done with this whole bookshelf-purging project, at least for a couple of years.

As it turned out, the little stack of books she was actually willing to part with included two excellent but duplicate books she had bought for friends only to find out they already had them, a joke book someone gave her that she never found funny, and a book about fishing. She didn't even know where that book had come from, since she didn't fish and didn't intend to start. There were also condensed books, three volumes' worth. She was not one to read condensed versions of things, so they could go. If Phil was bossy about her books, she could fling these at him and say, "Take this! And this! And this! Have some cookies. Now, go!"

Phil buzzed at the door more or less on time and she let him in. Apparently it had started to rain, which was far from unusual in Portland. He had a messenger bag slung over his shoulder and he and the bag were damp-speckled all over. She escorted him into the living room and waited for the inevitable.

"It looks like a library!"

There was a short laugh from the bathroom. Dan called, "I know, right?"

"I feel right at home here." Phil beamed at her. Usually first-time guests followed the it-looks-like-a-library comment with something else. Most people were polite enough to add an adjective like "cozy." Then there were the usual questions about whether she had actually read them all, followed by the names of books they had read in common. For someone to say they felt at home there was new.

"This isn't all of them." Coral gestured to the hall. Phil stood in the opening, nodding at the shelves. Coral said, "Keep walking." He turned to look back at her. "Go on."

When Phil reached the end of the hall, his eyes swept over her bedroom and then he turned back. "You have a lot of books. What's the stack on the floor? Ones you don't have room for?"

"Ones I haven't read yet."

"So I won't be selling you any for a while."

"Oh, you never know. I never let the fact that I already have a lot of unread books stop me from buying more. Can I make you some coffee or tea? I have regular and herbal. There are cookies on the coffee table."

"No, thank you. Well, actually, coffee would be nice. Black."

"Dan, do you want some coffee?" Coral called into the bathroom.

"No thanks."

"Are you about done in there?" She slipped into the bathroom and whispered, "You don't have to stay if you're done. I think this guy is okay."

"You sure? I was starting to run out of screws to tighten. Anything you need looked at in the kitchen?"

"No, it's good. Thanks for coming. I really appreciate it. Take some cookies with you."

Dan packed up his toolkit while Phil browsed the shelves in the living room and Coral went out to the kitchen to make coffee.

"Have you read any books that you *haven't* kept?" Phil called.

"Sure! Some of the ones we read in school were from the library and we needed to give them back. People have loaned me some here and there. But I prefer to own my own copy."

Dan emerged from the bathroom. He didn't look like a stereotypical plumbing-fixing landlord. He was about 40 years old and was wearing a shirt with a collar and slacks every time Coral saw him. His honey-colored hair was tousled in a way that would defy Portland weather to mess it up. He grabbed a couple of the cookies and let himself out the door. "Holler if you need anything."

"Thanks, Dan," said Coral before turning to Phil. "Landlord," she explained.

"Why do you like to keep the books you've finished?"

Coral had been thinking about how to answer this question, figuring he would ask. "Because if I don't it's like deciding to forget them. If I get rid of a book I feel like I'm throwing the memory away. Nullifying it." She didn't want to get into all the stuff about the memory loss with Phil. She barely knew him. The panicky feeling she got when she thought about forgetting even more of her life was her business. "It isn't really about needing to reread them all again. I do want to reread a lot of them, and some I already have. But when I read a book and live in that world, it's mine." Coral carried the steaming cup to Phil and set it on the coffee table, along with one for herself.

"They all change you, don't they? Every book, even the ones that aren't as good, let you into someone else's world. Their world becomes a part of me. They're all additions to who I am."

"Exactly. I understand that." Phil nodded gently, gazing at his coffee cup. "It's the ideas, though, not the paper."

"The paper is the gateway. Why would I deliberately shut the gateway? Look at all my gateways!" Coral's eyes swept her apartment walls lovingly.

"I think you need gateways that don't take up as much room."

"Sounds like you're promoting e-books. That's an odd thing for a used bookstore owner to do."

"I wonder what it would cost for you to replace all of these with e-books. Some you wouldn't be able to find electronic versions for anyway."

"That's not going to happen."

Phil set down his coffee and pulled the messenger bag he'd brought onto his lap. It looked very lightweight and flat.

"I have something that may help you. It's helped other people in the past."

Coral wondered what could be in the bag since it appeared to be empty. She looked at him quizzically.

"It's a way to help you sort out the book problem."

"I've already done that." She waved her hand at the little pile on the coffee table with an attempt at triumph, despite how meager it looked. "You can take those back to the shop with you. I don't need those."

"Okay. Sure. I can probably sell those for you. But hear me out. I bet I can help you clear out more than that." Coral stared at him with compressed lips. "I have something that will give you clarity. Plus it's fun."

What could he possibly have that would give her clarity? Sounded like either medication or religion. Would someone describe religion as 'fun?' It had to be some sort of high. "So you're a drug dealer? You deal drugs out of your bookstore? It's a front?"

"What? No!" Phil looked at the ceiling as he replayed what he'd said in his mind. "Okay, I can see how it could have sounded like that, although that was quite an imaginative leap. It's a messenger bag. Just a bag. See?" He held it up and opened it so she could see it was empty.

"That's going to bring me clarity?"

"It is. Here's how it works. Put a book into the bag. Any book, it really doesn't matter."

"Pick a book, any book?"

"Do I sound like a magician?" His eyes crinkled easily when he smiled. Clearly this was a man who had smiled a lot in his life. "But seriously, you put in a book and something amazing will happen that I am not even going to begin to describe. You'll have to see for yourself."

"Right now?"

"We could, or I'll give you instructions and leave the bag with you. Pick out any book and place it in the bag. Don't drop it in; you have to place it all the way in so your hand is touching the bottom of the bag."

"Okay, then what?"

Phil grinned enigmatically. "Then wait."

"For clarity?"

"Yes. You may have to do it more than once."

What was that supposed to mean? It didn't make any sense. Put a book in a bag. Take it out. Rinse and repeat. Then: clarity.

Coral was disappointed. Phil had seemed like such an interesting and intelligent old guy. They'd seemed to have a lot in common and she'd started to look forward to a continued friendship with him. She liked her work friends, but they were a motley bunch of accountant-jocks, programmer-jocks, engineer-jocks, and jock-jocks. She was the only bookaholic-jock. Most of her college friends had moved away and now it took effort to stay in touch beyond social media. She was beginning to scrape the bottom of the barrel when it came to people she could have literary discussions with, at least in person, but now Phil, so full of promise, was turning out to be kind of a weirdo.

He had been watching her face. "I wouldn't believe me either. But try it. A simple thing. One book. Place it in the bag. That's it."

He pressed the messenger bag upon her. She took it reluctantly. "One book in the bag. Then clarity. Got it. Would you like a cookie before you go?"

He looked at her skeptically. "I'd kind of like to be here the first time after all. I don't think you're going to do it."

"Why don't you just put these books I pulled out into the bag and take them with you?" She tried to slip them into the bag but he stopped her.

"Wait!" A sigh. "Just one at a time, and something you like."

Was she going to have a hard time getting him out of her apartment? Maybe she should have had Dan stay after all. Would he leave sooner if she did what he wanted with the bag or if she just bodily threw him out? He may have been a man, but he was past middle age and she was much stronger than she looked. She decided that keeping the encounter on a friendly basis for as long as possible was the better course of action. "Okay, fine."

A book she liked? Reaching into the closest shelf, which was loaded with horror novels, mostly by the prolific King and Koontz, she pulled one out at random and glanced at it. "I probably won't read this again anytime soon. There are always new ones. It's hard enough to keep up with those. I guess I could consider getting rid of this."

Phil frowned. "Um, I understand your reasoning. There's one other thing I need to tell you first. And you may not want to start with that."

Coral glanced at the lurid fangs on the cover and pushed it deep into the bag.

Then she was driving on a winding mountain highway at night, and something was coming. . .

6 A VOICE FROM NOWHERE, CONT.

She had placed a horror novel into the bag and then the kid appeared and the trees came down and there was fire. Now that she remembered the sequence of events that had gotten her into the book, she had a new problem. A bigger problem. How was she going to get out? The little boy in the car next to her—was he real or was he a character in the story? Whatever he was, he was terrified.

"Isaac, don't worry. None of this is real. I promise."

But his eyes widened in terror as he glimpsed something behind her.

Falling trees and fires were nothing compared to what she now saw: an animal the size of a bus, with reptilian skin that glittered and gleamed orange in the light of the fires it had set. Its head was lowered to the ground like a bull about to charge. The neck stretched out, bringing one red eye close to the window, peering in, only a foot from Coral. She recoiled until the seatbelt stopped her, then unhooked it and scrambled to the other side of the car, wrapping her arms around Isaac.

The ground shook as the monster circled them, at one point losing traction on the soft side of the road. A wing shot briefly out from its side to steady it. The creature was longer than she first thought. Its tail went on and on.

What Coral didn't understand was what this dragon had to do with the book she'd placed in the messenger bag. That had been something to do with mutant children who moved into the crawlspaces of houses in a small town in Montana, luring children to their lairs and eating them. It was popular about ten years ago and people were still quoting a tagline to each other: "Come to the dark place where we can play." The book she was in, however, had a winding mountain road in Oregon, a dragon, and a frightened little boy.

And it all felt real. Isaac smelled like little boy sweat and dirty hair. The dashboard was cool under her fingers. In the darkness at her feet she could barely make out fir needles and ground-in mud on the beige carpet, and a candy wrapper.

But it couldn't be real because this was not her life. She had a job at a fitness center, a married sister, and an apartment full of books. She couldn't think of a reason why she would go to Medford.

A sudden thought had her pulling the passenger sun visor down and peering in the mirror. She saw her own eyes looking back at her. They were darkened pits in the night but they were undoubtedly her eyes wearing her glasses. It was her hair too, straight and dark. Coral was still Coral.

Placing a book into Phil's messenger bag had thrown her into a book, but not one she'd read before. It was the same genre, though—a horror novel. Now the question was how to get out.

"Oh no." Isaac cowered in his seat. Coral turned in time to see the dragon's mouth open and a blast of orange fire hit the car broadside. The blast seemed to go on a long time, but was probably under five seconds. That was long enough to bring the internal temperature shooting to a nearly unbearable level of heat, and to set windshield wipers, and no doubt tires, ablaze.

Gasping for cool air, she tried to roll down the opposite window, but the electronics had been fried. She managed to pop open the door a crack and felt a bit of cooler air enter the compartment. This book may not have been her real life, but it felt like it was.

If they ran out of the opened door and up the hill, the dragon would easily get them, its talons wrapping around their waists, puncturing intestines as it brought them to its ravenous mouth. They couldn't stay in the car much longer, though—the heat would kill them. Isaac was already going limp.

"Isaac? Isaac? Don't worry, we'll think of something."

How would someone in a book get out of a situation like this? Surely a writer would have planned some kind of escape. Someone would rescue them, perhaps. What happened to that narrative voice the whole thing had started with, the voice that was warning her about something that was coming and told her it had awakened and was hungry? Shouldn't the voice be giving her some helpful tips about now?

The dragon turned around. Was it leaving? *Was that the writer's plan all along? It just gave up and left?* No, it had turned to swing its long tail into the car like a battering ram. The car jumped and twisted as the tail made contact over and over. The hood popped open and the airbags deployed with a bang, briefly trapping Isaac. When they deflated he was completely unconscious, his head on the armrest of the door, and his feet twisted around awkwardly. Even if she'd thought it was possible to escape the car she would never be able to carry him far if he was out cold.

With a tremendous roar the dragon ignited a row of trees it had been facing on the downhill slope, then turned and peered into the car again.

That writer had better come up with something soon, Coral thought. She leaned on the horn. She didn't know why. Maybe that would scare it away. Or maybe it would draw someone's attention—someone who would rescue them. Instead, the horn didn't work: another victim of extreme heat.

The ravenous reptilian monster slammed one mighty, clawed foot on the roof, caving it in and shattering every window. If it blasted them with fire again there would be no protection at all.

Coral shrank down below the steering wheel. *She did not want to be in a horror novel. She was a real person. This was enough. She wanted out and she wanted out now. She was simply going to refuse to participate.*

What did the novel want? To scare her. She would not be scared. She would not.

What could she do to break out of the book? She looked over at Isaac, helpless on the seat. Was he even real? She couldn't tell. A deep rumbling shook the car. It seemed the dragon was getting ready to blast it one more time.

Well, she was done. The door was bent, but a sharp kick with her legs forced it to open with a screech. She climbed out of the car and strode resolutely to the dragon's enormous face.

"I'm done! I don't want to be in this stupid horror novel anymore! I refuse to participate. I AM NOT AFRAID OF YOU!" The dragon looked at her with curiosity as she drew back her arm and punched it right in the nose.

7 TRUST

And then she was back in her apartment, on her sofa, and Phil Reddington was looking at her with concern. "I am so, so, so sorry. Are you okay?"

"What was that?" Coral pushed the messenger bag off her lap with a shudder and jumped to her feet. "What did that do to me? It's like I was there. It was all real. What *was* that?"

"I'm so sorry I didn't tell you how to get out before you went in. A horror novel! What was I thinking, letting you do that! Are you all right?"

"I don't even know how to answer that question."

"You just kind of popped it in there. I should have stopped you. I was starting to tell you something else, and then I got worried about it being a horror novel, and then it was too late. Completely my fault. How long were you in there? It was about three minutes out here."

"Three minutes? *Three minutes?*"

"It seems longer when you're living it. A horror novel. Oh, wow. How long did it seem?"

Coral looked at him incredulously. "Are you kidding me? I didn't time it. What was that? It was so intense."

"Right as you were putting the book in the bag I was going to tell you how to get out. But by then it was too late. You were sitting here unresponsive."

"I was?" In a way that was just as creepy as having been tricked into thinking she was in a book. She was not in control of herself in front of a man she barely knew. Was it like a date-rape drug? Her clothes were intact and nothing on her body felt wrong.

"I owe you an apology."

Coral paced her living room with her arms crossed in front of her chest in a defensive posture. "Where did you get that thing? What is it anyway?"

"It's very, very valuable, and one of a kind. Very few people in the world know it exists and it's imperative that it remains that way."

So it was a seemingly impossible, intense, *secret* messenger bag? "What do you mean?"

"There will be time for that later. Right now you need to process what you saw. It was meant to be about clarity, remember? Also, you need to decide whether to forgive me for not telling you how to get out. At least you figured it out on your own."

"Phil, it's not just about how to get out. You didn't tell me anything. I had no idea what to expect."

He looked sheepish. "I know. I should have given you more of a warning. But what if I'd said, 'I have a way for you to actually step inside books and live in them as though they were real?' Would you have believed me or would you have asked me to leave?"

"So tell me now. You can't just do that to me and say, 'I'll tell you later.'"

"I can't tell you exactly how it works, but I do know this: it was tested extensively and has never hurt anybody. It's also not something the general public knows about yet, but they will. You're being given a special opportunity."

"Does the government know about it?"

"Not yet, but when they do, I don't anticipate there being laws against it. That was a very intelligent question."

"Intelligent? I don't get anything that happened. I put one book in the bag and then I thought I was in a different book."

"That sounds normal."

"*Normal?* Huh! So let's pretend for a second that it's normal to think you're inside a book. Which it's not! But let's pretend. Does it work, like, a genre at a time? Because the place I went to is nothing like the book I put in the bag. It was horror, but something I don't remember reading."

Phil beamed. "I know! That's the beauty of it! You won't go into a book you read but instead one that's similar and new."

Coral was rubbing her neck.

"You look tired," said Phil. "We should talk about it later."

"'Tired' is not really the word to describe how I feel. 'Freaked out' is more like it."

"It's a little disconcerting the first time. And you started with horror. I really shouldn't have let that happen. That was completely my fault. I should have taken it out of your hand or something." Phil frowned at her sympathetically, but grew firm in tone. "Listen, I need to ask you to do something for me. The bag is very, shall we say, important. I need to know that it will be safe with you if I entrust it to your care."

Coral was incredulous. She was important to her own self too. He was expecting she would trust him. Why would she entrust herself, as he said, to *his* care?

"The bag belongs safely with me," Phil continued. "I'm willing to loan it to you temporarily if you promise me that no harm will come to it. Unfortunately this means not telling people about it. You get that, right?"

"How do I know it isn't some addictive drug? How do I know my brainwaves aren't being scrambled? I don't know what this thing is or how it works. I don't know you and you're asking me to trust you. You seem like a nice guy, but since you aren't telling me anything at all, I'm starting to wonder if I should just call the cops."

Phil laughed. "I've been down that road before: 'Officer, there's a guy with a bag that puts me into an alternate universe.'"

"That didn't end well for the person who made the call?"

"He wasn't taken seriously. And later, when he understood what was going on, he felt bad about the call and more awestruck about the opportunity he'd been given."

"He also needed help sorting books? This doesn't even make sense."

"No, nothing like that. Your real problem is not that you have too many books."

"Then what is it?"

"How do I know? We just met."

Coral merely blinked at him. Another non-answer.

"Maybe I should be more plain. Using the bag has a way of allowing you to sort yourself out. It's like therapy in a bag."

This was on the verge of getting awfully personal. "I would fire a therapist who did nothing but put me in a dangerous situation like that dragon attack."

"A dragon, huh?"

"It's more like I *need* therapy after using the bag. There was nothing useful about it."

"So far. Nothing useful that you can see *so far*. Like I said, it takes a few tries before you can really tell what's going on."

"That's not going to happen. You should just take your bag and go."

"I'm really sorry. This is my fault. I should have warned you. It shouldn't have been a horror novel. I'll just take one of these delicious-looking cookies on my way out." He popped one in his mouth, picked up the bag and began to head for the door. "Unless you want to give it a try one more time with something that isn't frightening, just a lot more fun. It'll be easier the second time, now that you know what's happening."

Coral had to admit to herself the idea was tempting. A totally immersive experience in a different sort of book could be fantastic. "I... don't know."

"Here's an idea! How about if I use it here, right now."

"Uh." She wasn't sure how to respond. Using it would show he wasn't afraid of it. She wasn't sure she wanted some old guy sitting unresponsive in her living room though.

"I won't stay long, just long enough for you to see I can go in and come out with no harm done. With all your books I'm sure I can find one I'd like to put in the bag."

"Okay, said Coral. If it was a bluff she was going to call it. "You do that."

"Great!" Phil looked over her bookshelves for a moment and selected *Great Expectations* by Charles Dickens. "Hey! This could be fun. I've never done Dickens before!"

Then he composed himself on the sofa, slipped the book into the bag, and went still.

Coral watched Phil. His eyes were closed and his breathing was regular. He looked like someone who had fallen asleep sitting up. She poked him in the arm and got no response. A scant two minutes later he opened his eyes and pulled the book out of the messenger bag.

"It's nice to finally be warm!" Phil rubbed his arms as though trying to get his circulation going. "I was freezing there. And what is it about orphans? Always orphans. Fun though. I was right there."

"You're not freaked out?"

"Nah, had a great time."

"Were you Pip?"

"Pip? Oh, that's right, the main character in *Great Expectations.* No, it's never the same book you put in the bag. Just similar."

"You're not going to start jonesing for your next fix of this thing are you?"

Phil smiled and shook his head. "It doesn't work like that. I'm happy to leave it here with you for as long as you like. I don't need it."

"I don't need it either and I don't want to start needing it."

"You're cautious. That's wise. Now you have a decision to make. Either I take it with me when I go and you can forget all about it, or I leave it with you and you can take your time deciding if and when you want to try it. I feel certain there's something going on with you that this messenger bag can help you sort out, and it's not about the books. If I do leave it with you I need you to promise me you'll keep it safe."

Should she actually consider doing this crazy thing? He found it enjoyable. If she'd put a different book in there it would have been a very different experience. She was starting to feel tempted. "I guess. I won't throw it out or anything."

"If you don't want it you know where my shop is."

"Yeah. I guess I might like to try one other book and see what it's like."

"Have a warm bath and get some rest. Give it another try tomorrow. Let's see, you figured out by yourself how to get out again so I don't need to tell you that. Just - *take care of it.*" He was looking at her anxiously from under worried eyebrows. "I believe you wanted me to take this little stack of books to sell at Red's Reads? Great cookies." He picked up the stack, stuck one more cookie into his mouth for the road, and walked backwards out her front door with a wave of his hand.

He was leaving? Uh, bye? Just like that? She was torn between wanting this weird guy to go away and making him stay to clear some things up. She had so many questions. First and foremost: How did it happen? Was it the latest update to virtual reality gaming? Not only sight and sound were included, but touch. She'd felt the heat of the fire blast and the scaly sharpness of the dragon's nose when she'd hit it. A quick inspection of her hand showed it was intact. If she had really punched the dragon, her hand would be bruised and bleeding. What she had done in the novel hadn't affected her real body at all. But at the time she could even smell things! She'd smelled the burning trees.

If something like this was possible, why hadn't she ever heard of it before? Was it some secret development, maybe from the military? You'd think any sort of virtual reality would have required climbing into equipment, but there had been nothing like that. Phil had said to put the book in the bag. So she did. And poof, new reality.

On closer examination, the bag was simply a brown messenger bag of the exact kind that was widely available at bookstores or office supply stores. She recognized the brand name. She used a backpack from the same manufacturer. Hers was an ordinary backpack. The only thing special about the one she used was that it had a pocket dedicated to music players and a hole to snake your earpieces through, but the backpack wasn't the slightest bit unusual. It was so much like everyone else's she'd decorated it with Sharpie pens to make it unique among all the other backpacks. She'd also sewn a bit of Velcro inside one of the pockets so she could adhere a little nylon bag she had that kept credit cards and some cash safe. That got her thinking—maybe this messenger bag was also tricked out somehow. It had to be.

Carefully feeling inside revealed nothing. She turned it completely inside out to examine the lining. At the bottom was a dull, reddish brown plasticized panel that stiffened the base so it would stand flat. Turning it right side out again, she saw only nylon, stitches, a long brass zipper at the top, and six brassy-toned feet. In other words, it looked perfectly natural.

Who wrote the dragon book she had entered, since it wasn't the one she had put in the bag? Isaac had felt very real, but he couldn't have been any more real than the dragon.

The only one with answers to her questions was Phil. But he was right. She needed to take a long, hot bath, get into bed, and zone out.

8 A DEFINITE DECISION – MAYBE

Zoning out in bed was easier said than done. The spy novel was not holding her attention. Her eyes moved over the paragraphs in their habitual way, but no information entered her brain. There was a white page and there were black squiggles. No amount of retracing the squiggles on the page could milk meaning out of them, because the images in her head were too bright. Her thoughts were shouting at her. She was, frankly, uninterested in the book compared to what she was already thinking.

Laying the book aside, switching off the light, and pondering the day's events in her darkened bedroom were the only solution. How did that bag work? Who was Phil Reddington, really? She got out of bed and did a quick Internet search, but could find no "Phillip Reddington" who seemed likely to be the guy she'd met. Should she be afraid of him, and of the bag? How was that supposed to have given her clarity? What book had she been in, and how did it really end? Did she want to do it again? Would she always be able to get out?

She decided that whether or not she wanted to do it again all hinged on being able to get out. To get out of the horror novel she had done something nobody ever does in horror novels: she had refused to be afraid and attacked the monster. She had, in effect, broken the genre conventions. That had booted her right back into her own world.

But did it give her clarity about what to do with her many books? Not in the slightest. One thing was clear: a horror novel might be an interesting place to visit, but she wouldn't want to live there.

It was kind of funny to think she'd duked it out with a dragon. Pretty gutsy. By then she knew it wasn't real. But even before that, before she remembered about the bag and the book, when she was being hemmed in by burning trees and thought there was a psycho with a chainsaw running around, she hadn't really felt as afraid as she would have felt in real life. She'd been logically prioritizing her fears. Let's see, is a chainsaw psycho more or less frightening than dying in a forest fire or being crushed by a falling tree? It was almost like a slumber party game. She should have known then that something was up when her emotional reactions were not as intense as they would normally be.

There was no position in bed that was comfortable that night. Isaac, the frightened little boy, kept filling her mind.

She sat up in bed with a start. She hadn't taken notes on any of this. She needed to record it all. If there was one thing she hated, it was forgetting things. She'd been so distracted by her confusion that she hadn't even logged the experience. Perhaps journaling would be just the brain dump she'd need to relax and go to sleep.

It helped somewhat.

The bag sat in her living room, waiting for her. Did she dare try it again? Phil not only thought she would do it, but thought that she *should*. If she did, should she tell Pearl and have her watch over her? That conversation wouldn't go well. Pearl was somewhat deficient in the whimsy department. The bag wasn't dangerous. Probably. Phil would have told her if it was. She hoped. He *seemed* like a nice guy.

The thought of sitting there unresponsive in front of anybody at all gave her a bad feeling. If she was going to do it, she would do it alone. It could be very brief. She would enter a book, take a look around, and do something that went against the genre's conventions to quickly get out. It couldn't be too dangerous if she didn't stay long, right?

After a tremendous amount of flopping one way and another, she made a decision that allowed her to drop off. She would try the bag again one more time. She would just hope there was nothing dangerous about it.

She didn't have to open Strong Body Cooperative the next day, so she was able to get in a little later. When she went for her morning run she took a different street from the one that contained Red's Reads. Even though she had a lot of questions she wasn't ready to interact with Phil just yet. Likewise, coming home she gave the used bookstore wide berth. Her run afforded her the opportunity to think about which genre she would like to try next. Horror had been way too much. She wanted something gentler, even comforting, maybe something with a hero so she'd have someone to lean on if things got weird. A blissful encounter with *Lonesome Dove* in high school had started her binge-reading Westerns for a while. There were Wallace Stegners on her shelf and a whole bunch of Zane Greys. Those always have heroes.

That evening when she let herself into her apartment she stopped just inside the door. The messenger bag remained on the coffee table looking empty and ordinary but inspiring in her a sense of mingled excitement and dread. She took her time in the shower, using the time-consuming deep conditioner on her hair, all the while knowing the messenger bag was out there. Then she puttered about in the kitchen scrambling eggs and making a salad big enough to last two days, constantly keeping the messenger bag in sight as though it might suddenly move. A check of her voice mails led to a bit of web browsing and a game on her cell phone.

Was she going to do this or wasn't she?

If it worked like her experience with the horror novel, it wouldn't matter which book she put in the bag, so she selected one at random, and making herself very comfortable on the sofa, checked the clock. It was ten past eight in the evening. She knew the date too, September fifth, although her experience with the first book led her to believe she wouldn't be sitting there that long. In a last-minute fit of nerves, she started to dash off a note to pin to her chest in case she didn't come back, then realized she was stumped about what to say. She eventually wrote the phone number to Red's Reads on it.

It was then a quarter past eight. She slowly slid the book into the bag, continuing to push it in until she felt the plastic piece at the bottom.

9 LAWMAN OF OREGON TERRITORY

Deputy John Marsh figured it wouldn't be long before ol' Sheriff Light found himself a split second slower than a plug o' lead and he himself would be called upon by the good people of Oregon City to cool the fighting passions of every no-account traveler who passed through that burgeoning hub of the West. Light was known throughout the Oregon Territory for keeping the peace to the extent that peace could be kept, but also for the quantity of whiskey he took each evening as a preventative against the diseases of the wilds, which were mostly mental. If the whiskey didn't kill him directly, the disharmony of certain of his familial relationships surely would, and Deputy Marsh was standing by to keep the city from going the way of so many other settlements in the West: fit for no man of conscience.

So if it happened that standing by meant serving as a chaperone to an orphaned young lady newly stumbled off the Oregon Road, then that was what he would surely do, with honor and respect. They had ridden south through the verdant valley since sunup, stopping once to chow down a picnic lunch of bread and apples, as she chattered away about narrative voices, primary and secondary characters, third person point of view, and other strange matters that the deputy figured she'd learned back East. He kept to himself out of politeness that none of that book learnin' would do her a lick of good out here.

This time of year showed the territory in its best light. Crops had been taken in, hay had been mown, and the light had a golden cast as the sun grazed the tops of trees that turned orange and brown in the waning light. Soon would come the dad-blame rain that seemed unceasing, and that could drive some folks to fits of melancholy, sometimes the kind of fits that kept already-hardworking deputies working extra hard.

It would be a few more days before Deputy Marsh would be able to deliver his beribboned package to the girl's uncle. How many days depended on how well she withstood the rigors of the road. He was feeling peaceful in his heart about it all, though, since she hadn't complained as females often do.

As the sun grew close to the Coast Range, Marsh drew up alongside the girl. "Let's set up camp here. There's a creek nearby for water."

The girl nodded, dismounted without any assistance, handed the reins to Marsh, and went off in search of dry kindling for a fire without being told. Marsh found a sturdy oak for tethering the horses, unloaded Maisie the packhorse, and got them water. By the time his care of the horses was complete, the girl had made a ring of rocks, laid out the wood, and gotten a little fire going. Her face glowed orange as the daylight began to fade.

"I reckon you're a handy thing to have around, ain't you?"

"My backstory is that I just got off the Oregon Road. Apparently I had to do this every day, otherwise I wouldn't know how to do any of that." She poured bean water out of a cook-pot that had been strapped to Maisie's back, added new water, and hung it over the flames. "This should be ready in about an hour. I don't have any pork fat to put in. That makes it nice. But I do have salt and some molasses."

"Much obliged, Miss Ambrose." Hunger was gnawing at his vitals as he spread out the bedrolls. For all her helpfulness, there was something sad about her around her eyes. She stared into the fire with a blankness that made him feel like he had when his best friend died. "Miss Ambrose, I hope you don't mind me askin'..."

Her eyes darted up to his, glittering in the firelight.

"This Jeb Ambrose I'm takin' you to, he's your kin, right?"

"My uncle." Her hand moved to her face as though to adjust glasses she wasn't wearing, a fact that seemed to puzzle her.

"He your pa's brother or your ma's? If you don't mind me askin'." Marsh had a kindliness that people warmed to. People looking into his blue eyes, be they criminals, victims, or women, tended to open up to him. They saw in the sandy-haired lawman a gentle giant. That is, until they pushed him too far.

"My father's. We were heading out to join him but my father and mother both died of the fever along the road. I had nothing else to do but keep coming all the way to Oregon, and I guess I may as well go to Uncle Jeb's like we planned. I reckon it's good as anywhere."

"I hope he takes real good care of you."

Her eyes returned to the fire, no doubt speculating about the matter herself. "Thank you."

With cat-like swiftness Marsh wheeled where he sat and grabbed his gun, springing into a crouch. There had been a noise in the underbrush behind him. He didn't know if it was man or if it was beast, but whatever it was he didn't want it to get a jump on him. A little voice said, "Mister? Don't shoot."

"Show yourself." The bushes vibrated and a boy of about eight years stepped out, eyes wide with fear. Miss Ambrose gasped.

"What are you doin', creepin' up on people like that? You coulda got shot. We coulda thought you were a deer and shot you for supper."

"Don't shoot me, mister. I got a heap o' trouble." He fell to crying like a baby, in a way that he would later deny to any of the other fellas.

Marsh put his gun back in the holster. "What's the trouble, son? I'm a deputy. Deputy Marsh out of Oregon City. And this young lady is Miss Coral Ambrose. Who might you be?"

"Isaac."

Miss Ambrose made a small sound like a laugh and shook her head.

"You know this boy?"

"No. Just going along with it. Go on with your story, Isaac." Miss Ambrose watched him with shining eyes, almost the way a person would wait for the punch line of a joke if the boy hadn't looked so pathetic.

"It's my pa. A dragon got him. Kilt him dead." Fresh tears ran down his face. He wiped his nose on his sleeve.

Deputy Marsh shook his head. It was one thing to have a boy talk about dragons and another matter entirely to have a young lady mutter "not again" as she'd seemed to. "A dragon, you say? I never heard tell of a dragon around these parts. You wouldn't be telling a tall tale now, would you, son? Because I'm an officer of the law and I don't take kindly to people trying to make a fool out of me. Your pa, is he dead or alive?"

"Dead."

"Did you see him dead or you just misplaced him?"

"I was in the hills and I come back and there was blood on the ground, a whole mess of blood, and no pa."

"Where's your ma?"

"Dead. She died having my sister."

"Where's your sister?"

"Dead too."

"You're by yourself now?"

Isaac nodded silently, tears making mud rivers down his dirty face.

"What's your family name, son? It wouldn't be McAllister, would it?"

"Yessir."

"Keep a sawmill, don't you? Sure, I've seen the wood your pa's been millin'. Never met the man, though. You keep a place down near Two Bit Higgins." The boy nodded in mute sorrow. There were a lot of ways a man could die in Oregon Territory, but a dragon attack wasn't one of them. A bear attack wasn't uncommon and could account for all the blood on the ground, but a deputy would be remiss in his duties if he didn't think there had been a fight between neighbors, knowing that McAllister was a neighbor of Two Bit.

Marsh rocked back on his heels and gave his britches a tug. "As the law around here, I need to get to the bottom of this. Nothin' we can do tonight, but at first light I need to check out this boy's story. Miss Ambrose, I promise I'll get you safe to your uncle's place, but we're going to have to take a little detour. I'm mighty sorry about that."

"It's perfectly fine. I'm not in any rush to get there and it's your job. Here, Isaac, sit down with us. We're going to have beans pretty soon and there's plenty for you."

The rest of the evening passed without incident until Miss Ambrose disrupted the relative placidity of the night by saying, as she lay snug in her bedroll, "I wonder what will happen if I fall asleep? Will I still be here?"

It was another puzzling thing to say and Deputy Marsh did his best to convince her that he and his six-shooter were more than enough to protect her and the boy from animals, outlaws, and even dragons. Then he lay awake awhile thinking about Two Bit. The Higgins family had a dark, fighting nature to them that made it hard for them to stay on good terms with anybody. When Two Bit's pa had married the kind-hearted Risher girl, everyone thought that would breed some gentler manners into their children, but it was not to be so. Two Bit had come out as cantankerous as his old man, but twice as likely to run off. The running off had suited everyone just fine, except his ma, who cried for him until he was returned, red-faced and swinging.

Two Bit had bought out an early partaker of the government land giveaway and moved south five years ago.

Marsh whispered, "Isaac? You awake?" There was no response. The little fella was tuckered out, curled on the grass like a wadded-up rag, with his head on his hat. He'd find out what the fight had been about in the morning. Because sure as shootin' there was bad blood between Two Bit and Isaac's pa. There was bad blood between Two Bit and everybody.

The aroma of baking bread and boiling coffee made for a good way to wake up on the trail, and it wasn't something Marsh was used to as a general rule, since he didn't keep a female around. He would like to get used to it. While he ate, she was chopping up and boiling carrots and throwing them in the pot with some dried meat.

"You're making stew? We ain't gonna be here that long."

"Pasties for lunch later on." She inclined her head to the boy. It would be a treat for the orphan. Seemed she was feeling sorry for him. As an orphan herself, she no doubt felt a special kinship. There was some logic to it, but it took a lot longer to pack up and head out than he'd planned. While all this domestic work was going on he questioned Isaac about his pa and Two Bit.

"My pa's been running a sawmill on the creek since before I was born. A couple of weeks ago we started seeing fires up in the hills. My pa thought it was lazy hunters too stupid to put out their campfires. Said one of them might burn us out. But one night we saw something in the sky. Something dark that made the stars go away, like a bird that was big. It was a dragon."

"A dragon?" cried Miss Ambrose. "I hate dragons."

"Come on, Isaac. Ain't no such thing."

The boy stuck his lower lip out obstinately. "We both saw it, my pa and me."

"Your pa said it was a dragon?"

"He didn't say nothin' but he saw it. You don't gotta believe me but my pa is dead."

"Let's talk about your neighbor, Two Bit Higgins. Ever have any trouble with him?"

"I wish the dragon et him instead. That varmint was always givin' my pa trouble."

"What kind of trouble?"

"Two Bit lives up the creek from us a piece. There's a wheel in the water that turns and the blade goes up and down, so the creek moves the saw blade, you might say. Well, Two Bit started watering his cattle right up the creek and the cattle turned it all into a soggy swamp. It isn't a creek anymore. So the mill won't work. Pa went over to talk to him. When he come back he was mad as a bull. Two Bit wouldn't stop watering his cattle right there even though he coulda done it someplace else. Pa didn't know what he was gonna do."

Deputy Marsh took off his hat and ran his fingers through his hair thoughtfully. That was a motive for murder he could understand, but Two Bit would have been the victim.

"The day your father was killed, did you hear any shots? What day was it, anyway?"

"Day before yesterday."

"Day before yesterday? It took you that long to find help?"

Isaac nodded.

"You poor thing," said Miss Ambrose. She seemed awful protective of the boy. Marsh reckoned it was female instinct.

"What about the shots? Hear any?"

"I was out in the woods hunting for squirrels with a bow and arrow my pa made. And suddenly I hear *bang! Bang! Bang!* And then my pa yellin' like he's in pain. So I come runnin' back quick as I could and all I could see was bl- bl- blood on the ground. And I run around and called him and he was gone. Didn't answer me."

"So you didn't see Two Bit shoot him?"

"Two Bit? No. The shots were my pa firin' at the dragon. At least that's what I think it was."

"Isaac, I want you to consider another possibility. Not sayin' you and your pa didn't see a dragon, but what if the shots you heard were someone shootin' at your pa?"

"You mean Two Bit?"

"He's the only one around there and he's the meanest cuss you'd ever meet."

Isaac's eyebrows met in the center of his face. "I want you to string him up, Deputy Marsh."

"Well, deputies don't string people up, but I'm going to get to the bottom of this."

They rode in silence until they crested a small ridge. In a field ahead they could see a little house, squat and squalid. Cattle grazed, unfenced but not unbranded. Each one bore the same brand, TBH. So Two Bit might be many things, but he wasn't a cattle rustler.

As the horses drew near the shack, picking their way through the mud, a reedy voice called out, "John Marsh, what are you doing on my land?"

"Come on out here, Two Bit. I need to talk to you."

"How about you get off my land and talk to someone else, like that fancy lady you got with you?"

Miss Ambrose didn't shriek or pretend to faint or any of the things some of these fine Eastern ladies do, just pursed her lips.

"Two Bit, you get out here right now and apologize to her! I said right now! Would you call your mother a fancy lady?"

A slovenly man with several days' worth of beard and clothing that may once have been different colors but was now uniformly the color of the mud they were trampling underfoot came from around the other side of the house. "You watch your mouth if you know what's good for you," he said to Marsh.

"You watch your mouth. I hear you had a conflict with this boy's pa."

"Oh, that four-flush fool come around here tellin' me what I can do on my own land. I told him to get the hell off. I got no problem with him anymore."

"How come?"

"How come? Because he got the hell off, that's how come."

"So you didn't have anything to do with shootin' him?"

"Shootin' him? He got hisself shot? Wasn't me. Probly someone else whose business he was gettin' into."

Isaac cried out, "You're lying! I heard the shots and I saw the blood. It was you!"

"It's okay, Isaac. You just let the deputy do his job," said Miss Ambrose. "You and I will stick together, that all right with you?"

Two Bit gave Isaac the same look you might give a pile of manure you just stepped in. "When was this?"

Marsh said, "Day before yesterday. You hear anything?"

Two Bit's brows lowered over his close-set eyes as he thought. "As a matter of fact I did. Heard a couple of shots and some yelling. I figgered it to be a bear. Been havin' bear trouble in these parts lately. Must be a big'un. Took one of my heifers almost fully growed."

"A bear, huh?"

"Bear trouble and some damn fool startin' fires in the woods." He stared at Isaac and scratched the side of his face with a loud *scritching* sound. Isaac stared back, his mouth agape.

"Okay, that's all I can do here right now. But Two Bit, don't you be goin' anywhere. I may have more questions for you."

"I'll do what I damn well please, John, and you'd do well to remember it."

"You'd do well to remember I represent the law of the Oregon Territory." Marsh spurred his horse. "Let's go take a look at the boy's house."

It was a short ride downstream to the McAllister place. They passed the swamp where Two Bit's cattle had churned up the creek and turned it into a muddy mess. Marsh nodded at Isaac, then turned to Miss Ambrose. "You'd think nobody would have to fight about water in Oregon."

"I heard it's worse in California."

"Sure, they hardly have any water in California. Here we have too much."

The McAllister home was well built and maintained, though not large. The mill itself consisted of a large open barnlike structure perched over what was left of the creek. There were logs stacked around drying, but no cut lumber. Isaac's father must have sold off the last of it.

"Looks like he had started to dig a mill pond to even out how much water ran through the mill," said Miss Ambrose, pointing to a digging project in the creek that had scarcely been started. "I wonder how I knew how mill ponds work."

The deputy looked at her from under his hat. "Be nice to have had a mill pond, but I guess it don't matter now."

It hadn't rained in a couple of days and the bloodstain Isaac referred to was still plainly visible in the soil near the front door. The quantity of blood left no doubt that McAllister was dead. Marsh knocked on the door and entered. There was, of course, no one there. The remains of a breakfast were on the table. Two beds stood unmade. Other than that, the place was neat and homey.

"I don't think we're going to find his—find him right around here. Someone needs to come down and spend more time looking around, and pack up the place for Isaac. You'll have to live in town now, Isaac. We'll find a family who can use an extra pair of hands."

Isaac looked grim.

"Of course, the land belongs to you, and it's worth something. Have to go to Oregon City to settle all of that." Marsh nodded as he thought. "I'm going to take Two Bit back with us. Let the judge sort it all out." He turned to Miss Ambrose. "And there's you."

"Let's get Isaac into town. I don't mind. I feel sorry for the boy. We're only a day outside Oregon City. I just spent four months on the trail. Another couple of days one way or the other doesn't mean much to me."

John Marsh looked at Miss Ambrose with appreciation. She was kind of skinny and her hair didn't curl becomingly, but she was solid when it came to heart and fortitude. He nodded. "I appreciate that. It could be unpleasant on the trip back with Two Bit but I won't let him hurt you."

Miss Ambrose smiled. "He should be worried that I might hurt him."

Perhaps she had a little too much fortitude to be attractive.

Collecting Two Bit involved a tricky bit of roping, but this was something Marsh had practiced since he was a boy and he had a knack for it. Soon the party consisted of Marsh on his horse with Isaac perched behind him, leading Two Bit on foot, wrists bound, spitting and making every manner of threat, and Miss Ambrose riding sidesaddle, leading the pack horse.

The evening's repose was not particularly restful with Two Bit kicking like a mule and trying to wriggle out of his ropes and away from them. Dawn's light was much welcome.

It was late afternoon the following day when their party trotted and stumbled into Oregon City, causing a bit of a stir at the Sheriff's office.

"We didn't have enough trouble with Two Bit when he lived here? You had to go outta your way to bring him back?"

"He may have killed McAllister, who ran the sawmill. This boy's pa."

Two Bit was covered in grime kicked up by the horses and smelled like an outhouse. "It was a bear what kilt him! I keep tellin' this damn fool!"

Sheriff Light said, "Well, we'll see about that. Lock him up, and take the boy over to Mrs. Carlson. She's a God-fearin' woman who maybe can use an extra pair of hands, what with her husband laid up the way he is."

The sheriff settled himself in his chair and set his boots on his desk. "Good thing you came back when you did. We got trouble with this last gang off the trail. Meanest load I've seen in a long time. Someone told 'em we were givin' away Main Street for free. Last I heard they were over at the saloon gettin' drunk and fallin' off their chairs. Wilbur has the girls hidin' upstairs. Didn't want 'em to get roughed up." He glanced at Miss Ambrose dismissively. "Guess you'll have to find yourself another way to get to your uncle, if you're in a hurry, that is. You can take a room at the boarding house and find a job. Take in laundry, and do some mending. Wilbur may want another girl."

Deputy Marsh's face colored at that. "Isaac, you wait here a bit, will you? I'm gonna deliver Miss Ambrose and all her things to the boarding house for *ladies*, and then I'll come back."

Isaac seemed intrigued with the Sheriff's office and was content to remain for a while, studying wanted posters and giving the cabinet of rifles a thorough inspection.

Marsh took Miss Ambrose's arm like a gentleman and led her to the wooden sidewalk outside. "I apologize for the implication that you are anything other than a lady. Someone should be able to get word to your uncle and he can come and collect you. You'll be safe here."

Miss Ambrose, who was examining the filthy hem of her travel-worn skirt, smiled up into his honest face. "I know I would be, but here's the thing: I'm tired of being in a Western novel now."

"A Western what?" The deputy wasn't sure he heard her right.

"The West is a dirty, rough place. I mean, look at my clothes! I'm filthy! I've been sleeping in them, and riding a horse, and walking through who knows what in a long dress. It's disgusting!"

Marsh took off his hat and scratched his head in honest puzzlement. Hadn't she just crossed the continent in a wagon train? "You can get a bath first thing at the boarding house. Miss Violet will be happy to help."

"And everyone's shooting at each other, getting eaten by bears."

"You've had a rough time. I'll ask Miss Violet to give you some warm milk."

"I'm not even the main character in this story. It's in third-person point of view, but the main character is you. And don't get me started on how limiting all this is for women in general! I mean, I can't even go anywhere without some man, no offense. I appreciate the help, but I'm completely marginalized. I'm not sure what women are even here for. They're not a big part of the story."

"I'm not sure what you mean." He was distracted by the opening notes of "My Darling Clementine" coming from the saloon down the street, a signal he and Ernie the piano player had dreamed up one evening after a particularly rambunctious card party had turned from friendly to fierce. A timely intervention of the law would have kept five bottles of whiskey, three bottles of rum, a bottle of sarsaparilla, a large mirror, a painting of a woman in her undergarments, and a drifter named Cavalli from getting blown to smithereens. He needed to get over there before it all happened again.

"Deputy Marsh, you're a good man, and it's been my pleasure to get to know you—"

He blushed as he strode down the street, calling over his shoulder, "Thank you, Miss. And likewise, I can't say I'm sorry to have you around a mite longer."

"— but I think I'm done here and it's time for me to go." With a crash, the saloon door flew open and a knot of swinging, choking, punching men rolled out onto the wooden walkway, hollering and bellowing.

"You see?" Miss Ambrose called after him. "That's what I'm talking about! People solve their problems with their fists here! I mean, it's not like I didn't know that!"

Marsh reached into the knot of fighting men and pulled one up by his shirt collar. He was the very picture of a Western lawman, tall and brave, and doing what needed to be done. An angry mob had gathered around. Whatever had taken place in that saloon had riled a number of the citizens.

"Goodbye, Deputy!" Miss Ambrose called. *She thought she knew how to get out of a Western. It was obvious, really.* "I'm going back *East*!"

As the words came out of Miss Ambrose's mouth, a shot rang out from the crowd and hit Marsh in the chest. He toppled to the ground.

10 CLARITY

And Coral was back in her apartment once more. It was 8:21.
Seven minutes. She unpinned the note with Phil's phone number from
her shirt and put the Western novel back on the shelf.

Marsh! Was he dead? What happened back there? If only she
had stayed a moment longer, maybe she could have gotten him help.
Or better yet, left a moment earlier—then she wouldn't have had to see
that. After all, he was only fictional.

He may have only been fictional, but it bothered her. She liked
him.

This messenger bag and its ability to make characters, stories,
and settings seem so real was incomprehensible. She would never have
dreamed something like this could exist in real life.

Coral needed to take a few minutes and get reoriented to her
actual world. She used to think finishing a book she was reading left
her feeling unsettled during re-entry, but that was nothing compared to
the messenger bag. At least now she knew it could be fun. Really, really
fun. Even if she wasn't the main character.

And what was this messenger bag anyway? Who wrote the
books? The author recycled that Isaac character from one book to the
next through completely different genres.

The most logical thing to do would be to ask Phil Reddington
for an explanation again. But the man had given her what seemed like a
magic bag; maybe he himself was outside the realm of normal life. The
bag defied science and rationality. If he had a magic bag, what else was
magic about him? And was he good or evil? Okay, she had definitely
spent too much time in the fantasy genre. She was uneasy about him,
though, that was for sure, until she thought about his apparent concern
for her. That and his dad-sweaters.

What would Pearl do? Probably just hand him back the bag, say "thank you," and spend the rest of her life avoiding him. Or maybe contact the police. That would be the most responsible thing to do. She could say, there's a guy with a weird bag I think you should look into. It messes with your head. No, really.

That would be a very awkward conversation.

But if she was being honest with herself, she didn't want to give the bag back yet. Because this was ridiculously fun. The spy novel was waiting to be read but she wasn't too interested in it, something unusual for her. There was nothing wrong with the book; it was just bland in comparison to what happened when she placed a book in the messenger bag. Actually entering into books was an amped-up experience that made reading dull in comparison. Now that she could get in and out at will, this seemed like the very best blockbuster movie meets theme park meets role-playing game, and all for free. Who wouldn't be enjoying this? Think of all the books that would be fun to pop into that bag. It was just a matter of choosing what came next.

When Phil gave her the bag he said it would be fun. Fun: check. And that it would give her clarity. Clarity: no check. The exact opposite was true. What kind of clarity did he think she was going to get, anyway? Wasn't this about book sorting?

She already understood herself pretty well. She was a normal young woman with a job who was happy with her life. Sort of happy. If not happy, then making her way in the world as well as a person who came from a smashed-up family could. No, she wasn't happy, but what could she expect? She was an adult and adults work. She worked hard. She *worked out* hard at the gym. She worked to fight the feeling that she could be forgetting something else by keeping records. And when she had time, she read. Her job was going fine. She wasn't up all night flirting with strangers on the Internet or doing drugs.

It wasn't like she was in conflict with Pearl.

Pearl. James wanted her to move to Belgium. That couldn't be thought of. Too much loss. She would hang onto everything she had and never let go.

Other than that her only real problem was that she needed a bigger apartment to store all her books. Big deal. Lots of people collect things.

She liked to read more than others and people would probably describe her as an introvert, but there's nothing wrong with being introverted. She wasn't shy; that would be different. Shy meant afraid or timid. Coral wasn't that, not at all. With all her working out she was pretty confident in physical situations, and in emotional situations she didn't care enough about what people thought to be afraid of them. She'd never been like that because she was perfectly fine being alone. In fact, she often preferred her own company. It was when she was alone that she regained her equilibrium. People are fun and stimulating, but there came a point when she felt like enough was enough and she just wanted to curl up with a book. Nothing wrong there.

Was that the clarity she needed? That there was nothing wrong with her? Fine. Good. There's nothing wrong, at least not yet with Pearl still around.

Or was there some other kind of clarity she was supposed to be finding? She had presented herself to Phil as someone who had book storage problems, but he'd seemed to see past that to ... what? Something else. Her first assumption had been that if she put a book into the bag it would help her decide whether or not to keep that book, like a Hogwarts-style sorting bag. But then the plot of the book she became a part of was completely different from the book she put in. Same genre, different plot. Was she meant to keep or sell all the books in an entire genre? That didn't make sense. It seemed the clarity was supposed to be coming from whatever happened during the in-book experience itself.

Clarity or no clarity, maybe she would make use of the bag just to have fun until Phil wanted it back.

Time to write the Western story down so she didn't forget it.

11 ELIOT

After another restless night's sleep it was her turn at the front desk at work. It could be a boring job unless you had something else to keep you busy. She answered phone calls and checked people in. Sometimes someone would complain about a lack of towels in the shower room. When things were missing or forgotten, members always turned to her because she remembered everything thanks to her compulsive note-taking. And since she always had a book with her she didn't get bored when other people would.

She was staring blankly at a page in her spy novel, the words again not registering in her brain as it worked on the mystery of the messenger bag, when the glass doors opened and the new guy with dark hair walked in. It was the one she had noticed before, finally signing in when she had the desk.

"Hi, can I help you?"

"Eliot Marsh."

Marsh like John Marsh, but a common enough name. Still, a fun coincidence. He was wearing sweatpants and a bright blue sleeveless T-shirt that allowed her to see that he was no stranger to working out with gym equipment. "Got it. I'm Coral Ambrose, one of the personal trainers here. Did you get your free session when you signed up? I'm sure you have, it looks like you've worked out a lot."

Eliot had a quality of alertness about him. She had the feeling he had already sized her up. "Yeah, they told me about that. I may take you up on it later. Right now I need to get a workout in and get to work."

Coral nodded and watched him as he entered the gym, then resumed her ruminations.

The first two bag adventures had taken place in Oregon. Coral didn't know if that was a coincidence or some sort of theme. She could test the theory by selecting a genre that depended on the setting being some other place. There were so many to choose from. She could hardly wait to get home and try one out.

That evening she rushed through dinner, spent a couple of minutes deciding between a couple of very worthy authors, pinned the note to her shirt, got comfortable, checked the time, and dropped one of her favorites into the bag.

Nothing happened.

"Huh?"

Coral reached her hand into the bag to pull the book out and ...

12 JIGGERY POKERY: A MISS AMBROSE MYSTERY

Miss Coral Ambrose peddled her leased bicycle down the main thoroughfare of Cotsley-on-Windle, dinging the bell as necessary to ward off small running children and the occasional terrier. She was quite pleased with herself to have found such a charming village for her holiday and even more pleased that the weather was fine. It was just as likely that the weather would have been grey and damp this time of year, perhaps even stormy. She would have been sorely disappointed to waste her precious time off tucked up in an inn by a fire with only a cup of tea for company.

She was also pleased that the messenger bag was working again after the false start. What exactly had happened would require thought at some future date. She needed to make sure this book didn't push her to the fringe of the action like in the Western. Within the bounds of the genre she had selected, she didn't think it would. Would the narrative voice show up here, as it did in the horror novel? Only time would tell. In the meantime, there was a village to admire.

The gardeners of Cotsley-on-Windle plainly took pride in their craft. It was a bit early in spring to appreciate the full effect of their endeavors, but each house she passed had its small front garden filled with daffodils and smaller narcissi nodding drowsily in the sun, with the promise of peonies, bellflowers, and lobelia in the nascent forms of buds, sprouts, and shoots.

The village wasn't large and a brisk five minutes' ride took her clear out of town and into the country. There spread before her England's green and pleasant land—dotted with sheep, lined with hedgerows, and overlooked by the occasional house. Fluffy white clouds mirrored the sheep below. The river Windle, hardly more than a stream, wound its way through the rolling terrain in a pleasing way. Beneath her wheels were deep ruts made by farm carts and tractors.

Having decided after some time that road conditions made riding about in town preferable, she was turning her bicycle around to head back when she heard a cry.

A woman, out of breath and pale and dressed as a housekeeper in a dark blue dress with white apron and cap, was running down a driveway that ran perpendicular to the road on which Miss Ambrose was cycling. "Miss! Miss! You must 'elp me! There's a body in the master's study—a dead body! It's 'orrible!" She covered her face with her apron as though to ward off the memory of the gruesome sight.

Miss Ambrose pulled up alongside the housekeeper with concern. "Oh, you poor dear. Do you know who it is?" *The accent that issued from her lips sounded no more American than that of any young woman born and reared in the Harrow district of London in the early part of the 20th century. Being in a book had changed not only her location and her clothing, but also her accent. Did it change anything about her essential self, she wondered?*

The housekeeper naturally assumed that the look of astonishment on Miss Ambrose's face was caused solely by the revelation of the murder. "I don't. I didn't look too closely, but I could swear I've never seen the man before in my life."

"We must get help. I'll ride back to town and find the police while you stay here to let them in. Do you think you can manage it? Being alone with the corpse?"

The housekeeper gave a shriek at the word *corpse* but answered, "Oh, no, miss, I never ... I'll stay in the entry 'all is what I'll do."

"Good idea. Oh, they'll probably want to know your name."

"Violet Emerson. I'm the 'ousekeeper. Bless your cotton socks."

"Pleased to meet you. I'm Miss Ambrose. I'll have them here as soon as possible." With blessed socks, Miss Ambrose left Violet walking slowly back to the house, head down, as though walking to her own gallows.

Upon returning to Cotsley-on-Windle proper she inquired of the first person she encountered, a lad of about 15, "I say, would you know where I would find the constable?"

"He'd be at the station, wouldn't he, miss?"

"Where is that?"

Exerting as little effort as a 15-year-old can while continuing to remain upright, the lad pointed at a brick structure just off the main road, with "Cotsley-on-Windle Police" posted by the front door.

Miss Ambrose entered, and stopped dead in her tracks. Sitting at the desk was a tall man, sandy-haired, with kind blue eyes. He winced a bit as he rose. "May I be of assistance, madam? You're a visitor here, I believe."

"Indeed. I'm staying at the inn."

"I try to keep my detecting skills razor-sharp, and I deduced as much, having never made your acquaintance."

I believe you have, John Marsh, Coral thought. "That sounds advisable in your line of work. I'm just here on holiday from London, getting a bit of fresh air."

"Do you find our little village to your taste? I'm Inspector Marsh." It was then she noticed that his arm was in a sling.

"Miss Coral Ambrose," she said, extending her hand to shake, then realizing too late it was his shaking hand that was in the sling. There was a bit of awkwardness involving clasping his left hand, which prompted them both to turn beet red, and then Miss Ambrose said, "I only just got here last night and I find your village perfectly charming, and I've been having a splendid time, but I'm afraid I'm here to report a crime."

"A theft? Someone nick something out of your room?"

"No, you see, there's a body been found in one of the houses. A housekeeper came upon it. She's at the house now, somewhat hysterical and waiting for you to come."

"Do you know who it is? The person killed?"

"I don't, and the housekeeper said she doesn't recognize him either. I am sorry to trouble you."

"Nonsense. Let me just ring for the physician and I'll be on my way. Which house did you say has this body?"

"I didn't say, because I don't know who owns the house. I was pedaling my bike down the road when the housekeeper approached me."

"You'll have to show me then, if you please. One moment." He placed the telephone receiver to his ear. "Give me Dr. Bruce, please. Hello, Doctor, John Marsh here. Oh, not too bad, but that's not why I'm calling. There's been a spot of bother. Seems someone has turned up dead. No, I don't know who it is. I'll be by momentarily."

Inspector Marsh collected his hat and coat and slipped a notepad into his pocket. "You shall ride with the Doctor and me in his motorcar. There's plenty of room. Of course, there will be the matter of coming back."

"I can walk. The weather's fine. I don't wish to be a bother."

"Perhaps we'll think of something later. Coming?"

"I wasn't expecting to find a police inspector on short notice in Cotsley-on-Windle. I went looking for a constable."

"My territory is rather large and I'm not always here. It's my great good fortune that today I am."

"Good fortune indeed," said Miss Ambrose.

Dr. Bruce proved to be a garrulous man, somewhat deficient in vision, but making up for it with his superb oratorical skills. He was loading a medical bag into the boot of a large motorcar when they arrived. "It won't be a mystery for long when I've had a chance to examine the body. It's science. Scientific evidence. That's what's wanted at a time like this: microscopes and tissue samples. Of course if anything is at all dodgy no one will want a post-mortem examination. Mark my words."

Kit loaded, they all piled in and the motorcar started with an impressive roar, which required further conversation to be undertaken at a shout. "I dare not tell the families about the scientific post-mortem. Their refined feelings will be much too tender to think of cutting the man open, even if it means we find out once and for all what happened." On the road to the house a hapless sheep wandered across their path, unnoticed by the doctor, who continued both his monologue and his pace. "These are modern times, don't you know." The sheep was unnerved by the rumbling motorcar and moved out of the way in the nick of time. "I suppose they'd rather see criminals walk free in a village like Cotsley, eh?"

"Just turn here," Miss Ambrose interjected when they came to the lane where she'd met the housekeeper. "The woman I met is called Violet Emerson. I suppose I'd have prevented a lot of trouble if I'd thought to tell you that in the first place. I'm used to London where nobody knows anybody else."

The automobile swung around a large, circular drive and Dr. Bruce braked to a stop. Miss Ambrose stifled a sigh of relief at having arrived safely. Violet immediately opened the door for them, pleased no longer to be alone with the body. "Oh, do come in!" she cried, pointing to her right. "He's just in there."

The study contained a desk, two armchairs, a fireplace with tools, and a large, red, Persian rug on which was sprawled the lifeless body of what appeared to be a tradesman of some sort. His face was turned away from the door and one arm was raised above his head as though to ward off the blows that had clearly rained down upon him, seemingly from the fireplace poker, which was tossed haphazardly next to the body. It was apparent from the extent of the injuries to his head and the amount of blood that had seeped into the carpet that the man was certainly dead.

"Hold up a moment, doctor," said Inspector Marsh. "Let me observe what I can before we go in and disrupt anything. It isn't going to help the bloke a whit to get a doctor to him now."

Violet tut-tutted and said, "It's a good thing the master and missus weren't 'ere when this 'appened, or else the poor little boy may have been the one to find this."

"They're out, are they? Do you happen to know their whereabouts?"

"Went to 'er sister's for the day, didn't they? To visit the baby and do a bit of shopping."

"When do you expect them back?"

"They said they would have supper 'ere. That's all I know." She seemed to pull herself together. "Would you like tea?"

Marsh had the notebook out of his pocket and was trying to make notes, despite his injured arm. "That would be lovely, Violet. And have some yourself. You've had quite a shock."

"Indeed I 'ave." Violet bustled off to the kitchen, happy to be going through familiar motions.

Doctor Bruce was becoming impatient. "It's perfectly obvious what happened here, John. Someone broke the window. There's glass all over the floor, so you know it was broken from the outside. Then some sort of argument ensued. He picked up the closest weapon at hand, the poker, and hit the man over the head repeatedly. It was not premeditated. If it had been, the murderer would have brought his own weapon." The doctor was pleased with his deductions. "It's likely they both broke in together, perhaps to rob the house, and then quarreled over something. You'll need to find out what's missing."

Miss Ambrose spoke up. "That couldn't be exactly what happened, though, could it? The glass is on the floor, but it's also on the windowsill, along with a coating of dust. If someone had broken through the window with the intention of coming in that way, he would have rubbed off all the dust and glass as he climbed in. As a matter of fact," she said as she pointed to a place on the victim's trouser leg, "you can see some of the glass on top of the body. The window was broken after the deed was done, to cover up the fact that whoever did it had access to the house some other way."

"If you keep this up the village won't need me at all," said Inspector Marsh.

Miss Ambrose blushed. "Sorry. It seems I'm secretary to a solicitor. I type things and one can't help but read."

"The solicitor is a lucky man. Go on. What else do you notice?"

"Well, for one, the poker is not the murder weapon."

The doctor's patience was at an end. "I say, John, may I go in and do my bit now?"

"Of course. And what makes you think that, Miss Ambrose?"

"It isn't bent at all. That style of poker isn't wrought iron. It's brass, and not particularly thick brass. Using it for repeated blows on anything solid would leave it a bit bent. The blood was added later to throw us off."

Coral impressed even herself with this level of perceptiveness and wished it would carry through to her real life.

"Jolly good. I'd noticed the trickery with the window myself, but you were the first to notice the poker." Inspector Marsh nodded at her encouragingly.

"And another thing," she continued, stepping gingerly into the room. "Look at the blood. Not the blood on the carpet, but on the walls and this chair. It looks to me like the victim was sitting here, in this armchair, when someone crept up behind him and hit him on the head. The poor fellow then sank to his knees in front of the chair, and the murderer stepped around to the side and continued to hit him, spattering the blood on that wall there," she pointed, "and on the wall directly behind, leaving a clean area where the blood hit the killer himself, and never made it to the wall."

Indeed, it was as she said. Drops of blood had sprayed to each side of one chair, but there was a gap that made a sort of outline of the killer. "You should be able to roughly judge the height of the murderer by triangulation."

That really sounded like she knew what she was talking about! Coral was having so much fun.

Inspector Marsh, who was holding his injured arm gingerly, smiled warmly, and said, "You are a marvel. So it appears the victim was sitting in this chair as though he belonged there, with his back more or less to the door. Someone crept up behind him from the hall, and did the deed. The killer then tried to cover it up and left, and unless we find something else, took the murder weapon with him, pausing for all the jiggery-pokery with the poker, if you'll excuse the play on words, and creeping outside to break the window. I believe if we look at the flowerbed outside this window we'll find one set of footprints walking to the window and walking away again."

A motorcar could be heard pulling into the drive and Inspector Marsh looked up. "Ah, I believe that would be the lord and lady of the manse here to clear a few things up for us. They're actually a very nice couple, the Carlsons. Active in the parish. Adopted a little orphaned boy. I'll just nip out and warn them off the study."

An orphan boy in this story too? No doubt his name will be Isaac.

"It wasn't a poker that made these injuries." Doctor Bruce appeared to be muttering to himself as he worked with thermometers and stethoscopes. "It was something with square edges, like the pedestal of a piece of statuary. I'd stake my reputation on it." Noticing that Inspector Marsh had left and his only audience was Miss Ambrose, he said, "Of course I'll have to get the body back to my surgery to take measurements. I also notice quite a few cuts on his hands. Some of them are healing and others appear brand new."

"Why, he's a carpenter! Do you see the sawdust, just here, and here?" Miss Ambrose indicated small patches of it ground into his sleeves.

The doctor replaced the instruments in his bag. "Nothing more I can do here. We'll get to the bottom of things, my girl. You can rely on it. I'll be able to tell Inspector Marsh when he died, although I hardly think there's much of a mystery about the cause of death. I daresay I won't also find he was electrocuted and attacked by poisonous snakes, eh what? Hardly likely to find rat poisoning was slipped into his evening sherry. I wonder what became of that tea?" He stood up with a groan and went in search of Violet.

Miss Ambrose sighed at the body and wandering over to the front door, looked out. Inspector Marsh was addressing a smartly dressed couple standing next to a modern motorcar. The man's face was quite red, and the woman had pressed a handkerchief against her mouth. She glanced up, startled to see Miss Ambrose, a stranger, in her doorway. Embarrassed to be caught staring, Miss Ambrose lowered her gaze.

Marsh turned, and said, "Ah, Mrs. Carlson, allow me to introduce you to the heroine of the day, Miss Ambrose. She found your housekeeper in hysterics and brought us back."

"I'm hardly a heroine. More of a messenger."

Mrs. Carlson gave Miss Ambrose a brief nod and said, "Oh, poor Violet! Where is she? She must be frightfully upset."

"We left her making tea," said Miss Ambrose. Just then a small boy careened around from the side of the house, sending gravel flying everywhere with his shiny black shoes.

"Mummy! Mummy! Is it time for tea?"

"Isaac!" said Miss Ambrose.

Mrs. Carlson looked at her quizzically. "Do you know my son?"

"No, not at all. Someone must have said his name. You'll want to keep him away from the study."

"Of course. Such a dreadful thing to have in one's home." Her eyes filled with tears.

Inspector Marsh said, "If you could just stay out here for a few minutes longer, Mrs. Carlson. We'll be able to close the study door and—" he nodded in the direction of Isaac. "—I'll get the Constable out here to help carry him out as soon as possible. You'll have a bit of a mess, I'm afraid."

Miss Ambrose said, "I really should be going. No point in me cluttering up the place. I do hope you find out who, er, what you need to find out, so you can get your lives back to normal. Now I'll see myself back to town. It isn't a very long walk and the weather is fine."

Inspector Marsh said, "I'll be with you in a moment, Mr. Carlson. Miss Ambrose, may I have a word before you leave?" He drew her off to the side.

"I suppose you don't want me to leave town until this is resolved. After all, I was the first person other than the housekeeper to be involved."

Marsh shook his head. His face seemed paler than it should be. "I don't regard you as a suspect. I merely wished to thank you for your help and insight, and tell you we could use someone like you around here now and then."

"Thank you. I'm sure you have everything under control. I don't mean to be nosy, but is that arm of yours all right? You seem a bit peaky."

He made a rueful face. "It's not my arm. I took a bullet in the chest last week. It's a sleepy little village, with just the odd row and occasional peevish shivving, but last week there was an altercation in the pub and I went over to help the constable sort it out, and was shot for my trouble."

"How dreadful!"

"It's taking a beastly long time to heal. The doctor says it would heal faster if I would stay in bed, but that isn't likely now, is it?"

"I daresay you should listen to him. Good morning, Inspector."

"Good morning."

The walk back to the inn gave Coral time to think. She was delighted with this book and found everything about it perfectly splendid. Solving a murder mystery in a study with John Marsh was going to be fun, but now she also had another mystery. John Marsh was shot in the chest here, just as he was in the Western. And Isaac was here, adopted by the Carlsons. This was all very confusing.

Miss Ambrose tapped her foot restlessly on the floral carpet of the room in which she was staying, watching through the window as the local residents entered The Lion and Lamb across the street. She was quite a modern young woman and perfectly capable of going on holiday by herself, taking trains and checking into the inn, taking meals alone, but going out for a pint where she knew no one was one step too far. And yet there was no place she would rather be. The local pub would be awash in rumors and possibly even news of a factual sort about the murder. She would love to know if the victim had been identified and if Inspector Marsh had an idea about the killer's identity, or at least a motive.

Hobbled as she was by her singleness and sex, she took a moment to ponder the peculiarities of living in a book. For example, the time from having left the murder scene to being in a chair in the inn simply didn't pass in the usual way. If she thought about it, she could say that she'd walked back to town, taken her rented bicycle to a neighboring town where she'd whiled away the time browsing through the shops, pedaled back, browsed the Cotsley shops, eaten at the pub, and chatted up her landlord. But there was no feeling of having lived it. There were no details.

Now she could look around her room and take note of the turquoise chenille bedspread, the green striped wallpaper with floral accents that looked dingy near the light switch, the white curtains with eyelet trim, her carpetbag standing open on the floor, her hairbrush and hat on the dresser, and her coat on a peg on the back of the door. The room had a slightly musty but not unpleasant smell of mingled lemon oil, radiator, and rolls being baked for tomorrow's breakfast. It was a bit chilly. She could hear a muted conversation from the room next door: two women. The occasional motorcar passed on the street below. All of this felt very real, while the afternoon was glossed over. Nothing that happened during the afternoon mattered, but because this part was written into the book it apparently did. Something interesting must be about to happen.

While anticipating the interesting occurrence, she took a moment to examine her appearance in the mirror, pleased that again there were no glasses and she remained a slender woman in her early twenties. This time her straight, dark hair had been twisted into a chignon.

There was a gentle rapping on the door, followed by the voice of the innkeeper. "Miss Ambrose, you have a caller. I've left him in the breakfast room."

"Oh, thank you. I'll be right down."

John Marsh stood as she entered. "I hope I don't startle you. I'm not here to interrogate you. You're not a suspect."

"That's a relief."

"I rather thought you might like to ... well, that's rather forward of me. Since you don't have mobs of friends here, I thought perhaps ... how silly of me, you came here to be alone. I'll just be on my way."

"I would love to have a pint at the pub with you. Let me just nip up to my room to grab my coat and hat and off we'll go."

"Jolly good."

The Lion and Lamb was one of the old pubs that dot England, standing in place for hundreds of years, the center of town life, added onto and sometimes modernized a bit, but remaining essentially the same. Marsh had to stoop to get in the door, which opened into a room with a dark-beamed ceiling that was barely higher than he was tall. A large stone fireplace with a small fire kept the room cozy at one end, and a glossy but dented wooden bar kept spirits high at the other. There was room for a few small tables and booths, but it appeared most of the patrons sat in a more modern room through a door in the back.

Many curious glances were directed their way as they entered, but only a few members of the staff ventured a polite, "Good evening, Inspector."

"I hope you don't mind if we move through to the new room. I always feel I'm in danger of getting a concussion in here, charming though it is."

"I can see why. Men didn't grow as tall as you when this was built. How old is the new room?"

"Oh, it's been here only a hundred and twenty years or so. Would you care for something to eat? They have the usual here: steak and kidney pie, fish and chips, that sort of thing."

"No, thank you."

"Couple of pints?" he asked, raising his eyebrows at Miss Ambrose.

"Just a glass for me. I like to keep my wits about me."

"Two glasses then, Eunice." She nodded and headed back to the taproom.

"Don't let me spoil your fun." Miss Ambrose had never really looked John Marsh full in the face before at such close range. He had large, kind eyes that suggested he had been a very attractive baby, but his skin showed evidence of having been out in the sun and the cold, probably a remnant of his days as a constable before being promoted to inspector. His gaze was steady. He was a man who had learned by watching people, and diffident though his manner had been when sounding her out about the visit to the pub, he was not a shy man.

"Not at all. I like a lady who knows her limits."

"Thank you. I've been simply dying to know: What did the footprints look like outside the library window? And did Doctor Bruce learn anything surprising?"

"This is an active police investigation, and as such I'm afraid I'm not at liberty to discuss the particulars of the case."

Miss Ambrose smiled slyly. "You needn't answer. I merely stated that I'm dying to know."

"I would think the secretary to a solicitor would be aware that I couldn't discuss the case."

"Especially not if you think I had anything to do with it, and I wouldn't blame you one bit if you did. A strange woman comes to town alone. It's unclear why she picked this town. Suddenly someone turns up dead, and who should be in the thick of reporting it but our strange woman. Then she acts as though she has special knowledge about how the crime was committed. If I were you, I'd be very suspicious of me."

"I'm not the slightest bit suspicious of you. You work for the respected William Edgington, Esquire. He thinks very highly of you, by the way. You rode in on the 6:45 on Friday and checked immediately into the inn. You had a light supper in your room, took a stroll around the town, where you were seen by several people, and then went to bed, taking a cup of cocoa with you. I suppose you could have nipped over to the Carlsons' house that evening, bashed the man's head in, changed into clothes that weren't covered in blood that you'd thought to stash in the bushes, and gone back to the inn, but I find it highly unlikely in view of the trust your employer puts in you."

This was all news to Coral, but she went with it.

"So we can put that behind us."

"Indeed." The glasses of beer arrived. Inspector Marsh raised his and said, "Cheers."

A boisterous group of young men tromped in and threw themselves into a booth as though they hadn't sat down all day. One of them caught Miss Ambrose staring and gave her a wink, then noticed Marsh sitting across from her. "Evening, Inspector."

"Freddy. Lads."

Miss Ambrose whispered, "I'm going to go way out on a limb here, but were they involved in the bar fight when you got shot?"

Inspector Marsh shifted in his seat and gave her a nod. "Indeed, but they're good lads. It was some tourists who started the fight and did the actual shooting."

"I hope they were sentenced appropriately."

"Oh, yes. Now, about your questions. You would not have been surprised by what we found when we examined the footprints under the window." Miss Ambrose nodded. "Likewise, Dr. Bruce hasn't told me anything surprising."

"No tiny dart tipped with curare. But you still don't know who or why. Do you at least know who the victim is?"

"I have reason to believe, based on items found in his pockets, that he's a carpenter called McAllister."

McAllister!

The name set Coral's mind to work. McAllister was the name of the murdered man in the Western, the one killed by Two Bit, or if you believed Two

Bit, by a bear. Or if you believed Isaac, by a dragon. In the last book, McAllister had been Isaac's father. Perhaps he was here as well. The Carlsons were going to adopt Isaac when she left the Western genre, and in this book it appeared to have happened. Could it be that this Isaac's original name was Isaac McAllister?

"The Carlsons were expecting him to come on Monday morning to do some repair work in their greenhouse. They didn't recognize him because they'd hired him on the recommendation of a friend of theirs. What he was doing in their house on Friday evening remains a mystery."

"Did you find the murder weapon?"

"I really can't say."

"I assume, being a thorough sort of person, that you've tracked down both where he was staying and anybody besides me who isn't familiar."

"I've done that and more. The only things I've told you are what's going to be in the press soon enough."

She wondered if he had figured out that the victim was Isaac's real father. Had he gotten that far?

A whoop and then roar of laughter came from the table of rambunctious lads, which drew Miss Ambrose's eye. As she was looking in that direction, something else caught her attention: a man in the adjacent booth had pulled out his wallet to pay for his drink. The wallet was an unusual Oriental silk style with a golden dragon embroidered on it. It was quite gaudy.

She pointed him out to the Inspector as subtly as she could. "Do you recognize that man? Is he local?"

"No, must be passing through. What a peculiar wallet he has!"

Coral couldn't tell him about the dragon that had terrorized her in a different book but ...

"There's something wrong about that man. I can't put my finger on it. He seems out of place somehow." She downed the last of her beer and said, "Are you ready to go? We can follow him."

"Follow him? For having an ugly wallet? We just got here." Seeing the look of determination on her face, he bravely attempted to help her on with her coat, although it went rather badly with his injured arm. "I do still need to pay."

"You do that. I'll slow him down." The man had already walked out into the night. Miss Ambrose quickly followed.

"Excuse me!" The mysterious stranger turned in surprise. He was a small, wiry man with a flat nose and one eyebrow that ran across his entire forehead. His face was completely unknown to her. She had not seen him in a previous book. "Terribly sorry to disturb, but I believe you dropped this on the way out." She held out her own comb.

He shook his head. "That's not mine." His accent gave him away as from the north of England, possibly from Yorkshire. *Within the book she had the ability to recognize the different accents of Britain despite being American.*

"Are you sure? They all look rather alike. I thought I saw it fall out of your pocket."

He pulled his own comb from his pocket. "Aye. Mine is right here. That appears to be a lady's comb."

"Oh, silly me. So it is. I really should get my eyes checked. Now I wonder where John has got to. Sorry to disturb!" She gave him her sunniest smile and he ambled off just as Inspector Marsh appeared. "I'm afraid I'm frightening people by accusing them of dropping combs. I really should get my eyes checked."

The inspector's face clearly indicated a lack of amusement. When the carrier of the gaudy wallet was out of earshot, he whispered, "You should have your head checked. What if he were the killer? You shouldn't rush up to a suspect like that."

"I'm not the slightest bit afraid." *Why would she be afraid of a mere character in a book? Especially since she was also a character in a book she could simply leave?*

"I can see that, which is why other people need to do the worrying for you."

"So you agree with me that he may be a suspect. Look, he turned down that street." She scurried after him and turned the corner just in time to see him slip into a large, run-down house.

"I should have known." The Inspector drew her back around the corner out of sight.

"What is it?"

"It's a boarding house, very inexpensive and rather disreputable. As the constable will tell you, most of his calls involve people who live there."

"Does the house rent out rooms by the night, or do you think he moved in?"

"Hard to say, but the proprietors have been known to rent out rooms for a few nights here and there. They aren't supposed to do it, but that doesn't seem to stop them."

"Will you question the dragon wallet man tomorrow?"

"I can't exactly bring him in to accuse him of having an ugly wallet. I'll certainly make discreet inquiries."

The evening air was cool, but breezeless and pleasant. They continued their stroll along the main road and into the part of town where Miss Ambrose had noticed the well-kept gardens. People walking spaniels and terriers passed them, nodding at Inspector Marsh respectfully. The Windle drew quite near the backs of the houses here, no doubt affording a lovely view for those fortunate enough to live there. She wondered if there were swans.

"This really is a charming town. So very unlike where I live."

"You don't find it boring here?"

"I haven't been bored a bit!"

"We don't have murders every day, you know. This was a special entertainment just for you."

Miss Ambrose smiled. "I very much doubt the victim found it entertaining. Have you found out who let McAllister into the house? That seems awfully important."

Inspector Marsh looked at her sideways. "No we haven't, and it is awfully important. Violet would never have invited a strange man into the home with the Carlsons out."

"Does she sleep there or live elsewhere?"

"She lives with her sister in a cottage in the village. And you sound exactly like someone who practices law yourself."

"Sorry. Typing all the briefs and transcripts does have a way of focusing the mind." *Apparently her job in London involved typing briefs and transcripts, a fact she was just learning now simply by thinking about it.* "Did she lock all the doors before she went out that night?" They had made a loop around the residential area and were nearly back at the inn. "Would you care to come in for tea in the parlor? It isn't terribly late. I'm sure we can get some."

"So you can interrogate me further?"

"I'm afraid so. Once I get my mind on something I find it very difficult to think of anything else."

"Aren't you meant to be on holiday? Shouldn't you be bird-watching and visiting ancient ruins?"

"Do you have ancient ruins?"

"No, actually, if you don't include The Lion and Lamb."

It was apparent on entry that the kitchen was dark, the staff had left or gone to bed, and tea would be an imposition. Miss Ambrose said, "I appear to have misjudged."

"Not a bit like London, eh? Perhaps we'll meet again before you leave. Tomorrow, is it?"

"Only if you let me interrogate you further. Perhaps I will have thought of something during the night. Dreamed up new questions."

"You're a bit incorrigible, aren't you?"

Miss Ambrose was the recipient of many frankly curious stares from children, who were in turn the recipients of parental yanks by the arm, as everyone filed out of services at St. Agnes the following morning, which holiday visitors rarely bothered attending. The vicar was in earnest conversation with Mr. and Mrs. Carlson on the front steps. Isaac was jumping off the stairs, making a game of it. Jump off the bottom one, then the bottom two, then the bottom three, until he realized he couldn't jump any further without injuring himself.

"I think three is going to be your limit," Miss Ambrose said.

Isaac turned to his mother. "Mummy?"

Mrs. Carlson saw who Isaac was talking to and resumed her conversation with the vicar. "Don't be a bother, Isaac."

Miss Ambrose continued talking to the boy. "I was at your house with Inspector Marsh yesterday. You weren't expecting to come home to find police, were you?"

"They wouldn't let me see anything. They shut the study door and told me to go straight to my room. It wasn't fair." He had a Northern accent like the dragon wallet man. "I'm not afraid to see a dead body."

"How did you know there was a body?"

"I'm not stupid. I could hear them talk."

"I rather think they didn't mean you to hear that."

"And I'm not a baby!"

"You haven't always lived with the Carlsons, have you? Didn't I hear that you'd been adopted?"

"That's right. My real mum died when I was a baby and my father and me lived together and I saw lots of things."

"So we really shouldn't treat you like you're a little child, because you're a worldly young man."

Isaac looked off into the distance, as if mentally trying on the image of worldly young man. He seemed to like it well enough. "That's right,"he said.

"I guess you miss your father. What happened to him? How did you end up with the Carlsons?"

His worldly young man eyes became downcast little boy eyes. "I came home from school and my dad wasn't there, and he wasn't in the shop, and a man came and said he was dead, and he took me to his house, and the next day the Carlsons came and said I would be their son. Then we drove and drove."

"That must have been quite a shock. Were you able to pack a bag? Bring your toys and things? Photographs?"

"The man who came, the first man, packed my clothes and put some toys in the bag, but not my favorite ones. He put baby toys in there I didn't want anymore."

"No photographs? Of your mother and father?"

"No."

"That is a shame. Do you remember the name of the man?"

"He never said nothing."

"Isaac! I told you not to bother the lady." The Carlsons had finished their conversation with the vicar and were anxious to leave before being cornered by more of the townspeople. Having a murder at one's house makes a family more conspicuous than one would wish. Miss Ambrose had a few questions she would like to put to them herself, but merely walked on. Though she was dying to know more about the circumstances surrounding Isaac's adoption, here amongst the mingling denizens of Cotsley she would be unlikely to glean useful information. Timing was, as always, key.

There were a great many questions she would like to ask a lot of people, but there was a train to catch at 3:20. She would like to ring her employer at home and learn more about how adoption works. It wasn't normally his field, but he should know. Didn't people adopt from orphanages? It almost sounded like the Carlsons had bought Isaac from someone. Did they have any idea his father was still alive when it happened? Who were the friends who referred McAllister to the Carlsons for carpentry work? Was that just a happy accident, or had he been searching for his son? She was inclined to believe the latter.

Why weren't the police looking for Isaac? Or were they? She knew someone she could ask about that.

Back in her room at the inn, Miss Ambrose carefully packed her carpetbag so it would be ready to go and set off for the police station, nearly colliding with John Marsh at the door.

"Well! Isn't this a pleasant surprise!"

"Good morning. I'm glad to see you're still here, Miss Ambrose. I had a bit of news I thought you'd find interesting." His face seemed drawn.

"A police inspector willingly providing information about an ongoing case? That can't be it. It must be about something else. Did ancient ruins suddenly turn up?"

"That would be newsworthy, but no. It seems your friend, the one with the wallet, is rather a person of interest after all. After we left him, he scarpered off into the night, never to be seen again. The landlady of the fine establishment is keen to get her hands on him as he neglected to pay his bill."

"Were you able to get his name?"

"After a lot of whinging, she produced the name John Smith of London."

"Of course." That was very disappointing. "Perhaps it follows that it may be possible to deduce the likelihood of petty thievery on the idiosyncratic appearance of a person's wallet."

"How scholarly-sounding. I really must add this bit to the growing body of scientific knowledge about the nature of criminals being collected at Scotland Yard."

"You may have my contribution with my blessing."

"I also wish to thank you."

"Thank me?"

"You told me I should have listened to the doctor's advice about resting this wound, and you were right. It isn't getting better. Rather the opposite, actually."

"Oh dear! Do come sit down." She led him into the parlor of the inn.

"They're sending someone from London to take over my responsibilities, but in the meantime, there's still this McAllister affair to sort. I know you're leaving, but I've come to respect you very much. Do you have any ideas about the case? Anything that will help me unravel it while I'm still ambulatory? I'd hate to go toes-up with this matter unsolved."

"Just give me a moment to think."

She needed to break out of the genre eventually. Solving the case would certainly end a book, which she presumed would put her back in her real world apartment, but she didn't have enough information to do that. She thought she knew who the killer was, more or less, but not his real name, nor where to find him. If she followed the pattern of the genre, she could have one of those scenes, probably in a drawing room, where she would reveal all. All except, at least so far, the name of the real killer.

She would be able to tell Inspector Marsh that the dragon wallet man was from somewhere in the North because she had heard his accent, and based on what Isaac, who also had a Northern accent, had told her about what he remembered, he'd been kidnapped and sold. Since there were not infinite numbers of characters in any of these novels, no doubt it had been the dragon wallet man who'd had the idea of making money by kidnapping a child and selling him to a childless couple.

So he'd knocked out or restrained McAllister, kidnapped Isaac, and sold him to the Carlsons. McAllister had never stopped hunting for his son and had somehow found out where he was. That he would never give up looking for his son simply stood to reason. That the body in the library was McAllister she knew because he was involved with woodworking, based on the evidence on his body and clothing, and also because Inspector Marsh had identified him by name and profession through something he had in his pocket, she didn't know what. The McAllister in the Western had run a sawmill. Two books, one character. Two books with a father and son separated. McAllister had to be Isaac's father. She could say she knew it somehow, but that bit would be extremely difficult to explain in the drawing room scene.

Moving on, it logically followed that the dragon wallet man with the Northern accent who had kidnapped and sold Isaac tracked McAllister to town, picked the lock on the Carlsons' house, and let himself in. McAllister arrived, hoping to find Isaac and unaware that the Carlsons were not at home. He'd never intended to do carpentry for them, he was there to find his son so he hadn't thought it would matter when he arrived. He didn't recognize the culprit who answered the door because he'd never seen him, was ushered in, and then the dragon wallet man bashed him over the head, afterward trying to make the murder look like a break-in.

But of course, if the dragon wallet man was trying to make it look like a break-in, why didn't he steal something? Why did he leave the body there? He could have dragged it away somewhere. There would only have been a mysterious puddle of blood. Why both pick the lock and break the window? Was there someone in particular he was trying to frame? There were a lot of holes that needed to be filled.

She had made a lot of the necessary connections for solving the mystery in the usual way of the genre, where the reader has no idea what the amateur detective is thinking until the final pages, but the story was not sufficiently complete. She didn't know the real name of the dragon wallet man and all sorts of things that would take time to find out. Did she wish to stay with it to the end and see if she could get out of the story that way? How long would that take? There was, of course, another way of leaving: doing something that would never happen in a cozy English murder mystery. That was how she'd escaped the horror novel and the Western: doing something against genre conventions.

She was of two minds about the situation. She truly liked John Marsh and had enjoyed being an amateur detective, but this was not her real life. Her actual body sat elsewhere, vacant. In addition, she was beginning to think the best way to help John Marsh, who appeared to be badly injured, lay outside Cotsley-on-Windle.

Coral made a decision. She looked into the open, friendly face of John Marsh and with reluctance said, "I'm afraid I really can't help you. I'm just a secretary. I know I'm awfully nosey sometimes and it's my worst fault. You should have told me from the beginning to stay out of other people's business."

"Nonsense! You're very perceptive. If you were a man you'd be an inspector yourself. Possibly the Chief Inspector."

"Now you're just being silly. I really should go back to typing and leave the detecting to the professionals."

Inspector Marsh tipped his head to the side and looked at her quizzically, as a dog might. "What brought this on? You were keen to help before."

"None of this is any of my business. I shouldn't make a puzzle of murder, as though it were a game. People's real lives are at stake. Murder isn't for our entertainment. When it comes right down to it, I don't know the murdered man and I really don't care terribly much what happened, at least not as I should..."

With a jolt Coral was on her sofa in her own apartment, but only momentarily. She was just looking at the clock to see how long the experience had taken in real time when another jolt took her back to the parlor of the Cotsley Inn...

Marsh's face was undergoing a disturbing transformation. First incredulity, then disappointment in her, then the stony-faced reserve of a Buckingham Palace guard crossed his countenance. *Because he had become dear and she valued his good opinion of her, fictional character though he was, the effect was heartbreaking. Coral couldn't stand it.*

"I don't mean that exactly. It isn't what you think. I mean, I do. Oh, I don't know what to say."

"It appears to me you do have something to say. But as you like. It was a pleasure meeting you, Miss Ambrose. . .''

Another jolt and she was in her apartment clutching the messenger bag in confusion. Then there was yet another jolt, and she was in her chilly room at the inn collecting her packed bag with no sign of John Marsh. What she'd done to break the genre hadn't worked well enough to get her out cleanly. Instead, it had left her in some sort of transitional world, half in and half out. Perhaps it was a reaction to her double-mindedness. She hadn't been entirely sure she wanted out.

Another jolt and she saw her own glass topped coffee table in front of her. She was back to her apartment. She tried to insert her hand into the bag to pull the book out of the messenger bag, but she didn't act fast enough. Another jolt and she was breathing fresh air at the train station at Cotsley-on-Windle, wondering if this was what epileptic seizures felt like. But the roaring in her ears, eddies of wind, and vibration in her legs were not neurological in cause, but instead being caused by a train pulling into the station: her train to London. She remained in the fictional world long enough to see that among the milling people queuing to get onto the train was the man with the dragon wallet. Another jolt, and she was back to the warmth of her apartment. She tried again to pull the book out of the bag, but again there wasn't time. This time she was swaying in her seat on the train, which was flying down the tracks.

Perhaps she could be quicker and pull the book out next time. Or she could find another way to break the genre's conventions more completely. What else would never happen in a cozy English murder mystery?

The next thing that did happen was not as much a jolt but a flicker. It put her back in time to the moment when she had disappointed Inspector Marsh. He was looking at her with his blank Buckingham Palace guard face and saying, "It appears to me you do have something to say." *Would she need to live through all that over and over? Everything had gone so terribly wrong.*

But then there was another flicker and she was back in the train, in the same car, miraculously, as the man with the dragon wallet...

Afraid to waste time thinking, she leapt from her seat, swallowed her revulsion, and approached him flirtatiously. "Remember me? The comb? I have something for you. You're going to want this. Come along. Trust me."

He blushed, a twinkle appeared in his rabbity eyes, and he followed her down the aisle and out the rear door to the gap between cars.

"Close your eyes and pucker up," she said.

It's a fictional character, a fictional character, she thought. None of this is real. I'm not really doing this. She wrapped one arm around his back like a lover, then quickly got her other arm under his knees and lifted the small man bodily over the rail, pitching him off the speeding train to his death.

All that working out at Strong Body Cooperative had paid off. It allowed the amateur detective to murder the suspect.

13 CONTROLLING FATE

Coral was back on her sofa for good, aghast at herself for killing someone, or at least feeling like she had. Until the last disconcerting part, starting with letting down Inspector Marsh, then flipping in and out of reality, and eventually becoming a killer, she'd had a lot of fun.

She took her cue from the earlier tone of the adventure and made herself a cup of tea. Her time there had been a bit longer: thirteen minutes. While the water was heating in the microwave, she ransacked her cupboard for some cookies she could refer to as biscuits. But she felt as though she were on the verge of tears. It wasn't the unsettling ending of the Cotsley book, nor was it even the fact that she had just killed a man, because she hadn't. That was no more real than children playing space aliens, shooting at one another with their fingers. Pew! Pew!

It was John Marsh. She had disappointed him. Just when he thought he could trust her, and that they were friends, she had clammed up and not told him what he needed to know in order to solve the crime. She had ruined their relationship. He didn't feel like a fictional character somehow. She wanted to help him. It didn't make sense.

Of course, nothing that was happening made sense. Setting aside the problem of how placing a book in a bag could temporarily put her directly into a book of the same genre, why did some of the same people keep cropping up in her different adventures? She still had no idea who wrote the books she entered into. They had plot-lines she didn't recognize and recurring characters other than herself. It was almost as though the characters and their world were as real as her. Were they?

That raised a question. John Marsh was wounded in an Old West shootout that later turned into a British bar brawl, and the wound was not healing well. If it was infected, it could possibly kill him, at least in the time periods she'd been visiting. She didn't want him to die.

Perhaps it would be possible to bring him into a modern book where he could receive proper treatment. Or better yet, some time in the future when a wound like that would be no trouble at all. On the other hand, these books went where the author chose. Whoever the author was. She had no control over the fate of any of them. Maybe Marsh wouldn't be in the next one, only Isaac. Maybe neither.

There was one way to find out. Tomorrow.

In the meantime, she had a lot of notes to make.

This time she didn't bother pinning the note to her shirt. Coming back had been a bit awkward last time, but she had gained experience and now felt confident she could get out of one of these book adventures whenever she chose. It was getting in that worried her. It hadn't worked right last time. It hadn't been until she'd tried to take the book out that she'd found herself in Cotsley. What was it Phil had said that first day? Not to drop the book in but *place* it in. She'd dropped it in and it hadn't worked. What was the deal with placing the book, and why had it suddenly worked when she went to take it out? It seemed to have something to do with the book and the bag touching her hand at the same time. Or something. She didn't know.

She once again made herself comfortable, checked the clock, and this time *placed* a book deep into the bag.

14 ATTACK ON ARJEN-PRIME

Seventeen months out, and 17 months back. There wasn't any way around it. Arjen-Prime was off the beaten path. Even if they sent a distress signal that actually reached home, and even if someone there had the funding to send a ship, and even if a rescue party would be willing to spend nearly three years of their lives coming to their aid and returning home, it would still be 17 months before they arrived. Which effectively meant: if they had a problem, they had to solve it themselves.

But they would have been laughed out of the company if they'd said they needed rescuing just because they were all in a really, really bad mood.

They were holding together, but just barely. C-Wing, meant to be crew quarters, had never deployed properly, leaving the crew all crowded together like old-Earth submariners. Tempers had flared past the breaking point, and it may have been simply because they needed more room to get away from each other. Maybe. It was just such a conflict, this time over feet that were projecting into a walkway that led to a hip shove at the mess table, which led to a hand shove, which led to a fist in the face, which had eventually turned into a tachy blast in the ribcage for John Marsh.

Commander Light grounded everyone. Outside of meal breaks no one was allowed to be anywhere but sleeping area (solo), workstation, or bathroom, except during scheduled exercise periods, one at a time, strictly enforced. He was going to make them sweat the jumps and bites and blackness right out of themselves so they didn't beat it out of each other.

Marsh's wound wasn't looking good. The tachy had missed all of his internal organs; in that he was lucky. It had bounced off a rib and headed up, tearing his pectoral muscle and leaving his right arm almost useless. Doc had fused it, but some microbe, Terran or native in origin, they didn't know which, was eating at the flesh.

Ambrose entered the sparse infirmary and shut the door. "You have to do something about Marsh's wound."

Doctor Bruce looked annoyed. "And this is your business why?"

"It's all our business, Doc."

"Getting into other people's business hasn't been working out so well lately."

"I'm trying to help. That's different."

"You may be trying to help Marsh, but you're annoying me. You're assuming I'm not doing anything about his wound. That's getting into my business."

"Damn, Doc, you could have just told me you were on it. I'm glad you're working on it. Keep up the good work."

"Do you have something you need to see me about? Something about you?"

"No."

"Then get back to wherever you're supposed to be. You're violating Light's grounding rules."

"Okay, I'm going."

She was sick to death of her bed and the half-meter in front of it that she had to call her own. There wasn't much to see. Just a gray wall, color coordinated with the gray of the planet outside seemingly to remove all traces of color from their lives, and some postcard-sized art prints she'd brought from home. She was so tired of those art prints that when she got home she wanted to find the original paintings and blow them up.

Ambrose took the scenic route, such as it was, back to her sleeping area. This involved going left around the galley, rather than right, which was a straight shot. It added ten paces to the route. The galley wasn't more than a steel sink and short counter with a few appliances wedged in among storage lockers.

This was the scenic route because it took her past a window, where she dawdled. Then she moseyed. It appeared to be a fine day on Arjen-Prime, a fine day. If there's one thing to be said about having jack-diddly for atmosphere, it's that the view is always to die for.

Which was why she got a good look at an unexpected craft that was landing near the ridge to the east.

"Hey, hey, guys! Something landed! There's a ship out there!"

Forty-three men and women spilled out of their holes and jostled for position at the small window. "It's there. See where the ridge looks kind of like a woman lying down, and she has feet sticking up? It's by her chin."

"I don't see it."

"There's nothing there."

"No, really, look harder. It's a little hard to see now that it landed, but I saw it as it was coming down."

"Move."

"Get off my feet."

"Don't bother, there's nothing there. Just Ambrose wanting attention."

Light said, "The sensors would have picked up any ship that was headed our way."

Ambrose pushed her way back to the front of the jostling crowd. "It's right there. Right by the chin." She took a step back. She couldn't see it anymore either. "Well, I saw something land. You can't see it anymore."

Light said, "Hasagawa, you're at the sensors right now? Stay there. Higgins, Carlson, Emerson, and Cavalli: each of you take a window and look out. Everyone else get back to where you're supposed to be. Ambrose, my quarters, now."

Commander Light's quarters were underground, a sort of antechamber of the small mining operation that was part of their reason for being on Arjen-Prime. His intended quarters hadn't deployed any better than anybody else's, and when their first tentative forays into mining directly beneath the station had quickly hit a pocket of odorous sulfur, they'd cleared it out as quickly as they could, leaving a rotten egg stench that continued to permeate everything both above and below ground. However, a decent-sized room was left, which Light immediately commandeered. Gravel crunched underfoot as Ambrose followed Light into his rocky lair. Homey.

"That's two strikes in one day, Ambrose."

"What do you mean?"

"First you interfered with someone else's medical treatment."

Did he have a spy camera in sickbay? "Interfere? That sounds like I was trying to prevent Marsh from getting treatment. That's not true. That's the exact opposite of true."

"Well, what were you doing? Telling the doctor how to do his job?"

Ambrose could feel her anger rising. She controlled it the best she could. "I don't know how to do the doctor's job. I couldn't begin to tell him how to do his job. I saw Marsh's wound, and I saw how much pain he's in. I think he's going to die."

"Look at you. You're becoming hysterical."

Ambrose stared at him with narrowed eyes, inarticulate. She had not been hysterical. She had been defending herself against an unfair accusation. She held her hands up in appeasement. What could she say to this? "I'm sorry that came across as hysterical."

"Then you make a wild claim about a spaceship only you can see. There's something wrong with you. You're completely cracking up. That's all I need, someone getting everyone upset about an invisible alien attack." He rubbed his eyes in martyr-like weariness. "Okay, here's what I'm going to do. First, inform you of the facts. Fact one: John Marsh has been injected with a new antibiotic that Doc fabbed based on scrapings he cultivated. Doc knows how to do this stuff because, unlike you, he's a doctor. Marsh will be fine within a day or two."

Ambrose was relieved. Of all the people in the station, Marsh was the only one she actually liked, *and it was beginning to look like he was the only thing in this whole book that she liked.*

"Fact two: Now that you've made your invisible spaceship claim, I have to send someone out there to take a look. Whenever someone goes out, it endangers us all. We don't know what we might be letting back in. More microbes like what infected Marsh, or maybe something else, something worse. Not to mention the danger to the person going out."

"I'll go. Send me. I was the one who saw it."

Light laughed. "You'd like that, wouldn't you? Who would believe anything you said when you came back?"

He had a point. Someone else needed to see it.

"Fact three: You've upset morale. Morale was already upset and you've made it worse. I have to make an example of you. Until further notice, you're confined to the mining tunnels. I'll have a bed brought down."

Ambrose still didn't know what exactly she had done wrong, but it could have been worse. At least she'd be away from everyone else. "How long until you send someone out to see where the ship is?"

"That's none of your concern. Get into the tunnels now and I'll have your bed and some food brought down."

Just outside Light's room was an airtight steel door shielding his room and the station above from the tunnels below. The switch that controlled all the power, lights, air, and tools was on the wall outside. Ambrose switched it on and stepped inside. The commander shut the door behind her.

Then he turned off the power.

Fists pounding on the door, she yelled, "Light! Light! Put the power on! I can't see anything!"

He did not turn it on, even though he must have heard her. His mind was just as affected as everyone else's.

The darkness of the tunnel was beyond dark. It was a velvet canvas on which the rods of her eyes painted gray streaks and flashes. Gasping, she stumbled forward, arms outstretched, until her hands felt the rock wall. It was ice cold. She drew her hands back and tucked them under her arms. She was wearing only the station uniform: a pair of clingpants and a thin sleeveless tunic with a minecoat over it. Her heart felt like it was trying to double in size as it forced blood through all the body parts— legs, lungs, eyes, brain— that should be doing something to get her out of there.

At this point she decided she'd had enough of this book. There was not one pleasant thing about being there. Not only was she trapped underground in total darkness, but everyone she'd met had been excessively mean to her. She was on an unattractive planet and there were aliens coming. Everything smelled like sulfur. And everyone seemed to be losing emotional control.

The goal had been accomplished anyway. John Marsh was apparently on the road to full recovery. Nothing was keeping her on Arjen-Prime. It was time to leave the genre. She thought she knew how.

"Space travel like this can never happen," she said out loud. "Einstein proved that. We can't travel faster than the speed of light, so everything is too far away. It's a simple matter of physics."

Nothing happened. Blackness continued to engulf her.

I guess that doesn't break me out of the genre, she thought. Apparently that's been done before. Have to think of a different way, which is not going to be easy. Science fiction writers are too inventive, and there are so many of them, each needing to come up with something completely new in every book. Maybe that's the key. "Boring! Nothing new here. Not a single new idea. It's more boring than Earth, so I guess I'll head back now."

Nothing. She may just as well have clicked her heels together three times before she said it. Just saying it was boring didn't make it so, she thought. She needed to become boring. As boring as possible. If she'd had paper and light, she would have calculated pi.

"One hundred bottles of beer on the wall, one hundred bottles of beer. You take one down and pass it around, ninety-nine bottles of beer on the wall. Ninety-nine bottles of beer on the wall, ninety-nine bottles of beer. You take one down and pass it around, ninety-eight bottles of beer on the wall. Ninety-eight bottles of beer on the wall, ninety-eight bottles of beer. You take one down and pass it around, ninety-seven bottles of beer on the wall ... "

All one hundred bottles of beer were taken down and passed around and still she remained in total darkness on Arjen-Prime.

It took her a minute to recognize that masculine, resonant voice, the one she'd heard in the horror novel, and also to see how she was being cut off from escape. It was the narrative voice! The book itself was fighting her.

"Hold on a second, Narrative Voice. I've only gotten through ninety-seven bottles. Where have you been, anyway? There's a reason why I'm being boring. So you be quiet. Ninety-six bottles of beer on the wall, ninety-six bottles of beer. You take one down and pass it around, ninety-five bottles of beer on the wall."

And yet no amount of beer-bottle counting changed her situation, said the Narrative Voice.

"Hey! I told you to be quiet! It's not like you've been any help. Ninety-five bottles of beer on the wall, ninety-five bottles of beer. You take one down and pass it around, ninety-four bottles of beer on the wall."

Coral doggedly persisted until she realized it was futile, said the Intrusive Narrative Voice.

"As I was saying before I was so rudely interrupted: ninety-three bottles ... or wait, was I still on ninety-four? See what you've done? Ninety-four bottles of beer on the wall, ninety-four bottles of beer. You take one down and..."

On and on she droned until she finally ran out of bottles, asserted the Utterly Overbearing Narrative Voice.

"I haven't even gotten through the nineties yet. Just my luck, to get a Narrative Voice with attention deficit disorder. Ninety-three bottles of beer on the wall... "

Unaware that the Great and Omnipotent Narrative Voice was able to change her perception of time, Coral believed herself to have sung through the rest of the song. Victory!
Without warning the lights came on, seeming to sear her brain. A shriek escaped her and she pressed her hands over her eyes. The door clicked open.

"What's the matter? Oh, the light! I can't believe he left you here in the dark. I want to get my hands around his throat." It was the voice of John Marsh. Ambrose slowly removed her hands from her eyes and squinted, eyes watering, until she could see.

"I brought you a cot and blankets, and some food, and guess what? A bucket."

"A bucket. How thoughtful. How long does he expect me to stay in here, anyway?"

"He didn't say. Until you've learned your lesson, I guess." Marsh lowered his voice to a whisper. "I brought an opener for the door. Keep it hidden. I couldn't stand the thought of you being trapped in here all alone. But if I were you, I'd stay down here. Things aren't getting any better up there."

"What's going on?"

Loudly, he said, "Oh, I also brought you a little lamp so you aren't in total darkness." Then he whispered, "People are getting crazier and crazier. They're acting like they've been drugged. Everyone is angry about everything."

"Not you?"

"Yes, me too."

"What does Doc say about it?"

"You want to be the one to ask him?"

"No. Not doing that again. How's your arm?"

He rubbed it. "Better actually. I think Doc got it right."

"Good."

Light's voice bellowed from his quarters, "Get out of there, Marsh. That's a prisoner, not your private harem."

Marsh physically placed the lamp in Ambrose's hands and left, shutting the door behind him. There was a brief pause while Ambrose imagined Marsh starting to leave the power on and Light making him go back, and then the lights went out again. She switched her little lamp on.

Nothing that ends in distant black nothingness can be cozy, but the place right by the door where the lamp was had a warm-looking glow now that belied the frigid temperature. Ambrose sat on the cot and wrapped the blankets around herself. It really wasn't so bad. She could rest now on something fairly soft, and she could stay warm. There was food for later. And a bucket. Simple things. She also had the door opener. That made a huge difference from a mental standpoint.

Stretching out on the cot, she wondered why she had felt the need to try to be boring because truth be told, she was genuinely bored. There was nothing to do, not unless she wanted to take the lamp and go explore the mine tunnels. If she was stuck here a long time she would do that. In the meantime it was nice to just lie down and get warm.

It had to be morning, even though she could tell through closed eyes it was still dark out. *Her alarm hadn't gone off, so it must not be one of the days she was supposed to open at the gym. Unless she forgot to set her alarm. Her eyes flew open in concern. What time was it? There was no clock to her left, and no nightstand. Not her bedroom—rock walls— a mine tunnel! She felt a moment of confusion as she sorted out the fact that being stuck on Arjen-Prime was not going to make her late for work. She was still inside a novel. She already knew sleeping wouldn't remove her. She'd slept in Cotsley-on-Windle, a place she wished she had stayed.*

Did she still want out of this novel? She did. John Marsh was healed and there was nothing enjoyable about any of the rest of it. It hadn't been hard to break the genre conventions of the horror novel, the Western, or the English murder mystery. So for sci-fi, she simply needed to do something you would never see in a sci-fi novel. Just being boring hadn't done the trick. So the trick would be what?

After about an hour of ruminating, she was hungry and that bucket was starting to look useful to her. But she had two ideas to try. The first was going to involve Marsh's door opener.

There was no problem getting past Light's room. His snoring did not break in rhythm as she passed. In fact, most of the crew was asleep, and those who weren't remained confined, except the few who were stationed at sensors and windows. It wasn't going to be possible to sneak past any of them. There was nothing to see out there, at least as far as they were concerned. But present them with the one who got them stuck with such a dreary task, especially while they were hopped up on whatever it was that was making them all irritable, and the night would get a lot more interesting.

Ambrose gave it her best shot. She mimed "shush" to them as she walked through the common area. They would not be shushed. It didn't matter, she didn't need to go more than 30 meters and she was always a fast runner.

Higgins called out, "What are you doing out? You're supposed to be locked up. Does the Commander know where you are?"

People in all the beds crammed into every corner of the station began to murmur and sit up.

"Get her. Hold her down." Cavalli cut her off and grabbed her arm. She slammed his against the sharp edge of a cabinet and darted past.

Hasagawa pulled at the cabinet door. It was locked. "Anyone have the key to the tachy guns?"

Emerson said, "No, Light's the only one. We can handle her."

Ambrose made it to the airlock, banging her shin on a bedframe as she ran, opened it, and stepped inside. "Just look at how much trouble you're going to be in when Light finds out you let me do this."

Higgins sneered, "There's nowhere to go. You're such an idiot, Ambrose. You trapped yourself."

"Did I?" She shut the door leading inside. One more button and she would be out on the planet's surface, completely unprotected. She laughed as a look of horror bloomed on Higgins's face. "Bye, guys!"

Ambrose got into a racing stance, pressed the button, and ran out.

The first freezing breath without oxygen caused an instantaneous spasm in her lungs. Her throat closed shut like a drowning victim's. Though she tried to will her arms and legs forward, they became jerky and she quickly lost her balance.

It wasn't until then that she wondered what was happening to her real body. It was just sitting there in her apartment, right? It was too late now, there was no way back inside.

Small blood vessels around her eyes burst. She saw stars. Her heart felt like it was tearing in pieces as it tried to move oxygen-depleted blood around her body, which continued to flail in a completely uncoordinated way for a brief time, eventually stopping at about the same time as there was a blissful release of endorphins. Then she lost consciousness. Her final thought was: This is what it feels like to die. Somehow I always knew it would feel like this.

Being carried. Voices. Anger. Why do I know this? I'm still in the Arjen-Prime book. But why?

She sat up and gasped.

Doc, who had been bending over her, dropped his instrument and leaped back. Light, Marsh, and the others gathered around all jumped.

"How is it I'm not dead?"

Doc regained his composure first. "How indeed? You were dead. You were very dead. And now you're not."

Light said, "There is something seriously wrong here. I want her restrained. How do we know it's really her?"

Ambrose laughed at him. "There's something wrong here, all right, and it's not me."

"Restrain her!"

"Restraining is pretty much your answer to everything, isn't it?"

A look of pure hatred flickered across Light's face.

"Light, you used to be a good man. I respected you a lot. We all did. But something is making everyone mean and crazy, and that includes you. Me too. When I ran out there, that was crazy. Something is affecting our minds and something brought me back. Oh, and by the way, there is someone out there, you know."

"You don't have to tell me my job. I know something is affecting our minds. I'm handling it. It's one thing to act drugged and another thing when someone who's dead suddenly acts like it never happened. I don't trust you."

"Of course you don't. Go ahead and put me back in the mine tunnel. I understand."

"How did you get out?"

"You let me out, Light. Don't you remember?"

Light looked puzzled. "I did not."

"Sure you did. How else could I have gotten out with you right by the door?" Ambrose could see one of the unguarded windows from where she sat. "Oh, and you may want to take a look out the window now."

Light looked like he was about to strike her, but Marsh turned around and looked. "Oh," he said. Then they all looked.

Peering in the window, wrapped in a clear, flexible mask, was a huge reptilian face.

She had seen that face before, in the forest of southern Oregon. She had punched it.

Light yelled, "Get everyone armed! Hasagawa, take this key and start handing out tachy blasters. Why didn't anyone see anything on a sensor?"

In all the commotion, restraining Ambrose was apparently forgotten, although nobody gave her a blaster. She didn't feel the slightest bit afraid. She had just died. What worse thing could possibly happen? An alien attack? Bring it on.

Besides, she was still in a novel and all of that was their problem. Her problem remained: How to get out of said novel and back into her own life.

In retrospect, she should have tried her other idea first. That is, if she had her life to live all over again. Because dying hurt. She didn't want to do that again, ever. And of course it was perfectly natural for someone to come back from the dead in a sci-fi book. Why hadn't she thought of that earlier?

Her other idea was only the half-formed kernel of an idea. Sci-fi novels may be all over the place as far as ideas go, but one thing they always are is sci-fi. They don't suddenly turn into children's books or ... romance novels. That could work. Maybe.

Light was still barking out orders, trying to prepare them for first contact with whatever was outside the window. The people who had been sleeping were tipping the beds against the walls to make clear walkways and stowing their personal items in lockers. The stench of fear was filling the small station faster than the air system could filter it. Though the company had trained them for the possibility of first contact they were miners, not soldiers. Now they were mentally compromised miners crammed in a tight space with tachy blasters.

She sidled over to Marsh, who was holding his tachy blaster and manning the window she'd originally been looking out when the mysterious ship landed. Then she just stood there. *What could she possibly say to turn this into a romance novel? The basic format called for two characters who are attracted to each other, but kept apart by something, or by someone, or by their own natures. Then there is some sort of dramatic breakthrough, and it's the man who does the pursuing. Everything about this situation was entirely wrong. She and Marsh were not kept apart at all. She did find him attractive, in an*

I-know-you're-a-fictional-character so let's-not-get-too-carried-away sort of way. Did he find her attractive? He seemed to in the Old West and in Cotsley-on-Windle. Here they seemed to be more like brother and sister. She decided to try anyway.

"How's your arm?"

He kept his eyes on the area out of the window, watching for the dragon. "Better all the time."

"That's good." She grew increasingly unsure of herself. "Being dead like that sort of put my life into perspective. I'm seeing things in a new way."

"Oh yeah? What looks different to you now?"

"For one thing, you and I aren't really brother and sister, are we?"

He looked at her curiously. "No, we aren't."

"I was sort of thinking of you like a brother."

"I've never thought of you as a sister." His tone was suggestive.

Okay! There we go! Now to encourage him to do some romance-novel-style pursuing. "I'm awfully willful and tempestuous, you know."

Marsh raised his eyebrows in surprise. "Tell me more."

"No man will ever tame me."

"I wouldn't even try."

Wrong answer. The Shakespearean shrew-taming plot had served the romance genre well in many, many books, but she was trying too hard to condense it all down and get out of there in a hurry.

"We may all be in terrible danger."

A tentative smile was creeping across Marsh's face. "I think I understand what you're saying."

"You do?"

"This could be the end of us all, so what the hell? Am I right?"

"That's not exactly what I was thinking."

"I happen to know where there's a cot in a dark place where no one is supposed to go."

Wrong, wrong, wrong. That wasn't a romance novel, that was sci-fi again. Sci-fi is loaded with sex. It's all basically, "Hey, you want to have sex?" "Okay." So they do. In the kind of romance novels Coral had read, Marsh would now be the cad, which was too bad because Ambrose did like him. She wasn't going to be able to rely on any of the characters in this novel to help her out. They were all doing what they were written to do. She was on her own.

She had one more idea. After that she was stuck.

"Okay, everybody, I'm going to teach you all how to make pancakes. Everybody who wants to learn gather around."

Marsh looked stunned. He'd thought he was about to have a good time, and now this?

Cavalli said, "What the hell, Ambrose? You're crazy!"

"This makes eight servings."

Light said, "I don't know what got into you, but just stay out of our way. You got that? And nobody give her a tachy blaster."

Marsh crouched as the dragon-like alien could be seen through his window, circling their base. It was very long and all of it was encased in the same flexible transparent material, which was apparently a highly sophisticated spacesuit. Its scaly skin was mostly gray with golden streaks, and it had a silvery iridescence.

"These are the ingredients we're going to need: flour, baking powder, salt, sugar, dried milk, dried egg, water, and oil." She pulled all of these out of cabinets and set them on the counter.

Every time the alien passed a window, the nearest crewmember flinched and tightened his grip on his tachy blaster.

"In a large bowl, we will mix together a cup and a half of flour, three and a half teaspoons of baking powder, one teaspoon of salt, and one tablespoon of sugar. Then we'll reconstitute the egg and milk with water to give us a cup and a quarter of milk and one egg." As she worked, people looked at her incredulously.

"In the meantime we take a griddle, oil it, and heat it over medium high heat. It will be hot enough when water drops dance on the surface, but don't seem to explode."

"Can I have some pancakes when you're done?" Emerson asked. Some of the others glared at her. She smirked.

"While the griddle is heating, mix the wet ingredients, including the oil, into the dry ingredients until smooth. Scoop about a quarter cup of batter for each pancake onto the griddle. Flip when small bubbles appear on the surface. Brown on both sides and serve hot."

15 TERRA SWEET TERRA

Turning the sci-fi novel into a cookbook had done the trick. She was back in her very precious living room. This time she had only been gone about seven minutes. But she was starving. There was a pancake house a few blocks away where she could journal the experience.

And there was a bookseller she needed to talk to because she was mad now.

16 COMPLICATED QUESTIONS

This time she planted her shoulder against the old door and really threw her weight into it. It flew open without resistance, so once again she fell into Red's Reads, this time slamming into a table stacked high with marked-down items, sending a dozen or so to the floor. Would this store always keep her off balance?

"You really know how to make an entrance," Phil said as he scurried to scoop fallen books from the old beige linoleum and arrange them once again for display.

"You fixed the door."

"I'm afraid so. Sorry. But I can't wait to hear how your adventures are going. I kept thinking I'd see you sooner than this. Having fun?"

"Yeah, well, about that." Phil looked at her with concern. "Something happened that really scared me. I thought I was going to be stuck in a book forever. And not a nice book. This one was a very unpleasant place to be."

"That never happened to me. You couldn't find the book?"

Coral gave him a blank look. "What do you mean, find the book? What book?"

"Find the book you're in. When you pick it up, that's how you get out."

A long pause. "Again, what book?"

"You mean you never found the book? How did you get out?"

"You never said anything about how to get out."

Phil looked toward the ceiling and scratched his head. "Well, right. I mean you got out the first time. I guess I assumed. How many books have you done?"

She ticked them off on her fingers. "Horror, western, English murder mystery, sci-fi. Four books."

"And you never found the book you're in and picked it up?"

"No. I never saw a book like that."

"They aren't typically just lying around. You'll find it somewhere nearby, though. Usually in a logical place, like on a bookshelf. How did you get out if you didn't have the book?"

"I did something you'd never do in that genre."

"What does that mean?"

"I wasn't afraid of the monster in the horror novel, and when the going got tough in the Western, I went back East." At this point Phil started laughing. "In the English murder mystery I told the police it wasn't any of my business and they had to do the detecting themselves. That didn't quite do it, so I murdered the suspect." He was guffawing. "But when it came to sci-fi I got into big trouble." She was angry that he wasn't taking her seriously. That experience had been genuinely frightening. She had even experienced death. Not funny. "You mean to tell me there was a book somewhere I could have picked up and, poof, I'd be back in my apartment?"

"It must have been somewhere on a bookshelf or in a drawer. I always want to get a better look at the cover art, but the instant I touch it, I'm gone."

"Phil, Phil, Phil." Coral was very irritated. "You could have saved me so much trouble if you'd told me that one little detail."

"I don't know, it sounds like you came up with a very inventive work-around."

"Until I got to sci-fi."

"Oh?"

"How would you break sci-fi?"

Phil thought about it. "Well, it would be tough. Hmm."

"I now know what dying actually feels like."

"Oh, that's terrible. You had to die to get out of it? I'm sorry."

"It didn't work."

"It didn't *work?* How did you get out?"

"I turned it into a cookbook."

He looked at her in open-mouthed wonderment. "Of course you did! That's brilliant!"

"I appreciate your enthusiasm, but I'm still mad at you." A smile was forcing its way past her resolve.

"I'm really sorry I didn't mention how to get out. When you got out of the horror novel I assumed you'd found the book."

"I was in a car in the horror novel. Where would I have found a book there?"

"Did you ever look in the glove compartment for any reason?"

Coral shook her head. Why would she have? She hadn't known she was looking for a book. "I don't get this whole finding-the-book thing. Or any of it."

Phil thought for a second. It seemed he was deciding what exactly he wanted to tell her. "When you find the book and seem to physically touch it, you're establishing a strong mental link to the fact that where you feel you are is not the real world."

Coral replayed that sentence in her mind, trying to milk some sense out of it. "But I already knew I wasn't in the real world!"

"Have you ever been in a bad dream where you knew it was a dream and you needed to wake up? It's sort of like that. Finding the book helps you wake up. Forcing a genre change is brilliant. It shows strong mental control."

"Are the book adventures like a dream then? They sure don't feel like a dream." She still had a million questions and didn't know where to begin. "Is it changing my real body in any way?"

"No."

"What else don't I know?"

"Um ... not much. How to get in, how to get out. That about covers it."

"How about what this bag is, and how it's supposed to bring me clarity, and why you have a magic bag, and just who you are anyway?"

"Okay, fair enough. Except I'm not going to answer all of your questions right now." She began to protest. "Because—and there is a reason—because the whole point is to bring you clarity, right? If I just answer your questions you won't find the clarity you need. Also, I can't give you clarity because we don't really know each other very well. There are some things you just have to figure out for yourself."

"You sound like a character in a fairy tale. Was that any kind of an answer at all?"

"Probably not, but notice I said I didn't want to answer them all *right now*. But I can give you a clue. When you go into books, are you seeing any particular patterns? Any recurring themes?"

Coral thought about the kind John Marsh, Isaac the orphaned boy, and the murderer/dragon. "Yes. Some of the same people, especially, keep showing up."

"Pay attention to that sort of thing."

"I *am* paying attention. I'm noticing. But what is that supposed to mean? I don't get how this is supposed to help me decide which books to save and which to get rid of. That was why I came to you in the first place."

"You don't understand. Yet."

"So you're saying I should keep going? Stick in more books and look for patterns?" It seemed he wasn't going to demand his bag back immediately, and now that she knew she wouldn't be trapped again, she was at least reassured that she *could* keep going. "Another question."

"Shoot. I may not answer yet, but go ahead."

"Who wrote all these books? They aren't the same ones I put in the bag, and I don't recall the plots from anywhere else. Where did these stories come from?"

"That is the exact sort of question you need to be asking yourself."

"I'm asking you."

"Then you're asking the wrong person."

"Phil! You're very annoying sometimes!"

"I'm sorry. Tell you what. Stroll with me." Coral eyed him suspiciously. "Just around the shop. First stop, the fantasy section."

"Okay."

"If the bag were a book, it would not be in the fantasy section. It's real. It isn't magic." Next on his tour were the shelves marked "Self-help."

"I would shelve the bag here, because that's what it does best. I know you're not seeing that yet because it takes time." Coral followed him deeper into the shop. "Next on our tour is science fiction. A good case could be made for placing the bag here, except again, it isn't fiction. It's real."

Coral made a beeline for the stacks marked "Children."

"How about if we go here? Once upon a time there was a girl who met a strange man who sold her magic fairy dust, and being a foolish girl, she used it without knowing who the man was or what it would do."

Nodding, Phil said, "I get that, I really do. So come with me to the history section."

Now we're getting somewhere, thought Coral.

"We wouldn't file the bag here for one very big reason: We're only now writing its history."

"What does that mean? It's new? Then how do you know it's safe?" There were sections in the back of the store for technology and medical books. "Should our next stop be one of those?"

"Oh, probably, but for now," he waved his hand back toward the shelves near the front of the shop, "It's a mystery."

"So are you going to tell me the part of the history that you know?"

Phil winced. "See, that's a complicated question."

"I don't get why that's so complicated."

"Let me just say that I have your safety in mind."

"You're saying that if I know about the bag, I stop being safe?"

"There's the potential."

Coral was reduced to blinking at him stupidly. "I can use the bag safely in the self-help shelves unless I know too much from the history shelves?"

"You can use it safely either way. It's safe. It's knowing about the bag that may not be safe."

"But I know it exists. So is that not safe?"

"You know, you could be a lawyer. Have you thought about law school? I know some people. I could make some calls."

"Phil!"

"You're safe as long as nobody knows you have the bag."

"Even my family? Can I tell my family?"

Phil shook his head. "Don't tell your family."

"Because then they won't be safe?" Phil shrugged in response. "You're really creeping me out, Phil."

"My best advice to you is to use it for the purpose we discussed, and then give it back to me. Don't talk about it to anyone. Just use it. Things will all turn out well in the end."

That was the best she was going to get out of him. While walking home, a plan formed in her mind. If Phil was going to talk in riddles, she was going to have to do some detective work to find out what was going on. It all hinged on just who Phil was. She knew what sort of book would take her where she wanted to go. Tomorrow. After work.

17 THE CONFUSED CLIENT: A MARSH, P.I. MYSTERY

It was the kind of dump that still had tiki masks on the walls, and not in an ironic hipster way. A maroon carpet swirling with tropical leaves would still be on the floor if it hadn't been doused too many times with rum and tequila, both before and after they had been drunk. It had been replaced by vinyl that was meant to look like bamboo, but even that was old enough to be peeling. You walked into this relic of the 60s under flashing green palm branches with "Outrigger Lounge" written vertically in orange neon to form the trunk of the tree. Just above the door, a convulsing neon sign flashed "AIR," "CON," and "ION." There had once been other letters. When people came in off the sodden street, shivering in their hooded jackets, they didn't expect to feel like they had been lifted out of Portland and transported to Honolulu. They didn't expect much at all. But they all seemed to be waiting for something.

There was a glass in front of me, along with a little pile of garbage, namely a paper parasol, a pink swizzle stick, and a toothpick with a Maraschino cherry and a lime impaled on it. There had been a chunk of canned pineapple, but I ate that. I was having a drink or two to celebrate getting paid. Since I work alone, my celebrations are exclusive affairs. I was amusing myself, as I always do, by watching people.

Orange Lipstick was waiting for someone to come up and tell her she was pretty. She probably used to be pretty, 30 years ago. She would be waiting a while because it was going to take a lot of liquor before someone thought she was pretty tonight. Ring Guy was almost at that point. Marital difficulties: I can spot them a mile away. He kept taking his wedding ring off, fiddling around with it, and putting it back on. His drink had come with a red plastic sword stuck into a cherry, and after he had eaten the cherry, he slipped the ring onto the sword and spun it around. He glanced at Orange Lipstick a few times, but thought better of it. If he was going to blow up his marriage, it was going to be for someone younger than that. Never mind the fact that he was no prize. He was going to wait.

The bartender was waiting for someone else to order a drink. He wasn't one of the talkative bartenders. His face was inscrutable while he waited. He was an ex-con. I could see part of a prison tattoo on his neck, and he had the look of someone who knows down to his core that it's in his best interest to mind his own business.

I was waiting for something too, someone to change my job into something I could care about again. My last case involved a client who wanted to know if her husband was cheating on her. He was. She was also cheating on him, and with his best friend. The two of them had set up a fat overseas account unknowingly funded by my client's husband. I don't know if she thought I wouldn't notice or if she didn't care, but when you engage a private investigator, lots of facts tend to surface, and not just about the person being investigated. I gave her the information she requested and handed her a bill at the same time. I didn't have to like my clients. But when they were both unlikeable and boring, it left a bad taste in my mouth that no amount of rum would take away. It was always the same stuff: lust and greed. Nobody caring about anybody but themselves. I wanted someone to have some other kind of problem for a change. I sipped my frou-frou mai tai and waited.

The door creaked open and cool, damp air rushed in, along with some dead leaves that pasted themselves to the floor. A woman stepped into the Outrigger Lounge and closed the door. Orange Lipstick turned away in resignation. This was not who she was waiting for. Ring Guy slipped his wedding ring into the pocket of his jacket. Maybe. The bartender assumed a readiness position. The woman's eyes swept the establishment and locked with mine. She came over to my stool.

"Are you John Marsh?"

"Why are you looking for him?"

"I need his help. I have a job for him." She was looking at me as though she already knew me. It must have been my honest face. I have that sort of overgrown-boy face you sometimes see on people of English ancestry, and some people find it disarming. It's just physiology, but I can sometimes use it to my advantage when I want to get information. Sometimes I can even use it to interest attractive women.

I offered her the stool next to mine. "You found him."

I was hoping I'd found what I was waiting for. Her name was Coral Ambrose. Thin as a greyhound, with caramel eyes glittering from the twinkle lights around the bottles at the back of the bar. Straight hair the color of mahogany pulled back in a loose ponytail. A whiff of expensive perfume escaped when she opened her coat, revealing a fawn cashmere sweater and jeans that fit her just right. She planted her feet on the rung of the barstool and ordered a Glenmorangie, neat. This was not a white wine spritzer kind of girl. She was going to get down to business. It made me regret choosing a mai tai.

"Don't feel bad about your mai tai. That's a great drink to celebrate with." The girl gave me a saucy grin, but in my slightly inebriated state I almost wondered if she had read my mind.

She chuckled, enjoying herself for some reason I couldn't explain. "I *am* here on business. I need you to research someone for me. I can't find anything about him online and in this genre I'm marginalized again."

I raised my eyebrows in curiosity.

"In any case, I figure you have resources the rest of us don't have."

"I do. Why are you researching this guy?"

"That's the tricky part. I don't want to tell you the whole story. At least not yet. I don't mean to hurt him and I'm not a crook. I just got involved with him, but he's awfully secretive and I want to know what his background is. If there's anything weird."

Of course she was involved with someone. Maybe he would turn out to be a jerk and she would cry on my shoulder. "Involved?"

"Not like that. More as a friend. He's a lot older than me and he's asking me to trust him in ways that make me uncomfortable."

"Uncomfortable how?"

She swirled the Scotch around in her glass. "He's more like a counselor. But not a licensed psychologist, to the best of my knowledge. Maybe he is. That's the kind of thing I want you to find out. What's his background? Has he helped other people before? What became of those people? That's probably the most important question." She turned and looked me full in the face. "I need to know if I'm in danger."

I was in danger. My pulse had sped up and I was tingling. Let's just say alarms were going off all over my body.

In the peculiar light of the bar it almost appeared as though she blushed.

"I'll do everything I can to keep you safe. May I ask what kind of counseling he was giving you? Or is that what you want to keep private?"

"I'd rather not say, at least right now. It's nothing, really. I'm not a serial killer or anything." That was good. It was bad enough helping people who were cheating on their spouses, but helping serial killers would be too much. She sipped her Scotch.

"Give me the information you have on the guy and I'll look into him." I explained my fee structure and she gave me a slip of paper with the information she had. Ring Guy had given up ogling her a long time ago, but I was reluctant to see her walk out the door into the night with all its other Ring Guys and weird counselors. I was feeling very protective. "Do you have any questions for me?"

She gave me an elfin grin. "As a matter of fact, I do. Are you going to call me 'doll face' and check out my gams?"

It was my turn to blush. I hoped it wasn't obvious in the tiki lighting. "A fan of Bogart movies? Sorry, that was last century. I can if you really want me to."

"Just kidding. I know the private investigator business has changed a lot since the 1930s."

"Not as much as you'd think. We do a lot of it on computers, but more often than not, it still comes down to walking around and asking questions."

It continued to rain the next day, and despite a headache from last night I made my first stop: the address Coral said was hers. Problem was, it was a grocery store. She'd lied to me. There was an espresso place across the street. I ordered a large latté and sat by the window. I'd brought my laptop. You can sit for hours with a cup of coffee and a laptop. Nobody gives you a second glance. Plus, it gives me time to make notes. If there's Wi-Fi available, all the better, and this place had it.

I was able to spend a lot of time searching for Phil Reddington, and found absolutely nothing that seemed relevant. There was a Phillip Reddington who had died in Minnesota, preceded in death by, etc. There was a Phil Reddington who had come in third in an Arizona State track meet four years ago. One guy was a radio announcer in Mobile, Alabama, and a father-and-son team who both had the name sold insurance in South Carolina. Stanford University had a Professor P. Reddington. No middle-aged bookstore owner in Oregon.

People went into the grocery store and came out with bags all morning. A stream of pedestrians walked by, most with hoods up in the rain, but I got a good look at all of them. No Coral. After a couple of hours of nursing the one latté, I began to get dirty looks, and feeling I was pushing my luck hogging a window seat, packed up my laptop and left. By that time the sun was breaking through and I wasn't really happy about that. Rain can be a private investigator's friend. People don't look around much in the rain. They focus on where they're going and walk quickly. It's a lot easier to pull up a hood and follow someone in the rain without being noticed.

My next stop was the address for the bookstore owned by the so-called Phil Reddington. That address turned out to be a pawnshop. I was standing there feeling played when who should walk up but the player herself. She stood next to me, hands in pockets, and shook her head. "I'm sorry. I could have sworn it was here."

"I thought you said you'd met the guy here. How come you don't know where the store is?"

She had the integrity to look ashamed. "I'm sorry, I'm afraid I'm wasting your time. I'm trying to get answers to questions that ... what I'm trying to say is I'm looking in the wrong place."

If she was talking about the bookstore, she was looking in the wrong place all right, and if she was talking about getting answers from me, she was also looking in the wrong place because I can't help someone who needs a psychiatrist. "I'd like to help you, but I think you need a different kind of help."

"I know." Her eyes darted to something behind me and her mouth opened to issue a warning, but it was too late.

A strong arm wrapped in corduroy that smelled like burnt rubber and ham wrapped around my neck and I felt the barrel of a gun pressed into my ribs. When I tried to twist to see who was holding me, the gun was jabbed harder and I thought better of it.

"Who are you?" I asked.

"Just hand over your laptop and it's over. And don't follow me." He gave my neck a twist I knew I'd feel for a few days.

"Take it."

The hand came down from my neck and snatched the bag off my shoulder. "Follow me and you're dead." I turned around in time to see his back as he loped down the street.

Greasy black hair, round head, ridiculous sideburns. I recognized him immediately. "Two Bag Higgins. He's a runner for the West Side Dragons."

Coral was looking after Two Bag in shock. "What does he have against you?"

I rubbed my neck. "Did a job once for the folks of a kid they'd been supplying. Guess they're worried about how much information I have on them."

"That kid's name wouldn't be Isaac, would it?"

Who was this Coral Ambrose, and how would she know a thing like that? I needed to watch myself around her.

"Are we going to let him get away with that?"

"Yes, we are. He had a gun."

"Well, I'm not." She must have thought she was invincible because she started sprinting down the street after Two Bag, clutching her shoulder bag to her chest.

"Coral! Stop!" I ran after her. "You're going to get yourself shot!"

"Not worried about it!" She was running like an Olympian, really putting those greyhound legs of hers to good use. Two Bag had started with a solid lead on us, but not anymore. All his cigarettes, bong hits, and coke weren't aiding his athletic abilities. He wasn't running very fast— probably figured nobody would be so stupid they'd chase him down. But he had never met Coral.

Giving it all I had, I finally caught up with her, my only goal to stop her in time to keep her alive. While running she had unfastened one end of the shoulder strap on her purse, which she handed to me. For a moment I thought she was handing me her leash. Without slowing down she pantomimed throwing the strap over his head, with her on one side and me on the other. I pantomimed "no" as dramatically and decisively as I could while darting around other pedestrians and jumping up and down curbs.

When we got close enough to breathe down his neck, Coral threw the strap over his head, gave it a jerk, and he flew backwards. The only thought in my head was to get the gun. When Two Bag fell over, he let go of it and it hit the sidewalk with a crack. I kicked it into the gutter and flipped him on his stomach, pulling his arms behind his back. Coral grabbed my laptop bag off his shoulder.

"What were you thinking? It's just a laptop! You could have gotten us both shot!" Two Bag was breathing as hard as he could with my weight on top of him. I eased up a bit. Didn't want to kill the guy.

Coral picked the gun out of the gutter with two fingers and placed it in her purse. "The police will want this for evidence." Several people had gathered around, unsure who exactly the bad guy was in the situation. She addressed a large man with a face like a bull who seemed inclined to intervene. "Do you have a cellphone on you? You do? Can you call 9-1-1 please, and say we caught an armed robber? I'd appreciate it." The man seemed to be as disarmed as I was by her sincere brown eyes and did as he was told.

Two Bag was squirming around in an annoying way. Coral sat on his legs. "I messed up, John. I asked you to be a detective in a matter you couldn't be involved in. With nothing to detect, you were about to become boring. You were about to wander into unforgiveable territory, in book terms. When Dirt Bag here ... "

A muffled protest rose from the face pushed into the pavement. "Two Bag! My name is Two Bag!"

"So sorry. When *Two Bag* grabbed your laptop you couldn't just let it happen. That would be boring. You see?"

"You're definitely not boring. I'll give you that." Crazy though.

"And you just thought, 'crazy though.' I know your thoughts because this story is told in first person, and you're the person."

What the heck?

"You just thought, 'What the heck.'" Coral was rooting around in her purse, trying unsuccessfully to find something. "On that note, do you happen to have a book in your laptop bag?"

"A *book?* No, just a laptop."

"Let me see." A smile broke out on her face when she opened it up and peered inside. "Yes, you do! Ha! That's fantastic!"

"What book is it? I didn't put— "

18 RULES, PATTERNS, AND THEMES

Three minutes. Live and learn. She'd tried to use the skills of the fictional John Marsh, Private Investigator, to learn about the real life Phil Reddington, but it hadn't worked. Apparently the bag couldn't be used that way; you couldn't get new information about real life out of it. What a shame. That would have been a really handy tool in so many ways. She could have entered a book set in the future and while she was there researched stock trends in the current era and gotten rich.

Phil was right about the fact that the more she used the bag the more she learned. However, he was wrong about the supposed clarity it was going to bring her, at least so far. But she was learning things about the bag itself. That was something.

She started with a fresh page in her journal and wrote:

> *Rules of the Bag*
> 1. *In order to get out, find the book you're in and pick it up.*
> 2. *Fiction is fiction—you can't learn new facts about your real life.*

Remembering how she had been unable to turn the sci-fi book into a romance by changing her relationship with John Marsh, she wrote:

> 3. *You can't change people; they remain true to their story.*

This brought up a whole other principle that she took some time to word properly. She was trying to find a better way to say that if you broke the genre conventions, it kicked you out of the story completely.

4. *When given a story you must accept it as written, changing only that which is possible within the rules. In other words, play the hand you're dealt.*

5. *The point-of-view is consistent with the genre. When choosing a genre it's best to pick one in which I can be the main character.*

Was that the sort of clarity she was supposed to find? That she needed to play the hand she was dealt, not be a bystander in her life, and that you can't change other people? Because they weren't novel concepts. She could have gotten that from a television psychologist. There had to be more to it than that. She had come to Phil for help with a book storage problem, he had intuited that her real problem was something else, something larger, and thought she would gain clarity about her own situation from the bag. Coral doubted he expected she would receive only general principles of happy living.

The bag was wonderfully entertaining and it was easy to get caught up in that aspect, but she needed to continue to write her experiences down in an organized and analytical way. Phil had said she needed to pay attention to recurring patterns and themes. Maybe all she needed to do was that. On a separate page she wrote:

Patterns and Themes:
- *Usually happens in Oregon unless it can't*
- *A lot of the same characters*
- *John Marsh: nice guy, detective or something like that, likes me*
- *Dragon: actual dragon or references to a dragon all over the place, kills people*
- *Isaac: lost boy or orphan or in danger*
- *McAllister: his father, dead*
- *Light: older man in charge, could be good or bad*
- *Higgins: guy with a nickname, probably a bad guy*
- *Carlsons: take care of Isaac*
- *Violet: takes care of the house?*
- *Dr. Bruce: does his job but full of himself,*
- *Cavelli: ?*
- *Hasagawa: ?*

Writing them out didn't help at all. They seemed like a bunch of people she ought to know but didn't, with the addition of the dragon. The only items on the list that seemed to have any real relevance to Coral were the little orphan boy, Isaac, who could symbolize her murdered brother Jet, and the dead father. But as far as the Isaac and Jet connection went, there was a big difference between orphaned and dead. The rest of them? No connection she could think of.

And what was the deal with the dragon? The fantasy genre was one of her favorites, but she'd never liked the parts about dragons for some reason, and even less so now. Another one of her inexplicable quirks. Still, it seemed like it was a theme that needed exploring. It could be fun. A lot of fun. Except for the dragon part.

Dragons were not hard to come by. There were a number of books that featured dragons she could enter tomorrow, which she was happy to notice would be her day off.

That night as she lay in bed, again giving up on the spy novel that continued to fail to hold her attention, her drowsy mind kept wandering back to the book adventures she had already been in, but not to analyze or to deliberately think about anything in particular.

It was when she wasn't trying find a pattern that it dawned on her that all of the stories lacked closure. She had kept shutting the door on the rest of the story. Now she wanted to know what she was missing. Would there have been another way to survive that dragon on the road, and what would have happened next? What about Deputy Marsh in Oregon City after he was shot, and the girlfriend character she seemed to have been destined to become? Would she have settled in Oregon City instead of with her uncle? In Cotsley-on-Windle, Police Inspector John Marsh must have eventually solved the mystery of the dead carpenter in the library, with her help. Those books always end like that. What was going on in the space colony of Arjen-Prime that made them all go slowly crazy, and would the alien have gotten the miners in the end?

The story with Marsh as a private investigator was a mess. Nothing would ever have come of it because *she* was the plot line, wanting to know about things in the real world, and that was impossible. Ending that prematurely had been the right thing to do.

Coral threw back the covers and padded into the living room where her journal remained on the coffee table. She made another entry in *Patterns and Themes*.

- *Everything lacks closure*

As she drifted off to sleep she resolved to remain longer in the next book adventure and try to see it through.

Her last thought was that she didn't know how the story with Jet ended either. They had never caught his killer.

19 THE KINGDOM OF SILENCE

A couple of feet to the left and it was gone. A couple of feet to the right and it was gone. It would have been simple enough to keep walking straight if she hadn't been walking through a village with its inconveniently placed cottages, carts, horses, and people. When following the line led her directly to someone on the street, they assumed she was being friendly and were generally friendly in return. Nothingthrall seemed to be a pleasant enough place and she thought it was possible she would be happy she'd been sent there by her beloved mentor, Arnick of the Woes of the Council of Health in Moonfire, but something seemed slightly wrong. She'd never before seen adults walking around with what looked like pacifiers in their mouths.

The first person she saw with a pacifier, if that's what it was, was an elderly woman in black. She was slowly going about her business with downcast, red-rimmed eyes. If not for the pacifier, Coral would have thought she was in mourning for someone. Was the pacifier a punishment? Was that why she had been crying? Further down the village lane, however, was a pretty young farm girl with a pacifier who, when greeted by friends, calmly took it out of her mouth and started chattering away. Coral couldn't imagine what the pacifiers were for.

She was clearly the only one aware of the presence of the ley line.

The castle cast an imposing shadow over the village in the late afternoon sun. It was built of gray stone covered in the lichen and mosses of the centuries it had stood upon the plain of Windle. She didn't see any gargoyles or grotesques standing sentinel, but many flags and banners flew in the wind, which gave the structure an overall impression of cheeriness atop venerable solidity and courage.

The castle wall presented an obstacle to continued progress in tracing the ley line's route. There was nothing to be done about it but to enter through the gate, past the helmeted guards in their chainmail and blue tabards, to see where it led.

So far, so good. The writing of this genre was fairly straightforward and unobtrusive, and she appeared to be the leading lady.

The courtyard was a busy place. Knights wearing thick cotton padding were sparring and various servants and courtiers were giving them a wide berth. Feeling this was a wise course of action, she did the same, and was pleased to find the line took her close to the wall and out of harm's way. It did lead her directly to a small stone building nearly adjacent to the castle itself. Walking around the building to find where the line picked up again, she was startled to feel her feet resonating where they shouldn't have: at a point perpendicular to where the line she'd been following was. She circled the small building and confirmed that her feet resonated in four places around the perimeter. She'd found a ley line convergence!

"Why are you circling our woodshed?" A small boy dressed in dark green trousers with a white shirt and beige tunic, quite a bit cleaner than you'd expect a boy that size to be, gazed at her calmly. He was used to having his questions answered and didn't do what country children usually did when talking to strangers: cringe away in shyness or adopt a posture of aggression. Clearly the child was royal. And as he'd said "our woodshed," he was likely the prince himself.

"I'm looking for something and finding more than I expected."

"Unless you're looking for wood and spiders, there isn't much there to find."

"I sometimes find things that surprise people, and myself as well. For example, I found you."

"No, I found you."

"Your point is well taken. My name is Coral and I've only just arrived in Nothingthrall."

"Why are you here?" He hadn't introduced himself in turn, which could only mean one thing: he was indeed a prince. It was assumed everyone would know who the prince was. Princes needed no introduction.

"I was sent here by the Council of Health."

"Why did they send a woman here? We need a new physician."

"I am a healer."

The prince raised his eyebrows at that, and laughed. "I've never heard of such a thing in my whole life."

Coral tried hard not to laugh in return. It's funny when the very young talk about their whole lives to someone older. "The most famous healer who ever lived was a woman, Enna d'Ambrose. Have you heard of her?"

"No, but I'm sure my father has. He's heard of everyone."

"I can prove I'm a healer if you like. Do you have anything that needs healing?"

The prince pursed his lips and thought a moment. "No, I'm healthy."

"No little cuts or bruises? Most of the boys I know are covered in them from rough playing."

"I don't play rough. But Sir Cavalli did give me this when we were sparring the other day." He lifted his tunic and shirt to reveal a large bruise on his side. It had already faded to greenish yellow.

"That doesn't look too bad, but I can heal it the rest of the way if you like."

"I don't care if it's healed, but I'd like to see if you can. Bruce wouldn't bother with something like this."

Coral took a vial of lavender-scented oil from the purse hanging at her waist and put a drop on her hands, rubbing it in. She never told anybody that the oil's purpose was just to keep her hands from chapping. Everyone assumed it was magic healing oil, but it was all for show. Her real power came from the ley line at her feet. "May I touch it? It won't hurt."

The prince stepped forward and Coral gently laid a hand on his bruise, channeling the energy up through her legs and out her hand into his side. All discoloration vanished immediately. The bruise had been a minor injury and the location was powerful.

"That should do it," she said with a respectful bob of her head.

The prince looked at his side where the bruise had been, then rolled up a pants leg and looked at his knee. There was nothing there but a knee. "It's gone too! I felt something tingle there and then I remembered I had fallen on the stairs this morning and scraped my knee. It was bleeding. You healed them both. You didn't even know about the knee and you healed it."

"It was easy to do, and I'm glad to be of service."

"Your name is Coral, right?"

"I'm Coral d'Ambrose, the new healer for Nothingthrall." It was getting embarrassing to be talking so long to someone whose name she didn't know. "What would you have me call you? Your Highness?"

He smiled. "The 'highness' is my father. One day I'll be the 'highness,' but right now I'm the prince. You can call me 'the prince' but I let my friends call me Isaac."

"Am I your friend? I wouldn't want to presume."

"Of course you are! Unless I get mad at you. Then you are back to 'the prince.' Has my father met you yet?"

"No, I just arrived today and was looking for a good place to set up shop when you found me."

"In the woodshed?"

"Well, yes actually. This is a very powerful woodshed you have here."

He made a face, seeming more like a normal little boy than he had before. "The servants are afraid of it."

Coral wasn't surprised. There was a tendency for unusual things to happen along ley lines, and at the point of a convergence she couldn't tell what might happen. "I would like to speak to your father about the future of his frightening woodshed."

"Oh, all right. I'll take you to him."

See the king right then? She wasn't prepared. She hadn't thought. But she might as well. Getting a personal introduction from his son could make it all easier.

The inside of the castle proved to be well tended, and neither opulent nor spare. Tapestries of hunting scenes hung on the corridor walls as insulation against the winter chill that was just then beginning to loose its hold on the kingdom. The smell of something delicious cooking wafted up from the kitchens and made her stomach rumble.

Isaac located his father in his personal chambers going over some paperwork with an advisor, quill pen in hand. Above the desk hung a royal blue tapestry with the coat of arms of the realm: a crown-topped shield, burgundy drapes pulled back on either side, revealing nothing in the center. In Ambrosia the coat of arms had been a phoenix with shafts of wheat crossed behind the shield.

"Isaac! This isn't really a good time. I'm working."

"I'm sorry, father, I'll just be a minute. I have someone here you'll want to meet."

King Light, his face recognizable from Coral's Western book adventure and more recently from her hideous experience on the planet Arjen-Prime, looked up, clearly expecting to see a playmate of Isaac's and surprised to see a young woman. Coral curtseyed, hoping his kingly character bore little resemblance to the sci-fi commander who had thrown her into mining tunnels with no light.

"Father, look who I found! Coral, our new healer," said Isaac.

The king made a sour face and turned back to his papers. "I told you I was too busy for games, Isaac."

"It's no game, father. She's a better healer than old Bruce ever was. She already healed me."

"Don't be ridiculous. Bruce was a physician, not a healer. And you didn't need healing."

"I had a bruise and a cut on my knee. She made them go away in an instant."

"Women are not healers, not since Enna d'Ambrose."

"If I may speak, Your Highness, Enna was my great-grandmother. We learn a different kind of healing in Ambrosia, and it's always women who can do it. The Council of Health sent me to you after they received your request. If you prefer a physician who relies on herbs and leeches, then one will become available eventually."

She now had the king's full attention. "If you're a tenth the healer your great-grandmother was, then we'll be glad to have you, although I always doubted the veracity of some of the tales they told about her accomplishments. I assume you're staying in old Bruce's cottage."

"For the time being, but it doesn't suit me."

"It doesn't suit you? It suited Bruce well enough for 65 years."

"Your Highness, are you familiar with ley lines?"

"I've heard of them, yes. Not sure I believe in such a thing. They're meant to be some sort of energy conduit that runs along the ground, giving people magical powers."

"Not everybody, only those born to receive them. Most people can't sense a ley line at all. The ability runs in families. In Ambrosia many people can sense the lines and use them a bit, but my family is particularly attuned to their energy. They're the source of my healing power. I need to be on a ley line to do my best work."

"If there are ley lines around here I wouldn't know about them. Wouldn't have the foggiest idea which direction to point you in."

"That's not necessary. I know exactly where they are. There's one that runs straight through the village into the castle, and one perpendicular to it that crosses the fields. The two intersect in the courtyard."

"In our courtyard? The castle courtyard?" King Light turned to his advisor, who had withdrawn to the side during this conversation. "Walton, look in the records and see if there is anything about ley lines."

Walton said, "It seems like more than a coincidence that the castle would have been built at the intersection of two of them."

"It does. I wonder if they knew or if they simply sensed something." He turned back to Coral. "So you wish to be on a ley line, and you'd do your very best work at the intersection of two of them, I assume."

"Indeed. I could save lives there that..." Her voice left her and her eyes welled up with tears. She loved being a healer and the good works she was able to do. If she had routine access to that kind of power!

"Where exactly is this intersection?"

Isaac spoke up excitedly. "The woodshed! That's where I found her. She was tracing the ley lines to that very place."

The King smiled indulgently at his son. "The woodshed, eh? Well, I'm afraid I'm going to need to test her first to make sure she's as good as she claims. I wouldn't want to sacrifice a perfectly good woodshed for nothing."

His advisor spoke up. "May I suggest a test? Violet burned herself quite badly yesterday. Violet is our cook and much treasured for her expertise with fowl," he explained to Coral. "Perhaps you could help put her on the mend."

Isaac said, "Violet's been pointing at what needs to be done and yelling for other people to do them ever since, father. They're all getting quite cross with her. I usually get a little cake from her, but not today."

"We can't have that! There must be little cakes! Walton, fetch her to ... where should she go?"

Coral thought. "One of the lines does run through the castle itself, but I'm not familiar with the castle so I don't know where. I know where they are in the courtyard. Perhaps we should just meet there."

"I'll show her!" Isaac ran off to join Walton on his mission. He was obviously pleased to be playing an important role in bringing this exciting new healer to the kingdom.

The cook had coated her hand in grease and wrapped it in gauze. When Coral unwrapped the bandages Isaac's mouth fell open and he grew pale, but the king and Walton looked on unflinchingly. They had seen battle wounds many times, and as painful as this burn looked, it was nothing new to them. Coral withdrew the small vial of oil from her purse, rubbed some on her hands, and said to Violet soothingly, "I'm not going to touch that right now. Don't be afraid." Nevertheless, as her hand drew near the burned area, the cook flinched. Coral drew ley energy through her feet and let it pass through the air between her hand and the cook's. The king watched intently as blisters flattened and crimson skin paled.

"That should be feeling better now. Is it?"

Violet beamed and flexed her fingers. "It is! It doesn't hurt a bit. Thank you ever so much!" But when she noticed that the skin remained covered in what looked like old scars, her face fell.

"I'm not through with you yet. Hold still, and this time I will touch your hand." Coral took the scarred hand between both of hers and pressed it briefly. Upon release Violet's hand was good as new.

"I'm not sure I believe my eyes. You are seeing this, aren't you, Walton?" King Light seemed more puzzled than pleased.

"Yes, my lord. I would say it was a trick if it was someone unknown to us who appeared to be healed, instead of Violet."

"It's not a trick, Father, she can do it! Let her heal something on you. Then you'll know."

Coral said, "I would be honored to do this if it would put your mind at ease."

King Light thought, and while absentmindedly rubbing the knuckle of his thumb said, "There is nothing wrong with me that's within reach of a healer."

"Is there a problem with your thumb?"

"It gets a bit stiff is all."

"Allow me?" Making a skeptical face, the king held out his hand. Coral took his thumb and held it gently for just a moment. "Now, about that woodshed."

King Light was flexing his thumb and grinning. "Marvelous! That's been annoying me for years and just like that, it's gone. You want a woodshed? You may have 20 woodsheds."

"Just the one will do, but some strong men to clear the wood out of it first would be helpful."

"I'll put the best knights in the realm on it. Don't tell them, Walton, I want to tell them myself. I'll say, 'I have a new campaign for you, hauling wood.' They'll be furious." As King Light and Walton strolled away Coral could still hear the king laughing with his advisor. "No, wait, I'll say, 'I'm sending you all to the woodshed.' Ha ha!"

"He's going to *need* the knights to get the wood out," said Isaac.

"Really? Why is that?"

"The servants won't go in anymore. They stand in the doorway and drag wood out with a hook."

"They're afraid of something in there? What is it?"

"Spiders."

Sleeping on the floor of Bruce's cottage was preferable to sleeping on the straw and flannel covered pallet on which Bruce had slept for the past 65 years. He had probably died there as well. Coral wasn't squeamish about death, but the dim light in the cottage was enough to show that none of the dishes or tools of his trade were clean, and she had no reason to think that the bed was any better. She swept the floor and took her chances there, hoping the situation would be temporary.

By morning she was sore and hoped even harder that the situation would be extremely temporary. She made a little fire to take the chill out of the air, ate some of the remaining food in her bags, and took advantage of the morning light streaming through the east-facing window to take stock of the cottage's contents.

There were bundles of herbs hanging from the rafters, giving the warming air a pleasant scent. She recognized henbane, hemlock and bay leaves, sage, and her favorite, lavender. A table was stacked with tools of the physician's trade: basins for catching blood and holding leeches, a poker for cauterization, pliers, a drill, a saw, and a knife. Above the table were shelves of bottles and crocks, but most of these were empty. Others contained foul-looking liquids, and none of them were marked. No doubt Bruce had known what was in each container and had had no need to mark them. One bottle caught her eye because of the beauty of its contents. She picked it up and swirled it around. It was like liquid silver. She had never seen such a thing, but guessed it was mercury, which her mother had told her never to touch. She put the bottle down in a hurry.

The wall next to the door was covered with astrological charts. Other than knowing what they were, Coral could make no sense of them, though she was aware that physicians and healers of many schools relied on planetary alignment in diagnosis and treatment. The opposite wall, behind a writing desk, held a shelf with great, dusty tomes, some quite old and some that seemed newer. One was marked "Humours," and one "Spirits." It would be interesting to look through these one day when she had more time.

One particular book caught her eye because it was smaller and the cover was made of paper, rather than hide.

She was just reaching for it to get a better look when it dawned on her: that was the book she was in. She drew her hand back quickly. Apart from sleeping on the floor, this story was proving quite pleasant for her with her awesome powers. She wanted to stay a while longer. It seemed like it was just beginning. And where was John Marsh, anyway? It was good to know where the exit book was, but she had to avoid touching it until she wanted to.

She was just craning her neck to try to catch a glimpse of the title of the book in the dim cottage light when someone called, "Coral d'Ambrose!" from outside the cottage. Opening the door, she found a young man dressed in the clothes of a servant of the king. "You are wanted at the castle. The king said to bring your things. You're to be lodged there until the woodshed, er, the new, um ... "

"That's all right. I know what you mean. It will only take a moment. You needn't wait if you don't wish to, uh... ?"

"Dariel, m'lady. I'm to help you carry your things and show you to your room."

"Well, all right then, Dariel. You can carry this." She handed him one of the bags she'd brought, scooped up the very few other belongings she'd scattered about the dusty cottage and packed them into her remaining bag. "Perhaps you can carry a book or two with you as well. Maybe just that one right there for now. The peculiar paper one." Her exit book secured, she gave the cottage one last look. She was awfully glad not to have to stay there.

Strange things were known to happen along ley lines, and it stood to reason that an intersection could produce interesting effects that would be confusing and even frightening to people who had not been taught their science. No doubt this was the reason why young Prince Isaac had mentioned that servants were afraid of the woodshed, and why the king had said he would send in his knights to clean it out and not the servants. As Coral approached the woodshed, she observed a servant using a hook on a long pole to pull wood out, rather than going in to fetch it, just as Isaac had said. The servant propped the hook against the wall by the door and bundled his wood outside. Coral nodded to him as he left, and he gave her a frightened nod in return. He seemed about to issue a warning but thought better of it and bustled away.

The door opened with a creak and she stepped onto a stone floor covered in broken bits of bark. Though the shed was easily ten paces deep and nearly as wide and was meant to store a winter's worth of wood for the entire castle, the wood was piled only knee deep this late in the season, and not stacked neatly like people would ordinarily stack it, but as though it had been thrown in from outside. Spider webs were draped from wood to ceiling, making it even more obvious that nobody had been inside in a very long time. Coral stayed where she was.

A sense of tremendous strength coming up through her feet told her that the intersection of the lines was nearby. It wasn't a tingling or a sense of warmth. It didn't feel like a need for restless activity. The energy simply felt like a rightness, and that everything could now be done. She could feel the aches from last night's uncomfortable sleep dissipate.

Giant Juice Bag, you are trespassing in the Kingdom of Araneae. Turn around and leave. This will be your only warning.

Someone was speaking into her mind, just as the Narrative Voice had the first time she had entered into a book when it was warning her about the dragon. This voice was different—alien and screechy. She couldn't see anything in the gloomy recesses but tumbled wood and hundreds of black hiding places.

"Are you talking to me? I apologize. The Kingdom of Araneae? I didn't realize where I was."

It hears me? This has never happened before. But it's not leaving. They never leave unless we swarm. Swarm it, children.

At first it seemed as though the black hiding places were growing, but it was actually thousands upon thousands of spiders, a wave of tiny, glossy bodies heading toward her, going under her dress, and beginning to crawl up her legs. Coral shuddered but stood firm. "Stop that! This will only end in death! I will hurt your children!"

This Giant Juice Bag isn't running away. Head for its face. They hate that.

"I can hear you, you know. I thought we already established that." There was a pause.

If you can hear me, why didn't you leave?

"I was hoping we could talk like reasonable people."

Giant Juice Bags are never reasonable.

"Stop calling me that. My name is Coral."

We don't name food.

Coral laughed. "You can't eat me. It would take something a lot bigger than these little mouths to eat me."

You're right. It would. Something much larger. Something as big as this.

Bark chunks scratched the floor as feet, eight of them, crept out of the furthest recess of the woodshed. Light from the doorway hit two shiny black saucers, then forest-green tufts of fur-like hair. It suddenly leapt out of the darkness and landed in front of her, making her heart briefly stop. It was a spider the size of a goat.

Frightened now, aren't you? You ought to be.

She might have been frightened if the spider hadn't thought that into her mind. It seemed like it was trying too hard. "Startled is more like it." She took a moment to examine it better. Three more pairs of eyes completed its face, but what really caught her was the color of its back, an iridescent emerald green. "You're beautiful. And so large. I never dreamed a spider could understand what I said. Truly, I've never seen anything like you."

No one has.

Did she detect sadness in its thought? "I've never met a spider as smart as you either. It must be the convergence of the ley lines. Did that draw you here or did it make you?"

The Giant Juice Bag is talking nonsense. And now it will leave before I bite it and melt it from the inside out.

A chorus of thousands of reedy voices said, **Bite! Bite! Hungry!**

"You have a lot of hungry children." If Coral wanted to she could back out of the door, but she'd never talked to a spider before. *With the courage born of being in a novel she stood her ground.*
Yes. I will have to bite.
Despite its large size, it was apparently reluctant to kill her. Perhaps she was the only creature of comparable intelligence the spider had ever found. "Wait. Will you at least tell me your name? I told you mine."
I'm the Mother. That's the only name I have.
"Maybe I could help feed your children. I mean, if you kill me you eat for a week, but if I bring you food, you could eat for a long time." Coral could see many reflections of herself in the black saucer eyes as the mother spider studied her face. "A spider as large as you must need a lot of food, and you have so many children. I can help you. Don't bite me just yet. Give me a chance to prove I can do what I say."
Without eyelids or a recognizable mouth, a spider face is utterly devoid of expression. But there were worlds of nuance in the thoughts the mother sent to Coral. Fear of starvation for herself and her children, but no trust in this "giant juice bag."
I will give you a chance. Coral somehow knew the mother would not go against her word. She was a creature of honor.
"I'll be as quick as I can. But first tell your children to go play somewhere other than on me." All the tiny legs tickled unbearably as Mother's children scampered down Coral's legs.

A large number of people with anxious expressions were gathered around the woodshed, waiting for her to come out— or not. Just as she emerged, Dariel, the young servant who had collected her from Bruce's house, arrived with a knight in tow: quite tall, blond hair, an open, good-natured face. There he was at last. As she emerged a cheer went up from the crowd. "She survived! She survived the woodshed!"
John Marsh said, "I was led to believe there was a young lady in danger, but you appear to be unharmed."
"Perfectly safe, but thank you so much. Perhaps you can save my life another time."

"Dariel, you said she was in the woodshed. I was expecting the fight of my life."

"She was!" The crowd was eager to tell the tale of how Coral had gone in, talked seemingly to herself, and come out again.

"You're as brave as any knight in the kingdom," said Marsh. "Or are the dangers of the woodshed mere tales meant to frighten the servants and small children?"

Coral pondered a moment, trying to decide how to approach the situation so that she ended up with the woodshed as her home and everyone, including spiders, liking her. "It's dangerous, and I confess I'm a little afraid myself. But I have a plan. Don't let anybody go to clean out the wood until I say so. I need to take care of something first."

"Good afternoon, Violet. I see you're busy getting ready for the evening meal. I hope I'm not in your way."

"In my way? After how you helped me? Sit down at the table and let me get you something."

Violet wiped doughy hands on a rag, pulled a cake and some wine from an airing closet, and placed them in front of Coral.

"These look lovely, but I'm on a different sort of mission. I wish to borrow a plate, and this is going to sound odd, but I need some food that's rotting."

"Rotting food? In my kitchen? Never! What would you want with rotting food?"

"Not to eat. It's to be used for something else. Rotting meat or even a bone would be good. Anything with flies buzzing all over it."

Violet went back to kneading her loaf. "We certainly don't keep things like that in the kitchen. They're tossed out in the pit, out back." She pointed with her chin.

"I see now. Don't you get a lot of mice and rats and things keeping it so close to the castle?"

"We never do. I can't say why."

Perhaps that was what Mother ate, thought Coral.

"Back home we used to keep the garbage far way from the house, and then we had cats for all the rats," said Violet. "Don't seem to have that problem here, and I'm glad of it. You can take a plate from that cupboard over there." She indicated the nice plates used for meals.

"Oh, no, give me something suitable for garbage." Looking around the kitchen, she found a dirty old basket that had clearly been used many times for toting vegetables. "This would do, if you can part with it."

"Take it and don't bring it back. We have newer and better. What you're doing with all this I don't want to know."

At dusk, when most people were indoors eating, including several townspeople who had come to her for healing that day, Coral slipped into the courtyard, opened the creaky woodshed door, and stepped in. She hadn't wanted to explain to one and all what she was doing with odorous fly-encrusted meat scraps. Placing the basket on the floor, she took a skin of water from her sash and sprinkled the meat until the flies had all flown off of it. They didn't fly for long in the web-filled air.

Black saucers watched her from the corner.

You are a clever Giant Juice Bag, and you have kept your word.

"I believe I have earned the right to be called by my name. It's Coral. And now I would like to know something."

What is that, Coral?

"These flies are for your children. They're too small for you. Do you get enough to eat for yourself? I think you've been keeping the castle free of mice and rats. Do you need me to bring you something as well?"

Hunting juice bags is my delight. It's nearly time to go. I creep around until I hear their paws and pounce. I wrap them in webs and puncture them so they turn to juice. The next night I come back and drink. Delicious! And there are always more.

"All right then, I wouldn't want to deprive you of that pleasure. But I can keep bringing more flies for your children. We wouldn't want them to be hungry anymore."

Perhaps I like you, Coral. The other Giant Juice Bags just wanted to kill my children. They killed many of them.

"They can't hear your voice like I can. They're afraid." What must have been spider giggles filled her mind. "We can use that to our advantage, can't we? I have a proposition for you."

Do you wish to work against your own kind? If I had a kind of my own to work against, I would not.

"I don't mean to work against my own kind. I'm trying to make everyone happy. You and your children will stay hidden, and I will bring food and be your friend. I will have a house to live in. The Giant Juice Bags will stop throwing wood in here and trying to kill your children. To them I will be the woman who made the spiders leave, and you will be my eyes and ears if I need them."

"Your Highness, would you have any objection to making the woodshed, I mean the infirmary, taller? Adding another story on top?"

"A stone building located within the castle walls isn't good enough for you, eh?" King Light gave her the look one ordinarily sees on the face of a parent whose child is requesting two cakes when the others are having one.

"I don't have many personal possessions and I have no need of most of the tools of the trade that Bruce kept, but as a woman I require a bit more privacy. It wouldn't do to have wounded farmers sleeping right next to me in my house. For the sake of modesty, I would prefer to have my own sleeping quarters upstairs."

The king held up his hand. "Say no more. It should be a simple enough matter to add a wooden story atop the stone. But no," he thought a moment. "For the sake of the overall look of the courtyard, stone would be better. Walton, have the stonemason add another story. We'll find a way to pay for it."

"May I suggest selling Bruce's unused supplies? The quicksilver I saw in his cottage should fetch a nice price."

"Splendid idea."

The renovations proceeded much more slowly than Coral would have preferred. Her room in the palace, however, was more than comfortable and even afforded a view of the lovely but oddly named Dread Cliff to the west. Young Prince Isaac made a project of her, showing off the surrounding farms and woodlands. She was charmed by his solicitousness. Most of the townspeople paid her a visit while construction went on, since everyone had at least one ailment that had either occurred during Bruce's final illness or after his death, or was something he had been unable to treat when he was still working. For the most part they paid her with material goods and services, rather than coin. Her temporary room in the palace was becoming cramped from all the linens, wall hangings, cooking implements, and whatnots she'd received from the grateful populace.

Having everyone healthy delighted the king and he spurred the workers on toward making the former woodshed a new infirmary worthy of its healer and the grandeur of the castle itself. The builders remarked on how joints fused seamlessly and nails were always straight, as though they were better builders than they actually were. Even though they were unable to feel the power of the ley lines, that didn't prevent the lines from expressing themselves through inanimate objects.

The night before construction began, all but the night watchmen had been asleep when a long line of spiders had emigrated for a temporary life in the castle's dank recesses. The only one who had caught sight of the parade thought his eyes were playing tricks on him and spent several minutes rubbing them.

Every day Coral carried a basket of food scraps covered with flies far beneath the castle to a room where fresh water gurgled from an icy spring— water that was drunk by all the castle's residents. The room was lined with racks of wine bottles. Behind the racks were rocky niches, now filled with webs. This was where Coral delivered the flies for the children and where Mother carried web-encased juice bags for her own meals.

"What do you think of this staircase, Coral? Isn't it a beauty?" The balusters had been carved from the pale wood of a beech tree and capped with a handrail of ebony. The carved pinecone atop the newel was truly the work of a great artist. Each riser was pale beech and the treads themselves ebony. The woodworker was so proud of his efforts he didn't even notice the bloody gouges on his hands.

"I've never seen a more beautiful staircase. I can hardly believe it's to be mine." She rubbed oil on her hands and took his scabby, oozing hands in hers. He complied without comment. They were all used to her ministrations by now.

"Why don't you notice you're hurting yourself? Are you so absorbed in your work or do you not care?"

A stonemason working nearby called over, "He just wants you to hold his hands."

The woodworker nodded.

A farmwife stepped into the nearly completed infirmary holding her hand to the side of her face. She spit a pacifier into her hand and said, "Pardon me, but when you have time, would you please help me with my tooth? It's awfully sore. It's bringing tears to my eyes, it hurts so much."

"Of course, I would be happy to."

"I can't pay you today, but when the turnip harvest comes in I'll bring you a bushel. Two bushels. All the turnips you can eat. You write a note and I'll make my mark."

"All right, we'll worry about that later. First, let's fix that tooth." The woman opened her mouth and pointed.

All of her teeth were stained and twisted and Coral was jerked back to modern thinking again. Those teeth were disgusting. It was because people in this time didn't brush their teeth or floss or go to orthodontists. Did she want to leave? All she had to do was touch that book. No, not yet. She felt that something needed to be done. This story had scarcely started.

She lightly touched her healing fingers on the woman's cheek over the painful, rotten tooth and held them there for a few minutes. The healing of bone and tooth was more time consuming than mending soft flesh. "It's better," the farmwife said eventually.

"Just a moment longer." Then it was safe to press the cheek more firmly with the palm of her hand until she could no longer feel energy passing through her.

"Oh, thank you so much! Now I'm going to cry from relief. Write a note and I'll sign it."

"All right, I'll do that." She took a scrap of paper from the purse at her waist and scratched a tiny note that read, "Pay me what you wish," which she handed to the farm wife. "I never caught your name."

"Agnes."

"Agnes, would you mind if I asked you a question? I keep seeing people with pacifiers in their mouths, and I saw you had one when you came in. I've never seen adults using them anywhere before I came here. Why do you do that?"

Agnes shook her head. "It's not a pacifier. It's because my tooth hurt so much I was afraid of what I was going to say."

The other workers in the infirmary stopped what they were doing and listened with what looked like concern.

"What were you afraid you would say?"

Out of the corner of her eye Coral saw the stonemason give his head a brief shake. Agnes acknowledged the shake with a nod. "If all will live another day, we must be careful what we say."

Coral was puzzled. "What ... what aren't we supposed to say?"

The stonemason yelled, "Get help!" The woodworker bolted for the castle as Agnes scurried out of the door.

Sir Marsh, in his Nothingthrall tabard, strode into the construction zone, brow furrowed. "Is it too late?"

"I'm not sure. I don't think so." The woodworker produced a hastily carved pacifier. "Here, this should help. Just pop this in your mouth, Coral. It'll help."

Coral looked at them all in astonishment. "With what? What is everyone talking about?"

"No one is talking about anything." Marsh's open face had grown dear to her. When he smiled encouragingly she took the pacifier from the woodworker and tentatively placed it in her mouth, feeling quite foolish. It tasted the way fresh cut wood smelled.

"There's something you need to see. I'm really quite surprised no one thought to show you this before," said Marsh.

Coral followed Sir Marsh like a docile lamb, albeit a lamb who wasn't used to being a lamb and who would really rather be something with more self-determination, like a cat. They walked into the castle and through a number of passageways to a long gallery dubbed the Hall of Perpetual Silence. She had seen this place marked by a sign above the door when exploring on her own and had stayed away, unclear about its purpose. With such a name, it seemed to have some religious significance that she didn't understand. She certainly hadn't wanted to go in and start asking questions in a Hall of Perpetual Silence.

Which was why Sir Marsh surprised her by talking in a normal volume when they crossed into the room. "There's no reason why you can't *see* things. Start here and look at the paintings, and then go around the room from left to right, as though reading a book. It's a story, and it's all true. This is the history of Nothingthrall."

Coral pointed to the pacifier in her mouth as though to say, "May I take this out?"

"You're best off leaving it in for the time being. Here of all places. Ask me again when you get to the end."

With a sigh of resignation, Coral examined the first painting. It depicted a squad of nine knights of the realm in full mail, complete with the oddly blank tabard, bravely fighting against something that had not been painted. The parts that were painted were remarkably complete and detailed. You could see the links in the mail, the determined look in the eyes of the knights, gleaming white terror in the eye of one of the horses, and rivulets of blood running from a fire-blackened knight who had fallen in battle. The surrounding countryside was charred and twisted in places, lush and green in others. And yet whatever they were fighting was not painted. Much of the upper right quadrant of the canvas was completely devoid of paint, as though the artist simply hadn't gotten to that part yet, even though he had been so meticulous with the rest. It didn't take any great leap of imagination to think it must have been a fire-breathing dragon they were fighting. If not for the pacifier she would have said so, but instead she merely caught Marsh's eye and pointed to the void with a furrowed brow. He nodded. She moved on to the next painting.

In this one, the castle of Nothingthrall was laid to waste. Many of the stones were blackened and smoke curled from every window, and yet the walls stood. She could see her woodshed, minus its wooden roof. People were streaming out of the doorless gate clutching bundles in their arms. Their faces were frightened and defeated. This painting had no void places. She supposed it depicted the castle after a fiery attack that came from the air with devastating consequences.

The next painting showed what must have been the king of the day being held in the air by something not depicted— another void. It was clear he would soon be dead. Arrows by the hundreds fired up toward the void and fell again. Projectiles fired from trebuchets met the same fate. She shuddered at the horrible realism of the king's face and moved on.

Dread Cliff, which she could see from her room, was depicted next, but in the painting the face of the cliff was covered in writing the color of charcoal, each letter the height of a man. There was a poem written across its face:

Speak of me and I will waken
For every word one will be taken

A warning to all, seemingly carved into stone by blasts of fire. Fire produced by the dragon, no doubt. She had assumed the cliff was named Dread because it was so tall and sheer that it would be certain death to fall from it, but perhaps the name came from the warning.

Surely it was all a fairytale. The paintings were discolored and the paint was crackled as though they were very old. Even if there had been a dragon it must have been a long time ago and the dragon would be long dead. She'd only seen the cliff from a distance but had never noticed any writing. And yet the people persisted in keeping the topic unlawful, forbidden. Sir Marsh was gazing at her somberly. He took all of this very seriously. She pointed to the letters and shook her head at him. She hadn't seen the writing out her window. He said, "Over the years the letters washed away," and then gestured that she should move on.

The last piece of art was a diptych. On the left was a tavern with people laughing and drinking, except at one table, where a tipsy, red-faced man was saying something and the listeners in his immediate vicinity were making a lunge for him with expressions of alarm. On the right side a shepherdess was being held above stampeding sheep, blood staining her dress and dripping toward the ground. Her head lolled to the side. But, as in earlier paintings, it appeared as though the part of the canvas that would show what was killing the girl was simply never painted. The meaning was quite clear. If someone spoke of the dragon and woke it, it killed someone.

Sir Marsh said, "We must all be very careful at all times. People's lives are at stake."

Coral removed the wooden plug from her mouth. "So these are not pacifiers. I thought you were all a lot of babies."

"Did you really?"

"No, but I couldn't figure out what they were for. I've never seen anything like it."

"We call them stoppers. Sometimes people are overly tired or angry or in pain, and when they think they may not have complete control over their words, they pop one of these in their mouths to stop them from saying anything, or to at least make them take it out before they speak, which slows them down. Can't be blurting things out."

"I understand. I have a couple of questions and I'm working hard to ask them in a safe way."

"Be very careful, Coral d'Ambrose. It's better to leave questions unanswered if it means saving someone's life."

She pointed to Sir Marsh's tabard. "Was there once something else in the center of that design?"

"Yes. Now there is nothing."

Then it came to her: the name of the realm. It wasn't always Nothingthrall. She'd thought that was a rather inelegant name from the time she'd heard it. At least Dragonthrall sounded like a real place. "Nothingthrall."

"What of it?"

"Nothing." She measured her words carefully. "When was the last time someone blurted-"

Marsh spoke over the rest of what she was trying to get at. "I couldn't say. No one can say. It can't be said."

"Will it ever be over?"

"That's a good question and I have no answer."

"But what if it *is* over?"

"Some things are better left alone. We have a good life here. It's even better for us all since you came with your abilities. Guard your tongue and all will be well."

Coral knew she would be unable to think a single thought that didn't have a dragon at the center of it for quite a while, so she popped the stopper in her mouth and headed away from all the temptations to talk, all the way to Bruce's lonely cottage, where she worked on sorting out which of his books she was going to want to keep when she was able to move into the new infirmary.

Mistake number one had been thinking she would be able to sleep at a convergence of ley lines. Everyone had worked very hard on her behalf making the woodshed into a home and infirmary, and when she had waved goodnight to them all, gotten undressed, and pulled up the blanket for the first time, she thought at first that the alertness she felt was an afterglow from the informal housewarming party.

Unfortunately, it was not. It was the planetary force that spilled up through the shattered crust and beamed itself straight out into space while empowering anyone properly attuned to receive it. Once turned on, the attunement could not be turned off merely because someone wanted to go to sleep. She would remain awake as long as she stayed where she was. Physically she could go without sleep indefinitely while living where she was, but even an Ambrosia healer needed the mental rest of sleep eventually. It appeared that to sleep she would need to distance herself from the ley lines. Her room at the castle had been ideally suited for that. She'd slept well there. Fizzing with wakefulness, she envisioned a number of different scenarios for living in Nothingthrall. Perhaps she could remain awake here most nights and keep a separate sleeping place for off nights.

Mistake number two had been thinking she could even feel restful with thousands of tiny spiders— and one as big as a goat—a thin door away, for it had been moving day for them as well. And what was even worse was that she could hear the thoughts of Mother chattering away to her children.

Don't be lazy. Flies do not catch themselves. I want to see every one of you hard at work making wonderful dinner platters. I have a splendid idea! Let's have a contest. Whoever makes the biggest dinner platter may eat whatever he likes before anybody else starts. That's right. Very good. Yes, I do see yours, it's very nice. Oh my, now this one over here brings up a problem. It's not good enough to be large, is it? It has to be neat as well. There must be lots of silk to catch the flies or else they'll fly right through, and we can't have that. Fill in the gaps. Yes, all of them. That's right. Much better.

Since there was no chance of sleep she might as well be friendly. "Are you happy with your home, Mother?"

We are. It's going to take some work, but we'll get by.

"No one will throw logs at you, that's a good thing. And I'll bring flies as often as I can. I'm hoping for every day."

I don't know why a Giant Juice Bag would be so kind to us.

"I asked you not to call me that." Spider giggles filled her mind with screeches. "We may have many opportunities to help one another. If I ever need someone to do some spying for me I can imagine one of your children doing an excellent job. Spider spies!"

My children are brilliant spies. Just give us the word.

"I imagine you know everything that goes on around here."

We know everything we care about. We care very little about the relationships Giant Juice Bags have with one another. They seem to be obsessed with that.

"Are you familiar with the word we're never allowed to say?"

There are several words you aren't supposed to say but you do anyway, mostly when you're angry. Which one are you never allowed to say?

Coral whispered, "Dragon."

Dragon? Indeed. That enormous firefly put you all in your place a long time ago.

"So it would seem. Is the firefly still alive? Can you send out your spies and find out for me?"

There is no need of that. We've seen its bones in the place where there is no food. It is dead. Its juices are all dry.

There was now a third reason Coral would never be able to sleep that night. She had said the word. Would someone die because of her? Even if Mother was right and the dragon was dead, would its bones reanimate at the mention of the forbidden word? Pernicious curses can outlive their makers.

By morning light Coral looked alert and energetic, but she did not feel relaxed. She had said the word. Would she find out today that someone had been taken?

Being awake all day and all night, day in and day out, would allow her to accomplish much, but it would take an emotional toll, and she knew she would sometimes need to visit Bruce's greasy cottage for a nap. In the meantime there was a kitchen to arrange and cupboards to fill with several months' collected payments from her patients: extra bedding, woven tunics, and jars of jam and vegetables. As she worked she strained her ears for cries of lament over the death of someone from a fiery aerial attack. But whatever was happening in the village did not extend into the castle courtyard, and all remained peaceful.

That is, until there came a pounding on the door that made her drop a jar of pickled beets, which shattered on the floor. "Coral! You must come quickly! Oh, for the love of the moon!"

Gathering her oil and her shawl, she ran into the bright courtyard, leaving the beets like a pool of clotted blood on the floor. Ashen faces stared at her. It was the servant boy, Dariel, looking as though he might be sick himself. "You must come at once into the castle. The young prince has need of you."

"Of course." With heart pounding she was led into the great dining hall where a crowd stood around anxiously. On the floor near the fireplace was a tiny blackened lump of flesh. It was Isaac, burned beyond recognition, but blessedly unconscious.

"Everyone step back and give her room to work." Coral had never heard the king's voice sound weak before.

Touching the burned flesh was unthinkable; it would likely have come off in her hands. She took her oil and rubbed it in, then held her hands over the worst burned parts: his hands and forearms. She could feel the ley energy pouring out of her in a torrent, but they were not directly on a ley line in this room. He would need to be moved, but to touch him in any way would be torture. She was going to need to do the best she could with him first.

To the king she said, "This will take some time and more energy than I can give him here. He must be moved to my infirmary as soon as I do what I can here. Have them bring a cot and a sheet."

"Of course. Is there anything else you need? Anything at all?"

I need to go back in time and not say that word. This is all my fault, she thought. She shook her head no, tears stinging her eyes.

Someone in the crowd of onlookers whispered, "See how she cares for the young prince?"

Another whispered, "If anyone can make it right, Coral can." Their words were daggers in her heart.

Having spent the night at the crossroads of ley lines had filled her to capacity, and she made use of every bit of energy she had, eventually falling to the floor, exhausted. Isaac looked a bit better, but still ghastly. He remained unconscious, but the surface of his body was now flesh colored rather than oozing, cracked, and charred. He was missing much of his right hand and his left was not much better. His face was unrecognizable. He had no nose, nor any ears. The healing she had done was all on the surface for the purpose of transporting him. The servants were directed to tip his body to one side, lay out the folded sheet under him, tip his body onto it, and spread the other side of the sheet so that he could be lifted gingerly onto the cot.

A small and sad parade moved from the castle to Coral's house: Coral, the king, the servants with poor Isaac on the cot, and three other servants carrying baskets of food from Violet for Coral. Someone had cleaned the spilled beets and broken jar in her absence, for which she was grateful. Basket carriers got to work building up the fire, for the morning air remained cool, and one of them heated cider to revive

Coral, although merely being in the presence of the lines was doing the trick.

With the skin sealed, she was able to touch Isaac directly, which made the process much quicker. She started with his poor face because he was so hard to look at. The ley power surged up through her feet and passed through her hands with such intensity she thought it must be visible to all, and yet to them it just looked like she was caressing the boy's face.

No healer since Enna d'Ambrose had restored this much flesh to an injured person but Coral was pouring everything she had into the effort to save the young prince. The only thing keeping her grief at being the cause of this from overwhelming her was the knowledge that he was not dead, he was alive, and she was going to make him whole again. Still, he'd been through a terrible ordeal and she knew it was her fault. Would she ever dare confess this fact to anybody? What would they do to her? She would need to leave Nothingthrall, where she had been happy and had begun to love many people.

The open doorway darkened and filled with the large form of Sir John. "Your Highness, I just heard and came as quickly as I could. How may I serve you?"

"Sit down and rest, John. Coral has the matter well in hand."

John peered down at Isaac and gave a low moan.

"If you think he looks bad now, you should have seen him an hour ago," said King Light.

"What happened?"

Coral drew back her hands, her head sinking to her chest, as she waited to hear the story of how Isaac had been attacked by the dragon. She wondered how they were going to word it without saying the actual words.

"I hate to tell you."

Assuming the king would be unable to tell him of a dragon attack, Sir John said, "Perhaps there are no words to describe it."

"No, no, it's not that. It's embarrassing, really. We were eating breakfast in the dining hall and that little dog Boots came in, you know the one, the terrier with the brown feet, and jumped clear up on the table, grabbed the ham off Isaac's plate, and took off with it. I said, 'Don't let him get away with it or he'll never learn.' And Isaac ran after Boots to get the ham away. Boots went under the table and Isaac went after him, and when Boots came out the other side, Isaac stood up too soon and cracked his head on the underside of the table. He stood up and was unsteady on his feet, going this way and that and making a bit of a show of it, and to my eternal shame I laughed. But when he careened into a chair and fell down into the fireplace it wasn't funny, not at all. I jumped up to pull him out, and the servants rushed over, and he was pushing himself out, but his clothes had caught fire. Someone had the good sense to pull down a drapery and put the fire out, or else he'd be dead."

"I'm so glad!" Coral blurted. It wasn't her fault at all, it was just an accident! If saying the word 'dragon' to the spiders had caused the dragon to attack, it hadn't attacked Prince Isaac. She doubted it had attacked anybody, since the spiders seemed to know what they were thinking about. The others looked at her strangely. She clarified, "So glad someone had the sense to pull down the drapery!"

King Light nodded. "I didn't take note of who it was. I was distracted. I need to reward that person." The servants who remained pointed out Dariel. "Well, good man. You used your head in a crisis. When this is over we'll see how I can reward you."

Isaac moaned and stirred. Coral whispered, "Just lie still, Prince Isaac. This is going to take a while, but I'll have you good as new."

It was the height of the harvest season and every able-bodied man, woman, and child was working in the fields and orchards, or in the kitchens securing their meals for the coming year—all except the royals, some of the knights, and Coral. Even Prince Isaac, on his father's orders, was going from household to household, lending a hand with whatever needed to be done. His father wanted him to understand the lives of his future subjects. He had healed perfectly from his ordeal, with no scars on his body, but a large scar on his mind, the sort that turns the folly of youth into wisdom.

Sir John was on horseback patrolling the region when a dappled gray mare bearing Coral pulled up alongside him. "What brings you here? Is there trouble back at the castle?" he asked.

"Not at all; in fact, the opposite is true. I've been waiting around for a plowing accident or for someone to scald herself with canning water, but everyone has been very well coordinated."

"That's good, isn't it?"

"It is, if rather boring. I thought I'd take advantage of this lovely weather while it's still fine and go for a ride. And here you are."

"This is one of the times when being a Knight of the Realm has its advantages. Here I am riding about in the autumn sunshine while the others are doing back-breaking work."

"Sir John, I'm actually glad to have a chance to speak to you alone. There's something I want to tell someone and I'd like it to be you."

He tilted his head and waited.

"The day before Prince Isaac had his accident, I did something by mistake. I said the word. It just came out. So when Isaac fell into the fire at first I thought it was my fault and that he'd been attacked. Except that he wasn't. And now months and months have gone by and nobody has been attacked."

Sir John rode along in silence. "Are you sure you said it out loud? It wasn't a dream?"

"I did say it. I'm sure of it."

"Did anyone hear you?"

"Yes, well, sort of. Nobody who can talk about it. It's hard to explain."

"Either someone did or they didn't."

"I said it to an animal."

"Oh." He appeared to be pondering the circumstances under which one would say 'dragon' to an animal.

"But the point is: Nothing happened. Apparently the curse is over or broken or something. I'm sure of it."

"That would be very nice if it were true. However, I wouldn't want to test it. What if it were a mistake? What if someone had died and you simply hadn't heard of it?"

"The kingdom isn't that large. We know when anybody dies. There is no curse, not anymore. It's over, just like the words that have washed off the cliff."

"I will bring this before the king, but I doubt he'll be willing to risk anyone's life to test your theory."

Coral, knowing she was only a character in a book, was completely unafraid.

"I'll test it myself. I'm not afraid. Dragon!"

Sir John's face turned red in anger. "You may have just killed someone! How dare you take matters into your own hands like that?"

"I'm telling it to come after me, if it's even there. Dragon, come and get me!"

"That's not how it works, and that's two people you may have killed. It's not the speaker who is taken, you foolish girl." Sir John drew his sword. "As a Knight of the Kingdom of Nothingthrall, I arrest you in the name of King Light. If you say it again I will cut off your head where you sit."

Coral was horrified. Her friend was threatening to cut off her head? This was absurd. "Fine. I'm arrested. Now we wait to see that nothing happens, which it won't. And when you all see I'm right, the people of Nothingthrall will be free to speak about anything they choose.

"Will you follow me or must I tie you up?"

"I'll follow. It's me, not a petty thief. Throw me in the stocks if you like, but you'll see that I'm right."

The journey back to the castle was silent but for the clopping of hooves.

What had she done? This story was ruined.

It was bad enough that John Marsh was angry with her, but her reputation among the people of Nothingthrall would now be ruined. She'd been enjoying their high esteem so much. The fertile fields of Nothingthrall had never looked lovelier than they did on that sad ride back to the castle in the golden light.

The dragon would not come, of that she was certain, but being put in stocks would be distinctly uncomfortable. They were in the back of the castle, near the kitchen waste. She'd seen them every time she collected scraps for the spiders.

It had never crossed her mind she would be put there one day, but when it came right down to it, it wasn't necessary. She had an easy way out, and upon their arrival at the castle courtyard, Coral knew she would take it.

"If I'm to be put in the stocks, may I have a moment in my house in private?"

"Yes, of course."

She tiptoed upstairs. "Mother, I've come to say goodbye. I guess I won't be needing your spies after all. I'll never forget you."

Goodbye?

There was a box tucked under her bed. Coral needed to hurry before Sir John came in to fetch her. She opened it, reached in, and touched the book.

20 LITTLE HEARTS

That one had lasted a long time, 16 minutes. The main point of going into that book had been to learn about the dragon. Well, that and to have fun, and indeed she'd had a lot of fun, at least at first. She had stayed longer in Nothingthrall than she had anywhere else. And yet at the end it had all gone wrong and she'd felt she needed to flee.

Losing the good will of John Marsh was even worse in this book than in the English murder mystery. In that one she had merely disappointed him. In this one she had become an enemy of his kingdom. Her heart was broken.

Feeling the need to stop being emotional over a fictional character, she pulled out her "Patterns and Themes" list and modified it based on her most recent experience.

- *Dragon: a killer who threatens to kill again if spoken about (person? animal? thing?).*

She hadn't really learned much about this dragon at all. She wasn't afraid of it. People thought it could still kill them, but it couldn't. She continued with more generalized patterns and themes.

- *A little boy is orphaned or in danger. His father is dead. Someone else takes care of the boy. Except in Nothingthrall.*
- *Someone named Higgins looks guilty but isn't? Maybe not that important since he wasn't in Nothingthrall.*
- *The dragon is the bad guy but you don't need to be afraid??*
- *John Marsh is a hero! Make John Marsh like me.*

Coral drew little hearts around the word "hero." It was her journal and she could do that if she wanted to.

In fact, she remained mired in sadness that she had let John Marsh down again. She kept letting him down, over and over, in each book adventure. He always wanted something from her and she never followed through, even though she really liked him. There he was, a fictional character, and apparently she had a crush on him. How ridiculous was that? How utterly futile! But on the other hand, if she was going into these book adventures primarily for fun, why not? Why not get romantic with John Marsh?

She had books for romance.

The next day she looked forward to her next book adventure the whole time she was at work. That night she brought home a carton of takeout Chinese because it was fast, ate it, and got herself comfortable. The cover of the book she placed in the bag was very, very pink.

21 THE LOST LADY OF COTSLEY

Pursed lips and lowered brows, a furrowed face, and wisps of hair protruding from a worn checked kerchief: this was her first sight of her new life.

"Had quite a knock on the head, didn't ye now, ducky?" That would explain the pounding pain she felt from merely moving her eyes in an attempt to take in her surroundings. The pain brought forth an involuntary moan, which prompted a finger to wag in her face. "You must hold perfectly still, lass, there's a good girl."

"Where am I?" The sound of her own cracked voice surprised her; it was weak and high pitched.

"The Lion and Lamb. A gentleman has paid in advance for your room, so you mustn't fret. Just lie back until you feel like yourself."

Myself? What do I ordinarily feel like?

"Now that I see you've come back to the world of the living I have customers to look after, so I'll leave you to your rest." The owner of the pursed lips and furrowed brows bustled to the doorway and turned back. "Your name, Miss? What are we to call ye?"

She opened her mouth to answer, but no answer came forth for one ghastly reason: She didn't know how to answer.

Was she Coral Ambrose? Coral d'Ambrose? Miss Ambrose? This time she didn't seem to know anything about her backstory.

The landlady, for that is who she was, *(and also named Violet Emerson though Coral wasn't supposed to know that yet,)* gave her a sympathetic look and slipped out the door, closing it in a futile attempt to be quiet.

She needn't have bothered about that, as raucous laughter and foot-stomping was issuing forth from the lower regions of the establishment, loud enough to shake the floor of Coral's room.

Someone was tuning a fiddle, a harbinger of an even greater cacophony to come. Rest would be out of the question. Gingerly twisting her head allowed her to give the room a better inspection. She appeared to be in a bedroom of a plain country inn. It looked clean enough, but its furnishings, such as they were, spoke of utility with no eye for embellishment. She saw nothing in the room that belonged to her— that is, to the young woman she apparently was. She wasn't sure she'd recognize her own things. But there was no cloak, no bag of any sort, and no clothing.

With a start she felt under the blanket to determine what she was wearing. All she had on, however, was a thin cotton nightdress. Any hope of learning her own identity by her clothing was dashed.

Where was her clothing? And who was the gentleman who had paid for her room? She fervently hoped he was indeed a gentleman and not an opportunist who preyed upon young women in distress. What had happened to her? Was she far from home? Did someone miss her? Was someone looking for her? She suspected the answer to many of these questions lay with the gentleman, but having a conversation with him dressed as she was seemed to be out of the question. There was nothing to be done but obey the landlady and rest. She closed her eyes and felt a sense of relief. The room had been spinning, and she felt better keeping her eyes closed.

Morning light streamed through the small window as a gentle rap awakened her. What was this strange room and where was this strange bed? Vague memories from the previous evening came back to her, but nothing from before. "Who is it?"

"Mrs. Emerson, Miss. I've come with your clothes."

"Oh, do come in! I wondered where they'd got to."

"They were in a right mess, they were. When they dragged you in yesterday you were like a little lost puppy and you looked a fright. Got thrown from your horse, they said. Now they've been cleaned and dried by the fire. There's a bit of a tear in the sleeve just here, d'ye see?"

She looked closely, willing her eyes to focus. "No actually, I don't see where."

Mrs. Emerson looked triumphant. "That was me gran what taught me to mend like that."

"You've done a beautiful job. How will I ever repay you?"

Mrs. Emerson waved a dismissive hand. "It's all been paid for already. Now what can I get ye for breakfast? We've simple fare here, but I've a few eggs and a bit of bacon if you like."

"All paid for by the gentleman as well? Some tea and toast would be perfectly fine. I don't want to be a bother. By the way, I hope you don't mind me asking, but what is the name of my benefactor?"

Mrs. Emerson rolled her eyes. "I'm a bit dense sometimes, aren't I? Of course you'd like to know that. Why, it's Sir John of Marsh Hall what found you laid out insensible by the side of the road and carried you here."

Coral smiled inwardly. There he was. She wondered if Isaac, the Carlsons, and Dr. Bruce would show up. Perhaps she'd even see Higgins and Light. Would there be a dragon of some sort? But first things first: she needed to find out who she was in this story. She stretched gingerly, feeling stiff in a hundred places. "I don't suppose Sir John also bought me a hot bath?"

"Do you feel well enough for that already?"

"I think so." She stood up carefully, watching for lightheadedness. Other than a very stiff neck and a headache, she seemed to be all right.

"You can have a bit to eat while I heat the water." Mrs. Emerson scurried out of the room, seeming glad to have someone to fuss over like a daughter.

The bath water was not very deep, but it was deliciously warm. The brown soap smelled sharply of tallow and lye but it did its job well. She dressed in her newly cleaned clothes— traveling clothes they appeared to be, of a coarse brown fabric meant to withstand the rigors of the road and not to call attention to the wearer.

The room contained a tiny mirror, rather spotty around the edges and only big enough to reveal the part of a face a man would be shaving. Moving her head around carefully despite the soreness of her neck, bits and pieces of her appearance were revealed: emerald eyes, full pink lips, and wavy chestnut tresses.

All of this was extremely odd, because in her real life, Coral's hair was an ordinary brown and quite straight, but there was no other way to describe the color of the hair she had now but chestnut and the tumbling waviness demanded to be called tresses. So chestnut tresses they were. Her eyes would ordinarily have required tinted contact lenses to attain that emerald color, not to mention the visual acuity, and she enjoyed having them now.

Clean and dressed, she ventured downstairs to the common area to see if anything or anybody was familiar.

Making himself at home on a bench in the corner of the room, a man fiddled with the lace trim on his sleeve, his long blond hair obscuring his face. Her entrance caught his attention and he stood, sweeping the hair from his eyes, blue eyes that glinted in the morning light with an innate kindness. His nose was wide and not long, almost like a child's, but the massive neck and chest proclaimed him to be all man.

She wasn't used to seeing John Marsh with long hair and hadn't recognized him immediately.

"Please! Come sit down," he said, offering her a seat at the bench opposite his own. "I'm Sir John, the younger, not the elder who is quite in his dotage, don't you know." She offered her hand in greeting, but as she hadn't reciprocated with a name of her own, he ventured the question. "I hope you don't find me impertinent, but would you do me the honor of telling me who you are? I've been in a lather all night trying to guess what your name is. The later the night got the more ridiculous the names I invented. When I did fall asleep I dreamt of Rumpelstiltskin. Do put me out of my misery and tell me who you are and how a young lady such as yourself came to be traveling through here unaccompanied by a large contingent of fathers and brothers."

"I would be happy to tell you my name and anything you wish to know about me as soon as I learn these facts myself."

"What? Are you saying you've lost your memory? Well, that is a bit of a surprise. I'm very glad I didn't take anybody up on the wagers they were putting forth."

"You were taking bets on who I am?"

"I most assuredly was not. However, you must know you've made a bit of a stir in our sleepy hamlet. It isn't often we find a young lady unconscious on the side of the road."

"I'm glad to hear it. I'd hate to think I'd blundered into some dreadful part of the country where it happens all the time. Can you say what happened to me? I seem to have hit my head somehow."

"I was rather hoping you'd tell me. Now it seems we need to find some third party who can tell us both. What do you remember? Do you remember where you were going or who accompanied you? I'd be rather worried about that person. I hardly think anybody would have left you there of his own volition."

She thought hard. *She remembered her own modern life perfectly well, but of this life there was no backstory at all.* "I remember waking up and seeing Mrs. Emerson."

"Really? That's all?"

"I believe my name is Coral. But I don't know where I'm from."

"Coral! Well, that's something anyway. A lovely name." His eyes wandered over her clothing, no doubt trying to ascertain whether she was common or noble. The clothes themselves were well made, but clearly meant for traveling. "Would you mind terribly if I looked at your hands?"

"Not at all." She held them out. His hands felt cool as he felt for callouses.

"It's clear you've done nothing more strenuous than lift a pen and a needle with these hands. And see just here?" He pointed to small grooves on several of her fingers. "You were in the habit of wearing rings. They've left reminders in your skin. I wonder what became of them."

"Perhaps I was robbed. Perhaps I was traveling with someone who was beaten and kidnapped, or worse." She pressed her knuckles to her mouth in worry as she contemplated the horror of her situation. "I don't know who I am or where I belong, and I don't know if I'm supposed to be worried about someone. I don't know where to go or what to do next."

His glib attitude gone, a worried look settled on Sir John Marsh's face. "You *are* in a state."

"I can't stay here forever. I have no money to pay Mrs. Emerson." She took Sir John's hands and squeezed them with desperation. "I have nowhere to turn and no one to help me. You've already been so kind. I hate to prevail upon your good nature further, but I don't know what to do."

His face softened, revealing the melting of his innermost parts at her entreaty. What could he do but bow and place himself at her service? Seemingly fighting the urge to gather her in his arms, he instead left her to compose herself and went in search of a horse he could add to his own so that the two of them might scour the countryside in search of clues as to her origin.

149

He had no sooner left through the back door, heading toward the stable, when the front door opened with a crash and two rough-looking men stomped in, one completely unselfconscious in soiled and wrinkled clothing, clearly the leader, and the other possessed of the sort of snide face that's meant for making remarks intended to be witty, but only at another's expense.

Coral disliked them instantly, the more so since she recognized the first one. She wondered what his nickname would be this time.

He called out, "Emerson! Two pints of your finest, my good woman, and make it quick! There's thirst to be slaked and a ha'penny here with your name on it."

Mrs. Emerson took her time pulling the draughts. "We've only one kind here and ye know it, Horse Whip. You also know it costs more than a ha'penny."

So Two Bit was Horse Whip this time.

Coral quietly withdrew into a dark corner of the room, glad for her drab clothing. They had not yet noticed her presence. Horse Whip produced a purse from among the folds of his voluminous muddy cloak and waggled it in Mrs. Emerson's face, where it made a clinking sound. "Oh, you'll get your money, old lady. My lad and me have come into a bit."

"Good! Then you can settle up right proper. You owe me enough to buy me next two kegs." A sudden thought apparently struck her as her eyes darted from the coin purse to Coral in the corner. Thinking better of making any of the sorts of remarks that her thoughts may have prompted, she retreated to the safety of the kitchen, wiping her hands on her apron.

The look was not lost on Horse Whip's sharp friend. He didn't say anything, but merely took his beer and sat down with it, drinking in silence, yet keeping his eyes on Coral. Horse Whip, who had not yet noticed Coral, sat with his back to her and said, "So you never been in this inn, eh? It's the only one for miles."

The back door opened and Sir John's face reflected the distaste he felt for Horse Whip as soon as he strode in from his errand at the stable. "Horse Whip Higgins."

"Well, if it isn't the lord of us all himself: Sir John. Allow me to present my friend, Cavalli."

"Charmed. A foreign name is that, Cavalli?"

"Foreign to these parts, but known well enough where I'm from."

Horse Whip clapped Cavalli on the back and said, "He didn't have the pleasure of being raised in Cotsley like we did."

Cavalli inclined his head toward Coral and in a voice just loud enough to be heard by the men alone said, "Perhaps not, but a part of me is being raised right now with pleasure on its mind."

There was a moment of silence. Horse Whip was not a particularly bright man, so it took him a moment to understand his friend's quip. When he did, he turned around, spied Coral, and roared with laughter. John was frankly taken aback. He was unused to coarse joking of this sort in his presence, and looked like he had trouble believing his ears. He stared at Horse Whip's friend, aghast for a moment while sorting out how to proceed.

Coral was astonished when ale spilled everywhere as Sir John grabbed Cavalli by the collar of his shirt and lifted him bodily out of his chair. "How dare you speak of a lady in that manner? Apologize before I horsewhip you." He threw the scrawny Cavalli in the direction of Coral's chair.

Coral leaped up. "I ... I didn't hear what he said."

Horse Whip hooted. "Coo, Cavalli, you're in for it now."

"Silence, Horse Whip! You're the one who brought this bounder here. Shut it before I remind you how you got your name."

"Yes, sir."

Seeing his friend's rapid change of demeanor to obsequious assent had a dramatic effect on Cavalli, who shrank down upon himself, looked at his own feet, and muttered, "My apologies, m'lady. We'll be going now."

"What do ye mean '*we'll* be going?' I have a pint to finish." Horse Whip waved his friend toward the door and took a long pull of his ale.

Sir John took the glass from his lips, poured its contents out the front door, and said, "And now you're done and you can be on your way."

When both of the rough men were outside and the door shut behind them, however, their jocularity returned and gales of laughter could be clearly heard through the front window of the inn, which had been left open due to the fine weather. They seemed to be unaware of this and stayed a while on the front step, possibly to light pipes.

"We could have had her when she was lying senseless in the mud."

"Nobody would have wanted her then. Looked like a drowned badger."

"Cleaning her up did her a world of good. Must be young John paying for her then, since she doesn't have any money left. We made sure of that." That got a rowdy laugh from both of them. Since it was clear it was they who had robbed her, Sir John started for the door handle in pursuit, but Coral waved him to a stop. She put her finger to her lips. Listen!

"So it's come to this, has it? Young John paying for the company of a trollop? What do you think his old man will do when he finds out?"

Sir John turned bright red and made for the door again, but Coral once more intervened. She wanted to listen longer and find out what they knew about her. She could have been anyone, for all she knew.

"He certainly wouldn't be getting any from that London tart who comes to visit, now would he? With a face like a sheep? Take it where you can get it, I always say."

Sir John turned white with anger. He hissed, "This has gone on long enough."

Coral grasped his arm and whispered, "Wait just a bit longer—they may say more about what happened to me."

"Do you think John knows where this one came from? I daresay all those gents and ladies know each other from their parties and such."

"If he did he wouldn't keep her at the inn, now would he? She's a right mystery, she is. Lying sprawled out on the road for blokes like us to find. Good luck for us, I say. The less anybody knows the better, eh?" Their voices trailed off as they sauntered down the road.

Coral slumped on the nearest chair. "They don't really know anything. They just found me there and robbed me. And left me lying in the mud, unconscious."

"By the time I'm through with them... "

"They could have done worse, though. Have to look at the bright side."

"Are you sure they... ?"

Coral blushed prettily. "Completely sure. I would know if... "

"Hmm, yes." The turn of this conversation was obviously making him uncomfortable. "I will get your money back at least. Stay here. When I return, you and I will look around for anything else you may have lost, clothing or a horse. Perhaps we'll find clues about whomever you were traveling with and what attacked you."

He dashed out the door, leaving Coral wondering who the London tart with a face like a sheep could possibly be.

She wasn't destined to wonder for long.

A scant half hour later, John, as she had come to think of her protector, rode back to the inn, muddied but seeming to be otherwise unscathed, carrying the small purse Horse Whip had been seen flashing boastfully to Violet Emerson.

"This belongs to you. At least what's left of it. It's a good thing they hadn't long to spend more of its contents. They seemed determined to buy up every bit of alcohol and tobacco in the village. It would have been better had they bought a bath and some better clothes and perhaps repaid Horse Whip's debts. But we each have our priorities in life."

Coral accepted the purse humbly. "I can never repay you for the many kindnesses you've shown me."

John dismounted from his horse and handed the reins to a stable boy. "The best kindness anyone can show you would be to find out your identity and restore you to your people. Horse Whip and that ferret-faced friend of his convincingly persuaded me that they had nothing to do with your original misadventure. They were mere opportunists who found you on the road and who hadn't the decency to help you like any other person would, but thought to simply help themselves to your money. They're greedy bounders, but not murderers or kidnappers. Do you know they were actually the ones who first raised the cry about you? They came into town calling about there being an accident on the High Road, and left before anybody saw who was making the fuss."

"So they didn't mean for me to die, but they wanted my money for themselves. I dare say they felt they earned it for sending help."

"I rather think you're right."

In the bright midday light John's eyes were a clear blue, as blue as a bachelor button. Had she not noticed this before? And they seemed to be the eyes of a truly good and decent man. Absorbed as she

153

was in his eyes, she didn't notice the approaching pair of horses until they were almost upon them.

"There you are," a high-pitched female voice cried out. "Having a drink at the inn and wooing the village girls, are you? I can't let you out of my sight for an instant!"

Startled, John turned to greet the sheep-faced but attractive young woman and her riding companion, a stable boy from his own manor house. "Marie! Darling! What a pleasant surprise. I wasn't expecting you until tomorrow."

The rider raised one eyebrow and looked sideways at Coral as she adjusted her stylish riding garb. "I can see that you weren't. Aren't you going to introduce me to your friend, John?" She added teasingly.

"Of course. Coral, this is my betrothed, Miss Marie Walton who told me she would be arriving from London tomorrow, but ever the minx, has graced us all with her presence a day early. Darling, this is Coral, and that's all anybody knows. It's quite a story, really."

John was attempting to help Miss Walton down from her horse, but she waved him off. "Don't bother about that. I came to fetch you, not mingle with the locals. Is that your horse there? I'm eager to get back. Doctor Bruce and his group will be arriving at Cotsley tomorrow and I wanted some time alone with you first. Can you blame me, darling?"

"Yes, of course. I mean, no. Excellent notion." John mounted his horse. "Coral, I'm afraid the scouting expedition is off. But do tell Mrs. Emerson to continue putting your expenses in my name."

"But I have my own money."

"I won't hear of it. Oh, and I just had the most brilliant idea, if I do say so. You should come to the party tomorrow!"

Miss Walton paled in horror but said nothing.

"Oh, I really couldn't. I have nothing suitable to wear."

"Hm, yes. Well, that can't be helped. It's important for you to be seen, however. No good will come of you being shut up in a country inn. We'll have a fair number of people. Someone may know something. I'll have Edward here come pick you up around three o'clock. By then everyone will have arrived."

As Coral went back into the inn to safely store her little purse, she overheard Miss Walton shriek, "John! Have you gone mad? Bringing your little country trollop to our party?"

She couldn't hear his reply as she shut the door.

It didn't take long to make herself as presentable as possible the next day, given that she had exactly one dress to wear. She did manage to pin her chestnut tresses up into a becoming style that flattered her long neck. She was just putting in the final pin when Mrs. Emerson knocked on the door with something glowing bundled in her arms.

"Come in, Mrs. Emerson. What do you have there?"

Mrs. Emerson poured a river of emerald satin and frothy cream lace onto Coral's bed, and Coral gasped. "That's beautiful! Where did it come from?"

Mrs. Emerson was usually quite modest when complimented on her abilities as a seamstress, but with this dress she couldn't contain her pride. "It's me daughter's wedding dress. Only wore it the once and then off the happy couple went to a farm where a dress like this could only come to harm. Left it with me she did, for safekeeping."

"Oh, I can see why. It's breathtaking." Coral fingered the delicate lacework in amazement. "You did all of this yourself? You could be working at the palace. I'm so pleased you showed it to me."

"I'm doing more than showing it to you. I'm giving you the loan of it for the party."

"I couldn't! What if I ruined it somehow? It's so lovely. I might spill something on it or tear it."

"Cloth can be cleaned and mended." She looked severe. "I can't have a young lady under my care dressed inappropriately at Marsh Hall."

"But won't your daughter mind? It's her dress."

"She's a good girl. She'll be glad you have the use of it. Besides, after her three children she can't wear it anymore. It's too small for her now."

Coral stroked the satin in appreciation. "If you're absolutely certain."

"Let's see how it fits. After all my work I'll be happy to see it worn."

After the rough traveling clothes, the satin felt delicious against her skin. Mrs. Emerson chattered away happily as she got to work fastening a long row of buttons in the back. "My Mabel is smaller than you and the dress is going to be too short, but I can fix that. I have enough of the stuff left to attach to an underslip. It will look like a ruffle at the bottom. The fit is perfect at the waist. See? But tight through the bodice. She's smaller in the chest than ye are, or at least she was before all the nursing. I can only just fasten these buttons."

"Maybe it's too small. Maybe I shouldn't wear it. I wouldn't want to rip the bodice."

Right after she said that Coral was taken clear out of the moment. She was in a bodice ripper.

There was absolutely no stopping the short burst of laughter that erupted out of her.

"What's so funny?"

"Nothing, I was just testing to see if I can breathe and laugh without tearing anything. It seems to be fine."

Mrs. Emerson took her by the shoulders and turned her slowly around. "Lovely." Tears filled her eyes. "Ye remind me of my daughter on a happy day. Although there wasn't so much of her on display."

Mrs. Emerson gestured to Coral's bust, where two large mounds of bosom had been pushed up over the top of the tight bodice. "Oh, my! Is this even decent?" She strained to catch sight of this womanly marvel in her tiny mirror.

"The dress starts right where it has to: nothing indecent about it. But I daresay that even if the people at the party don't know where you came from, at the very least you'll find a husband."

When the butler took the cloak Mrs. Emerson had loaned her and ushered her into the drawing room, announcing her arrival, Coral's hopes of slipping in without a fuss were dashed. As she entered the room, all conversation immediately ceased and all heads turned. She blushed as she looked from face to face. There were several men she didn't recognize, and a few she did: Dr. Bruce and Mr. Carlson. Each wore a variation of the special face they showed to women they found attractive. The women included Mrs. Carlson and a few others she didn't recognize who were giving her mixed looks of greeting, wariness, and curiosity. Marie looked angry. John Marsh looked as though he might drop his drink.

An elderly gentleman came forward and extended his elbow to be grasped. "You must be the mystery girl. Come in, my dear, and allow us to get a good look at you. My son failed to warn us of your beauty. What a pleasant surprise it is. Perhaps one of us will be able to shed some light on your, er, predicament."

Because he had not bothered to introduce himself, Coral assumed he was John Marsh the elder, lord of the estate and father of the John Marsh she knew. He too had blue eyes, but was much smaller in stature.

"Thank you so much for allowing me to come."

"Not at all, not at all. Anything we can do to help."

Miss Walton trilled, "Yes, of course, the sooner we can get you back to your own people the better." Apparently realizing how petty she sounded, she added, "I should hate to not know where I came from. My family connections are very important to me." Even that sounded unkind, since her family connections were undoubtedly better than Coral's, known or unknown. John gave his betrothed a sideways glance.

Sir John the elder led her to Dr. Bruce. "This is Doctor Bruce, our family physician, who may be able to help you with your memory loss."

Dr. Bruce took her hand. "At the very least, you should be examined. Head wounds are not to be trifled with. I understand you were treated with rest alone and not seen by a competent physician."

"I would very much like it if you could help me recover my memory. It's really awful not being able remember anything about my family, or even where I'm from, or what I was doing on the High Road, or how I was injured. There may have been someone with me I should be concerned for, and I don't even know that."

A general sigh and tut-tutting went up from the assembled group. Mr. Carlson said, "I'm afraid I can't place your face. I wish I could help. Don't you remember anything at all?"

"Nothing. I woke up in the inn. That's my first memory. And my name is Coral."

Sir John continued introducing her around the room. Among the other guests were Miss Walton's mother, father, and older brothers. There was recognition on no face.

"I see no one knows her, then," said Miss Walton. "Anyone for cards?"

Mrs. Carlson said, "That's a lovely gown, my dear. Did you have that with you? Perhaps it's a clue. Not every seamstress does such lovely, fine work."

"Oh, no, the landlady at the inn let me borrow it so I would have something appropriate to wear when I came here. I was wearing traveling clothes when I was found. Those are all the clothes I have. They're very non-descript."

Mrs. Carlson reached a hand out to the lacy sleeve. "I had no idea landladies had such fine things."

Coral smiled. "She dresses herself like an ordinary country woman, but Mrs. Emerson is an excellent seamstress. She made this dress for her daughter's wedding several years ago. I think her talents are wasted running an inn. She should be working for the crown."

"Do you know who sews for the royal family?"

"Why, no."

"Ah, I thought I would try and trick your memory into revealing something."

"That was very clever. I wish it had worked."

Mrs. Carlson had been won over. "I do as well. Don't give up hope. We'll find your home."

"Thank you for your kindness."

Miss Walton's brothers, who were called George and Wilbur, were less than helpful. Wilbur said, "I daresay someone in our set knows her, and if they don't they wish they did."

George nudged his brother playfully. "I think let's not tell them. Rather keep her to ourselves, eh?"

Miss Walton's petulant voice could be heard from the other end of the room. "John, I want to play cards. Come with me."

"Not just yet, dear. Let's wait until the others are ready."

Coral said, "I'll play cards with you, Miss Walton. As you said, they either recognized me right off or they didn't. Perhaps something will come to someone when they've had time to think."

There was a short pause, and then Miss Walton replied, "Very good. Who else wishes to play? The card table has been set in the library." She strode out of the room.

"Isn't there tea? I believe we're having tea," said Sir John the elder. On cue, the butler returned and announced that tea had been laid in the dining room. Dr. Bruce escorted Coral in, and John dashed down the hall to corral the straying Miss Walton.

Coral intended to confine herself to drinking only the tea because of the tightness of her borrowed dress, but she was unable to resist one tiny cake with white icing and crystallized rose petals. The conversation continued to revolve around her unusual circumstances. One theory after another was put forth, but with no corroborating evidence the party remained at a loss. No one had heard of any family missing a daughter.

Miss Walton drank a cup of tea and nibbled her cake quietly. Her hair, which was blonde and curled becomingly, was evidently a source of pride for her, as she began to twirl some errant curls around her fingers while looking at John under her lashes. John, for his part, was either enjoying the tea or engaged in the speculative conversation and didn't notice. Eventually Miss Walton blurted out, "I rather doubt she's anyone in particular. I go to all the parties and I know everyone in London and Bath and I've never seen her."

Wilbur leaped to Coral's defense. "She needn't be from London. She could be from any number of places."

"I'm merely stating that ladies my age all come to London for the season, at least ones of our sort. If I've never met her, it stands to reason she isn't our sort."

Miss Walton's mother raised her eyebrows at that, but said nothing. It was apparent she had been letting her daughter speak her mind without censure or restraint for a long time.

Sir John said, "I believe my son is convinced she, well, he had evidence she isn't a scullery maid, eh?"

"It's her hands, Father. They've never seen hard work. They're clearly the hands of a lady. And you can see the marks where she'd been wearing rings. I see the marks have faded a bit now, but they were there yesterday. And her manner of speaking is hardly that of a laundress or a farmer."

"That's not evidence at all!" Miss Walton had become shrill. "Dance hall girls have soft hands. Women of ill repute may speak well."

"Marie!" John was aghast. "She's ... this is a guest in our home!"

Sir John the elder looked as though he had smelled something unpleasant and stood. "I believe I shall retire to my room for a short rest."

The rest of the company took their cue from their host and excused themselves from the table. Coral was at a complete loss as to what to do. Unlike the others, she had no room at Marsh Hall to which she could flee, and yet she was the one who most wanted to. Miss Walton's insinuations were painful and there was no way to repudiate anything. All she wanted to do was go back to her comfortable little inn in Cotsley to remove the tight dress.

She had perfectly good feet for walking and didn't need a carriage. She would simply leave John arguing with his jealous betrothed, walk out the door, and be on her way. No one knew her. There was no reason to remain.

On the way back to the inn there was supposed to be a mill, with a large pond with ducks. She'd seen it from the carriage on the ride to the manor house: a stone building with a wooden house attached, dark brown, with white curtains in the windows. Some children playing with a medium-sized dog. She could see all of these things in her mind's eye, but no amount of visualizing could conjure their actual appearance. The manor was miles behind her. There was only one explanation: She'd taken the wrong road and was now lost.

She would have cut across the fields and picked up the right road had she any idea in which direction it lay, and if she hadn't been wearing Mabel's satin dress. Being lost is a dreadful feeling, especially when a person is so lost she can't even hazard a guess about which direction will take her nearer to her goal. The village could be anywhere except where she was. The only thing she knew for certain was that Marsh Hall remained back along the road on which she had walked, miles away. If she walked all the way back, she would suffer the disgrace of arriving tired and disheveled and looking ungrateful for the help they'd offered.

With no houses about, though, there was nothing else to be done but head back. Perhaps she could slip into the stable at the manor house and borrow a horse unannounced. Granted, that was a euphemism for "stealing a horse." No doubt Miss Walton would not be so tactful when she heard about it. She would thrill at the chance of calling Coral a dance hall prostitute *and* horse thief.

Though in July the days were long, even summer days draw to a close, and it would be dark soon. Her feet throbbed at the thought of the long walk back, but that would be far less risky than pressing on alone off the road in the chill and darkness, especially knowing she had taken the wrong road once and wasn't clear in her mind which road would be correct. A brief rest would do her good. She looked about for a place to sit that wouldn't stain her lovely gown, finally seeing a group of stones that had apparently been of some significance in days gone by, but was now merely a pile of stones.

As she sat upon the rocks, she heard scurrying in the leaves at her feet and looked down in time to see a flash of gray dart under her skirts. With a shriek she jumped up. A mouse was trying to take refuge in her clothing. Or perhaps it was trying to get back into its home under the stones. She was probably sitting on top of a whole nest of mice hidden in the rocks.

Unable to rest and forced to tread on, Coral wept. She was lost and frightened. She didn't know where her home was, nor even who she was. The man who had been so kind was promised to another woman, a horrible one at that. There was little hope for relief from her current troubles and no hope for happiness in the future. And come to think of it, she was dreadfully hungry. She really should have eaten more than that one pretty little cake with rose petals.

If she had been in her real life she would have had soggy tissues piling up next to her, but within the interesting parameters of this genre, she cried prettily with no puffy red eyes and no swollen nose.

The distant sound of horse hooves brought her heart into her throat. Who could that be? Would they see her? Indeed, if anyone came down this road they couldn't fail to see her, with her brilliant emerald gown catching the last of the afternoon light. Perhaps it would be a farmer who could tell her the way to the village, or better yet, give her a ride. On the other hand, it could be whoever had hit her over the head and left her for dead on the High Road. She scrabbled furiously for a way to protect herself. There were a few fist-sized rocks along the edge of the road. She picked one up and clutched it.

The horse proved to be pulling a trap driven by Sir John Marsh, whose worried face turned to relief and back to concern at the sight of her distress. "Are you hurt?"

"No, just tired and lost."

"You most certainly are lost. I've been hunting all over the county for you. Let me help you in. We'll get you back to the house." He jumped down from the seat to attempt to help her in.

Resisting, she said, "No! I don't want to go back. Just take me to the inn."

"I feel absolutely terrible about Marie, terrible in every sort of way. How can I begin to apologize for her behavior?"

Coral's eyes were full of sincerity as she replied, "You owe me no apology nor any other thing. You've been nothing but kind to me, a stranger. I don't wish to disrupt your happiness with Miss Walton. Just take me to the inn. I can pay my own way, at least for a time. If I never remember who I am, perhaps I can ask Mrs. Emerson to teach me to sew. She's truly gifted and so good to me that I'm sure she'd do it. And then I can make my own way in the world."

John searched her face, seeming to memorize every detail of her. Her chestnut hair, now tumbling down from its pins, her tearful eyes, the pink glow on her cheeks from the long walk, her delicate white throat that led down to firm, ample breasts. His eyes finally rested on her soft, pillowy lips. His voice was quiet. "You're so brave— a young woman to be admired. How can anyone doubt that you're a lady? You deserve to be treasured. Would that I ... "

He turned away and kicked at a stone in the road. "I came to a decision today, one that has been a long time coming. It's very painful to admit that I've made a terrible mistake, but that is the case. I haven't spoken to my father, but he'll be in complete agreement. He can't abide Marie."

John waved his arm across the fields. "My family is responsible for these people. They work the land and we take care of them, employ them, and look after them when trouble strikes. It's been that way for centuries. It wouldn't do for the blacksmiths to stop smithing or the farmers to stop farming, nor would it do for my family to think only of ourselves. It's a good system really, but it only works when each of us plays the part we are given."

Coral had another out-of-book experience. She wondered if the farmers and blacksmiths thought it was as good a system as he did. If everyone were to suddenly take a giant step to the left and the lords became footmen and the footmen became blacksmiths and the blacksmiths became farmers and the farmers moved into the manor, would John Marsh still think the system was so good? Certainly the farmers would think so. It would be a long time before that happened, and when it did it wouldn't be pretty. In the meantime, though, she had a romance to live.

The young lord continued, "You wouldn't know it from today's performance, but Marie is very accomplished. Her sparkling conversation attracted me to her. I confess I sometimes find country life somewhat dull, and thought she would liven things up. What I hadn't realized when I proposed is the lack of depth she possesses when it comes to any subject that doesn't revolve around her or her interests. I noticed this only after we announced our engagement. It would have been better if I had noticed it before.

"The way she tore into you was unconscionable. We had before us an opportunity to help someone in distress, but the only thought in her mind was the undeniable fact that you are more beautiful than she."

Coral cast down her eyes.

"Our life in the country isn't taken up with fashionable parties and conversation. Much of it consists of plain, simple activities that don't interest her. And the worst of it is, as Lady Marie of Marsh Hall, she would be expected to involve herself in the parish, plan festivals and gatherings for the neighbors and tenants, and sometimes assist people in our employ. My mother was brilliant at this sort of thing and everyone loved her. The contrast between my mother and Marie is ... well, as I said, Father can't abide her. Mother's nanny lives in a cottage on the estate at our expense. It wouldn't do to put her out in the streets, but I can't imagine Marie ever caring about a servant in any way other than how well they're serving her."

He paused.

"What I am trying to say is that I've decided not to marry Marie.

"You're not a man to go against your word, John Marsh. I may have only known you a brief time, but this much I do know."

"You are right, but I do not think she would be happy to live as my wife. The trick of it will be to make Marie think she's the one throwing me over. It really shouldn't be that difficult. Once I caught on to the way her mind works, I realized it's very easy to manipulate her. That sounds awful, doesn't it?"

Coral laughed. "I don't think anything you do is awful. I think ... "

She was unable to finish that thought. John had put his hands tenderly on her shoulders, no longer the lord, but a man who was desperately attracted to a woman in an emerald gown. His eyes lingered on the cleavage that seemed to deepen in the waning light, then moved to her lips. She parted them and smiled slightly. It was all the invitation he needed. His lips were warm and the kiss soft at first, then urgent, as he drew her into his arms, his breath quickening. Eventually he pulled away.

"I'm afraid you'll think I'm taking advantage of you, a lady in distress. I'm so sorry. I'll stop."

Coral pulled him closer. "Don't stop." Her arms caressed his back and broad shoulders as she gazed up into his eyes, the blue of them now dark as the night sky.

"I've never felt this way about any woman. It's the oddest thing. It's as though I've known you all my life, even though not even you know who you are. It's like I was waiting for you."

"You should have waited a bit longer," said Coral, thinking of his engagement to Miss Walton.

"That I should have. I'll regret that for a long time."

"No regrets. Kiss me again."

He pressed his lips against hers, moist and hot, passionately seeking to learn her taste and her smell.

That was when she felt it pressing against her hip: his turgid manhood.

Right out of the moment she went. It was a turgid manhood. It wasn't any of the other names found in various genres: it was a turgid manhood. These were code words for what kind of romance novel she was in, since turgid manhoods only show up in one kind. Coral tried to remember exactly which book she'd put in the bag, but all she could recall was picking a pink one with a picture of a man in period costume and longish hair clutching a woman, also in period costume, with a tremendous amount of hair blowing in the wind, both with serious expressions on their faces.

But covers aside, romance novels vary a great deal in just how far they take sexuality. There are the ones mothers can read with their 12-year-old daughters and the ones mothers hide even from their husbands. On one end of the scale are sweet tales of new love and on the other are raunchy erotica, with everything possible in between, and supernatural ones in their own category. This turgid manhood placed Coral's romance with John around the conservative center of the genre. She wasn't entirely sure how she knew it was a turgid manhood, as opposed to one of the other names it could be called, but she did.

One of the many things Coral had learned from her book adventures was to stay true to the genre, so it wouldn't do any good to try to venture far from the turgid-manhood zone.

She tore herself from his arms and said, "We should stop. You need to break the engagement with Miss Walton."

"Returning so soon? How was the party?" Mrs. Emerson's kind face puckered in dismay. "No one knew you, then?"

"I'm afraid not. But I believe Dr. Bruce will be coming by tomorrow to see if he can help me regain my memory."

"That's something. I'm sure they all thought you were pretty as a picture."

"Your dress was very well received. I wouldn't be surprised if Mrs. Carlson had you make something for her. She was quite taken with it."

"I see the bodice didn't rip."

It easily could have on the road, Coral thought, if I hadn't put a stop to things. "No, it was sturdy and reliable. A marvel of construction."

"I don't know why you were so concerned. It wouldn't have been the first time that bodice ripped. I had to repair it the day after the wedding." Mrs. Emerson giggled. "Were there young men to fawn over you?"

"There was a bit of fawning, yes, but nothing will come of it. Brothers of Miss Walton. They seemed to be nice enough at first meeting." Coral knew it was prudent to keep her affairs with the young lord private until he'd had time to resolve his domestic problems quietly. "We went for a long walk, and now I'm more tired than I can say. I think I'll go lie down for a bit. Thank you again for the loan of the dress. It's so very beautiful."

Sinking gratefully into the downy bed, Coral pondered the future. If everything continued in the direction it was headed now, there would be a wedding and she would be Lady Coral of Marsh Hall. That sounded very good.

This was not a book she wanted to jump out of prematurely. Sitting downstairs, amidst a small eclectic assortment of books kept for Violet Emerson's traveling guests who found themselves at loose ends, was her escape. She could leave any time she chose, but not yet. There were still plot holes to fill. Who was she? Would Marie Walton break the engagement?

Hoof beats in the street were followed by the welcome sight of John Marsh striding purposefully into the Lion and Lamb. It had been a fortnight since she'd seen him and it was all Coral could do to keep from flinging herself into his arms. His face was nearly bursting with contained smiles.

"I've come to collect you for a picnic. The others are meeting us, so we must hurry."

"A picnic? What others? Will it be the same people I met at the party?"

"No, they've all gone. This will be a different group altogether."

Coral glanced down at her traveling clothes in dismay. "But I haven't anything to wear."

"You look perfectly fine. It's a picnic, not a ball. No one will care what you're wearing. You needn't bring a thing."

Coral was confused as John's trap approached the Windle River, where a blanket was spread but no one was about. "Will they be joining us later? Perhaps they wandered off."

John helped her down from the trap. "Oh, no. They're all here. Allow me to introduce you to Sir Blanket, Admiral Bread, Lady Fromage du France, the Grape family, and the Reverend Chablis. Ladies and gentlemen, this is Miss Coral of Nothingthrall."

"Nothingthrall?"

"I made that up. Nothing because we know nothing about you, and thrall because I'm completely enthralled by you."

"Ah. For a moment I thought you'd learned something. You didn't tell me the names of all the Grape family. I'm afraid their feelings will be hurt."

The bottle of wine had been secreted in a stone niche in the river to chill. John began filling two crystal glasses. "Will you be able to eat them if you know them by name?"

"You've made an excellent point."

"Be seated, my lady. There's business to discuss."

"Business?"

"First is the business about the color of your eyes in the light. They were green when you were indoors and now they are nearly aqua. How do you do that?"

"I suppose it's a reflection from the sky and the river. What other business is there?" Coral took a sip of wine, hoping he would get to the point.

"There's also the business about the color of your hair."

"The color of my hair? It's a perfectly ordinary brown."

"Ordinary? That it is not. From a distance a person may think it's ordinary, if he were unobservant. But there is some magic afoot that I confess even I didn't notice at first. On closer examination your hair is made of many different colors. There are brown strands, but also black strands, blonde strands, red strands, and some that gleam with rainbow iridescence in sunlight."

As he spoke Coral watched his lips with their playful upturn. When would she be able to kiss those lips again? "I have nothing to say about my hair. This discussion is dreadfully one-sided. Haven't you any other business to discuss? Anything involving Miss Walton?"

After taking a deep draught of wine, John spread cheese on a piece of bread and handed it to Coral, then took some for himself. "Nothing is exactly resolved. However, Marie has left in a snit."

"A snit? Is that some sort of conveyance? Perhaps larger than a trap and smaller than a carriage?"

"If you keep saying things like that I shall have to kiss you. Eat your cheese. As you know, Marie was jealous of you and immediately started a row when I returned after leaving you at the inn. I didn't speak of you, but instead took the opportunity to tell her she was not demonstrating the necessary temperament to be Lady Marie of Marsh Hall. You can well imagine how she took that. The next morning she delivered ultimatums. Ultimatums I do not intend to take. As she and her family packed to leave, several days early, I should add, I took the opportunity to elucidate the requirements of the position of Cotsley's lady to her further, to flesh it out in such a way that it would appear to be completely unlike anything she would ever wish to do, which it is. Truly I think it isn't something she would enjoy and she'd be happier with a London man."

"I take it you're in a sort of chess game and it's her turn to move."

"It *is* her turn. She'll do something cruel. She'll tell all of her friends some dreadful untruths about me and make it difficult for me with a certain group of people I care little about. I'm not afraid of Marie. I'll just be glad to be rid of her." He poured more wine into Coral's glass and his own. "There is something I'm much more afraid of." His sad eyes showed the sincerity of his statement.

"What is it, John?"

"I'm afraid of how much I love you. It's utter madness. I know nothing about you, your background, your family." Coral's eyes welled with tears. "Now I've made you sad and I'm sorry. It's a dreadful problem, though, isn't it?"

"Nobody knows that more than I do."

"I don't think you understand. As much as I love you, I cannot marry someone with no background. What if you're promised to another man? Or worse yet, already married? You'd been wearing rings when you were found."

Coral had no answer. This was indeed a horrifying possibility.

"Even if I were the sort of man who cared little for the rights of another man, which I am not, my father would never approve. He would cut me off completely. Then if I were to throw it all away, the title, the land, the people, everything that's been my birthright and all I've ever known and expected, and run off with you to live solely on our love, what would become of our children? They'd be brought up in poverty. It would be cruel of us." He dashed the last of his wine on the ground and caught her up. "Coral, you must remember! Remember who you are, oh my darling!"

The closeness and the emotion of his grasp were too much for both of them. Without conscious thought, their lips came together and they tumbled back onto the blanket. Coral's hand slipped down his back, past his waist, and beyond. His fingers gently stroked her neck and down her chest until his palm rested on her firm breast. Aflame, Coral cried, "John, John, stop! I can't bear it! We must stop now or we never will."

Exhaling gustily, John rolled to his back and threw his arm over his face. With a sob Coral stood and ran into the woods, only stopping when she realized that, blinded by tears, she was in danger of falling. She must remember her past! Her future depended upon it. What horrible force had been pressed upon her to make her lose all recollection of everything that had gone before? Her mother, her father, her childhood home—of all these things there was nothing. And now this man with whom she was deeply in love was prevented by his honor and his sense of duty, two of the very things she found most appealing about him, from taking that final consummating step of marriage. He was not to blame. It was she who held their future in her hands. There must be a way to regain her memory. There must!

Not far from where she stood there appeared to be a bundle of rags on the forest floor. Curiosity drew her closer.

Fate was most cruel, as inspection allowed her to make the horrifying discovery of the body of a young boy, dead.

Isaac.

Jet.

The body was that of Isaac, but seeing him lying dead in the forest, positioned exactly like that with a rope around his neck, brought back the memory of the worst day of Coral's real life, and what she saw the day Jet was killed.

She must have screamed because John ran to her. "What is it? Oh, the poor lad. Do you know him?"

"It's Isaac and it's just like Jet. My brother! My brother!"

"He's your brother? Come away. He's beyond our help. Come sit down, you've had a terrible shock. What else do you remember?"

"I don't know. It's all so confusing. I don't understand about the book and how it works. Why did it show me this?"

"Did you say how the book works? Perhaps some cold water on your face. Let me just dampen my handkerchief. There, is that better? So his name is Isaac? Who is Jet?"

"My brother."

"Then who is Isaac?"

"A little orphan boy, I think."

"So you say it's just like Jet to do such a thing? Is that it?"

"No! You don't understand. I don't expect you could. The boy is Isaac and the way he died is just the same as how my brother Jet died, only something is missing. The dragon. Where is it?"

A tender look of pity crossed John's face. "Let's get you back to the inn to lie down and rest."

"Yes, the inn. Please! I must get back."

She couldn't think about romance anymore. The bag, the patterns, the purpose for doing all of this: she had almost forgotten she was supposed to be seeking clarity. Now that she understood that the orphan boy Isaac, the boy who was always in danger and needing her help, was her brother Jet, she needed to think things through clearly. She couldn't do it within a book. She needed to get back to her real life.

The way home was on a shelf at the inn.

John Marsh was helping her into the trap with tenderness that bordered on reverence. His blonde hair gleamed in the summer sunlight, and his eyes shone with love for her. After he handed her up, she held onto his large hand.

Would he ever look so appealing in any other book? Or more to the point, would any real man ever love her like this? Would anybody's kisses ever thrill her beyond reason like his did?

"John, wait. Kiss me again. One last time."

"Gladly, my dear, if you think we both can bear it. But I hope this will not be the last kiss, but merely the last kiss for a short while and that there will be a lifetime of kisses ahead of us." He took his time, brushing his lips tenderly against hers while drinking her in with his eyes, and then more firmly as his passion grew. "Kisses and more."

Her passion rose to meet his, engulfing them both almost entirely, *leaving only one phrase to prevent her from losing herself completely.*

The phrase was turgid manhood. She had to get out of the turgid-manhood zone right now. "John, stop. Take me to the inn. We can't do this."

"You're right. You're so hard to resist."

The inn, the shelf, one last look at her would-be lover, and then she grasped the book and she was home.

22 NO FORWARD MOMENTUM

What had seemed clear in the romance novel didn't seem so cut and dried in her own apartment. If Isaac was Jet, who were all the other people? She had never known anyone like John Marsh, although she wished she did. Who were Violet Emerson, Dr. Bruce, and the Carlsons? Where were the other real-life people important to her, like her father and Pearl?

Up to that point she had not remembered what Jet had looked like lying dead with a rope around his neck. Now she knew that she had actually seen him like that when she was a little girl, and even as an adult the thought left her feeling ripped to shreds and powerless. Perhaps her childish mind had simply decided that it didn't like what it saw and it wasn't going to retain it. But what made her forget everything else from before? Most people remember lots of things from early childhood, but she didn't. There had to be something else. Something more. Something worse. Did she really want to regain whatever memories she had repressed?

The Coral of this romance novel adventure was being prevented from moving forward in life, getting married, and living happily ever after, because she couldn't remember the past.

It was true though. She had to admit it to herself: she wasn't moving forward with her life. She wasn't really free. If Pearl and James moved away she would be forced to make changes, but it was unthinkable.

Like it or not, she needed to remember those lost years. There was only one person to ask for help.

23 THE OLD NEIGHBORHOOD

The sweatshirt she was wearing was in no danger of being torn open by her normal-sized breasts and her eyes remained brown and behind glasses. But her hair was now a rich shade of chestnut, or "Cinnamon," as the box in her bathroom trash said.

"Has James come home yet?" There was a sound of exasperation on the other end of the line. "I'll take that as a 'no.' Or did that mean he came home and was so annoying you want to send him away again?"

"He has to stay in Europe another week. Oh well, I'm fine. I'm used to it. I have plenty of work to keep me busy."

"Don't be too busy because I want to talk to you."

"Oh yeah?"

"You want to come over here again?"

"Why don't you come to my house this time? What's this about?"

"I'm sick of not remembering anything from before I was 6. I want you to help me remember. You're the only one who was there."

There was silence on the other end of the line. Then: "If we want to do this properly, we should go back to the old house."

Nobody had answered the bell. Probably at work. The sisters stood at the foot of the driveway, feeling awkward. If they'd been dressed better they would have looked like a pair of Jehovah's Witnesses. "I wonder how many of our old neighbors still live here."

"No idea."

"I hope nobody calls the cops."

"If they do we'll just tell the truth." That would be a peculiar conversation: We're trying to remember forgotten things.

Pearl cast an appraising eye on her old home. "They changed the color. It was gray when we lived there. Not sure I like this color, sort of Army green. The trees have grown. There used to be a hydrangea there. Why would someone take out a hydrangea? Hydrangeas never hurt anybody. And jeesh, they ought to give mandatory pruning classes every time they sell someone pruning stuff. You can actually damage the trees by pruning them that badly. Dad would have been appalled. He was very good with landscaping. I do like the flowers in the pots by the door though, that's a nice touch. Good curb appeal. So, recognize anything?"

"Of course I do. We lived here for three years after Jet was killed. I need stuff that's going to prompt memories from before."

"Okay, I was thinking. This cul-de-sac makes a nice circle, right? When you were about 4 you used to run around and around it like a track star. Why don't you run around and see if anything comes back?"

"Why don't *you* run around the cul-de-sac? I'm not going to do that, I'd look like an idiot."

"If anybody comes out we'll just tell them the truth, remember?"

The sisters looked at each other and laughed.

"Okay," said Pearl. "But nobody is going to come out, and if they do, maybe we'll know them and it will be a big reunion. Go on. On your mark, get set... "

"Fine." Coral began to run clockwise around the circle until Pearl protested. She needed to run the other way. Apparently that was the way she used to go.

Lap one, nothing. Lap two, nothing. During lap three, fragments of memories popped into her head. Right after the mailbox there was supposed to be a bush that stuck out and it wasn't there. Then came the house with the barking dog, only there was no barking dog. Pulling up, Coral asked, "Did there used to be a bush there, and did that house used to have a barking dog?"

"Misty, yes. Hated that stupid dog. I can't remember about the bush. I'm not sure if those memories are from before or after, though."

"Okay. So that was a waste of time."

"I'm helping you. Stop complaining. See the front steps on our house? You jumped off them one time and skinned your knee really badly when you were little. Remember that?"

"Nope."

"Hmm, okay. Let's walk around to the park. At least we won't feel so conspicuous there."

"I hate the park." The place where their brother was murdered could never be a comfortable place to visit.

"Me too."

What they called the park was really an unbuildable ravine full of native Douglas fir trees and prickly mahonia bushes that ran along the edge of their neighborhood, ostensibly giving the development the name Crystal Woods, although what was crystal about the woods was unclear. Crystal was probably the name of the developer's daughter. All it really meant in practice was that a small brick wall announced the entrance to the street with "Crystal Woods" spelled out in tarnished brass.

The parks district had not bought the land and no one maintained it. It was just part of the watershed, but it did give the houses along their side of the street a nice view of greenery instead of more suburban houses. At the end of the cul-de-sac, between the last two houses, was a little path leading into the ravine. Neighborhood children apparently still used the area as their private world away from adult eyes. Pearl and Coral could see the detritus of youth scattered around the area: candy wrappers, the homework page that would later be reported to the teacher as lost, a small plastic catapult from someone's castle set.

"After Jet was killed, the neighbors came through here and cut out most of the bushes so it wasn't so dense and nobody could hide in the woods. They thought some homeless guy had been camping here or something," Pearl recalled. "Looks like a lot of them have grown back."

"I guess people forget. Time passes, people move out, new people move in, and hardly anybody remembers the little boy who was murdered."

Pearl struck off through the trees to the base of the ravine. In wet weather it was a flowing creek, and in dry it made a nice silted path. There were lots of footprints in the soil here, a busy place. Soon Pearl pointed up the hill. "The back of our house is right about there. I never actually saw where they found him, you know. But I have a pretty good idea where he was. I think it was a little further along."

Coral followed silently as her sister continued along the bottom of the ravine.

"I snuck away one time a few days later when nobody was paying attention and came down here. They'd already taken him away. The police were gone. But there was crime-scene tape all around this area over here." She stopped and looked around, remembering. "See that sort of gully where the water comes down from the other side? I think he was in there. I think the killer hid him in there."

"No, that's not right, he was here." Coral pointed to a grassy place, exposed and flat like a tabletop. "He was there, with a rope around his neck."

Pearl's head whipped around in astonishment. "What else? What else do you remember?"

"I wasn't alone then, I was showing him to someone else. To Dad."

"Go on."

"He looked like a bundle of rags." After a long silence Coral shrugged. "That's it."

"That's something, though! At least you remember something, even if it's that. I'm sorry, sis, that's a horrible image to have in your mind."

Coral rubbed her eyes. "If I can only remember one thing from the whole first five years of my life, why does it have to be that?"

"Maybe more will come back to you now that you remembered even one thing. I'm going to choose to think of it as a little crack in the armor. What I don't get is this: you remember showing his body to Dad. So you knew where Jet was first, before anybody else. How did that happen? Did you see something? Did you find his body, or did you even see it happen? Maybe you saw it happen and it traumatized you so much you lost your memory."

Coral shrugged. "I don't know. I just don't know. I have that one image: Jet on the ground with the rope and Dad is with me because I brought him there. He made a noise, Dad did. A noise I never heard him make before."

"That's horrible. You were just a little kid."

Coral shrugged again. There was nothing to do or say.

24 AN EXPERIMENT

Tired, but feeling somewhat reckless that evening, Coral did something different from what Phil had suggested. There was an old birthday card from her sister on a shelf. She wondered if the bag would work on writing that wasn't a novel at all. Snatching it up, she thrust it into the bag.

25 HOW THOUGHTFUL

It was a lovely room, with sunlight streaming in the window and illuminating a table with a vase full of flowers in colors not found in nature. Shiny blobs like glass droplets stuck to the petals. There was what appeared to be tea in an old-fashioned china cup and saucer on the table, but when she picked up the cup, what had appeared to be liquid was actually a solid.

The flowers spoke in a purring, feminine voice.

With Deepest Sympathy. May you find comfort and solace in this time of lost memory.

26 IT'S NOT ABOUT THE BOOKS

With a jolt she was back in her apartment. The bag had kicked her out on its own. It did work on other kinds of written material, and she had also learned something else. Apparently it was possible to come to the natural end of a piece of writing and leave that way. She'd been wondering about that but had always bailed out before the end.

Even more importantly, however, a greeting card only has one point to make, be it happy birthday, congratulations, or get well soon. Greeting cards don't make several points and they aren't confusing or symbolic. This one was sorry she had lost her memory.

"Okay, bag," she said out loud, very aware that she was talking to an inanimate object. "I get one thing. You've convinced me that my memory loss is very important." She *wanted* her memory back, her memory of her very own life. What written material could she put in the bag that would help with that?

She needed to find something that took her back to her own childhood.

Then she had an idea. She'd been a reader since she was five and still owned many of those early books. Which ones would be good for solving a mystery?

There was a certain mystery series she still kept on her shelves. She had a dozen books in nearly identical jackets to choose from, each numbered, but not sequentially, as she owned only a fraction of the available series. She picked one at random.

27 THE MYSTERY OF CRYSTAL WOODS

Coral Ambrose pulled into the driveway in her powder-blue convertible and saw her best friend, Violet Emerson, and her boyfriend, John Marsh, waiting for her on the front porch. "Oh, no!" she cried in dismay. "I'm sorry I'm late. I hope I didn't keep you waiting long."

"Not at all," said John, happy to see her.

"Besides, you aren't late. We got here early. Just couldn't wait to see you, I guess," said her plump friend cheerfully.

"Come in out of the hot sun and let me fix us all some lemonade," said Coral warmly.

John thirstily replied, "Sounds good to me."

Mr. Ambrose was sitting in his easy chair reading the newspaper and smoking his pipe when the trio entered.

"Hi, Dad!" said Coral as she gave him a peck on the cheek. "Would you like some lemonade? I'm making some for all of us."

"Welcome home, and yes I would, thank you," he replied gratefully. Then his smile of welcome turned to a frown. "I was just reading something very sad in the newspaper. Do you remember the little boy who was killed a couple of years ago in the woods near here? They've written a follow-up story about how the police never did find out who his killer was."

"Oh, that's awful," said Violet sadly.

"I wish there was something we could do to help," offered John. "Coral... ?"

"Maybe there is!" she cried excitedly. "Even if the police couldn't find the killer, it may take someone else snooping around to find some clues they missed. Game for some sleuthing, chums?"

John smiled at her proudly.

"You bet we are!" enthused Violet.

"I knew I could count on you two. Now before I go make that lemonade, there's something I need to do." Coral walked over to the bookcase in the tidy living room, gave it a quick inspection, and reached in to remove a book.

28 TOO OLD

Back in her own apartment, simple as pie.

She hadn't gone back far enough. She'd been reading those after, well, after she learned to read, and that wasn't until after Jet was killed. By then her memory was already lost. She needed to find the kind of book that had been read to her when she was really little. She didn't have many of that kind of book because they hadn't just been her books; they had belonged to all the Ambrose children and Pearl had half of them at her house. But there were a few to choose from. Coral picked one.

29 THE PLAYFUL PUPPY

One day the Playful Puppy wanted someone to play with.

"Will you play with me please?" she said to the Curious Cat.

"I'm much too busy watching the mouse," said the Curious Cat. "Go find someone else."

"Will you play with me please?" she said to the Scampering Squirrel.

"I'm much too busy finding nuts for the winter," said the Scampering Squirrel. "Go find someone else."

"Will you play with me please?" she said to the Beautiful Bird.

"I'm much too busy listening for worms. Go play with your brother. He's in the woods. I saw him when I was flying."

The Playful Puppy was not allowed to go into the woods. She ran to the edge of the woods and called his name. "Perky Puppy! Will you play with me please?" But he did not answer.

Perhaps he didn't hear me, she thought. She called louder. "Perky Puppy! Will you play with me please?" But he still didn't answer.

She called as loud as she could: "PERKY PUPPY! WILL YOU PLAY WITH ME PLEASE?" When he still didn't answer she became very cross.

She put one paw into the woods and nothing bad happened. She put another paw into the woods and nothing bad happened. She put another paw into the woods and nothing bad happened. Then she had all four paws and her whole self in the woods and nothing bad happened.

So she ran, ran, ran into the woods and
down
down
down a hill.

And there was her brother with a leash around his neck!

"Help me, Playful Puppy! I'm trapped here! Get this leash off of my neck!"

So the Playful Puppy used her sharp little teeth and chewed and chewed until the leash came off.

Then Playful and Perky Puppies ran
up
up
up
and all the way home.

"Hooray for Playful Puppy!" said Curious Cat, Scampering Squirrel, and Beautiful Bird.

"Hooray for Playful Puppy!" said Perky Puppy. "You are my Best Friend!"

30 TOO YOUNG

When the story came to its natural end, Coral the playful puppy was back in her apartment. It had been moderately fun to be a playful puppy, although somewhat tedious with all the repetition, but she hadn't learned anything. She had not really rescued Jet from the rope around his neck. That was nothing more than wishful thinking.

She had tried a children's book that was too old and one that was too young, and like Goldilocks, now she wanted one that would be just right. She had books of fairytales aimed for many different ages, from the cleaned-up versions for little kids, to some that had been distorted into cartoons and turned back into books as merchandising tie-ins, and all the way to the intense original stories that were so dark you wondered why anybody ever thought they were children's stories in the first place. She selected a very old book that seemed like it could be age-appropriate for a 5-year-old, made a wish, and slipped the book into the bag.

31 CORAL HOODIE

Coral Hoodie lived in a house made of books at the edge of the deep, dark woods. One day a mockingbird sat on her windowsill and sang a song that sounded just like the cries of a small child. It was a terrible sound to hear. It was soon joined by another mockingbird, who sang:

> *Please help me, I beg you!*
> *Please help me, I beg you!*

Knowing mockingbirds only sing what they hear, Coral Hoodie put on her hoodie and rushed off into the deep, dark woods to hunt for the small child. As she went she called:

> *Little child, little child, where do you hide?*

After she had been hunting for many hours, she became hungry and tired and sat down on a log to rest. When she did she heard again the crying of a child:

> *Please help me, I beg you!*
> *Please help me, I beg you!*

Very frightened for the crying child, she put aside her hunger and got up again to resume her search, this time calling:

> *Little child, little child, where do you hide?*
> *I hunt and hunt for you far and wide.*

Suddenly there was a tremendous rush of wind and the earth shook as a fearsome dragon landed on the forest floor in front of her. Coral Hoodie shrank back in terror. The dragon roared a terrifying roar and said:

> *Go back to your house. Your search is in vain.*
> *I've killed before and I'll do it again.*

Coral Hoodie ran back to her house of books as fast as her legs would carry her. When she got home she closed all the books around herself and vowed never to go back to the woods again.

But all the next day she was tormented by the mockingbirds and their piteous cries. She knew there must be a child in the woods in horrible distress.

So Coral Hoodie put on her hoodie and went back into the deep, dark woods to search for the little child once more. As she searched she called out:

> *Little child, little child, where do you hide?*
> *I hunt and hunt for you far and wide.*

Only this time more quietly, hoping the dragon wouldn't notice her. He must have had very good hearing though as once more he landed in front of her with a great rush of wings and an earth-shaking thud and said:

> *Go back to your house. Your search is in vain.*
> *I've killed before and I'll do it again.*

So Coral Hoodie once again ran home as fast as her legs would carry her and closed herself in her house of books and cried.

The next day Coral Hoodie put on a different hoodie, a green one like the forest, and green pants, and pinned leaves all over herself so that she looked like a bush, and went back into the deep, dark woods. This time she did not call out anything at all, but only walked on her tiptoes and listened.

After she had been walking for a long time, she heard the sound of the child crying in the distance. Following the sound she came upon a little cage standing in a lonely clearing. Inside was a small girl wearing a hoodie the color of coral. The child said:

Please help me, I beg you! You must find the key!
When the dragon comes back I'm afraid he'll eat me!

Just then there was a rush of wings and the earth shook as the dragon landed in the clearing. He roared his most terrifying roar, uprooted many trees, and said:

Ignore her cage and ignore her cries.
The girl is mine until she dies.
With tooth like sword and claw like knife
I will keep that girl and take your life.
It's time for you to run in fear.
You made a mistake by coming here.

There was nothing left to do but run, so Coral Hoodie ran home to her house of books as fast as her legs would carry her.

She spent all the next day and the day after that thinking what she could do. The little child who looked just like her would be stuck in the cage at the mercy of the dragon until she could find the key, and she didn't know where to begin looking for it. The deep, dark woods were very big.

On the third day, Coral Hoodie put on her green hoodie and put more leaves all over herself and went back into the woods in search of the key. She searched and searched and did not find it. She searched the next day and the next, and the day after that. She searched for days and days, then weeks and weeks.

Sometimes she snuck to the clearing to tell the little girl not to lose hope because she was still looking.

But the seasons changed and changed again and then years passed.

Coral Hoodie grew older and older.

The little girl, however, remained a little girl of exactly the same age the whole time.

When Coral Hoodie was a very old woman and her hood covered white hair and her footsteps on the forest floor were unsteady, she realized that her life would soon be done, her house of books would soon be a coffin of books, and she would never get the little girl—for a little girl she remained—out of the dragon's cage.

So Coral Hoodie reached for one very special book on her wall and touched it.

32 JUST RIGHT

Coral shuddered. What a horrible story! She would never go into a fairytale again. They were not all princesses and fairy godmothers. At least no one was actually eaten in this one.

She felt like curling up in a ball and crying. It wasn't the fairytale's characteristics that upset her, though: It was the futility. She had been trying to rescue her little-girl self and never did. It was too hard. She couldn't do it. She wanted to stomp around and throw things. It wasn't fair. It wasn't fair!

And there she was, the little girl Coral, crying about fairness. That kid lived in her still. It seemed that little Coral wanted to be found.

She had to keep looking.

There had to be a different genre that could reach her. Her bookshelves were so full of every kind of book. Lots of them had nothing to do with children, but she had read a number of books where the author seemed to remember what it felt like to be a child. Perhaps that would be better: to have an adult telling about childhood.

33 A PINK SUIT AND RED DUST

The boy was the first to see a plume of red dust come toward their place, and he hollered to his sisters to come and see. The littlest sister came right out of the house.

Her age seemed just about right, with hair cut in a short bob. This could work.

She'd made a jail for the cat out of an overturned laundry basket and he'd finally gotten upset and left. She was looking for a new diversion. Then the older sister came out of the screen door, which banged behind her, jingling the hook, and lowered her eyebrows at the trees that stood like a jagged wall in front of the ridge where the road was. They couldn't see what was coming yet.

The big sister was wearing an undershirt of her father's like a dress because all of her clothes were out on the line. She hoped they weren't going to have company today with her looking like this, especially not someone from school. "Can you still see it from up there?"

He was sitting in what he called his tree fort, but was really just a single board he'd nailed himself between two pine branches. His legs dangled down, skinny and white with red scratches and scabs. "No. Get Daddy."

"He's sleeping. Leave him alone. May just be someone lost the highway." They could hear the engine now, a deep rumble like a ball going down the lane about to hit a strike. The children waited, their eyes glued to the place where the bend in their long driveway would reveal whatever it was that was coming.

A bright yellow taxi with impressive fenders appeared, kicking up baked clay, and rolled to a stop. A woman's face could be seen peering out from the back seat. This sent the big sister into a fit of jumping. "Mama! Mama! Mama! Mama!" The driver got out and walked around to the back and opened the door. Two legs in silk stockings and high-heeled shoes came out, followed by a woman in a smart pink suit with a round hat on her head. She smiled a quick smile toward the children and opened her shiny pocketbook with a snap to pay the taxi driver. "I'll be needing a ride back again. You'll come pick me up, won't you, way out here?"

The driver was looking at the red dust that had turned his cab more orange than yellow and said, "Not sure if it'll be me or not. You got to call this number and they'll send someone." He eyed her up and down as he handed her a card.

"All right." She turned her full attention to the children. Her eyelashes were blacker and stiffer than what they were used to seeing and her lips were painted dark red like a movie star's. The boy had come down from his tree fort and was standing shyly behind the jumping girl who hadn't left off saying "Mama! Mama!"

The little sister started jumping too. She thought it was sort of a strange game to start playing when they had company, but she figured Violet knew best. "Ma-ma-ma-ma-ma-ma!"

The lady said, "This cannot be Violet! My word, child, how you have grown! You must be, what, 7 now?"

"I'm 9!"

"And this grubby thing can't be Isaac. I declare, this cannot be the tiny boy I used to hold on my lap. Come out from there so I can get a look at you." He withdrew further behind Violet.

The little sister was still playing the jumping game but she'd made it her own now and was jumping around in circles. She'd turned "ma-ma-ma" into "ba-ba-ba" and "la-la-la."

"I want to see my baby!"

That got her attention. She wanted to see the baby too. She was looking around to see where the baby was when the woman took ahold of her shoulder to make her stop jumping. "Baby Coral! Come say hello to your mama!"

Coral looked up at the lady in horror. "I ain't a baby and you ain't my mama! I ain't got a mama." Then she punched her in the stomach and ran into the house. The screen door slammed behind her.

The lady looked after Coral with pursed lips. "I can see her daddy hasn't been telling the truth. Now come and give your mama a hug, you two. I came a long way to see you." Violet hugged her but

Isaac hung back. "Oh, that's all right. You just stay right there. I don't want all that dirt getting on me."

Isaac's face got red, like he was trying not to cry.

The screen door banged again and their daddy was standing there. He'd combed his hair and put water on it so it would lay straight. "Didn't expect to see you today, Rose. How long are you staying?"

"Aren't you going to invite me in? You need to teach the children some manners and the first thing you do," she smiled and nodded at Violet to signify that this was something Violet should always remember, "when you have callers is invite them in and offer them something to drink."

Violet used the voice she used when playing tea party with her dolls. "Would you like to come in, Mama? May I get you some tea?"

"Only if it isn't any trouble." The lady strode into the house as though she owned it, flung her handbag on a chair, and looked around. "You didn't hire a cleaner? Well I can hardly blame you. Good help is *so* hard to find. If they aren't being lazy they're stealing. Now Isaac, you should offer me a seat."

He took ahold of the back of a chair and said, "Here's a seat."

The lady laughed a short forced laugh and said, "Why thank you, young man, I do believe I shall." She scrutinized the chair before sitting on it.

"What brings you here after all this time?" Daddy was still standing, ill at ease. He was seeing the house as she saw it: the gray doilies on the armchairs, the piles of books and papers on the table, the windows that made every day look like it was foggy outside.

"Let's just have a nice visit before we get to that. Now Isaac, tell me about school. What do you like best in school?"

Isaac wasn't looking at her. There was a gap in the floorboards where he was standing and part of the rubber had come loose on the edge of his shoe. He was trying to see if he could slip the strip of rubber into the gap. "Recess." It was the standard answer all the comedians in his class gave and the first thing that popped into his head. He really liked almost all of it. He was a good student and got along with everyone except the mean cusses who didn't like anybody.

"Oh, my. 'Recess.' Sounds like your daddy. Violet, what about you? What do you like best in school?" Violet had come back with a glass of sweet tea for her. She'd wrapped a scarf around her waist like a belt, trying to turn her father's undershirt into a white party dress.

192

"Well, I have a lot of friends and we have fun." She was also a good student.

The lady was delighted. "That sounds like your mama! A lady can go far in life with good connections. Always remember that. Now you should ask me how I do."

"How you do what?"

"Why, ask about my health and if the weather has been fine in Charlotte, that sort of thing."

"How is your health?"

"I'm quite well, thank you. How good of you to inquire."

"What's the weather like in Shawlit?"

"We've had a touch of dampness this spring."

Daddy had had enough. "Elna Rose, how you do go on! 'A touch of dampness in Sha-a-a-wlit.' Just how many syllables are there in Charlotte, anyway? I don't know whether you're fooling anybody there, but you're not fooling me."

The lady squinted her eyes at Daddy briefly, then turned to Violet. "Your daddy has always been happy with the simple things in life. Give him a stick to whittle and a chaw of tobacco and he's happy as a pig in mud, bless his heart."

Isaac piped up, "Daddy doesn't chew tobacco. He won't let me do it neither and he won't let it in the house."

"That's good, Isaac, never do that, it's a filthy habit. A gentleman would never spit in public." She snapped open her purse and pulled out an enamel cigarette case. "I don't see an ashtray, Violet."

Daddy said quietly, "Just get a saucer."

The lady lit the cigarette with affectedly delicate movements of her fingers, which were tipped with scarlet nails. Spying Coral watching from the hall, she gave her a wink. "Will you come out of there if I promise not to call you a baby? You may not have a lot of chances to see your mama."

"I can see you." Coral slipped past the front room and into the kitchen to find Violet. "Hey," she whispered.

"Hey."

"It's my fault that we ain't got a mama."

"How do you reckon?"

Coral's mouth went into the small square shape it made when she was trying not to cry. "She had you and she stayed, she had Isaac and she stayed."

"You hush now." Violet carried the saucer in to her mother.

Daddy pulled out a dining chair and sat down, facing the lady head on. "Tell me what this is about."

"You're all business, aren't you? Will wonders never cease! All right, then, I'm getting married and moving to Texas. I wanted to see y'all one last time before I go. It may be a long time before I come back this way."

"Married? How can she get married?" Isaac cried. "She's married to you, Daddy, ain't she? Ain't you two married?"

"You didn't tell them? Oh, for pity's sake." Her face took on an exaggerated look of concern. "Coral, you come in here, sugarpie, I have something to tell you." Coral came in, curious what this strange creature would do next. "Your father and I got a divorce. We were married when we had you and we aren't anymore, according to the State of Georgia. And now I'm marrying someone else."

Coral scowled in disapproval. She'd heard the word 'divorce' before, but people said it like it was a dirty word. She was surprised this lady would say a bad word and even more surprised that her daddy let someone smoke and say dirty words in his house without doing a thing about it.

The lady went on. "His family has oil money."

Daddy interrupted. "I don't want to know about him or his oil money, Elna Rose."

Violet had put her hands over her mouth, as though she'd been notified of a death. She finally said, "Are you fixing to have other children?"

The original Elna Rose broke through the Charlotte version she'd made of herself with a slap on her knee. "Hooo-eee! Not on your life."

There was a moment of silence. Even Coral heard that message loud and clear. The crease between Daddy's eyebrows deepened. He seemed to be on the verge of saying something when the Charlotte version of Elna Rose attempted to redeem herself. "What do I need other children for when I have the three of you? Now where is your telephone? I should call the taxi company now. Who knows how long it'll take them to get way out here?"

Everyone in the room pointed to a small table in the hallway where the telephone stood.

After she placed the call she said to Violet, "That was a very nice glass of tea. Now you should ask me if I would like another."

"Would you like another?"

"No, thank you kindly." She smiled beatifically and smoothed Violet's hair. "What are you wearing? Don't you have any real clothes?"

"Yes, ma'am. They're out on the line. I didn't know we were going to have company."

"A lady should always be ready to entertain." Striding out to the clothesline through tall drooping grass that released a lovely fragrance when crushed but was growing in soft red clay, the lady twisted her ankle several times in her high heels. She tutted as she fingered everything that was hanging. "I don't know what your father is thinking, dressing y'all like this. You tell him you need new clothes and I said so. Isaac, leave off doing that." He was rubbing his hands in the dirt to soak up the pine sap he'd picked up from his tree fort so it would come off.

"Coral, have you ever had new clothes in your life?" the lady asked.

"Nope."

"No, ma'am."

"No, ma'am. I mostly run around butt nekkid." Coral careened around the yard, shrieking the way she imagined people would shriek at her in Shawlit if they saw her running around butt nekkid.

"Why, she's just a wild animal! Well, maybe the school will do something with her." Dismissing her youngest completely from her mind, she focused her attention on Violet, the only one of her three children who was still listening, and drew herself up regally. "I'd like to leave you with a legacy. A legacy from your mama. You'd like that, wouldn't you?" Violet nodded. "I'd like you to have good manners and to be cultured and to appreciate the finer things in life. You understand what I'm saying?"

Violet nodded at her soberly.

"Say 'yes, ma'am.'"

"Yes, ma'am."

"As a young lady you should be able to comport yourself in society, and eat crêpes Suzette."

After an eternity, the taxi finally arrived and the family lined up on the porch to see her off. The lady said, "I will miss you so much! I'll think of you every second! Will you miss me too?"

Isaac said, "No."

Coral pulled a face, making her eyebrows low and sticking out her lower teeth. She said in a monster voice, "Nooooo."

Violet stepped forward and threw her arms around her mother for a brief squeeze and said, "Goodbye, Mother," in a formal voice. The lady looked at her strangely for a moment, then nodded.

"Taxi's waiting, Elna Rose." Daddy wasn't making any effort to disguise his happiness that she was on the way out.

"You get these children some decent clothes, you understand?" He didn't reply. "Remember the legacy, Violet!

The plume of red dust glowed like a pillar of fire disappearing into the setting sun. Bullfrogs began to sing down in the creek, sounding like single notes on a double bass. A cool breeze blew up from the lowlands, smelling like everything in their world was growing and green. Daddy sat down on the porch swing and Coral crawled in his lap. Isaac sat on the steps picking scabs on his legs until Violet told him to cut it out, that he was going to get infected and they'd have to saw his legs off.

Coral said, "Daddy, how come I don't have a mama?"

"That was your mama."

"How come I don't have a real mama?"

Daddy was quiet a minute. The children waited. "She wasn't as real as I thought she was, I guess."

"Did she leave because of me?" Coral's voice was quiet, terrified.

"What? No! What makes you think that?"

"She had Violet and she stayed, she had Isaac and she stayed, and then she had me and she left."

"Give me your shoe a minute." He tied her lace and double knotted it, which bought him time to think through how he was going to answer. "The thing is, and I don't know if Violet remembers this or not, but she wasn't ever much of a mama. Sometimes that happens with animals, you know. A mama will ignore her baby and you have to give it to another mother or it'll die."

"You didn't get us another mother."

"We're not animals, Coral. It's different with people."

Isaac said, "Why did she have three of us if she didn't want to be a mama?"

"I don't know, son."

Violet said fiercely, "You don't need a mama, Isaac, you have me. I'll look after you."

"And I'll look after you," Isaac pointed to Coral.

"And I'm taking care of you," said Coral, pointing at Violet, who joined in by pointing at Isaac so they had a Mexican pointing standoff.

Daddy said, "I'm taking care of all of you. Me and Jesus."

Coral didn't know this Jesus. Was Jesus a who or an it? She'd never met anybody named Jesus so she thought it must be an it. "Is Jesus the checks that come from the government?"

Daddy craned his neck around to look her in the face. "We don't get checks from the government. Where did you get that idea?"

"The kids in kindergarten get checks from the government."

"I don't think they all do, just the ones who don't have parents with jobs. I work in the sawmill."

Isaac had gotten all his scabs off and was engrossed in watching a trickle of blood run down one shin. "Is she going to change her last name?"

"Yeah, I expect she'll change it when she gets married just like she changed her name to McAllister when she married me. Guess she decided to keep that name after the divorce. Can't say I blame her. If she'd gone back to her maiden name she'd be Elna Rose Bottom again."

The children shrieked with laughter.

"Yep, Bottom. She thought she was really coming up in the world when she married me."

"Ha, ha! Bottom!"

"I guess you don't remember Meemaw and Peepaw Bottom. They followed Elna Rose to Charlotte. Heard she wasn't too happy about that."

They were all going to die laughing. Coral fell off the porch swing dramatically.

When the laughter had gotten to the point where it began to sound forced, Daddy added, "Not only that, but her mama named her after a sewing machine. Elna was the kind of sewing machine she wanted. Saw it in a catalogue."

Eventually the children grew tired of laughing and the frogs decided it was safe enough to croak again. Daddy pulled Coral back onto his lap. "Now I just had a very interesting thought. I've been sending alimony checks to Elna Rose, and once she's married I won't have to do that anymore. Then maybe I can buy you some new clothes so you don't have to run around butt nekkid."

"What if we like to?" Isaac asked as Coral slipped off Daddy's lap and skipped into the house.

Coral had had enough. It was time to hunt for the exit book. She found it in a stack of early readers in the bedroom she shared with her sister.

34 SEMI-PRECIOUS

Coral was gutted. Who wrote this story that was about her life? It told the truth. That was what it felt like anyway. She remembered now. The truth was in the emotion, even though the facts themselves must have been wrong. They lived in Oregon, not Georgia, and she wouldn't be born for many years after the fifties, when the story appeared to take place. But it was truth nonetheless. Their mother had abandoned them because she hadn't cared about her children, but the three of them, the semi-precious gems, had vowed to look after each other, and their dad had watched over everyone. They had filled the void of being without a mother by protecting each other.

Ultimately it had gone wrong. They couldn't do it. Jet—Isaac—was lost. The young Coral who was still locked away felt responsible for them having no mother. And she finally saw that Violet, who always took care of things, was Pearl.

How had she not seen that before? Pearl was only five years older but had stepped up and been responsible when Jet was killed and all that sad time when their father wasn't coping well, and then had taken over as her legal guardian after he was killed as well.

Now that she knew who Isaac and Violet were meant to be, who were all the other characters? And who knew enough about her to write these stories?

35 CORAL DEMANDS ANSWERS

"Is anybody here?"

Someone else was monitoring the front desk at work, so after teaching a couple of self-defense training sessions, Coral had the rest of the day off, which she intended to use by modeling assertiveness at Red's Reads.

"Regrettably, no. This location seems to be off the beaten path, which is probably why the rent was so attractively cheap. Your hair looks nice. You did something."

Coral slapped her hand on Phil's check-out desk in a way that showed she was done with his coy games. Actually, she wanted to slap it, but after Phil's cheerful greeting it was more of a tap. Still, her face conveyed her feelings. "What are you doing to me?"

Phil's expression became serious as he gauged her mood. He replaced the book he'd been holding onto a cart of new additions and walked over to where she stood. "I don't know, what *am* I doing to you?"

She had rehearsed this conversation in her mind. "You've given me some sort of, what, alien technology? It crawls around in my head and stirs up feelings I didn't know I had. You won't tell me what it is or where it came from and yet I trusted you like a fool. Now I'm going to need to get counseling to recover from what it's done to me."

"Oh." Phil flipped the sign on the front door to "Closed." "Let's sit down," he said, gesturing to a pair of sofas near the center of the store where people were encouraged to sit and read, should any customers actually venture into his little out-of-the-way shop. "I won't flatter you by saying you're too smart to continue with this blindly. Instead I'll say I was too stupid to realize a smart person wouldn't go along with it, at least not for long. I'm sorry. Sharing it is new."

Coral sat on the sofa opposite him, upright and far from relaxed.

"Is it dredging up painful memories for you?"

"Something like that. Never mind exactly what. I want to know how it works, like who writes these stories. I feel like some *thing* is crawling around in my brain and I have no reason to believe that it has my best interests at heart."

"Okay, let's start there. Full disclosure. Nothing is crawling around in your brain. You're writing the stories yourself."

"I am? How can that be? I don't feel like I am, and I'm constantly confused by what's going on and surprised when things happen."

"That's what the process feels like. It's one step at a time. Lots of times the next step surprises you or you become confused about what the next step should be. Authors do say they surprise themselves when they're writing books."

"But what about the passage of time? These book adventures all pass in a matter of minutes. I could never write a story that quickly."

"You probably couldn't without the use of the messenger bag. That's true. But it's all coming from you. Have you tried to get information during one of these adventures that you didn't know before?"

The John Marsh she'd consulted in the modern-day detective novel hadn't known anything about Phil she didn't. "Yes. It didn't work."

"Exactly. If it wasn't in your brain in the first place, it won't be there at all. The bag doesn't make you clairvoyant."

"Okay, but what *is* it doing? And how?"

"It's exciting the parts of your brain associated with memory and emotion, called the limbic system. People have been trying to do this sort of thing with hypnosis and various kinds of therapy for hundreds of years, with limited success. When you go into a book adventure, you're entering a state almost like dreaming. As you may know, dreams that seem to last all night really only last for a few minutes. Your time with the bag is like that. In dreams we're working to solve problems too. "

"These aren't like dreams, though. They make more sense. They hold together better. And why am I putting in a book and going into a different book of the same genre?"

"Your brain is using the book you put in as a launching point, then writing its own book based on whatever you have kicking around inside you."

"Why did you say it would help me decide which books to keep and which to get rid of? I don't see that at all. What's happened has nothing to do with that."

"I bet it has, or it will eventually. When you first came into my shop you were extremely emotional about even a terrible book. I could see there was something else going on there. I thought the book hoarding was a symptom of an underlying problem."

Coral's face reddened, but he was right. "You sound like a psychologist."

"Well, to be forthcoming, I am a psychologist. Or I was." He paused and ran his fingers through his graying hair. "That's a whole other story that you also deserve to know. But let's save that for later."

"No, tell me now. Were you kicked out for malpractice or something? I have a right to know."

"No, nothing like that. I quit ... I quit, actually, to protect the bag. As I said, it's a long story. I was a professor of psychology at Stanford University. If you wish to do a computer search on me when you get home, go right ahead. As you say, you deserve to know."

Hadn't a P. Reddington been a university professor that she'd found when she was searching for his background before? She would definitely investigate that later.

"I'll do that. So how did you get this bag?"

"I took an artifact and made it into a bag. It wasn't originally a bag. If you turn it inside out and look at the lining of the bottom, you'll see that there's a panel made of a different material that looks like plastic."

She remembered that she had turned the bag inside out and had seen that plastic piece and assumed it was there to stiffen the messenger bag so it would stand straight.

Phil went on. "That material is what really does the work. We originally called it 'the artifact.' Touching the artifact caused the effect you've seen. The bag was a convenient way to hold it, and also to make it look like nothing at all, just an ordinary messenger bag like many people own, especially on college campuses."

Coral was puzzled by the word "artifact" but there were so many questions to ask. "When you say 'we,' who are you talking about?"

"The ones who made it in the first place, plus a couple of my colleagues who were tasked with studying how the thing worked before information about it got out. Can you imagine what the world will do with this? Best therapeutic drug in the world for psychological problems, but it can be used recreationally. We felt we needed to understand it before—" Phil's attention was drawn to the front door as the tiny bell jingled, and he grew pale as he stood. "Oh, no. Just walk out of here like a normal customer. Don't attract attention."

Coral's brain was spinning. With everything she'd needed to take in, she wouldn't have been surprised to see centaurs walk in the front door. Instead it appeared to be two ordinary men in their 30s. With no better plan in mind, she decided to play along. She picked up a stray book that was sitting on the table between the two sofas, handed it to Phil, thanked him, and walked out. The men glanced at her, but their attention was focused on Phil.

Pausing outside to look back at the shop, she wondered if she should call the police. Phil had seemed genuinely frightened. Then another thought struck her. The two men had walked right in past a sign in the window marked "Closed," but as far as they could tell, so had she. Had they noticed she was out of place?

Who were they? This was something else to worry about when she already had so many things on her mind. She had to prioritize her worries. First things first: Keep an eye on Phil. Those guys had really creeped him out. She had her cellphone with her and could call the police and say—what? Some guys looked creepy? They hadn't done anything but walk into a store.

Directly across from the used bookstore were a wig shop, a place that had gone out of business, and one that sold crystals and New Age stuff. She ducked into the New Age shop to watch through the window.

The proprietor, a woman in a floor-length embroidered dress with her hair in a large number of braids woven through with strips of cloth, said, "Let me know if I can help with anything."

"Yeah, sure. Okay." Coral browsed around in the front of the shop, avoiding a rack of dragon knick-knacks she wouldn't buy in a million years, and picked up some pretty rocks that were in a bin.

Fingering them as though carefully considering whether their energy was going to balance hers, or whatever they were supposed to be doing, she kept her eyes fixed across the street. She couldn't see anything happening.

"Rose quartz. The love crystal. It also soothes and comforts. What are you looking for?" The proprietor was tiny, with catlike movements, and Coral hadn't heard her coming until she spoke.

"Soothing is good. Do you have anything to bring back lost memories?" She thought she could see movement inside the bookstore, but it was so hard to tell what was going on.

"Not a crystal, no, but let me think. There are other ways. That one you're holding now is obsidian. It's about change. I always like these." She fished around and pulled out a lavender one. "Amethyst. They're used for wisdom and guidance."

"I thought amethysts were darker and cost a lot more money." Phil and the two men had moved up front, closer to the cash register. They were just talking, but Phil was making lots of gestures of denial and negation.

"The ones jewelers sell, yes, but those parts are only a small fraction of the whole crystal. They regard what we have as without value, but we know better."

Coral wanted the woman to stop babbling at her so she could watch Phil's store in peace.

"You're going to need a healer to help with lost memories. The energy of a crystal is more subtle, at least by itself. I know a few people I could recommend. Why do you keep staring across the street?"

Coral turned and looked at her directly. "There's someone in that store I'm trying to avoid. Would you mind if I just stayed in here until they leave?"

"I don't want any trouble."

"That's why I'm staying in here, to avoid trouble."

The proprietor pursed her lips and closed her eyes. She may have been consulting a spirit guide. "I'd like you to leave."

Coral was fed up. "Look, I'm sorry I'm harshing your mellow or whatever, but I'm going to wait here until those guys leave. If you want me to buy something, I will. I'll buy a rock. One of these bigger ones over here." There were large chunks of naturally formed quartz crystals sparkling in a display case. "I can use it to bash them over the head."

The little woman gasped. "That's not what they're for!"

Coral was on the verge of answering back that it would be for whatever she said it was for after she'd paid for it when she noticed the sign in the case, which read: "Quartz Clusters - Protection and Amplification of Energy."

"They're for protection and increasing strength?"

"That's right. No! Not like that."

"How much is this one here?" It was one large crystal, rather than a group of smaller ones and would fit nicely in the palm of her hand.

"Two hundred seventy-five dollars."

"Seriously?"

The door of Red's Reads opened and the two men came out. They stood in the doorway for a moment, looking up and down the block but not talking to each other, then walked over to an old Mustang. Before they got in, one pretended to shoot at the store with his fingers. The other man laughed and they drove away.

The shop proprietor was watching too. "Those were the guys?"

"Yeah."

"Should I be worried if they come here? The sisters have to look out for each other."

Suppressing a very strong urge to roll her eyes at this sudden claim of sisterhood when a moment ago she'd been willing to throw her to the wolves, Coral replied, "I really don't know. Thanks for your sanctuary."

The "Closed" sign remained up, but Phil had not locked the door. She found him sitting on the sofa, obviously shaken.

"Who were those guys? Are you okay?"

Phil jumped up. "No, you shouldn't have come. Did they see you? Did they see you come in?"

"Calm down, Phil. I watched them drive away. There's no way they saw me come in. What did they want?"

"Them not knowing anything about you is the best thing that could happen."

"What are you talking about? What do I have to do with anything?"

"You have the bag and they don't know that. They don't know you exist."

Phil had said knowing about the bag was dangerous and she had blown it off because it seemed hyperbolic at the time. Now she realized he had been very serious. "Apparently I'm involved now. You have to tell me everything you know."

He sighed in defeat. "I agree. But first I'd like a cup of chamomile tea. Would you like some?"

"That sounds like a good idea. Want me to get it for you? You can sit here and calm your nerves."

"Oh, it's easier if I just do it than telling you where it is. Come with me to the back."

"All right." She made a detour to lock the front door after carefully peering out at the street to see if the men were out there watching.

The back of the store contained, surprisingly, a sofa. Perhaps Phil stretched out on it and took a nap when business was slow, which seemed to be most of the time. He had a little kitchen setup as well, with a dorm-size refrigerator and a one-cup coffeemaker. Coral saw a box of pods for the coffeemaker.

He said, "You can have coffee or whatever you like, it doesn't have to be chamomile tea. Here's dark roast, decaf, hazelnut."

"Ooh, I'll try that. On second thought, just decaf."

As Phil filled the water tank from the sink in a tiny bathroom, Coral said, "I'm not sure whether to say 'start from the beginning' or to keep asking who those guys were. I'm still not entirely sure who you are."

Phil handed her a steaming cup of coffee and got to work on his tea. "Let's start with that. I've told you the truth about myself from the beginning, and if you think about it, you know much more about me than I do about you. I'm actually entrusting something extremely valuable to your care and I know very little about you."

Coral was somewhat taken aback. Looking at the situation from his point of view, it made sense. Who was she to him, anyway? He knew almost nothing about her except that she was an athletic but emotionally fragile young woman who was addicted to books like some people are addicted to heroin. He knew nothing about her family. He hadn't asked what she was learning from the book adventures and she'd assumed it was out of politeness. That he hadn't wanted to pry.

"That's fair. So who goes first? I tell you about myself, you tell me more about yourself, or more about the bag, or who those guys were? Seems to me you have more to tell."

"But I've already told you a lot and you've told me nothing."

"Again, that's fair, and I have nothing to hide." Coral took a sip of the hot coffee while she organized her thoughts and attempted to curate her life for the situation at hand. Her athlete friends weren't very interested in what she'd been reading and her college friends weren't interested in hearing about her friends from Strong Body unless they hoped she would start actively dating one of them. She generally left out the bit about Jet until she got to know people a lot better because talk of a murder tended to pull all the focus onto itself, even though she'd worked so hard to make her life about more than that. Her current audience was a college professor and a psychologist—someone new. She took a deep breath and started talking.

"I'm from here originally. My dad was a stay-at-home dad who took care of us, and my mom was a sales rep who was always traveling for business. They divorced when I was very young. I have an older sister named Pearl and I used to have an older brother named Jet. So we were all named after semi-precious materials used for making jewelry. Our mom was Ruby, and I think that says a lot about how she felt about her kids. She was precious, but we were only semi-precious. In any case, she was literally never around. It was like we didn't have a mom. But we had our dad, and he was a great dad.

"Then, when I was 5 and my brother was 8, he was murdered in the woods behind our house."

"Oh, I'm so sorry!"

"They never knew who did it. I have no memory of that or anything that happened before it. Actually, now I have one memory. A bad one. That's what I've really been sorting out with the bag adventures. Trying to get my own memories back. I've been doing everything I can to journal and hold onto the memories of everything I've ever read because there's a huge area of my memory missing and I'm afraid of what else I'll lose. But I'm tired of it. I'm tired of writing it all down. I'm tired of needing to keep everything. And I want to remember my brother, and not just dead with a noose around his neck."

Phil was quiet a moment, his face full of compassion. "Such a burden for one so young. You sound remarkably self-aware."

"I have the bag to thank for that. Before it was just... " She waved her hand over the top of her head.

"I'm glad it helped. Someday I'll tell you how it helped me. But go on with your story. What happened after Jet was killed?"

"My life became really ordinary after that. Went to school. My dad went into a major decline after Jet died and sometimes drank too much and crashed his car and died when I was 17."

"That's not ordinary!"

"But by then Pearl was 22 and legally old enough to be my guardian, so we just stayed together until she got married. She was always my mom, really. She taught me to read and did all the stuff moms do."

"Are you and your sister still close?"

"We are. I love Pearl. I can count on her. I can also count on her to annoy me, but I think that's how sisters are."

"Seems to be. Wait a second, if Pearl was your legal guardian, what happened to Ruby?"

"She moved to Australia. We get cards with checks in them sometimes. Honestly, the woman means nothing to me. I think Pearl resents her because she at least remembers her, but I don't really. She's a stranger to me. Looking at her with adult eyes, I just have to put her in the category of people who should never have had children they didn't want. Dad loved us. We were okay."

Phil nodded.

"So, I graduated from high school, went to U of O on a track scholarship, and got a degree in Human Physiology."

"Human Physiology! I would have thought Comparative Literature or English or something like that."

"Because there are so many jobs in those fields?" Coral raised an eyebrow. "Pearl and I had some insurance money and Ruby's checks, but nothing else to fall back on. We knew we'd be taking care of ourselves. I was always good at track and liked working out and staying fit and thought with all the gyms around, I could always find work as a personal trainer, and that's exactly what happened. I work over there." She waved in the direction of her place of employment. "I didn't need a teacher telling me I had to read this or that. You at least knew that about me."

"Of course not. Makes perfect sense. How do you see the future?"

"Oh, I don't know. Does anybody my age know what the future looks like?

"How would you *like* the future to look?"

Coral wasn't sure how to answer. Maybe she wanted to understand more about her past so she could do ... something else. Something in addition to working and reading. She went for the easy answer. "I want to live in a bigger house to store more books. A huge house with whole rooms devoted to book storage."

"You could live in a library. How about that?" He nodded in encouragement, but the twinkle in his eye conveyed that he knew she wasn't telling him the whole truth. Then he just got very quiet and waited for her to speak.

"I also want ... I want to be able to remember that part of my life that's a blank. The first five years and what happened to Jet. That's what I'm using the bag for now."

"It's going to work," Phil said with conviction.

"You think?" Coral's eyes filled with tears. "But I'm conflicted about it. I'm not entirely sure I even want to remember. I think I forgot something for a reason."

"You had a reason to forget? You made a choice? The reasoning ability of a 5-year-old is generally not as good as that of someone your age. If you're saying you chose to forget something when you were 5 perhaps you can choose something different as an adult."

That was a little hard to argue with. "So you're saying I should decide for myself, my adult self I mean, what I should and should not remember? And using the bag is going to help me with that?"

"If you keep at it long enough, it will. It always does. We just have to make sure you keep at it. That you're able to. That nobody takes it away. That's what I'm trying to prevent. We have the most important therapeutic breakthrough in the history of psychology—in fact, one of the most significant inventions in the history of mankind—and we're trying to make sure it's used to benefit everyone and doesn't fall into the hands of people who would just use it to get rich."

Coral paused to let this soak in. "So why don't you just publish how to make these things? I mean, translate it into every language and put it on the Internet? Boom! There it is, out there for everyone to see."

"We would if we could, but there's a small problem. We don't actually know how to recreate it. The material in the bottom of the bag is one of a kind."

36 BRAIN LIGHTS

"It was a failed experiment. It was meant to be a conductive polymer to be used by industrial robots, but instead of allowing electrical charges to pass in an infinite number of directions, the polymer had the effect you've experienced. The same thing happened years ago with the guy who invented sticky notes. You probably know the story. The glue in sticky notes was supposed to be really strong, but instead was weak. Rather than regarding it as a failed experiment, however, he had the foresight to realize people don't always want glue to be strong, and an industry was born.

"When the artifact solidified, our chemist tested its conductivity and quickly realized it hadn't done what he'd hoped it would do. But then someone happened to be holding the artifact in one hand and a book in another, and you can imagine what happened."

"My colleagues and I were called in to try to figure out what the heck was going on. The team touched it with various items like coffee cups and pencils and a metal ruler. Oh, and they tried blindfolding someone, putting a book in one hand and the artifact in the other, with the person not knowing what was in the book. They tried having two people hold a book and the artifact at the same time. All sorts of things. What worked was for a person to touch the artifact with bare skin while also holding reading material they were familiar with. That was why I had you push a book to the very bottom of the bag, so you were touching the artifact with your hand.

"It was so bizarre that as a psychologist I had to fall back on one of the most basic definitions of what psychology even is. It's something I taught in Behavioral Psych, which says the purpose of psychology is to describe, predict, and control behavior. I had to leave *how* the artifact did what it did to the neurologists, but I could set up scientifically valid test procedures to describe, predict, and ideally control what it was doing to people."

Coral was shaking her head. "Wait a minute. That's all psychology is? I don't believe it. What about all the therapists and the couches and talking about feelings?"

"Every freshman says the same thing until they realize that studying psychology is mostly studying all the contradictory theories from Freud, James, Skinner, Rogers, and the others. I started studying the artifact using the behaviorist model and hoped to move on from that eventually."

"Okay, I don't know who most of those people are, but I get that."

Phil nodded briefly, seeming like the professor in the classroom once more. "I devised rigorous scientific test protocols, always keeping in mind the ethics of using human test subjects, and convinced them to stop the improvised experiments. We realized pretty early we needed to keep the test subject group small because it seemed like we had something with amazing potential on our hands and didn't want the news to get out, and also because we didn't know if there would be any ill effects. To make a long story short, there sometimes were ill effects of the same sort one sees from people undergoing psychotherapy. Temporary ones. I recognized the similarity right away. With these people, their boat has been rocked. But if they stayed the course, they came out healthier on the other side." He gave Coral a nod of encouragement. "You're in the rocked-boat stage right now. Do you see that?"

She shrugged.

"Ah, it's my fault. I shouldn't have let you do this with no warning. Granted, we had no warning when the artifact was first being tested, but we all had each other, and you were alone."

"Wait a second, why do you call it an 'artifact?' I thought artifacts were things dug up by archeologists."

"The word means something made by people, so yeah, archeologists dig up artifacts, but this is also an artifact."

Coral rolled her eyes. "The things that were going through my head! Alien artifacts. Something dug up from an ancient tomb."

"You read a lot of books, don't you?"

"As a matter of fact, I do."

"Back in the land of reality, at least as much the land of reality as Palo Alto ever is, we tested the artifact every which way we could think of and knew we had something absolutely amazing on our hands, something that could change how therapy was done and make it much more effective. And being a cynical lot, we also began to be concerned that someone would try to keep it all to themselves and make a lot of money off of it. And we were right to be concerned."

"That's who those two guys were."

"Yeah. And they aren't the only ones. Word about the artifact got out."

"Darn."

"Yeah."

"And you still didn't know how to recreate it?"

"Recreating it was never my job, but the chemist and his part of the team worked and worked but nobody's been able to do that yet. Determining that it worked by stimulating areas of the brain in a pattern they don't normally form was about as far as the neurologist got. Even that was interesting, though. Certain regions of the brain are involved in a natural dream state. In the limbic system, for example, the hippocampus lights up during REM sleep, the time a person is actively dreaming. That part of the brain is involved in most emotions, memory, and patterns. The amygdala is also involved, and that part of the brain is where you find fear and aggression. That's where the bad dreams come from, all those fight-or-flight feelings. Also, in normal REM sleep the frontal cortex, which you can think of as the reasoning part of the brain, is pretty quiet. This is why dreams can be so crazy and not make any sense. Your frontal cortex is taking a little break. The artifact triggers a brain state that's similar in many respects to REM sleep, but also differs in some important ways. First, it doesn't stimulate the amygdala. You didn't experience much fear or anger, did you?"

"In that first book, when I was in the horror novel, I was afraid at first, but not as much as I would have been in real life. And eventually I just walked up to the dragon and punched it. So I would have to say that's true. Then in later books I was doing all sorts of things I would have been afraid to do in real life. I just figured it was because I knew I was in a book and nothing was real."

"Right, you punched a dragon. Love that."

"Yeah."

Phil nodded at her in admiration. "See, that makes sense. That shows the second difference between what the artifact is doing and what normal REM sleep does. Instead of the frontal cortex taking a rest, it stays just as active as it does during waking hours. So the overall effect is that you're revving up your emotional, pattern-making, memory-making, and retrieval center, and keeping your ability to make sense of what you find in a calm and even happy way."

"Let me see if I have this straight. My logical part is working, my memory part is working, my pattern part is working, but my fear part is not."

"Highly simplified, but that's basically it. No part of a brain ever shuts down completely. Everything is connected. It's just a matter of which areas are more or less active."

"So my brain is thinking up new, logical stories using patterns from my memory and not letting fear get in the way. It basically made me super creative for a couple of minutes, and in those minutes I had written a book, or at least most of a book."

"That's one effect it can have, yeah. And your creativity is coming from your memories."

"So how did it end up in a used bookstore in Portland?"

"When we saw we were in danger of having the artifact stolen out from under us, I made a run for it, basically. I told everyone I wanted nothing to do with any of it—everyone except two people I utterly trust—but took it and split."

"*You* stole it."

"I'm protecting it from the people who want to steal it. When it's safe, I intend to continue research and get the technology available to everybody."

"Phil, Phil, Phil. You make a very bad thief. Why didn't you change your name when you came up here? You aren't hiding very well."

"If I looked like I was trying to hide, they would have been all over that. As it is, I'm just a burned-out psych professor who decided to spend his golden years running a little bookstore. They have no proof I have it. And I can honestly say I don't. I could pass a lie detector test."

He didn't have the artifact because he had given it to Coral.

"This is why you don't want them to connect you and me. Okay, I'm with you on that now." What if they had seen her and began to follow her? What if they broke into her apartment? She wasn't willing to die to protect this thing. Would they go that far? She needed to put it someplace safe, away from where she lived.

"Do they know what the messenger bag looks like?"

"I don't know for sure."

"Would you mind if I hid it someplace else? To be safe."

37 IT WOULD BE GREAT TO LOOK YOU OVER

If someone broke into her apartment, they wouldn't find the messenger bag. She had hidden it someplace completely inaccessible. It wasn't with her at work that night either.

The possibility of being stalked by thieves was a lot more frightening in real life than it would have been in a book adventure with her amygdala dampened. Now her amygdala was doing whatever it is amygdalae do. But she didn't think the two guys had paid close attention to her and didn't know she had the artifact. She hadn't seen any sign of them when she'd left Red's Reads. They didn't even know for sure that Phil had taken it.

It was a slow night. People in Portland practice a carpe diem philosophy when it comes to weather: When it's nice out, as it was that evening, they were going to be outside enjoying every minute. All too soon the drizzle would start again and hardly let up for months. With few people coming into the gym, there was plenty of time to think about what she'd learned from her book adventures and what she still wanted to know.

Up to this point, the only early memories she'd been able to glean included the sense that she and her family had been very protective of one another after her mother left, that she had known where to find Jet after he was killed, and what he had looked like lying there dead. Now that she knew the bag was acting like souped-up hypnosis in freeing memories of the past and then putting a dreamlike spin on them, she had hope. Surely everything that had happened as a child was still in her mind, locked away, and she only needed to keep chipping away at the barriers to find answers. She was certain the answers would be painful, but she needed to know.

When she dared to use the artifact again, what sort of book should she give it? A psychology textbook? Another fantasy? She was getting awfully tired of dragons, but a dragon often played a part in the story so it was clearly important. Maybe another mystery, since everything hinged on Jet's unsolved murder.

The door opened and a fresh breeze blew in, along with Eliot Marsh, the dark-haired guy with the same last name as John Marsh. This time he had on a button-down shirt and khakis, like he'd come from work.

"Eliot Marsh," he said, checking in.

"I remember. You'll almost have the place to yourself. I guess everybody decided it was too nice out to get stuck in a stuffy gym."

"If I didn't have to do this, I'd be out there too." He turned his head to look out the door. His dark hair was cut very short in back.

"You have to do this? How come, if you don't mind me asking?"

"I'm up against some guys who think they're real badasses sometimes. Have to make sure I'm tougher than they are."

"You are? How does that happen?"

"Portland P.D." A police officer *and* named Marsh! Had she met Eliot before? How did a police officer named Marsh get into her book adventures?

"Oh! Th- that makes sense," she stammered. "Have to be the baddest badass of all. I almost said 'have to be the baddest ass of all' and that would have been rude. Don't mind me." Coral shook her head and rolled her eyes at herself. She was a lot cleverer in the book adventures. In real life she remained a rather gawky, bespectacled bookworm.

He stared at her, unsmiling. "Didn't you say you teach classes here or something?"

"I'm a personal trainer. I mostly work with people who are just getting started, but it would be great to look you over and check out your form and stuff. I mean make sure your technique is optimal. Sometimes we get into some sloppy habits. It would be a nice change of pace for me to work with someone who already knew what they were doing, that's what I'm trying to say." What was she trying to say? If a guy had said he wanted to check out her form, she would have given him a curt "no thank you" and been on her way.

"All right, let's do that sometime." Eliot gave her a nod and headed into the men's locker room.

Those eyes of his! They were like laser beams. They didn't miss a trick. If she'd been a crook she would have confessed to everything instantly. She was on edge when he was around. A Portland police officer was a far cry from her idealized John Marsh with his gentle manner, the one who loved her. Real life versus fiction: score one for fiction.

Come to think of it, she *had* received stolen goods, sort of. Maybe she should stay away from Eliot Marsh. He would look down into her heart and know she was hiding something. She would just stay at the front desk and think about what sort of book adventure should come next.

38 ONE PROBLEM DOWN

No one had trashed her apartment. Everything appeared untouched since she'd left it earlier that evening. She was probably being excessively paranoid. The drawback to her paranoia was that now she had to wait for the mail to come before she could go into the next book. That did give her time to make a pile of books on the coffee table.

The longer she spent looking over the spines of her many books, the bigger the pile grew. Eventually she realized she would need to divide the pile into two stacks: one stack of books that were most likely to yield information about her childhood, and another that just looked like they would be fun to have an adventure in.

Two long days passed. Pearl was tied up with house hunters who were proving picky and demanding so she was no use as a distraction.

Coral was afraid to visit Phil in case she was seen, but worried that the men may have come back. She had to assume they were tech savvy enough to find her through her IP address if she emailed him, and of course phoning was out of the question. She entertained thoughts of strolling by in a wig and sunglasses, hoping to catch a peek of him through the window, but that seemed to blur the lines between something a real person would do and something only a person in a book would do. Those lines were already plenty blurred. Would he contact her eventually? Should she do anything at all about Phil?

Phil wasn't her only worry. There was no sign of the envelope. On the third day, a sinking feeling settled in Coral's stomach. What if it had gotten lost in the mail? One of the most important developments in the history of mankind and she'd just stuck it in a mailbox? What had she been thinking?

That evening, Dan the landlord knocked on her door, looking tidy as usual.

"This didn't fit in your mail slot and the guy left it lying on the counter underneath. It looked like it might be important, so I picked it up for you. Didn't want someone to walk off with it." He placed the envelope in her hand.

"Thanks, Dan," she said, trying not to sound excessively relieved. "You're the best! Anything new with you?"

"S.O.S. Same old stuff. That toilet working okay now?"

"It's perfect. Thanks again for doing that."

"No problem."

No problem. If only that were true.

The artifact had come back to her and was not lost in the mail. Coral tore open the package. It appeared the same dull reddish brown color it had always been, with no dents or tears. That was one problem down, but how many left? There was Phil's safety, and by extension, hers. There was the fact that she was using this technology they hadn't finished testing, and even though Phil was convinced it was safe, it was definitely messing with her mind.

Pearl and James might be moving to Europe, leaving her all alone.

Her best friend was a fictional character, which probably meant that Pearl was right: There was something very wrong with her social life, which was entirely her fault.

Of course there was the ongoing problem. Her brother had been murdered, nobody knew who did it, and she couldn't remember anything about him or a lot of other things.

Coral got a carton of coffee ice cream out of the freezer and ate the whole thing. It didn't help. It only gave her time to look around and bemoan the fact that she still had just as many books in her apartment as when she started. And now she had a stomachache.

She wanted to escape the old fashioned way—into a book.

With the artifact back she could do that, only better. Phil had told her it didn't need to be in any sort of bag at all. The first experience had happened when someone happened to touch it while holding a book. That would be all she'd have to do.

Looking over the piles she'd made, she chose a genre that had nothing to do with families, dragons, or feelings. A genre completely unlike her life.

A place where she could be tough and brave.

39 A PLOT THREAD WITHOUT CORAL

When General Albert Light summoned you to his office by yourself, you weren't getting invited for a drink, you were getting called onto the carpet. The men under his command dreaded receiving an order to appear before him that way and he was glad of it. When he had good words for someone he generally said them in...

(And so forth. This had nothing to do with Coral.)

40 ANOTHER PLOT THREAD WITHOUT CORAL

"You're home early." Amanda had on shorts and a T-shirt and her hair was pulled back off her face in a damp ponytail. She'd just come back from a tennis lesson in the afternoon sun at the China Lake Naval Weapons Center. "What's up? Don't you feel well?"

"Pack your bags, honey, we need to get out of here." He was tossing their empty suitcases down from the searing attic.

"What are you talking about? I haven't even showered yet. I'm doing a... "

(And so forth. Still no Coral.)

41 THESE MUST TIE TOGETHER EVENTUALLY

"Dead," Dr. Bruce said, pressing into the flesh with his serrated blade. "Dead and gone. Expired."

"Oh, what a shame. Do you want us to wait for you?"

"Of course not. You go right ahead." He took a sip of Scotch and waved the waiter over. "Based on my extensive medical training I pronounce this piece of beef lost to us forever. Would you please take it back to the kitchen and tell the cook that 'medium' does not... "

(And so forth. Coral was not present at this dinner either.)

42 THE GANG'S ALL HERE EXCEPT CORAL

Half Baked Higgins waited in his rental car in the parking lot of the civilian supermarket across from the China Lake Station main gate, keeping his eyes fixed on the cars coming down the main road. This was going to be the easiest job he'd ever done and he was thanking his lucky stars. He didn't know who had hired him and he didn't ask why they wanted...

(And so forth. Again.)

43 AND THERE'S HER SISTER

What they'd ordered and what was delivered did not match. When you work in the White House Mess, even something as simple as expecting sweet potatoes and receiving yams sends up a red flag. Violet Emerson, who had cooked for the last two administrations, outlasting the "official" White House chefs...

(And so forth. Come ON.)

44 IN ALASKA?

Captain Hasagawa had been right to call him to The Rock, the U.S. Coast Guard's base on Kodiak Island, Alaska. Something about this so-called trawler boat captain's story didn't add up, and John Marsh was tasked with deciding just how seriously the Department of Homeland Security was...

(And so forth.
Maybe she could take up knitting.)

45 CORAL ENTERS THE STORYLINE

Special Agent Coral Ambrose had been pacing laps around "C" ring corridor at the Pentagon for a very long time and was already annoyed.

She didn't care about Hasagawa, Higgins, and those other guys she'd had to wait through. And finding out that John Marsh was in Kodiak, Alaska and not part of her storyline, at least not for the time being, was even worse. She wondered how long her piece was going to last now, and then how many more pages of story would leave her twiddling her thumbs until it was again her time to participate in the plot. Would she get a whole chapter? Was she a main character or wasn't she?

There was nothing to be done about it. She had a meeting to attend.

The banner on the door of the conference room read, "Top Secret, Security-Compartmented Information." Being top secret meant in part that the door did not announce that the meeting was an Interagency Working Group on Emergent Science (IWGES), much less that this meeting had been hastily called. A small table in the entry held a sign-in sheet, where she was required to list not only her name and organization but both her regular and secure phone numbers and her regular and secure email addresses, all under the watchful eye of a Pentagon Security Guard.

Pitchers of cold water and glasses were in place on the conference room table, and attendees were milling about waiting to see who else was coming before choosing a seat, as at any point someone might enter who would require even high-ranking officers to come to attention. Coral recognized all of them, of course, but few recognized her. As a Secret Service agent, it was her job to become the anonymous face of protection for not only the President and Vice President of the United States, but also visiting foreign dignitaries and esteemed personages. She was one of the people in a dark suit with a wire in her ear, that's all. She didn't know why she was here, but this time it was not to protect the others. She had been inexplicably asked to attend.

Warren Glass, Director of the Secret Service and Coral's boss's boss, entered. Quickly spying her standing with her back to the wall in a position she was used to among the powerful, he approached.

"Good. You're here, and no doubt wondering why. You and I need to talk after this. Sorry we couldn't do it beforehand. The information presented here is going to be vital to your continuing role with the Secret Service."

"Yes, sir."

"Sit directly behind me when everyone finally sits down."

There were 10 chairs arranged around the table itself and 10 chairs pushed against the walls. "Yes, sir."

At exactly 1000 hours, General Light and his aides entered the room. He told everyone to take their seats, and took his own place at the head of the table. The others immediately organized themselves according to rank and sat down as well.

General Light said, "I'm not a man with answers today, I'm a man with questions, and I need you to supply the answers. But first I need to show you what we're talking about." He pressed a clicker and one of the large screens arranged around the walls of the windowless room lit up, showing a pastoral scene of goats grazing. A timer ran in the upper right corner. There was no audio.

The only sound was a fly in the room that had somehow made it all the way to "C" ring.

"You know where this is."

Coral didn't know where it was.

"See the goat in the lower left with the 'x' painted on her side? Keep your eye on her." The goat's tail flicked, and then it was gone—it had simply vanished. "Looks like something out of early Hollywood, doesn't it? You take a movie, then you stop the camera, remove something, and start the camera again and it looks like the thing you removed disappeared. That's not what happened. The timer just keeps moving in real time because what you saw is exactly the way it happened. I saw this demonstrated live with my own eyes." He replayed the scene several more times. "Watch the other goats this time. Their movement stays smooth, no sudden jerks. Watch this. Nothing. No reaction. There was no sound, nothing like an explosion or a shot. They didn't even notice. They kept eating the grass."

The fly was silently crawling along the ceiling above their heads as the others quietly waited for an explanation.

"The good news is, this is our technology. Came out of China Lake Naval Weapons Center. The bad news is that you're dead, Bob." He was looking at General Roberto Chavez of the U.S. Army.

Chavez felt the back of his neck and pulled off a small black object. It was the "fly" that had been hanging around by the ceiling. "I felt this thing land on my neck." He looked at it more carefully. "I'll be damned. It's a drone." He passed it around the table. "Since I'm not dead, I assume it's a targeting device."

"Wrong. It's the actual weapon. Not that one, it's for demos. If it were the real thing it would have hit you with a tachyonic pulse so strong it would separate every cell in your body from every other cell. And completely silently."

"We can do that?" Colonel Ross Black of the Air Force was holding the tiny device. "Holy lord."

"We can now."

"Separate the cells? What does that mean? I don't understand how that works. What are the underlying physics?"

"I'm not sure I understand it myself," the general replied. "It's just as well that we don't. The fewer people who know how this thing works, the safer the world is."

"Does it matter what size the target is? Does it ever leave part of a person behind? What about clothes?"

"All good questions. It disrupts all the cells of one contiguous, integrated biological organism. It's been tried on a whale swimming in the water. The whale was gone, a gaseous bubble rose to the surface, and water rushed in to fill the gap. Nothing happened to small fish that were in the same tank. They put clothing on a goat. The goat disappeared and the clothing fell to the ground.

"This is where you come in. How long did we have the atomic bomb all to ourselves? You get my point. Our guys just invented the ultimate assassination technology. How we're going to use it isn't a problem. We're already so legally constrained it may never get used. We can't assassinate foreign heads of state, no matter how much they deserve it."

Knowing chuckles rustled around the conference room.

"Sure would have liked to have had it when bin Laden was alive, right? Think again. Suddenly nobody can find the guy. What kind of justice would that have been for the families of the victims? They needed to see the raid. They needed to see a dead body, know he was afraid, and understand the implications. We'll have other people working on that. That's not my question for you. What I want to know is how we're going to defend the United States of America *against* this weapon."

Warren Glass rubbed his forehead and turned to catch Coral's eye. A little piece of hell had just been unleashed on the Secret Service. How could they protect anybody against that?

General Chavez said, "We have the Navy to thank for that." It didn't get a laugh.

"What's being done to keep this from getting out?" Colonel Black wanted to know.

General Light responded, "Security at China Lake is among the tightest of any facility in the nation. As you know, China Lake is way the hell out in the Mojave and has excellent physical security. Moreover, they successfully ward off literally millions of cyber assaults on their information systems *daily*. The problem is that these things are developed by people, and people have families that can be gotten to. If a scientist is told, hey, we know your kids are Billy and Suzy and they're at this school and take this bus, and we'll torture and kill them if you don't give us this tiny piece of information, just this one tiny piece of the big puzzle, what would you do?"

"I guess this time calling in the Marines isn't the answer," said David R. Brown, Commandant of the United States Marines Corps. He didn't get a response either.

Light continued. "My point is that once these things are out of the bag, there's no putting them back in. We could burn all the records and lock everybody who ever worked on the damn thing in an underground bunker and it would still show up in Russia, China, somewhere worse. I don't expect you to have answers today. But I thought I'd give you something to keep you awake."

"What's the name of this thing anyway?"

"NAPdrone. Nullifying Anti-Personnel Drone."

"Nullifying?"

General Light stood up. "You saw what happened. You have a better word for it?"

Later, back in the corridor of "C" wing, Warren Glass pulled Coral aside. "That was a great way for you to start, wasn't it? I just threw you right in there."

"Start what, sir? I still don't know why I was there."

"I've just promoted Anna Griffith to be my Deputy Director."

"Oh good for her. She'll be great." Most recently, Griffith ran ongoing site protection training for agents of all levels at the James J. Rowley Training Center just outside of D.C. She was known and well respected by all.

"That left a hole at JJRTC, but your boss said he was ready to do something different and decided to step into that role. He recommended you for his position as SAC of the Presidential Protective Division."

Becoming Special Agent in Charge of an office as important as that at her age was unheard of. Coral was floored. "I'm honored. Thank you very much, sir."

"I'm not sure thanking me is the appropriate response now that you see what you're going to be up against."

The JJRTC was going to have to come up with a whole new class now: how to protect against the NAPdrone threat. In the meantime, the safety of the POTUS had just become her responsibility. This was something straight out of a fever-induced nightmare: it had to be done, but was impossible.

Despite her efforts at maintaining a poker face, Director Glass saw her alarm. "I'm glad to see you recognize the gravity of the situation. If you didn't, I'd think we'd put the wrong woman in the job. The NAPdrone can kill people one at a time all around you and you won't even see it coming. And then it'll get you too. This isn't an instrument of war. It's the most dangerous assassin the world has ever seen. The time when we all blew each other up with bombs seems like the good old days. Then we had bigger bombs, and the nukes that took out whole cities, but they also destroyed everything worth taking. Nobody wanted to use them. Then we had terrorists who were sneaky and effective, but most of the time they had to kill themselves to get the job done. Terrorism was self-limiting.

"But what will stop a NAPdrone? One individual can take out every head of state in the world simultaneously if he has enough of them. Then make his demands, follow it up with a thousand more assassinations, and he owns the whole damn world. Life as we've known it is over. We've just entered the NAPdrone age."

46 NOT THIS AGAIN

They were arguing in whispers, keeping their voices low enough not to wake up Isaac, who was sleeping in the back seat of the car racing toward Oregon.

"They'll find us. We can't get away from them."

Dr. Carlson's hands gripped the steering wheel tightly. "I don't know what else to do. You don't know what I'm dealing with... "

(And so forth. Coral gritted her teeth.)

47 SUFFICIENT INTEL FOR AN EXIT STRATEGY

President McAllister would arrive in the motorcade at 1805, greet the people waiting near the loading bay of the hotel, and walk to his reserved suite, arriving at 1820. He would then have 10 minutes of downtime to review his notes, have a drink, or whatever he wanted to do. He would then be escorted to Ballroom A at 1830 and be seated at his table. All areas had been electronically swept and locked down and metal detectors were in place. A few early attendees had begun to trickle in and were being processed. There was nothing else for her to do on this end but wait and receive communication from the agents who were traveling with the POTUS.

Coral had a few moments to think.

She knew she should probably be grateful she had only needed to wait through one other storyline this time before it became her turn again. Nevertheless, it was hard to imagine living through an entire lengthy book like this. Since the President's name was McAllister, he was probably going to end up dead since he'd been dead in most of the other stories. This time she would be blamed. It looked like a NAPdrone was going to start killing off the characters.

She supposed she could wait around and find out. On the other hand, her intention in choosing this genre had been to have fun, but now it seemed that the name of her brother's killer might have just been dropped on her lap. The killer, the real killer, not some guy called Two Bit or Half Wit or whatever his name was, was called something like NAPdrone. That didn't make sense in the real world, but she doubted it would make more sense if she stayed here.

In the suite reserved for the POTUS she greeted Agent Cavalli and opened up her briefcase.

Inside was a book wrapped in a towel. She'd used oven mitts to wrap it.

Cavalli watched her curiously. There was no point in saying anything, no goodbye, no "keep up the good work."

She touched the book and got out of there.

48 NAPDRONE?

The search engine could find nothing like "napdrone." It tried to help. It thought perhaps she meant "naphyrone," "naperone," "padrone," or "popdrone." She didn't, of course, but she did become curious as to what all those other things were. The first was a drug. Jet had not been killed by a drug, he had been strangled. The second was the Finnish word for toddler, "padrone" meant innkeeper or boss in Italian, and the last was a music website. None of these seemed helpful. She'd hoped it would be someone's name.

Thinking that perhaps it wasn't the person's actual name but similar to his name, she tried to think what that could be. The paper telephone directory worked better for this purpose, because she could visually scan large quantities of names in a way the Internet wasn't equipped to allow her to do. It wanted to do all the scanning of data itself. After several minutes of flipping back and forth, she gave up. Nothing seemed to be close.

Exasperated, she reached over and touched the artifact with the phone book still in hand.

49 PORTLAND A-Z

And immediately regretted it.

She was standing in a long, long, long line of people. They stretched out, single file, both directions, further than her eyes could see. There was nothing around the people. It was all white. Just a line of people in a completely blank world.

She wasn't going to find a book to touch to get out of there.

Coral sighed.

"Hi," said the woman behind her. She had her telephone number on her shirt. Coral looked down and noticed that hers was on her shirt as well. "I'm Cyndie Ambrose. What's your name?"

"Coral Ambrose. Glad to meet you."

"I live at 4329 NE Taylor Street in Portland, Oregon."

"Oh, my address is unlisted."

"Okay."

After that they didn't have anything to talk about.

"Hi." Coral said to the man in front of her. "My name is Coral Ambrose."

"I'm Carl Ambrose. I don't think we're related."

"Neither do I. My address is unlisted."

"Mine too." They nodded to each other briefly but could think of nothing to add to the conversation. Name? Check. Phone number? Check. Address? Optional, and check.

With no book to touch, she was going to have to get out of here the way she used to. She was going to have to break the genre conventions or something. An idea occurred to her. It would be simple as pie.

Coral darted out of the line. "I'm heading for the N's," she called out to Carl and Cyndie. "Nice meeting you!"

"Stop!" cried Cyndie in horror. All of the other Ambroses were aghast, and even some of the Amhersts.

Carl acted like he wanted to step out of line to grab her and pull her back, but he didn't dare. "You can't do that! You have to stay in line."

"Byeeeeeeee!"

50 WASTING TIME

Okay, that was a big waste of time. She turned to her "Patterns and Themes" notes and updated the character portion.

- *John Marsh: nice guy, detective or something like that, likes me, I keep letting him down*
- *Dragon: a killer who threatens to kill again if spoken about (person? animal? thing?) "NAPdrone"*
- *Isaac: Jet*
- *Light: older man in charge, could be good or bad*
- *Higgins: guy with a nickname, a bad guy, not the killer*
- *Carlsons: take care of Isaac*
- *Violet: Pearl*
- *Dr. Bruce: full of himself*
- *McAllister: probably Dad*
- *Rose: Ruby (Mom)*
- *Hasagawa: ?*
- *Cavalli: ?*

Her mother wasn't exactly a pattern in herself since she had only shown up the one time, but she was part of the bigger pattern: book characters were representing significant people from Coral's life.

She needed a break, to just curl up in bed with a book she wasn't in and read until she fell asleep. During the days she had been waiting for the artifact to return in the mail she'd actually made progress in the spy novel she'd been trying to read. Perhaps tonight she would even finish it. She had to open at work in the morning anyway.

51 THE VICTIM

The spy novel came to an end and the book she'd selected to read next was one she'd been assigned in college: a prose translation of *Beowulf*. Quite fascinating. But nothing was just reading material anymore.

When she was reading she couldn't help but imagine how it would be to live the book. If she jumped into her own version of *Beowulf*, would she become Coral Ambrose, brave shield maiden, gracious in word and deed and bearing the jewel-encrusted battle necklace worked with gold? Because if she was honest with herself, that sounded awfully good to a personal trainer with nobody to train who was sitting at the front desk of an urban gym waiting around for someone to come and check in. Who wouldn't want to protect the great homeland of the Scyldings with sword and bow against the claw of Grendel, in the company of mail-clad chieftains and warriors? Would she find herself speaking Anglo-Saxon the way she'd effortlessly spoken early-20th-century British English in Cotsley?

It was settled. She was reading it now and would jump into it later. There were probably all sorts of interesting facts she could learn about her so-called dragon in the great homeland of the Scyldings.

This train of thought may have been why, like a brave shield maiden, she sensed danger when the door opened and two men walked in. Later Coral would think about how her body had reacted before her brain. First her blood ran cold while her brain was still mistakenly thinking they were new people who might want to sign up. Then her brain caught up and she realized they were the men who had been harassing Phil.

It wasn't all that warm out, but they looked sweaty and rumpled. They approached Coral at the desk with great machismo, no doubt hoping they looked like picadors in the bull ring, although they really just looked like a couple of used-car salesmen who had been standing in the sun waiting to corner potential customers. And then maybe rolled down a hill a little bit.

"Just give us the thing Phil gave you and we'll leave. Simple as that."

How would fictional, fearless Coral handle this situation? Because real Coral was mostly good at running away really fast, or in a pinch, using Aikido. One thing was certain: She couldn't just hand over the artifact.

"Phil who?"

One man, the guy with the narrow face and dark circles under his eyes, said, "Don't do that. You know who I'm talking about. We saw you come out of the bookstore and followed you home."

"The bookstore? Which one? Do you mean Powell's or Red's Reads? Who put you up to this?" She swallowed her fear, made her best skeptical face, and looked him right in the eye. "I can't even think of anybody who would do something stupid like this. None of my friends are dumb enough to find this funny. Who are you?"

"Red's Reads. What did he give you?"

Would it be stupid to be the brave, fictional Coral? Should she show the legitimate fear she was feeling or stand her ground? Real life had consequences she didn't face in a book. Maybe courage in the face of danger was something she was meant to be learning. "He gave me change when I bought a book, douchebag, what do you think?"

"What book? This one?" The other guy, with tightly curled dishwater hair, grabbed Beowulf off her desk and flipped through it. Coral reached for the phone. Curly slammed the receiver down. "We saw you come in with a backpack and a gym bag. Where are they?"

"None of your business. Get out of here."

Circles spied the keys around Coral's neck and snatched them away, scratching her neck when he yanked the lanyard over her head. "Let's see, this will be front door, this is probably interior offices. Maybe they're in there. What's this?" He watched her eyes as he fingered the keys. "There we go. It's a locker key. She locked the bags in a locker. Must be in the ladies' room." The two strode toward the door, calling, "Cover up, girls, we're coming in."

"You can't go in there!"

Curly came back and grabbed her arm, jerking her away from the phone and forcing her to go with them.

There was water running. Someone was in a shower, apparently oblivious. Coral hoped she stayed there.

Circles read the number on the locker key. "One-one-one. One-eleven. Where are you? Here you are." Circles inserted the key in the lock and turned it. "And here we go." He dumped the entire contents of the locker on the floor, pulled out her backpack, and turned it inside out. Curly kicked the contents around while Circles even opened up a cosmetic bag. "It's not here."

"If you'd tell me what you're looking for, maybe I could help you and you could stop spreading my stuff all around."

"It looks like a piece of plastic."

"Like packing material?"

"Flatter. But I think you know exactly what it looks like."

Coral shrugged and scooped up her cell phone. Curly snatched it out of her hand and threw it against the tile wall, where it broke apart.

"Hey!"

Then he took hold of her wrist again. "We're going to look around and you're staying with me." Coral failed to mention to him how strong she was and let him lead her around to the various classrooms and offices like the weak little girl he assumed her to be. She didn't need to fake the trembling.

There was another bag she'd brought, a gym bag with a towel in it, in the manager's office with a note tied to the handle that read "Hold for P. Riley." There was no P. Riley. When they got to the manager's office and Circles spied the gym bag on the floor he let out a whoop and whipped the towel out, then turned it inside out and felt the lining. He was puzzled. "It's not here. It's not here. This is the one she brought in, but it's not here."

She had been too smart to carry the artifact around with her in any sort of container. This time she'd put it where responsible adults are supposed to put things they don't want other people to be able to steal: A safe deposit box at a bank. She'd used this gym bag, all right. The messenger bag had looked tampered with on the bottom after she took the artifact out—a dead giveaway that she'd once had it, so she'd taken the messenger bag and placed it in the gym bag, brought the gym bag to work, removed the messenger bag and stuck it in a different locker, and put the key to that locker in the tampon machine. Hooray for the spy novel she'd just finished.

"It's okay, Ray, we didn't look through her desk."

"No names, idiot. Take her with us."

With Coral struggling slightly, the three reentered the lobby.

Eliot was standing at the front desk, looking around for someone to check him in. He took in the scene of the two angry men and Coral being held by the wrist and immediately frowned at Coral as though to say, "Just how bad is this?" With her chin she pointed at Circles, then turned her eyes on Curly, who had shifted his grip on Coral to her hand and was now smiling like they were all great friends.

This gave Coral the opportunity to knee him in the groin, get on his back with one arm circling his neck in a very uncomfortable way and the other pinning one of his arms behind him. She then kneed him to the ground. Circles was so astonished at this sudden turn of events that he didn't see Eliot coming and was soon on the ground himself.

"Burglars?" Eliot's voice was calm. He brought guys down all the time. It was his job.

"Maybe. Lunatics would be more like it. I *do* want to press charges."

Curly's voice was muffled. "Aw, crap. We weren't going to hurt you. This is crap."

It was a moment she would reflect on later and wish she'd said something like, "You're right, you wouldn't have hurt me. I was *letting* you drag me around. I could have gotten away from you anytime I wanted." Then she would have sounded really tough. But her heart was still pounding too hard to come up with bold statements. Instead she said to Eliot, "You wouldn't happen to have handcuffs in your gym bag, would you?"

"No," he said, opening a pack around his waist and removing a Portland Police-issue Glock. "But they aren't going anywhere. Can you phone 9-1-1 and tell them we need a squad car here to pick these guys up? Then you need to tell me what happened."

After placing the call, she sat at her desk waiting for the officers to come and desperately wanting to take a shower. It felt like there were creepy-guy germs all over her. It dawned on her that the manager ought to know what was going on, so she called him. When he came she could go home.

As Eliot arranged both men on the floor next to each other with their hands on the backs of their heads, he gave an appreciative nod in Coral's direction. "Nice take-down. Are you ex-military or something?"

"I'm a fitness instructor. I teach self-defense, kick-boxing, all sorts of things. They picked on the wrong girl."

"Ha! Nice. What were they doing?"

"Looking for something. They said they followed me home and then followed me here." Home. Oh, no. They hadn't arrived at work right after she did, but about two hours later. "Maybe they went to my apartment first. Maybe they broke in."

"What about it? Did you two knuckleheads go to her place first?" The guys weren't talking. To Coral, "I'll go back with you."

"Would you? I'd feel so much better." This was almost like hanging around with John Marsh. She was starting to like this guy. "I'm sorry this is messing up your time off."

"It's not your fault. If I didn't want to help people I wouldn't have taken a public service job, right?"

There was already a cruiser outside the apartment building in the shade of the trees she loved to see through her window, but she didn't lose hope until she turned the corner in her hallway and saw Dan the landlord was peering through her open doorway. He almost jogged to stop her, seeming to want to soften the blow, his face stricken. "Coral."

"No, no, I know, someone broke in."

"I had the deadbolt on there and you locked it. It's not your fault. They tore the lock right out of the wood. Everybody was out. Nobody heard it. Smashed the wood in that old door. It was a good deadbolt, I put it on there myself. And you locked it. Not your fault either. It was a good lock. Broke the wooden frame." Dan was babbling from nerves.

It was worse than she could have imagined. The responding officers were having a hard time walking across all the books scattered five deep across every inch of the floor. Some of them had been torn open. The shelves had been toppled. Coral backed up and slipped down the hallway wall to the floor, putting her face on her knees.

"Aww, Coral, let me get you something. Some tissues or something. I'll be right back." Dan scurried off to his own apartment.

"Hey, Mark. Andy," Eliot called to the responding officers.

"Hey. What are you doing here? We didn't call for backup."

"The guys who did this went to the victim's workplace and tried to shake her down there. I just happened to be in the right place at the right time."

The *victim*.

Coral hated that word possibly more than any word she knew. The victim just sat there and did nothing. The victim got hurt and tortured and robbed and scammed and killed. She did not want to be the victim, and she didn't want to be called that. The victim was an 8-year old male Caucasian found in a ravine behind his family home. The victim was a 5-year old female who had her memory ripped away. Victims cried. She wasn't going to cry. She was going to sit there on the floor until her brain worked again and she knew what to do next. Stand up? Say something? Go somewhere?

In a fierce whisper Dan was saying to Eliot, "She's not a hoarder, she's a book collector, she collects books. Like a librarian."

Eliot glanced over his shoulder at Coral, filing away the new information: She's like a librarian.

The officers were trampling all over the books, breaking their spines and twisting their own ankles. She should pick them up and make neat piles. As she started to stand up she realized she was holding a glass of water. "Why am I holding a glass of water?"

Dan said, "I gave you that."

"Why?"

"I don't know. They always give people a glass of water, you know."

"Okay, thanks." Coral took a little sip to show appreciation, then put the water down on the hall floor. "Can I make piles of the books so they stop walking all over them?"

Eliot stuck his head in the door. "Hey, the owner would rather we didn't walk all over the books. Any reason why we can't pile them up somehow and make pathways or something?"

A voice from the bedroom called, "That would help. We can't even tell if she's been robbed."

Dan said, "I can help. Let me help. I'll set the shelves back up and we can just put the books back where they belong."

"Probably best if we just let the homeowner and the police do it, sir," called the voice.

"I trust Dan. If he doesn't mind helping, I'm okay with that," Coral said to Eliot.

"She's okay with it and we know who did it. We have the guys in custody," Eliot called.

With five people working, it only took about 15 minutes to get all the shelves back up and loaded. None of the books were in any kind of order, but that didn't matter. A pile was made of books that had been destroyed which Coral was averting her eyes from. She didn't want to know what she had lost. It was too much all at once.

"Ma'am, can you tell what they took? Jewelry? Any cash you may have kept?"

The jewelry box contained the same minimal amount of costume jewelry it always did. The small roll of twenties she kept rolled up in a sock was still there, although on the floor. All the electronics were there. They seemed to have taken nothing but any sense of security she had in her home.

When Dan left to get a replacement door and frame and the responding officers were getting ready to temporarily secure the apartment the one Eliot had called Andy asked, "Who were those guys you arrested? What was this all about? I'm not going to be able to fill out a report until I coordinate with you on this, Eliot."

"Yeah. And there are still huge unknowns on that too." He shook his head. "What were they trying to do, Coral? What exactly did they say?"

"They kept saying I should give them the thing that Phil gave me, that they knew I had it, and I kept saying 'what thing?'" Eliot was just asking her who Phil was as a look of horror spread across Coral's face. "Eliot! We need to check on Phil! If they did this here what have they done to him? Oh, why didn't I think of that sooner? He could be in horrible danger."

"Give me the address."

52 SHOCK UPON SHOCK

It wouldn't be possible to stay in the apartment that night, or, given the way she was feeling, possibly ever again. She was going to need to go to Pearl's. She gathered a couple of things, left the securing of the place to Dan, and headed out in her asphalt colored crash-mobile by way of the bookstore. The crystal vendor across the street peered through her window with a look of disapproval on her face. If she hadn't been dressed like a neo-hippy she would have looked exactly like a cranky old schoolmarm. She wasn't going to put up with goings-on like this in her neighborhood, no indeed she wasn't! It was going to take hours of chanting to clear this mess up!

Red's Reads looked like Coral's apartment had. She called, "Phil? Phil? Are you okay?"

Eliot had maneuvered his way to the back office. "There's no one back here. I don't think anybody is here unless he's under all of that." He gestured to piles upon piles of books. "We should probably call in a K-9 unit. Coral, do you have a friend's house you can go to? This is going to take a while."

"I'm on my way to my sister's. Can you call me when you find Phil? Or, wait, my cellphone—they smashed it at the gym. I can give you my sister's number. Or I can go get one of those pre-paid phones. I'll do that. I'll be right back."

There were doubtless other stores closer that carried pre-paid cellphones, but Coral didn't want to think through exactly where those could be and simply got into the car to drive to a big box store she knew carried them on an end cap near the registers.

Cheap phone secured, she pulled back into traffic and was driving through a green light when the passenger window to her right suddenly filled with something white - an oversized SUV. There was a

247

huge metallic bang and the sense of going sideways. Her side air bags deployed and then deflated.

The first thing she saw was the shocked face of the driver of a car that was heading toward her. Her car had been pushed partway into oncoming traffic. If she had been driving in the countryside that could have been the end of her, but in downtown Portland nobody could drive very fast with all the stoplights, heavy traffic, and constant lane changes. The driver who was heading her way easily stopped in time, put on his emergency flashers, and stepped out of his car to see if she needed help.

She didn't know if she needed help. She was unclear about everything. She should probably move her car. The man from the car who hadn't hit her was rapping on her window. She rolled it down.

"I'm sorry. I move. Gonna move. Out of the way." She sounded like she was drunk.

The guy looked like a college student with curly hair and a scruffy beard. "Are you okay? You seem a little dazed."

"I'm okay. I need to move my car."

The driver of the white SUV got out and walked over. "I'm okay! In case anybody wants to know." She looked to be about 18 years old and had a cellphone in her hand. She started busily texting something. Probably telling her friends she had just been in a car accident. She may have been texting when she'd run the red light.

The college student seemed to be on top of things, which was very good because Coral's brain had gone into slow motion. He pointed to a parking lot on that block and said, "Why don't you pull in there, if you can move the car?"

The car made a ghastly noise, but she managed to pull it into the lot. The college student apparently directed the girl in the SUV over to the same parking lot, then negotiated an insurance information swap, made sure Coral could walk and had a phone, and took off without leaving his name. He was one of life's kind people who just happen to come along at the right moment, and this was all a very good thing because Coral had gone beyond her ability to deal with anything. The other driver's car was less damaged and she drove off with no word of apology. Coral had the sense that she should have been feeling some strong emotion about that girl, probably anger, but she felt nothing. Various onlookers slowly wandered off, some after leaving phone numbers, ready to testify about whose fault the accident had been.

Coral wondered if she'd had a stroke or something. Her thoughts were not forming properly and she had a hard time talking. All she wanted to do was run. Just run away home. Not her apartment home—that had been trashed. She wanted to run home to Pearl.

She ran home to Pearl and Daddy. She was 5 years old and terrified for Jet and she couldn't say anything.

The parking lot belonged to an ice cream shop, which had a brightly colored bench outside. She dragged herself to the bench and sat down, with an odd jangling feeling, like her entire nervous system was sending random pulses through her body.

A mom came out of the store with a toddler and sat next to her. The mom held a cone of pink ice cream and was trying to show the toddler how to eat an ice cream cone. "See, like this. Watch mommy lick it. Now Molly do it." She put the ice cream up to the child's face. "Lick it. Go on. Stick your tongue out. Lick it, Molly. That's right!"

Another image came to mind unbidden and a wave of nausea nearly overcame Coral.

Lick it, doggy. Go on.

She didn't know where to go if she was actually going to be sick but in front of an ice cream shop would be a bad place.

Lick it, doggy. Go on.

She got up and ran, a horrible image in her mind.

She knew now. She knew what she had seen all those years ago.

The day had heaped shock upon shock, turning her into a victim, like she'd been when she was 5 on the day, that horrible day, when her world had ripped apart. She was resonating with her younger self. Five-year-old Coral had finally woken up to say what she knew.

Her running slowed but she kept moving. She felt there was someplace up ahead she needed to go.

Three blocks down, she came to a funeral home set back from the road with parking running down the side. Something made her stop and look at it. It had perfectly trimmed shrubbery and a manicured lawn. Flouncy curtains obscured the windows. The paint looked new, and even the roof tiles all matched one another perfectly. It looked as though it was completely untouched by the effects of time, as though when you stepped onto that property you were entering a bubble of eternity, where the flowers would be real, but would never wilt. An italicized sign placed low on the front lawn read, "Carlson's Funeral Home: Our family caring for you since 1963."

"It's all right, Coral, the Carlsons will take really good care of Jet." Daddy is holding her and she's fighting him.

The Carlsons who were always taking care of Isaac in the books were the staff at Carlson's Funeral Home. Jet's body had been placed at Carlson's Funeral Home and they had handled the memorial and burial. At five she had been unclear about what "taking care of Jet" had meant. She'd thought at first he had gone to live with them, and it wasn't until later that she'd understood he was dead, or even what "dead" really meant. When you're 5, "dead" means you lost the game and you lie there on the ground for a little while making a face with your eyes rolled back and your tongue lolling to the side, and then you jump up and play again.

It was coming back now, when her brain was already overwhelmed with grief over her home, worries over Phil, the car accident, and even confusion over what to tell the police about the artifact. It was coming back now, when she was a *victim*. It took being a victim again to find the little girl who was hiding. Little Coral the victim and Big Coral the victim, not quite the same person, yet running and running, running away to Pearl, and speaking victim-ese to each other.

Coral sat down on the lawn of Carlson's Funeral Home and cried as though she would never stop.

Pain upon pain, she remembered it all.

A few passersby noticed the crying girl, but because of where she was sitting, assumed she was crying about a death and left her alone with her grief.

She wanted to be with Pearl. She pulled out the cheap phone.

53 THE BIG BOY

The two sisters waited at the police station in an alcove set apart from the main hall in chairs bolted to the floor. They sat with big eyes, doing what they'd been told, watching the people walking by and wondering which were criminals, which were victims, which were lawyers, and which were police.

Then John Marsh walked up to them, a real person, as though he hadn't been living in Coral's book adventures.

His hair wasn't what she was used to. It was light brown on top and gray around the temples. His large features looked less childlike, with deeper furrows under his eyes and extending from his nose to the corners of his mouth. He had a bit of a paunch. Not much, but it was there. He was 20 years older, but it was the same guy with the open face.

"Pearl and Coral Ambrose? There you are, the semi-precious gems all grown up. Sergeant John Marsh." He extended his hand to each of them. When Coral stood to shake the offered hand, she got another surprise. Her John Marsh had always been tall, but the real John Marsh was only slightly taller than she was.

"I was one of the officers assigned to the case 20 years ago, and if you have new information for me I would love to hear it. This case has been eating at me for a long time."

It was all too much to take in at once. Here was the living, breathing, real-life John Marsh, only he was an old guy. He must have seemed taller to her when she was 5. Back then he had been a kind, heroic policeman and she'd had a big crush on him, and at the time felt bad about not telling him the truth. Little Coral let him down. Then the artifact had turned him into her buddy in the book adventures. The things she had done with this man in the romance novel!

Embarrassing! Coral tried to suppress a smile, but the sergeant noticed. "Something funny?"

"I just remember you, that's all." She had to start thinking of him in a way that was more in tune with reality. What she was there to do would help. Time after time she had let him down in her book adventures. It was finally time to make that right.

"I'm surprised. You were only 5. You *are* the younger one, right? I reviewed your file when you called to say you were coming. You said you had new information for me?"

Pearl spoke up excitedly. "She remembers now. It's coming back to her. She had no memory of anything for the longest time, and now she remembers what happened. But she won't tell me and it's driving me crazy."

"I just want to say it once so I'm remembering the real memory and not remembering telling you." Coral knew Pearl didn't understand and disliked being left out. "If that makes any sense."

"Are you afraid you may change your story?" Sergeant Marsh asked.

"It's not that at all. I'll be telling the truth. I just want the truth to be as unadulterated as it can be after all these years. I want to tell you what I remember and not tell you what I remember telling someone else. Maybe that doesn't make sense to anybody but me."

"Actually, it does make sense to me. Memory is an elastic thing." Sergeant Marsh led them to a plain and dreary interrogation room that looked a lot like the ones on television. The walls were painted a misbegotten green and there was a feeling in the air that no one was ever happy there. "Step into my parlor, ladies. May I offer you some tea?"

"I just love what you've done with the place," quipped Coral, immediately regretting the joke afterward. It had come from nerves.

"It smells funny in here," said Pearl.

"Unfortunately I have to spend a lot of my time in places that smell funny. It's part of the job. Have a seat. Seriously, can I get you something to drink? There's a soda machine in the hall."

He may have been older and shorter than she expected, but he was still nice. "No, I'm fine, thanks."

"Me too," said Pearl.

Sergeant Marsh set his case file next to him and took out a pad and pen, which he set on the desk in front of him. "This case bothered me in part because I have a son the same age as your brother." He shook his head bitterly and clapped his left hand to his chest, over his heart. "It wounded me personally. I kept thinking it could have been my boy."

John Marsh's chest wound. This was a gesture he'd used even during the investigation, and young Coral had interpreted it as a real wound.

The Sergeant flipped open the notepad and began. "So let's review the facts. Unpleasant, I know. Are you ready? Little Jet Ambrose, age 8, was found strangled to death in the ravine behind the family home by his father, who went looking for him when he didn't come home for dinner. We had one guy in custody for a while, a transient named Harcourt Higgins who went by the street name Hard Core."

Higgins! There really was a Higgins. Someone who looked guilty but didn't do it.

"With a name like that, I would have changed it too, but not to 'Hard Core.' Anyway, the guy was a real prize but we couldn't get any solid evidence against him. He sure looked guilty, though.

"The case got a lot of media attention and we followed hundreds of leads, but nothing ever panned out. In the meantime we had the family to talk to, and there was one person who seemed to know more than she was saying. That was the youngest daughter, Coral. That was you."

"Yeah, you talked to me a lot. I remember you. You were really nice to me. You told me to call you John."

"You seemed to be afraid and I thought maybe you were afraid of the police."

"I wasn't afraid of you, I was afraid of something else."

The sergeant leveled a steady gaze at her and nodded slowly. "I also wondered about that. Anyway, I'm going to let you tell your story now."

"Okay." Coral took a deep breath and went for it. "These memories are like little pieces. They don't play out like one flashback scene from a movie. They aren't connected. I'm trying not to embellish by saying what must have happened in between, but if I do I'll say that's what I'm doing, okay? Like I assume I had nobody to play with because Pearl had a friend over and she told me to get lost. I do remember I couldn't find Jet. I assume Dad was busy doing something.

So I thought I would go looking for Jet. I went out of our yard into the park area back there and down into the ravine. I wasn't really allowed to do that, but I did it anyway."

This was going to be the hard part. Coral took a deep breath to relax herself and pressed on. "When I got down near where the creek is I heard this voice saying 'Lick it, doggy.' I wanted to see the doggy, so I crept along as quietly as I could using sneaking feet."

Coral paused and lowered her eyebrows. She was feeling her confusion all over again, despite having an adult perspective. "There was a big boy there with Jet. Jet had a rope tied around his neck. I thought they were playing a doggy game. The big boy wanted him to lick something. He was going, 'Lick it, doggy, go on.'"

Pearl looked confused at first, and then sick. Sergeant Marsh remained silent, his eyes fixed on her face.

"I didn't understand what I was seeing at all. I was really mad at Jet for doing such a bad thing. I yelled, 'Jet, stop that! I'm telling Daddy!' And then I could see that Jet had tears all over his face. He was coughing and pulling at the rope around his neck. Then I don't remember exactly what happened, but I must have started to run away because the next thing I remember is that I'm yelling 'Daddy! Daddy! Help!' And the big boy is holding me from behind with his arm around my waist and he puts his hand over my mouth." She had unconsciously slipped into the present tense.

"Oh my God, Coral." Pearl's eyes filled with tears.

"But that's not what happened, not what you think. I guess he didn't like little girls. And he says to me, 'If you ever say anything about what you saw I'll kill him, you understand? Nod your head yes.' And then he forces my head to nod, which he could do because he has his hand over my mouth."

Coral's head went up and down as though forced.

"Then he goes, 'And then I'll kill your family and make you watch. And then I'll kill you too.' I'm having a hard time breathing because I'm crying and my nose is stuffed up and he has his hand over my mouth. He goes, 'You're not going to remember anything you saw, right?' He shakes my head no. He goes, 'When they die it'll be all your fault. You better just forget everything that happened, understand?' And I can't breathe and the edges of the world are turning into black dots and all I can see is right in front of me. Then I may have blacked out or something, I don't know. Then I'm running back to the house as fast as I can. I'm thinking about how I'm not going to remember anything I saw. You were still playing with your friend in our room."

Pearl interjected, "Then I asked you where Jet was and you pointed at the park."

Sergeant Marsh nodded. "I have that in my notes. You were dirty. You were probably on the ground at some point."

"Then I crawled into my bed and thought nothing was real and I went to the very bottom of it and stayed there."

"I remember you doing that. We thought you were really weird, Megan and I. You stayed there a long time."

"I stayed until Megan went home. Eventually you told me to come out of there. I was worried because I had pointed at the park. Would the big boy know I had done that? Would he kill Jet because I had done that? Then later Jet was dead—"

A sob escaped her. She closed her eyes as tight as she could and plowed on.

"—and it was my fault. All I did was point but that was the same as telling so that's why he killed Jet. And then he was going to come after the rest of us and it was my fault."

Coral hugged herself to keep from shaking. "Anyway, I *felt* like it was my fault that Jet died and like I had to protect everybody else. Wow, how dumb is that? That big boy couldn't have known I'd pointed at the park."

Sergeant Marsh shrugged. "You were 5. That's how 5-year-olds think."

Pearl was rubbing Coral's back.

"This 'big boy' you're talking about, would you recognize a picture of him?" Sergeant Marsh may have been hoping she would pick Hard Core Higgins's face from a stack of mugshots, even though he'd been in his early 30s at the time, and not someone anybody would call a 'big boy.'

"I think so. Yeah. One more thing." Coral fumbled in her handbag for a tissue, hands shaking. "He was a dragon."

"What do you mean?" Sergeant Marsh asked in a very quiet voice.

"He was a dragon, so he was magic and could do anything. The other kids called him a dragon."

Sergeant Marsh looked at Pearl quizzically. "Do you remember a kid the other kids called a dragon?"

She shook her head. "Not that I recall."

"No, this is good. We're getting somewhere," Sergeant Marsh said encouragingly. "What I really need to know is who that big boy was. You did recognize him from before that day, right, Coral?"

"Yeah. He lived a couple of blocks away. I didn't really know him. He was in high school, or maybe college."

"What was his name? Or do you at least remember which house?"

"I don't know which house and the name I remember can't be right. His name was something like Napdrone. Dragon Napdrone?"

Sergeant Marsh turned to Pearl. "That ring a bell at all?"

Pearl shook her head, thinking. "Dragon Napdrone. No."

"Maybe a nickname? Or something that sounded like that?"

Pearl was quiet.

Sergeant Marsh continued to prod. "She was only 5 and she didn't know him. She probably just heard his name once or twice. Try saying it out loud a time or two."

"Dragon Napdrone? Dragon Napdrone." Pearl repeated. "Dragon ... Draeger. Draeger Natherone. It sounds like Draeger Natherone! It was *Draeger Natherone?*"

The sergeant looked at her quizzically.

"He was a big kid, that's right, maybe college age but lived at home. He may not have been in school at all. Sort of a unibrow and big nose. I didn't really know him because he was way older. I got the feeling the older kids thought he was weird, not cool."

Coral's stomach turned. Coming out of Pearl's mouth it sounded right. Draeger Natherone had killed her brother and she had seen it. He had stolen away the first part of her childhood and turned her dad into a drunk who wrecked his car and died.

John Marsh nodded thoughtfully. "Sure, I can see how a little girl would hear an unusual name like Draeger Natherone and think his name is Dragon Napdrone and that he really is a dragon." Scribbling the name on his pad, the sergeant looked hopeful. "I hope this pans out. Twenty years is too long for that little guy to wait for justice. Do you have any idea where he is, Pearl?"

Pearls voice got very flat, something she was prone to do when she was angry. "No idea at all. He—he came to the house with his mother to drop off a casserole before the memorial service. He told

Dad he was going to hunt all over until he found the guy, you know, bragging. In fact he was always buzzing around the house for a while."

"I know he was! Scared me to death!" Coral had withdrawn deeper and deeper into her own world rather than risk going outside and running into him. Every time she'd seen him around, she was afraid he had come to kill another member of her family because she had pointed at the park.

She had been so afraid then, and now she was very, very angry.

"That's not uncommon. We always take a hard look at the guy who's injecting himself into a crime scene where he has no reason to be. I'm surprised I didn't notice him at the time."

"If you find him I want to kill him." Pearl hadn't thought that statement through carefully. They needed to get out of there.

"Never say that to an officer of the law," Sergeant Marsh said kindly.

"No, I didn't mean it literally." She clapped her hand over her mouth.

"Go back to the waiting area. If he did something like that when he was a teenager, there's no way he doesn't have a record. Guys like that don't just stop offending. I'll find him."

Pearl gathered her little sister in her arms and just held her in the waiting room, not knowing what to say, but finally settling on, "Thank you."

"I wish I would have remembered sooner. They could have caught him. That asshole really put a whammy on me."

Pearl frowned. "A whammy, huh?"

"Well, I don't know what to call it."

"For once you're at a loss for words." Pearl released her and looked intently at her face. "It's not your fault. It's not Jet's fault, Dad's fault, my fault, the police's fault. It's totally his fault, Draeger Natherone."

"I know." Finally there would be justice, and it was only the two of them left to see it. "You're my best friend, Pearl."

"I know."

"Coral? Did something else happen?" Eliot was walking down the hall in uniform and approaching her with concern in his face.

"Eliot! No, I'm here about something else. Hi." Coral took a swipe at her damp eyes with a tissue. "This is my sister, Pearl." Pearl smiled at Eliot. At last her reclusive sister knew a guy. "Still no sign of Phil?"

"No one knows where he is. You'll let us know if he contacts you, won't you? We've escalated this. So... everything okay?" No doubt he was thinking that people don't just wander into police stations and hang around for the ambience. "Anything I can help you with?"

"No, we're already being helped." It sounded like Coral was fending off a sales clerk at a clothing store that paid on commission. "We're here to see Sergeant Marsh."

Eliot was interested. "Oh yeah? What do you want with my dad?"

"Your *dad?*" Coral turned to Pearl. "This is Eliot Marsh, the sergeant's son, and being incredibly stupid I didn't make that connection." She'd noticed the name back when she first met him, but never knew what to make of it. It was a fairly common name and besides, at that point John Marsh was a fictional character. Or so she'd thought.

"Why would you?" Pearl asked. She didn't know about book adventures and the fictional John Marsh. "We just met his dad for the first time since we were little kids."

"You and I haven't really known each other very long," added Eliot. "You knew my dad when you were kids?"

"I'm going to go out on a limb here and guess that you're exactly three years older than Coral," said Pearl. "Because he said he had a son the same age as our brother. Unless you have another brother, he was probably referring to you."

"I get the feeling there's quite a story here."

"You have no idea." No matter how good-looking he was Coral was in no mood to hash it all out for someone she scarcely knew. It had been an emotionally draining day and she had the feeling there would be more to come. "I'll tell you later sometime, if you're interested."

"I'm interested." He was looking her right in the eyes. "Right now I need to go. Let me know if you hear from Phil."

Pearl nudged her in the ribs as Eliot headed out the side door that led to the squad cars. "He's interested."

Even with all of this going on, Pearl was playing matchmaker. "I heard. Cut me some slack, I kind of have a lot on my plate at the moment."

Pearl was looking over Coral's shoulder. "Hello, Eliot's Dad."

"What?" Sergeant Marsh hadn't expected to be greeted like that when he returned with what he'd found during his search.

"We just met your son. Well I did. Turns out Coral already knew him. Isn't that weird?"

"Where do you know Eliot from?"

Coral pretended to pick a piece of lint off her shirt, acting casual. "He works out at the gym where I work and he's been helping me with a different police matter. Some guys trashed my apartment."

"That was you?" John Marsh looked as though she was a discordant note in a symphony. "Why are you here telling me about your brother now?"

"Because—because I didn't remember anything for so long and then being scared and violated like that made it come back. Like all I could think about was being helpless and afraid, like that was all I was and all I could remember being. And it all came back to me. It's like I had to be a victim to remember."

Pearl was murmuring to her, stroking her shoulder. "You're not, you're not. You're strong and brave. They're not going to get away with this."

"Okay. I guess I can see that. Come back with me to my desk. There's something I want to show you." Sergeant Marsh led the mute sisters to his computer, where he had info on Draeger Natherone already displayed.

There was a classic mugshot, front and side views, of a sad-looking man with a beaky nose, one eyebrow that ran across his entire forehead, scabby skin, and long wispy hair. "Is this your former neighbor?"

Pearl was disgusted. "Yes, that's him. Older and even stupider looking, but that's the guy I remember." She turned to Coral, who was trying to understand why her hands felt like they didn't belong to her and why blood was no longer going all the way to her head. "Coral? Coral? Are you okay?"

The sergeant sprang into action. "I'm going to put your legs above your heart. You'll be okay in a second." He caught her in his arms like she barely weighed a thing, using those big shoulders she remembered, and laid her down on the floor with her feet on her chair.

Coral looked around at the police station from that odd vantage point and felt extremely conspicuous. A pair of uniformed officers paused, determined everything was under control, and moved on. Other people went about their business as though people took a little rest on the floor all the time.

"I'm better now. I'm okay." She pulled her legs off the chair and sat up.

"All right, but take it slow. Just stay down there a minute and then let me help you into the chair. I think I know the answer to the question, but I have to ask." The sergeant pointed to his computer screen. "Coral, is that the man who killed your brother?"

"Come on, just help me into the chair. I feel stupid." When she was sitting normally she felt more or less fine. "I didn't see him kill Jet. What I saw was him sexually molesting Jet and choking him with a rope around his neck, and he threatened to kill him and my whole family. Then Jet was dead within an hour. So I would say yeah, the guy in that picture killed Jet. Where is he?"

"I'm going to find out."

54 JOHN MARSH'S SON

After one more day of eating pastries from Cornish's and drinking wine at Pearl's, Coral was more or less ready to begin making her apartment habitable again. At least she had backup.

"You don't need to do this. We only just met."

Coral and Eliot were standing in the doorway of her apartment, surveying the damage. Dan, ever efficient, had replaced the door and frame. The new door was a lot more solid and had a peephole, chain, and deadbolt. After it was painted it would look nice. With most of the books put back on the shelves, albeit randomly, you'd hardly know about the break-in from just looking at the living room—if it weren't for the pile of torn books in the corner. Of course, once you saw the kitchen, bathroom, and bedroom, you'd have no doubt. Every drawer had been overturned and every cabinet emptied by the two goons.

Eliot was wearing neither his uniform nor his workout gear. He had on a black U2 T-shirt and dark jeans.

"This will give me a chance to hear the story about how you know my dad. I can probably get the dishes washed and put back pretty quickly, which will help a lot. I'll leave your clothes to you, and your bathroom with your girl things."

Maybe he was a caring guy, like the kind she was looking for. He had already been a hero. She wondered how he felt about bookaholics.

"I sort of feel like I want to burn it all. Is that normal?"

"I think that feeling passes." Eliot, no stranger to dealing with people in crisis, got to work loading the dishwasher with whatever wasn't broken.

"We don't have to do it all right now. Pearl and her husband James are coming over too."

She paused, hoping she wasn't about to make a horrible mistake. Full disclosure now, before she got in over her head? Yes. The longer she held this back, the worse he would take it when he realized she had not been totally forthcoming.

"There's something I need to tell you about the guys that did this. But first I should say that I made the wrong decision when I was 5. I knew who killed my brother and I didn't tell your dad because I thought I was protecting my family. Now I'm afraid to tell you something because I want to protect Phil."

Eliot stopped working and looked at her silently with a dishrag in his hand.

Those eyes of his really bored into a person. Again she was ready to confess even things she'd never done.

"I trusted your dad then, and I trust him now. I thought about going straight to him, but this is your case, so I guess I should tell you. And you're his son, so I'm hoping you're his son. I mean, just like him. The thing is, I know what the guys were looking for, and I do actually have it. It's not in my apartment. I put it someplace safe because Phil was afraid of those guys and thought something like this might happen to him. He didn't think they'd come after me or that they even knew about me. I stuck it in a safe place because I was being cautious."

"So you lied to me before." He didn't yell or turn red in the face, but he was clearly angry. Maybe she shouldn't have told him. He was first and foremost a cop. She needed to remember that. But who knew what the thugs were saying in jail and whether anyone would believe them? Better to come clean. Or had she only told him because she felt attracted to him? Maybe that was his schtick, like good cop/bad cop. He was hot cop who could get the girls to tell him everything.

"I didn't actually lie, only by omission."

Eliot's cell rang. After a quiet conversation in the kitchen, he returned to her and said, "My dad is downstairs. He's coming up."

"He is? What for?" John Marsh was on his way? She had to get over the feeling that he was the fictional character from her book adventures and was her friend.

"Says he has news for you and Pearl. I said Pearl was on her way here, so it looks like he's saving you both a trip to the station. We can all tell each other the things we need to know at the same time. How about that?"

"That would be fine, except there's something I don't want Pearl to know because I don't want to put her in danger."

"I see. Well, if you talk fast you can say what you need to say to both of us before she arrives."

Eliot and Coral worked silently for the few minutes it took for John to arrive. Coral continued to get a bit of a thrill at the sight of John Marsh, even if he was not really the John Marsh of her books. Seeing father and son next to each other proved there was a family resemblance, but Eliot was taller, had dark brown hair, and not as much of the open, child-like face of his dad. In a way, he was better looking in a classic sense, and younger, of course, but with the same broad shoulders.

He was also real.

"Those guys really trashed your apart— you sure have a lot of books! It's like a library in here." So now the real John Marsh had said it too. Everybody did.

Eliot filled his father in on the plan for Coral to tell them something before Pearl arrived.

"What is it you wanted to tell us?"

The words tumbled out of Coral quickly. She knew how it was going to sound. "I know what they were looking for, and I do have it. Phil gave it to me for safekeeping. It's a piece of advanced technology."

Father and son looked baffled. A used bookstore owner with advanced technology?

"A revolutionary piece of gear. The guys who invented it want to make sure it's used appropriately. It's something that could really benefit humanity. If it got into the wrong hands, someone could make a ridiculous amount of money off of it and the benefit to humanity would be lost."

She watched their faces as they weighed whether she was delusional or whether she was telling the truth. Telling it like this sounded so James Bond. She wouldn't be at all surprised if they didn't believe her.

Eliot asked, "What does it do?"

"In the right hands, it's a tool for psychological healing. In the wrong hands, it's a psychedelic drug. Phil knows more about this than I do. I wish he were here so you could ask him."

"So it's a pharmaceutical invention." The sergeant addressed Eliot. "We may need to bring in the DEA."

"It's not really a drug, though. It's a polymer. It looks like a piece of plastic, about three inches by eight inches."

The resemblance between father and son grew stronger when both were obviously attempting to determine whether or not to call in Social Services instead of the DEA. Finally Eliot asked, "How does it work?"

"I don't know, and Phil said the guys who invented it don't know either. They were just starting to study it when they realized the secret had gotten out and they had a big problem on their hands. See, they didn't invent it on purpose, it was a fluke." She spoke quickly, trying to get the story out. "They were trying to recreate what they did and the last Phil heard they hadn't been able to reproduce it yet, so the one he gave me is the only one of its kind, and Phil was keeping it safe. He sort of put himself in his own version of witness protection. All of this happened at Stanford. Am I explaining this very well?"

"Go on ... "

"Phil let me try it. It's amazing! You wouldn't believe it! It makes you think you've entered into a fictional world, really entered into it, better than virtual reality, more immersive." She was pretty sure they were now labeling her a 'drug addict.' She needed to show she was talking about a scientific advance and not the latest legal (so far) high. "It puts you into a state sort of like a dream or a hypnotic trance where you can sort things out and get clarity. You feel like you've entered into a book, but it's a book you wrote yourself. I didn't believe it at first either. I don't blame you. But the thing is, that's what those guys are looking for. I know where it is, but it's important that I keep it safe."

As the police officer in charge of the investigation into the break-in at Red's Reads, Eliot was going to let the question of Coral's character slide for a moment. He had a job to do. "So where's Phil?"

She wished she knew, but as of an hour ago, all she knew was that he was safe.

"Phil is all right. I don't know where he is, but he did contact me."

"He contacted you and you didn't tell us?" The flatness of his voice showed that any pretense of Eliot the friend was gone at that moment. He was just Eliot the cop.

"It just happened. I am telling you." After no body was found underneath the books in Phil's shop, Coral had become optimistic that he had gotten away. When that morning she'd received an email from an address she'd never seen before, she knew for sure he was all right. It read:

Hi, Coral!!!! LTNS, huh? I still have that book you gave me, the one where they burn the car and then drive around in it and everyone is all emo all the time. Ha ha! LMAO. Bet you thought you'd never get it back, huh? Write me! Miss you!

The writer was describing the book she'd brought Phil the day they met that was so bad it needed to be thrown away, which was something only Phil would know. He seemed to be trying to sound like someone her age, probably a girl. He had been a college professor, so he'd spent a lot of time listening to young people, clearly people younger than she was. But the good news was: Phil was all right. He didn't say where he was, but he was worried about her. She'd hit reply, channeled her inner 18-year-old, and wrote:

Hi back!!!! You can keep that book, it's okay. I still have your book too. Ha ha! Remember those jerks we met and couldn't get rid of? I saw them again! BARF!!! My friend scared them off so it's cool. Call me when you come to town.

"It's sad to think he's afraid to email from his own address, but maybe he thinks someone got hold of my laptop."

"I'm going to want to see those emails," said Eliot.

"Of course. I know you think I'm crazy or something, but please go ahead and check on the facts I have. Phil was a Stanford psychology professor until recently."

"I already knew that part."

"Oh! Of course!" He'd done his research as part of the ongoing investigation. "He left sort of suddenly after working in a think tank with some other guys on a secret project."

"Through SRL."

"What?"

"They weren't working at Stanford, per se; the think tank was at Stanford Research Labs in Menlo Park."

"Oh. Okay. Well, I don't know the names of any of the other guys involved, but I got the feeling Phil trusted the ones on his team. They may be in danger."

"How long did you know Phil?"

"Not long at all. Maybe two weeks."

"You seem to have gotten awfully close in two weeks."

"It was an intense two weeks. You have no idea."

Eliot's face betrayed no emotion. "So he was your boyfriend?"

Sergeant Marsh watched the exchange carefully, no doubt curious about the relationship between Coral and his son.

"What? No! He's older than my dad would have been! He was a friend. He was acting like a psychologist which I didn't even know he was at first."

Sergeant Marsh said, "I'm going to want to see this polymer thing."

"That's fair. It's not here right now, but I can get it."

Eliot and John Marsh had decisions to make about the legitimacy of the artifact, so she was going to have to give them the opportunity to learn more about it, probably try it first hand. In the meantime, she hoped they kept Pearl out of it.

The new front door swung open. "Ho. Lee. CRAP."

Pearl and James had arrived and were standing in the kitchen, looking shocked, even the usually unflappable James. He had traded in his normal business-casual attire for a plaid flannel shirt that was apparently left over from his days as a grunge rock fan in preparation for what he thought would be a little straightening up. This was their first sight of the trashed apartment. Pearl darted down the hall to Coral's room.

"Are you *kidding* me? Are you *kidding* me? Why? Why did they do this? Who were those guys?"

Eliot spoke up. "We have them in custody. They were looking for something they thought Coral had and when they didn't find it here, they went after her at work."

Eliot didn't tell Pearl about the artifact. Coral had a flash of hope.

"What were they looking for?"

"I told you already, they thought this bookstore owner I had just met, you know, the one who wanted to buy some of my books, had given me something. Weird, huh?"

"You're pressing charges, right?"

"*Oh*, yeah."

Pearl fist-bumped her sister. "Good. Oh, I'm sorry, James, this is Sergeant Marsh, the policeman who was trying to find out who killed Jet all those years ago, and his son Eliot, who knows Coral from her gym."

James gave a little wave and went back to examining the destruction.

"I'm surprised to run into you here, Sergeant," said Pearl. "Nice-surprised, though. Hey! I have a question for you. Did you name your son after Eliot Ness?"

"Everyone always thinks that, but no, Marie is a big reader and named him for the writer T.S. Eliot. People think Eliot Ness was the greatest cop ever because of that TV show, but most of it was made up."

"Marie is your wife?" Coral asked. John Marsh nodded.

Coral actually found the name very amusing. In the romance novel Miss Marie had been the evil rival for Sir John Marsh's affections. Apparently as a little girl with a huge crush on the nice policeman, she'd heard the name of his wife and decided she was an enemy. Now it seemed she would like the real Marie Marsh if they were to meet. After all, Marie was a reader.

"Marie Marsh. Pretty name. Which reminds me, at some point I want to ask you about some other names that popped into my head. I was wondering if you could help me make sense of them."

"How about now?"

"Didn't you come here with news?"

"Yeah, but let's save that. Shoot."

"Was there a boss named Light or something? In the police department?"

"Light? No. There used to be Police Commissioner Linfield Lype. I doubt you would have met him, but he was on television a lot talking about the case. He retired 10 or so years ago."

When she was 5 she had probably heard "Lype" as "Light."

"Was there a Doctor Bruce?"

Sergeant Marsh frowned and shook his head. "No, no doctors except the medical examiner, but I'm sure we didn't let you girls anywhere near them when they were working."

"I keep thinking there was a Doctor Bruce who was kind of full of himself."

The sergeant smiled. "I know who you're thinking of! Sure! The FBI sent a criminologist to work with us and he told us all to call him Doctor Reynolds. Now that's funny. Even a 5-year-old girl could see he was full of himself. Bruce Reynolds, yeah, that was his name. Maybe he told you to call him Doctor Bruce."

Pearl nodded. "Doctor Bruce! I remember that guy. He seemed pretty sure he was going to get more information out of us, especially you, Coral."

"He wasn't a medical doctor then? I guess when I was little I didn't know about the Ph.D. kind of doctor. What about a Hasagawa, or a Cavalli?"

Sergeant Marsh frowned in concentration, trying to place the names, but Pearl jumped in. "I know who they are! They were neighbors we used to have."

"They were? I don't remember them."

"They both sold their houses. I guess it was right after Jet was killed." Now that Pearl was not only an adult, but also a realtor herself, she was beginning to see the situation in a different light. "Huh. They probably moved because of Jet's murder. Didn't want to live where the boy had been killed. Either they didn't feel safe or it creeped them out to see us coming and going every day. These names just sort of popped into your head?"

"Something like that, yeah. They weren't attached to any real memory. I couldn't figure it out."

"Any more names? No?" Sergeant Marsh said. "I'm so happy to get this resolved—you can't believe it. We were following so many leads and nothing panned out. At one time we were even wondering if there was some significance to your brother's name, that's how desperate we were."

The sisters and James looked at him blankly. "It's kind of an unusual name, but why would that get him killed?" James asked.

"It was some crazy idea someone had. I don't even remember off-hand who brought it up. It may have been an anonymous tip. Someone noticed that you were all named for semi-precious materials, things you'd make jewelry out of. Up to that point I'd been thinking of the name Jet like a jet airplane, but jet is also a kind of stone. That's where the term 'jet black' comes from. You know that of course. Whoever it was looked it up and discovered it's the—"

Coral and Pearl spoke in unison. "Stone of mourning."

Pearl went on. "We know. We found that out ourselves years later. Back in the days when widows would wear nothing but black, the one kind of gemstone deemed appropriate for them on brooches and rings was jet because it was also black."

"We think it was just life being freaky. Did you think it actually meant something?" Coral was puzzled.

Sergeant Marsh shrugged. "Who would name their kid after the stone of mourning and then take off the way your mom did? Something never seemed right about her."

James jumped into the conversation. "I have to agree with you there. I met Ruby once and she's a real piece of work, but I think she's just a selfish woman who wasn't interested in her kids. She was the precious stone and her kids were semi-precious. I think that about sums it up. I doubt she's educated enough to know jet is the stone of mourning. She probably looked at a list of semi-precious gems and said, let's see, what can you name a boy? And it was either that or Jasper. Fifty-fifty chance, and Jet it was."

"Did you really suspect our mom?" asked Pearl.

"Your mom, your dad." He looked at the sisters and said nothing, but the look told them everything. He had suspected them too. It wouldn't have been the first time a childhood fight had ended in death. "It's my job to get to the bottom of whatever happened, and that means everyone is a suspect. People tend to think of a child killer as being a stranger, but in reality it's usually someone the victim knows well, and often a family member. Those are the facts we work with. The bit about the name sounded far-fetched from the moment I heard it, but it was the sort of little idiotic thing that kept us chasing our tails when we couldn't come up with any solid leads. Drove me around the bend. Until now." Sergeant Marsh smiled warmly at Coral. "We found your Draeger Natherone."

Coral caught her breath and Pearl reached for James's hand.

"I didn't want to say anything yesterday because sometimes parolees aren't where they're supposed to be, but the cops in Fort Wayne picked him up and he's in custody now. He was living as a registered sex offender after doing 15 years for molestation. They didn't get a confession. But we still have Jet's clothing to check for trace evidence, and the chance is very good we'll find something that belongs to Natherone on it."

"Thank you, thank you. Best news ever," said James, as he squeezed his wife around the shoulder.

"Don't think this is all sewed up. I got to warn you. They may not find any trace, and even if they do, it takes a long time to process. TV shows have everyone convinced it only takes 15 minutes. It's going to be weeks before we hear anything, you understand? And in the meantime, he may even be let out on bail. This is the point where the lawyers get involved, and since he was living out of state it's all going to be a pain in the ass. You understand? Just so we're clear on that."

Coral nodded mutely. Pearl said, "Thank you."

"He was living in a trailer park and doesn't seem to have money, so he'll have a public defender. They're going to try to make you look like a liar, Coral. Why would you suddenly come forward now, after all this time? They're going to make you look like a liar and a crazy person. You should probably know that going into it. A lot of the case is going to hinge on your testimony. You have to convince a jury you're not making this stuff up."

"I'm not!"

"I believe you. I'm just saying that's what they're going to do."

"Yeah. I can see that. So my job is to look sane."

Pearl interjected, "That shouldn't be hard. You are sane. It's not like you're crazy. There's nothing the matter with you." Coral was grateful that she left out anything like 'except you keep too many books.' It probably also didn't hurt her case with Eliot to have her sister defending her like that.

55 CORAL PARTS WITH BOOKS AT LAST

Books were again stacked all over Coral's living room floor. On one side of the room were stacks of books that were broken and needed to be put out for recycling. It was sad how many there were, far more than she'd thought that first horrible day when the artifact goons had broken in. Additionally, after she moved back to her own place and begun putting the books in a logical order, she found that the oldest paperbacks weren't worth saving.

She had a lot of old paperbacks.

Because her finances had always been limited, over the years she'd taken to scouring garage sales and thrift shops for books. Many of the books she'd read, in childhood especially, were old enough that the glued bindings were failing. They looked fine on a shelf, but when you actually opened them up pages immediately began to fall out. Hardcover books will last for many decades, even centuries, but paperbacks were not meant to. Maybe some day she would like to reread *The Wind in the Willows, Catcher in the Rye,* and all the others, but it would have to be a different copy because these were ruined by time. Oh well. She'd probably only paid 50 cents apiece for them in the first place.

On the other side of the room were stacks of books she admitted she was never going to reread because she hadn't liked them that well the first time. Or because, in some cases, the author kept writing new books so quickly she couldn't keep up with his or her new works. She may just read a few favorites a second or third time, letting others languish. It occurred to her that maybe someone else with limited funds like her would enjoy these books if they had the opportunity. It would be better for the books to have new readers than to fall apart until they were fit only for recycling, as happened with the paperbacks she'd hoarded.

The books worth selling were going in boxes to be stored in Pearl's attic until Phil came back and reopened Red's Reads. She would sell them to him. James was coming over the next day to collect them.

It was okay. She didn't need to hang onto every single thing she'd ever read anymore. As bits and pieces of her own early childhood kept filling in, she didn't have that same panicky feeling about forgetting things.

She was going to take the rest of the broken books to the recycling center, but not in her asphalt colored crash-mobile, which had a bent frame and was effectively totaled, but in the loaner car from her insurance company.

That left a lot of empty bookcases.

And that was why Coral was very happy to hear the intercom from the front door of her apartment building buzz. "Hello?"

A voice came through the speaker sounding like a cross between a large bee and John Marsh. "Marsh Moving Company. I understand you have some bookcases you want moved."

Eliot came to the door with a dolly and straps like a real mover. Marie was going to take all of the bookcases that had been crowding the hall, which still left plenty of empty shelves in the apartment in anticipation of future reading material. Eliot was not the John Marsh of her book adventures, but who can match someone's dream? The real Eliot had a solid feeling to him, like someone she could count on. He hadn't run away when he found out she was involved with the artifact. In fact, he was curious to try it. And for the first time, Coral didn't feel like running away either. Maybe nothing would come of the relationship, but at least she was finally willing to consider the possibility that he was a caring hero, or whatever it was she had been too confused to articulate to Pearl. The way his laser beam eyes focused on her it seemed he was considering possibilities too.

John Marsh, the married and older real guy, followed his son, carrying a very small box. "Your landlord handed this to me when he saw we were coming up. Said it came for you in the mail."

The return address was a post office box in Colorado. Coral got a pair of scissors and sliced it open. Inside was a brass door key and a note.

Coral,

I hate to dump this on you too. I'm presuming too much. Not sure what else to do right now. This will let you into Red's Reads. Don't worry, I'm not asking you to run the place or anything. Not that it was a lot of work with no customers. Ha ha! Could you just keep an eye on the place a little bit until I come back? Not exactly sure when that will be. Trying to figure out how to get back to the study. I'll be paying utilities and so forth, so don't worry about any of that. BE CAREFUL! We really don't know who else is out there. Hope I'm not asking too much. Mostly keep the ARTIFACT safe, right? This note will self-destruct! Maybe you're too young to get that reference. I should be able to call you. Sorry I'm such a pain! All you wanted to do was sell me a book. -Phil

She wanted to talk to Phil and tell him how his artifact had helped her. He would be so glad.

Were Pearl and James moving to Europe? That remained unknown. If they did, Coral would miss them like crazy, but she would think of some way to survive. Maybe she'd go with them. Maybe she'd manage Red's Reads.

Of course, Coral still had the artifact and fully intended to use it.

The Novel Life Of Coral Ambrose
Book Club Questions

1. What do you do with books you've finished reading, and why?
2. What sorts of things do you keep because of a strong emotional connection? What wouldn't you wouldn't dream of giving up?
3. We're all shaped by our past, and most of us have a pretty good idea of why we feel the way we do based on our life experiences, but we don't remember every single thing that ever happened to us. Do you have any irrational fears or longings you can't explain?
4. Coral is able to do things in these book adventures she normally couldn't or shouldn't do. What genre would you pick that would free you to do something you wouldn't do in normal life? And what genre would you pick to stay in for a long time?
5. What fictional character from any book would you really like to know in person?
6. Coral jumped into many genres. Do any of the books remind you of specific authors?
7. Small children often blame themselves when things go wrong, simply because they are egocentric enough to think things are all about them. Can you think of anything from your own life where you felt like you failed when you were a child, but looking back you realize either it was never your fault in the first place, or you were just doing what was age-appropriate?
8. How has Coral changed while she's had the artifact?
9. If everyone had access to an artifact how would it change the world?
10. Looking beyond the end of the book, what should Coral do next? What should she tell Pearl? What do you think will happen with Eliot?

ABOUT THE AUTHOR

Bonnie Ballou attended the University of California at Davis and lives in Oregon with her engineer husband, a bookaholic like herself. They have two sons. A job involving rental properties allows time for indulging in an array of creative hobbies, such as painting and gardening. She has written, directed, and performed in theatrical sketches, one of which won the Best Comedy award from CITA in 2002.

Find her at BonnieBallou.com

www.ingramcontent.com/pod-product-compliance
Lightning Source LLC
Chambersburg PA
CBHW062136170626
46813CB00002B/721